ENEMY OF ROME

www.transworldbooks.co.uk

Also by Douglas Jackson

CALIGULA
CLAUDIUS
HERO OF ROME
DEFENDER OF ROME
AVENGER OF ROME
SWORD OF ROME

For more information on Douglas Jackson and his books,
see his website at www.douglas-jackson.net

ENEMY OF ROME

Douglas Jackson

BANTAM PRESS

LONDON · TORONTO · SYDNEY · AUCKLAND · JOHANNESBURG

TRANSWORLD PUBLISHERS
61–63 Uxbridge Road, London W5 5SA
A Random House Group Company
www.transworldbooks.co.uk

First published in Great Britain
in 2014 by Bantam Press
an imprint of Transworld Publishers

A CIP catalogue record for this book
is available from the British Library.

ISBNs 9780593070567 (cased)
9780593070574 (tpb)

Addresses for Random House Group Ltd companies outside the UK
can be found at: www.randomhouse.co.uk
The Random House Group Ltd Reg. No. 954009

The Random House Group Limited supports the Forest Stewardship Council® (FSC®),
the leading international forest-certification organisation. Our books carrying the FSC
label are printed on FSC®-certified paper. FSC is the only forest-certification scheme
supported by the leading environmental organisations, including Greenpeace. Our
paper procurement policy can be found at www.randomhouse.co.uk/environment

Typeset in 11½/15¼pt Electra by
Kestrel Data, Exeter, Devon.
Printed and bound by
CPI Group (UK) Ltd, Croydon, CR0 4YY.

2 4 6 8 10 9 7 5 3 1

For Mr and Mrs G. T. McKay

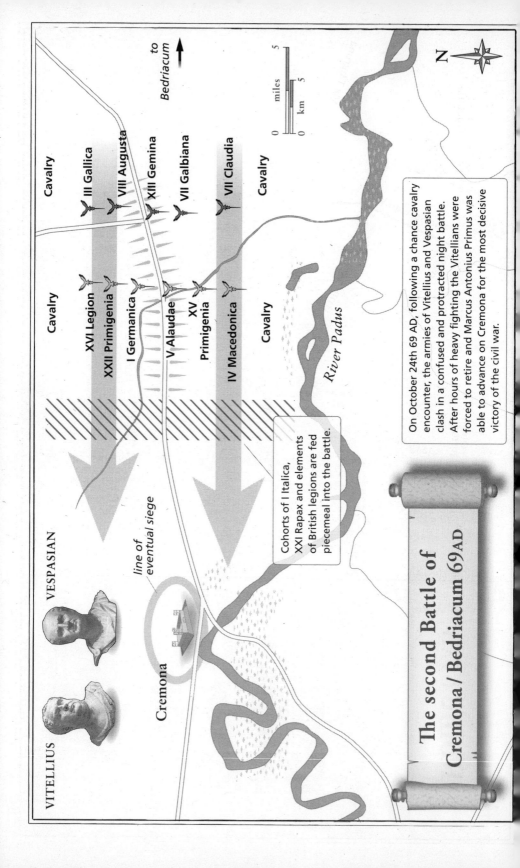

VITELLIUS

VESPASIAN

line of eventual siege

Cremona

River Padus

to
Bedriacum

N

Cavalry

III Gallica
VIII Augusta
XIII Gemina
VII Galbiana
VII Claudia

Cavalry

XVI Legion
XXII Primigenia
I Germanica
V Alaudae
XV Primigenia
IV Macedonica

Cavalry

Cavalry

miles   5
km   5

Cohorts of I Italica,
XXI Rapax and elements
of British legions are fed
piecemeal into the battle.

On October 24th 69 AD, following a chance cavalry
encounter, the armies of Vitellius and Vespasian
clash in a confused and protracted night battle.
After hours of heavy fighting the Vitellians were
forced to retire and Marcus Antonius Primus was
able to advance on Cremona for the most decisive
victory of the civil war.

The second Battle of
Cremona / Bedriacum 69AD

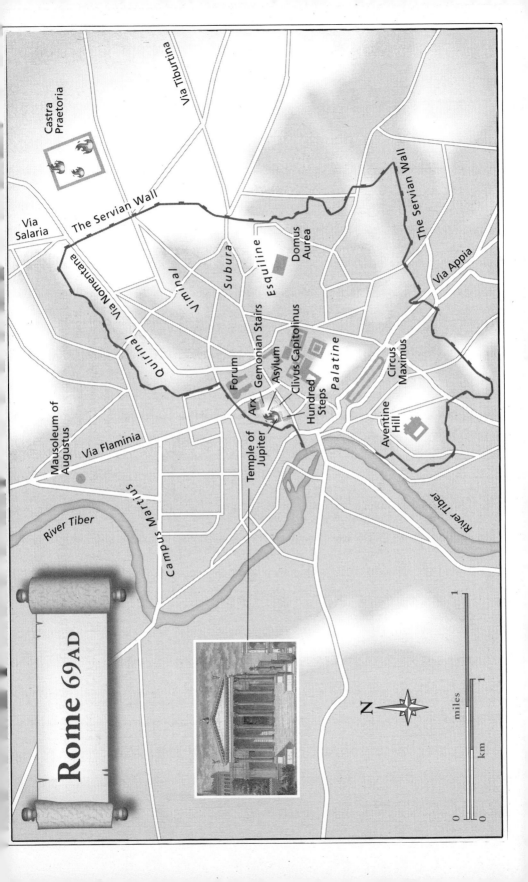

Once before, the Capitol had been consumed, but then only through the crime of individuals; now it was openly besieged, and openly set on fire.

Cornelius Tacitus, *The Histories*

I

Western Pannonia, August, AD 69

'You are sentenced to death.'

The verdict sent a jolt through Gaius Valerius Verrens as if he'd been drenched in ice melt. All the air seemed to be sucked from the sweltering tent and the three officers facing him behind the rickety campaign table shimmered like a desert mirage. In the centre, Vedius Aquila, commander of the Thirteenth legion, continued to outline the prisoner's crimes. Valerius could see his lips moving, but their meaning was lost in the void between. This couldn't be happening.

The civil war that had torn the Roman Empire apart since the death of Servius Sulpicius Galba almost nine months earlier should have been over. Galba's murderer, Otho, was dead, his army defeated on the damp plain between Cremona and Bedriacum by forces loyal to the governor of Germania, Aulus Vitellius. Now Vitellius sat on a golden throne wearing an Emperor's cloak and an Emperor's laurels, his position confirmed by the Senate and people of Rome. Division, deception and the betrayal of old loyalties are the very stuff of civil war. Valerius Verrens counted Vitellius as his friend, but he'd fought for Otho at Bedriacum, as deputy commander of the First Adiutrix legion. He'd watched the First fight like champions, but its cohorts had been annihilated when the army's left wing collapsed. An eagle was won, but the First's eagle had been lost, and the loss of an eagle was the loss of a legion's pride, its honour and its soul. Valerius somehow escaped the final massacre, only to discover that another man now disputed Vitellius's claim to the throne. That man was Titus Flavius Vespasian, proconsul of Judaea, whose Egyptian and Syrian legions, preceded by a vanguard from Moesia and Pannonia, were now marching on northern Italia.

After Bedriacum, Valerius, branded a traitor to Rome, fled east to join Vespasian's forces. Bearded, stinking and looking more like a one-handed goatherd than a holder of the Corona Aurea, he'd been arrested as a deserter by the first soldiers he'd encountered. When Aquila had recognized him, Valerius believed his ordeal was over. Instead, it was just beginning.

'. . . you are stripped of your honours, your rank and your possessions. Be thankful that I give you a soldier's death, rather than the coward's you deserve.'

'It is not true. I—'

'Silence.' Valerius clamped his lower lip between his teeth and drew himself up to his full height as Aquila continued. 'You will be taken from this place and paraded before the leading cohorts of this army to your execution.'

Strong hands pinned Valerius's arms to his sides, but he shrugged them away. 'There is no need to bind me,' he snapped. 'I am not afraid to die like a soldier.' He met Aquila's stare, and the men holding him relaxed as the legate nodded. Valerius continued to hold his gaze. 'This is wrong, general. I hope you can live with it.'

The narrow, almost skeletal features froze, but Aquila's expression remained implacable. 'Take him away,' he said tersely.

They emerged into the sunshine, and the summer heat of Pannonia struck Valerius like a blacksmith's hammer. He blinked as his eyes struggled to adapt to the change from gloom to searing brightness. When they cleared he wondered how it was that, when a man's life could be counted in moments, every image seemed so sharp, every colour so vivid, deep and intense. He hesitated, taking a deep breath, but a hand shoved him roughly in the back and sent him staggering towards the open square, where two thousand men waited to see him die. His left hand instinctively went to his throat, but the gold charm had been taken when he was captured. At least they had dressed him in a clean tunic and allowed him to shave, so men could see him for what he was: a knight of Rome. A member of the senatorial class that had ruled long before Augustus proclaimed himself Emperor. More important, they had left him the carved wooden fist that was as much part of him as the original, now a pile of mouldering bones lying in the burned-out ruins of a British villa.

That memory strengthened his resolve and he raised his eyes so as not to miss a moment of what was to come. This was meant to be a humiliation – the shaming of a coward and a deserter. Yet he felt their gaze on him and he knew they were seeing a soldier. A tall man, his gaunt features scarred by battle and more wounds hidden beneath the crow-dark hair; eyes filled with defiance burning from a face marked by sorrow and loss. Gaius Valerius Verrens was not afraid to die. He had faced death many times: in the smoke-filled darkness of the Temple of Claudius; on the dusty golden plains of Armenia; and, more recently, on the blood-soaked sands of the arena at Cremona, where another man's sword had carved him open. He had known triumph and defeat. He could face disaster. But he would not feel shame.

The four guards steered him up the first leg of the square and he recognized the roaring lion symbol of the Seventh Claudia on the line of shields. Campaign-hardened faces stared out at him from beneath polished iron helmets, their expressions varying from tense to bored. These men were veterans; they had better things to do than stand in the sun and watch a stranger die. A few showed sympathy, and some of the younger eyes glittered with anticipation. These would be the newer recruits, soldiers who had not yet witnessed the lake of blood a man couldn't avoid during a lifetime marching behind the eagle. Valerius was surprised at how little he felt on this day of his death. A hollow emptiness inside. A slight numbness of the mind. A tickle at the neck in anticipation of . . .

He pushed the thought to the back of his mind and concentrated on the faces of all the friends who had preceded him on this journey: Falco, commander of the Colonia militia, who sacrificed himself and his men to delay Boudicca a few more hours; Maeve, the Trinovante girl who had loved, then betrayed him; Lunaris, defender to the last at the door of the Temple of Claudius, and Messor who risked his life in vain in the tunnels below. Marcus, the old *lanista*, who led his gladiator cohort to its death at Bedriacum, and Juva, the big Nubian who captured an eagle there. All gone. All sacrificed to Mars. Why should Gaius Valerius Verrens be any different?

His eyes drifted to a cloudless blue sky marred only by three black specks circling lazily over the distant hills. The sound of buzzing insects filled the air and the occasional chink of metal on metal drew a hissed rebuke from a centurion. A new shield, and another lion, but this time with the rays of the sun shining from its maned head. The symbol of the Thirteenth, who had fought on the right flank at Bedriacum, led by the man who had condemned him. Vedius Aquila believed he had been betrayed, not defeated, and these men were desperate for another chance to show they could fight. Their commander had been reprieved, but their most senior centurions were executed in the aftermath of the battle on the orders of Vitellius. Aquila felt the shame of Bedriacum more deeply than any man, and he blamed the First Adiutrix for breaking. The First's legate had died in the battle, but not before Valerius's unorthodox tactics had gained him the enemy eagle captured by Juva. They might have won the day if he'd been supported. But Aquila, an old-fashioned commander, blamed Valerius's impetuous tricks for the defeat, and believed he had abandoned his men. That wasn't true, but it didn't matter now.

As he walked barefoot through the dried grass the stems crunched beneath his feet and the sandy soil was almost painfully hot between his toes. For the first time he noticed the bare-chested soldier waiting patiently in the centre of the square leaning on a long cavalry *spatha*. A burst of energy surged through him and he felt the men beside him tense and move closer as they sensed it. He almost smiled at the thought that they believed he might attempt escape, but he felt betrayed by his body's reaction. Why feel fear at the sight of a sword?

14

He had sent more men than he could count to the Otherworld with point and edge. Better to die in battle, but no soldier should flinch at the sight of the blade that would kill him. Another turn and he was marching along a wall of shields painted with the emblem of a red bull. Seventh Galbiana, then, the legion Galba had formed in Spain, that had accompanied him on his fateful, and ultimately fatal, march to Rome. In the centre he recognized a face beneath a centurion's distinctive helmet, with its transverse plume of scarlet horsehair. He tried to place the man, whose serious eyes followed every step of his walk of doom. Then it came to him. An attack on a British hill fort in the months before the Boudiccan rising. A young *optio* who had sweated beside him in a *testudo* during the assault. Yes. Atilius Verus; he would recognize that eagle's beak of a nose anywhere. The man must have been one of the centurions transferred to the Seventh to stiffen the backbone of raw Spanish recruits. Their eyes met and something indefinable made Valerius smile. The faint breath of fear that had stayed with him since the first sight of the sword faded. Verus straightened and nodded approvingly in a show of respect as good as any salute.

A final turn and he was walking in a dream towards the man at the centre of the square. For the first time, the movement brought a reaction from the three cohorts of soldiers brought here to witness the execution of Gaius Valerius Verrens. Just a soft rustle as two thousand men shifted uneasily, but proof that not every legionary here supported the condemnation of a Hero of Rome. He took a deep breath and concentrated on his executioner. A big man, with curiously sensitive eyes but powerful shoulders and the muscles of an athlete or a wrestler. Stripped to the waist, his brick-red face and forearms contrasted sharply with the fish-belly white of his torso. A legionary seldom removed his tunic, except to sleep or bathe. Valerius remembered a man condemned by his general for daring to work naked apart from his sword, and the incongruity of it made him laugh.

The executioner's face hardened at the unlikely sound. This wasn't what he expected from his victims. A simple man, born and raised on an Etrurian pig farm, he was only doing his job, and he liked the proceedings to pass with dignity for all concerned. Valerius nodded gravely in greeting and the peasant face relaxed as the man returned it. The escort moved away.

'Kneel, facing in that direction.' The soldier pointed towards the men of the Thirteenth.

Valerius obeyed, wincing as his bare knees sank into the burning sand. He sensed the man moving into position behind him. Suddenly his throat felt as dry as an Egyptian salt pan and he would have given anything for a last drink of cool water to send him on his way. In contrast, his whole body felt liquid and sweat started to pour down his face. He told himself it was not fear, but a natural reaction to his situation. He prayed there would be no others.

'Steady, lad. I've done this a hundred times.' The voice was surprisingly soothing and Valerius was reminded of a sacrifice where the young *victimarius* had whispered into the bull's ear right up until the last moment. 'Just keep your head up and you won't feel a thing. Good lad.'

Valerius closed his eyes. He felt the soft, experimental touch of the blade on the back of his neck before it lifted for the last time. His father's face swam into his mind, inspiring a sudden burst of panic as he realized his sister Olivia would be all alone now. He imagined the man behind choosing the perfect spot between two vertebrae, his muscles rippling as the sword rose. He gulped a final breath. A silence like no other filled his world.

'Hold!' The sharp command was accompanied by the thunder of hooves. 'I said hold,' a voice accustomed to authority snapped a second time.

Valerius heard a murmur of confusion run through the massed ranks in the square, instantly silenced by the snarl of centurions and *optiones*. He sensed the moment the executioner took a step back, heard Aquila's outraged tones in the distance. 'What is the meaning of this?'

The owner of the first voice didn't reply immediately. Instead, Valerius heard the sound of a single horse approaching and felt a shadow fall over him. 'You can open your eyes now.'

16

Warily, Valerius did as the speaker suggested. His head swam as he looked up to see a travel-stained young man in a simple tunic gazing quizzically down at him from the saddle of a fine milk-white stallion. Only the scarlet band at his waist identified him as a legionary legate, and the equal in authority of any man here; perhaps superior. He sighed. 'Trouble follows you around the way a seasoned bitch attracts every dog in town. Get up, man.' He grinned. 'There's no need to kneel to me. At least not yet.'

'Titus?'

II

'This officer has been found guilty by a military tribunal of cowardice and desertion and sentenced according to military justice.'

'I do not dispute that,' said Titus Flavius Vespasian, son of the man whose legions were now converging on Italian soil to depose an Emperor. 'I dispute your right to carry out the sentence without confirmation from my father. Gaius Valerius Verrens is a Hero of Rome, a holder of the Gold Crown of Valour. He has done certain services for the Empire – and for my father.'

Aquila spluttered and Valerius looked on dispassionately as the two men debated his fate. Titus, seated behind the campaign table where the tribunal had passed sentence, was of a similar age to the one-handed Roman. He'd be almost thirty now, though he looked younger. Each had a background in the law, and they'd both served in Britannia during the Boudiccan uprising. That shared past provided a connection after Titus had saved Valerius from dying of thirst on an Egyptian beach after shipwreck. It developed into friendship later, when Valerius had spent six months in the desert helping Titus train Vespasian's Nubian cavalry. While Valerius tried in vain to prevent civil war, Titus had been adding to his laurels in Judaea as commander of the Fifteenth Apollinaris. Vespasian had wanted his son to become Galba's heir, but Galba had died before Titus reached

Rome. Now the father was bent on taking Rome for himself.

Movement in the corner of his eye alerted Valerius to a newcomer. He looked beyond Titus and Aquila to the doorway and found himself the focus of a pair of the most malevolent eyes he'd ever seen. They smouldered with the primeval menace of a starving leopard and belonged to a tall, whip-thin savage in a ragged tunic. The apparition had a face that belonged in Hades: all dangerous shadow and razor edge, meshed with lines that looked as if they'd been scored with a knife point. His thin lips were drawn back in a permanent sneer and his shaven head glistened with the puckered scars of past battles.

Titus ignored the newcomer. 'You say the verdict cannot be changed and the sentence stands. I say the verdict is not legally binding until it has been ratified by my father, and the sentence cannot be carried out until it has been confirmed.' He graced Aquila with a courteous smile. Valerius knew he disliked using his father's authority to further an argument, preferring reason to brute force, but in the end he was his father's son and would deploy whatever weapons were to hand. 'Since the verdict and the sentence cannot be changed, I suggest that they be suspended—'

'What? Military justice—'

'Suspended until they are confirmed by the Emperor,' Titus continued. 'In the meantime, Gaius Valerius Verrens remains under sentence of death. The punishment is to be carried out only after the Senate and people of Rome formally agree my father's position and he ratifies the sentence. Thank you, Aquila, for your time and your patience.'

Aquila spluttered with suppressed rage, but he was general enough to know when he'd been outmanoeuvred. He rose from his chair and bowed, and stalked out of the tent, not even deigning to glance at Valerius.

Titus sighed and called for wine. A young slave brought a silver jug and placed it on a table beside four pewter cups, pouring one for the young legate and vanishing behind a curtain at the rear of the tent. The young aristocrat closed his eyes and savoured his drink. 'I do so hate disagreements.'

'You'll forgive me if I'm glad you had this one.' Valerius reached for the jug and poured two more cups.

'I'm not sure a convicted criminal is worthy of this vintage.' Titus fixed him with one weary eye. 'But your Spanish wolf is certainly deserving. Without him the gentleman with the sword would have gone about his business and I would be having this conversation with your head.'

Valerius carried a cup to the ragged figure who still lounged by the doorway. Serpentius, former gladiator, his freedman and his friend, took the cup and sniffed it suspiciously. Valerius laughed. 'None of your usual tavern horse piss.'

'It smells like fruit,' the Spaniard grumbled. 'What's the use of wine that smells like fruit? It should make your eyes shrivel and your balls explode. That's proper wine.'

'So what took you so long?'

Serpentius lifted the cup unhurriedly to his lips and drank, his nose twitching at the unfamiliar sweetness. 'That first day, when they caught us by the river, I wasn't too worried. I thought you'd talk your way out, the way you always do. So I just followed and watched when you were taken into the Thirteenth's camp. As time passed, I realized you were in a bit of trouble.' Titus laughed at the understatement and poured himself another cup. The Spaniard continued. 'I managed to make friends with a couple of the guard detachment . . .' He saw Valerius's look. Making friends had never been Serpentius's greatest talent. 'I taught them a few gladiator tricks,' he said defensively. 'The old sword spin, and that belly punch that makes you piss blood for a week before you die. Anyway, they were happy to talk and I found out where you were being kept. They said you were a dead man walking because Aquila blamed you for Bedriacum. I thought about breaking you out . . .'

'You were too closely guarded,' Titus interjected. 'So he decided the only way to save you was to find someone with more authority than Aquila and plead your case.'

'I managed to reach the army's headquarters at Poetivo . . .'

'But Primus, who commands, kicked him out on his skinny Spanish arse because Primus is a proper patrician and your friend looks like a mongrel mix of rag salesman, latrine cleaner and hired assassin.' They waited for some reaction from the Spaniard, but Serpentius only rolled his eyes and took another drink. 'Somehow, he discovered I'd just arrived in the camp, found his way past my bodyguard – which they'll regret for all eternity – and you know the rest.'

'And he has my thanks for it.' Valerius raised his cup, eliciting a shrug from the former gladiator. 'What I don't understand is how you happened to be here. I thought you would be back in Judaea by now. Oh, and Primus? That's not Marcus Antonius Primus, I hope?'

Titus frowned. 'It is. Why would it matter to you?'

'Because I prosecuted him in a fraud case. He and his friends forged an old man's will so his nephew would get the proceeds of his estate. They threw him out of the Senate and banned him from Rome. Will that cause you a problem?'

The young legate waved a hand airily as if the fact had no import. 'To answer your first question, I was in Cyprus waiting for my father's instructions when word arrived that Primus had come out in support of him with his Pannonian legions. Vespasian is aware of, um . . . certain character defects in his most enthusiastic champion.'

'You mean he's a fraud, a liar and a thief?'

The other man smiled. 'I was thinking more of the fact that he is reckless. The message I brought is that my father wishes him to delay here and conserve his forces until Licinius Mucianus arrives with his Syrian legions. You remember Mucianus from Antioch?'

A narrow, ill-tempered face swam into Valerius's head. Sculpted patrician features with dark unforgiving eyes. Valerius had been sent to Syria to spy on Nero's eastern commander, Gnaeus Domitius Corbulo, only to discover that his real mission was to provide cover for the man sent to assassinate Corbulo. When Mucianus had taken command after his fellow general's death Valerius had become a hunted man. 'I don't forget people who want me dead.'

'One among many, it appears.' Titus raised a cultured eyebrow. 'But I believe he is no longer a threat to you. In Antioch he was Nero's man, and once you had outlived your usefulness he would naturally have had you killed.' His tone was utterly detached, as if he was discussing the price of grain, and Valerius was reminded that Titus was now a prince of Rome, and, if Vespasian won the throne, heir to the Empire. 'His loyalty now lies with my father, and my father has made it known he owes a debt of gratitude to Gaius Valerius Verrens.' He smiled. 'What is done is done; we have new battles to fight.'

'But I'm still under sentence of death,' Valerius pointed out. 'I won't be of much use to your father dead.'

'Suspended sentence,' Titus agreed. 'But Vespasian will never confirm it. In any case,' he added cheerfully, 'by the time he gets the opportunity you may actually *be* dead.' He paused and took another sip of wine. 'Soon I must return to Judaea, where my father has work for me. He will want all the information I can provide on Aulus Vitellius and his forces. Your Spaniard said you were at Bedriacum and Placentia, but he is as mean with words as he is free with his sword.'

Valerius nodded to Serpentius and the Spaniard slipped soundlessly out of the tent. When they were alone Valerius took the seat Aquila had vacated and told the younger man about his attempt to persuade Vitellius to give up his claim to the throne. He and Serpentius had been forced to flee to Placentia, where they'd manned the city walls against the might of two legions, then escaped to join Otho's army in time for the horrors of Bedriacum. 'We hurt them at Bedriacum, but we were defeated because of bad generalship and Otho's insistence that the army take the offensive over ground that was more suitable for defence than attack. If he'd waited until the Seventh and the Fourteenth joined us it would have been different.'

Titus nodded, noting the grey pallor and new lines around his friend's eyes that had nothing to do with his months in captivity. He had seen it before in the East, in the aftermath of military defeat. Gaius Valerius Verrens looked like a man worn out by war, or worn out by life. The melancholy thought made him frown. 'And now Vitellius sits in Rome and my father must force him out or . . .' He shrugged. They both knew that if Vespasian failed the most likely outcome was death for the entire family. 'He will make a fine Emperor, Valerius. He will be fair and just and wise. A new Augustus.'

Valerius remembered another man who had spoken of becoming the new Augustus. *Our ambitions are the same, Valerius. A strong Rome, a prosperous Rome, a Rome untainted by the stain of corruption.* 'Vitellius may wear the purple, but the real power lies with his generals,' he said carefully. Titus's head came up and his eyes glittered with new interest. 'If you can split him from them, I suspect his enthusiasm for his new position would be fatally weakened.'

Titus nodded carefully. 'I will think on that; we can discuss it more fully later. Now, you must leave me. I have letters to write to my father and my brother Domitianus.' He was already reaching for his stylus and missed Valerius's startled reaction. Titus's brother was Valerius's rival for the affections of Gnaeus Domitius Corbulo's daughter, and the last time they'd met Valerius had threatened to remove certain parts of Domitianus's anatomy and make him eat them. 'He is trapped in Rome, but under the protection of my uncle Sabinus. I—'

A bustle of activity from the doorway made Titus look up, and Valerius turned as a heavy-set, older man in a legate's sculpted breastplate and red sash entered the tent. Titus smiled a welcome. 'Marcus Antonius Primus, commander of the Danuvius legions.'

The big man nodded, but a frown shadowed his face as he noticed Valerius for the first time.

'Don't I know you?'

III

'I do not believe I have been able to convince him.' Titus outlined his problem the next day as his entourage prepared to leave for the East. He kept his voice so low Valerius had to strain to catch the words. 'My father did not wish to give a direct order to a commander in the field, because he is aware how quickly conditions can change and opportunities arise. In an experienced and thoughtful general that would be well enough, but Primus is a gambler by nature. My greatest fear is that his impetuosity could place this army in danger. We can win, Valerius. We will win. But to do that we must husband our resources, and the battle-tested troops of the Danuvius frontier are our greatest asset.' He looked Valerius in the eye and his next words contained a challenge. 'I rely on you to be my agent in this.'

Valerius almost laughed. 'What makes you think Marcus Antonius Primus will listen to me? The man blames me for destroying his career. Even with Serpentius watching my back I'll be lucky to last a week without having my throat slit or hemlock slipped into my wine. What was it he said when he recognized me?' He shook his head at the memory of Primus's violent reaction; the bulging eyes, the purple distended features, the hands that had twitched for his throat. '"If I had known you were in Aquila's custody I would have had you strung up by your own intestines and personally lit the fire beneath your feet."

Those aren't the words of someone who'll thank me for giving him military advice.'

Titus smiled. 'It's true his initial reaction wasn't encouraging, but I've spoken to him. He's not a fool, Valerius. He knows this campaign is his opportunity to return to high office, but the only way he'll ever wear a consul's toga and march behind twelve lictors is if he wins victories. I've told him my father values your services, and that he should keep you close for your knowledge of Vitellius and his generals. He understands the importance of your experiences at Placentia and Bedriacum. Your rank of *tribunus laticlavius* is restored and the Spaniard appointed your servant and personal bodyguard. Primus will never like you, Valerius, but he will be happy to use you. As long as you are of use to him, he'll keep you alive.'

'It'll be like being chained to a tiger with toothache.' Valerius knew he protested in vain. 'And the outcome is likely to be just as painful.'

The other man laughed. 'Yes, that would sum it up rather well. But Gaius Valerius Verrens has experience of riding tigers. You survived Nero's enmity while men like Corbulo and Seneca were swept away. You alone paved the way for Galba's march on Rome. Who else but Gaius Valerius Verrens would have dared to demand that Aulus Vitellius give up the purple?' Valerius stifled a denial. They both knew Titus was exaggerating. He had survived Nero by fleeing with Vespasian's help. Other men had guided Galba to the throne. Honour and duty had dictated he must approach Vitellius, but he had not been alone. None of that mattered. He was here and he was available. Titus placed a hand on his right arm. 'I would not ask this of anyone else, Valerius.'

A young aide announced that the preparations were complete and Valerius accompanied Vespasian's son to his horse.

'I haven't made my oath to your father,' he reminded him.

'And he would not demand it.' Titus smiled. 'He knows he is not the Emperor until he has convinced the Senate and the people to affirm it. We will make that pledge together on the day he dons the purple and Valerius Verrens receives the honours he deserves.' As the escort moved off he leaned down from the saddle and whispered, 'Tame the tiger for me, Valerius.'

'Let me be very clear.' Marcus Antonius Primus sniffed his contempt. 'I would rather feed you to my dogs than have you on my staff.'

Valerius held the other man's poisonous stare during the long pause that followed. The last time he'd looked into those eyes had been during his brief return to the law after returning from Britannia. He'd been selected to prosecute three senators on a charge of falsifying a will and forcing it on an elderly man. The evidence against Primus, and his fellow defendants Valerius Fabianus and Vincius Rufus, had been overwhelming, and though they tried every trick, legal and otherwise, to have the case dismissed, they were found guilty. All three were already rich and the only motive for the crime was naked greed. They'd been dismissed from the Senate under Lex Cornelia Testamentaria and banished from Rome. Nero's death and the short-lived rule of Galba had seen Primus reinstated and given a legionary command. Aulus Vitellius had been one of the senators who had banished him, which forced him to throw in his lot with first Otho, and now Vespasian. The headquarters tent seemed to strain with the power of his anger, and for a moment Valerius thought the general would break the metal stylus in his hand.

Eventually Primus managed to regain control. 'However, I am a servant of Rome, and if I am to ensure Vespasian takes his rightful place as Emperor I must use every weapon at my disposal, no matter how distasteful. Your rank and privileges as senior military tribune are confirmed.' Valerius bowed his thanks for this grudging concession as Primus continued: 'You know the false Emperor Vitellius personally?'

'I served with him in Africa,' Valerius admitted.

'And your assessment of his military capabilities?'

Valerius almost smiled. His old friend Vitellius's greatest military capability was to eat a full century's rations at a single sitting and still be demanding more. 'He is no soldier,' he said, 'but no fool either. He will leave the fighting to his generals.'

The legate nodded slowly. 'And who commands, Valens or Caecina?'

'I believe neither will willingly yield to the other. Both have an equal influence on the Emp— on Vitellius and he chooses not to choose between them for fear of alienating the one or the other. Caecina Alienus is a charming rogue who milked his province of Baetica dry and would have been prosecuted' – he saw Primus wince at the hated word – 'but for Galba's death. I have never met Fabius Valens, but I know him by reputation. A hard man and a good soldier who personally cut the head from the former governor of Germania Inferior. The only thing that unites them is their ambition.'

Primus chewed his lip thoughtfully. 'And which is the greater threat?'

Valerius remembered a short-lived negotiation before the walls of Placentia; Caecina, flamboyant in his colourful barbarian costume, a wild excitement in his eyes, his beautiful wife at his side. 'Valens,' he said emphatically. 'At Placentia, Caecina should have waited until he deployed his artillery. Instead, he threw his best men at strong stone walls without support and lost thousands. I doubt he has the patience or the wisdom to be a great commander.' He hesitated, waiting for a reaction to what could have been a criticism of the man before him, but Primus didn't respond and he continued: 'Bedriacum was Valens' victory. He fought a clever battle over difficult terrain and used his reserves skilfully. With enough men, Caecina could hurt you, but Valens could destroy you.'

Primus looked up sharply, wondering whether to be insulted by the suggestion that either man could defeat him. Gradually he relaxed and his face twisted into what was almost a smile. 'Yes, I see why Titus suggested I could use you. Honest to the point of foolishness. Brave enough not – quite – to be despised. A man never likely to play the spy.'

This time it was Valerius's turn to flinch, but he was careful not to show it. Primus believed himself a fine judge of character, but he was wrong. Valerius had played the spy for Nero, for Galba and for Otho, and played it well. He had no doubt Titus wanted to be kept informed of Primus's moves, but he thought it unlikely the legate would give him the opportunity. 'I am happy to serve the general in whatever role he feels me best suited,' he said carefully.

27

'A lawyer's answer.' Primus's mood changed in an instant. 'Venus's tits, I hate lawyers. Your *role* will be to be at my orders day and night, and if I tell you to jump off a bridge you will ask me which side is my pleasure. You will be part of my council, because that is what your *friend*, Titus,' the word 'friend' was given an emphasis that made Valerius want to take the other man by the throat, 'has *suggested* and for the moment Titus has his father's authority, but you will keep your ugly face and that crippled arm out of my line of sight until you are called. I have been advised to stay on the defensive, but that will depend on the reports I receive over the next few days. If the conditions are right, we will march on Rome. We will fight this war, you and I, and we will defeat the enemy, but by the end you will wish you had died under the executioner's sword. Do not be deceived by my gentle manner today, Gaius Valerius Verrens. When this is over there *will* be a reckoning. Now get out.'

Valerius bit his lip to stifle words that would put him under another death sentence. He slammed the wooden fist against his chest in salute and marched from the tent. Outside, he found Serpentius waiting on the other side of the Via Principalis. 'By the look on your face I'd say that went well,' the Spaniard said.

A bitter laugh escaped Valerius and he looked out over the familiar lines of tents to the grey hills beyond. 'Remember that time we crossed the Danuvius and were ambushed by the Dacians? I think we were safer among the savages and their skinning knives than we are here.'

Serpentius shrugged. 'In that case we should get out the first chance we have. You don't owe these people anything.'

Valerius shook his head. Titus had saved his life; and there was another, more important reason. 'Primus may be a complete bastard who would like nothing better than to see me hanging from a cross, but he's more of a soldier than I gave him credit for. Vespasian has advised him to stay here and wait for our old friend Mucianus.' He grinned, and his voice took on new energy. 'But I think he's already made up his mind to fight his way to Rome, and Rome is where I want to be.'

Serpentius shot him a worried glance at the sudden change of mood, but Valerius was too lost in thought to notice. He was already thinking on the battles ahead, and the enemies in front and behind. Titus had asked him to tame the tiger – the problem was to avoid being eaten first.

If Valerius was right, the tiger was about to march on Rome.

And in Rome, Domitia would be waiting.

IV

The great house on the lip of the Esquiline slope in Rome reminded Domitia Longina Corbulo of her father's palace in Antioch: designed to be full of magical light and wonder, the rooms adorned with works of art and treasures from Asia, Africa and the East. The only difference was that she had felt safe in Antioch.

Walking along the pillared corridor in the villa gardens, she fought boredom as the toga-clad patrician beside her insisted for the fourth or fifth time that she could rely on his family's protection. The years had made Titus Flavius Sabinus pompous and exaggerated the vanity for which he was famed. He must once have been considered handsome, she thought, but the strong features had blurred with age and his broad forehead now stretched all the way back across his scalp. Sabinus had a thick neck, wide shoulders and a conspicuous paunch that he carried in front of him like a basket of loaves. If he lacked the calm assurance of his younger brother Vespasian, and the signs of nervous stress were unmistakable, it was hardly surprising given his position.

'As urban prefect I must be seen to be above politics,' he explained, the thick lips pursing in a worried frown. 'I am responsible for Rome and I take that responsibility seriously. I hope that whatever issues exist between my brother and the Emperor can be resolved without further bloodshed, but if not I will do my utmost to safeguard this city and its people.'

Domitia nodded gracefully as if she accepted the explanation without question, but she wasn't sure she believed him. Sabinus's main aim was to secure his family's power base in Rome whatever the outcome of the Imperial struggle. He also had the predatory eye for an opportunity that was characteristic of all the Flavians. Vespasian's decision to remain in Alexandria might be designed to keep the two branches of the family from meeting in combat, but if Vitellius showed any sign of weakness she suspected Sabinus would try to take advantage. Sabinus continued speaking, filling the unacceptable silence with words as was his habit. Domitia glanced over her bare shoulder.

He was still there, of course, three or four paces away, watching. Sabinus's nephew Domitianus had appointed himself her protector on the long sea voyage back to Rome after her father's death. No, call it what it was, despite the fact that Gnaeus Domitius Corbulo had taken his life with his own hand. It had been murder. Nero had murdered her father and left her an orphan. At first Domitianus had been like an adoring puppy, happy to be blessed with a nod or a smile, but all that changed when they reached Rome. Even when she'd married the elderly aristocrat Lucius Aelius Lamia, he'd continued to haunt her footsteps. After the wedding, Lamia had made it clear that the marriage was purely one of convenience. He'd cheerfully set off to take up his praetorship in Sicilia and left her to Domitianus's mercy with instructions not to shame the family name.

Tall, pale and slim, with sandy, tight-curled hair, a weak chin and narrow eyes that never left her body, Domitianus caught her eye. His lips twitched. She flinched away and tried to turn her attention to what Sabinus was saying.

'The Emperor,' he grimaced as if the word was a betrayal of his brother, 'has assured me that he understands and sympathizes with my situation. He is grateful for my support and the work I have done in past years.' He turned to her with a resigned smile that made her like him more than she had. 'As a former consul Vitellius knows the pressures of my position; the minutiae, the delicacy required when dealing with so many different personalities and classes. The provision of grain and the policing of the streets take up much of my energies, but in a time of civil . . .' he hesitated, apparently not able to bring himself to say the obvious word, 'strife, my responsibilities are multiplied. In many ways it was much simpler to command the Fourteenth when Claudius invaded Britannia. A man knew his place then.'

'Then I will try to be as little a burden to you as possible, sir.' Domitia bowed her head respectfully. 'And you have the thanks of myself and my husband for your offer of protection in these troubled times.' She imagined she could feel the heat of Domitianus's fury at the use of the word 'husband'. 'I am sure he will insist on expressing his gratitude personally when he returns from Sicilia.'

Domitianus's affection had grown into obsession when Marcus Salvius Otho ordered him to escort her back to Rome on the eve of the battle of Bedriacum. But when news came of Otho's defeat it quickly became clear that obsession had been replaced by ownership. Domitianus assumed she was his for the taking, and all that was required was for her to recognize the fact. He still followed her around like a puppy, indulging what he believed were her needs, but now there were additional irritations. Little 'presents', compliments whispered just too low for Sabinus or his servants to hear, and the occasional inappropriate brush of the fingers that she met with a stare of outraged dignity. When patience ran out and word of the true scale of the disaster had arrived in Rome she'd screamed at him to leave her alone. He'd only laughed and said she was a typical woman, overwrought and prone to exaggeration. Sabinus suspected something, but had clearly decided that whatever it was was between his nephew and Domitia. But there had been times recently when the look in Domitianus's eyes frightened her; moments, when he thought she wasn't looking at him, when warmth was replaced by a diabolical rage, devotion by lust, and tenderness by the threat of violence.

Sabinus stalked off. A second later she felt hot breath on the back of her neck, and she wasn't sure whether she heard the whisper or only imagined it. 'You will be mine. It is only a matter of time.'

She had to get out of here.

But only one man could help her. And for all she knew that man was dead.

Aulus Vitellius Germanicus Augustus felt an ominous liquid gurgling in his lower stomach and fought to conceal the look of unease that was the natural result. His digestive system, so reliable for so many years, appeared to have become confused or unbalanced by the strictures imposed by his new eminence. He'd always been known for his gargantuan appetite and was aware men called him the Emperor of the Dinner Table, but it didn't concern him. A man should enjoy his food, and if the consumption of it gave him a presence to match his appetite, then so be it. Nothing had spoiled his pleasure, until now. Who would have thought that after so many years of bequeathing vexatious decisions to those more able to deal with them, he should have managed to elevate himself to a position where the problems of the world were the sole province of a single, unlikely, and, he feared, singularly ill-equipped personage. Not that you would know that from the reaction of those in the Senate, who hailed his tormented, hard-won decisions as god-inspired works of genius. Yes, he'd managed to make one or two patently sensible changes. He'd earned the gratitude of his soldiers by outlawing the selling of furloughs and exemptions by centurions. The populace applauded his order to cast every astrologer and like charlatan from the soil of Italia. After Nero's suicide, Galba's murder, and the demise of Otho, the mob were happy with the prospect of stability, the games he'd promised, and bread in their stomachs. True, he had made mistakes. He should not have blurted out that Otho's grave marker was a little tomb, fit only for a little man. In retrospect it was unfitting, had been said in anger at the trouble Otho had created, and he regretted it. Still, the Senate would support him as long as the army did, and the army would support him as long as they were paid – and as long as they were winning.

The thought generated a new spasm and he forced a smile to disguise the discomfort of the moment from the two men who shared the room with him in the great Golden House Nero had built to reflect his glory. Each was clad in the purple-striped toga of a senator, but

33

worn in the distinctive manner, tied at the middle with the *cinctus Gabinus*, that marked a serving consul of Rome. Suffect consuls, it was true, filling a prescribed role for a prescribed period of time, but consuls no less. When they marched north, the *fasces* borne by their dozen lictors would carry the axe heads that proclaimed their right to put to death the enemies of empire.

They were the generals of his armies: Gaius Fabius Valens and Aulus Caecina Alienus. His greatest strength and his greatest weakness.

Valens was the elder and normally a man of frighteningly violent disposition. Thin and spare as an unsheathed *gladius*, blank-eyed, with a nature as vicious as his weaselly features, he was as feared by his officers as he was respected by his troops. Yet the grey pallor and pink eyes staring out from beneath drooping lids took the edge off the threat. He looked old; old and worn out.

'A tincture with your wine, general?' Vitellius suggested. 'My physician can mix it up in an instant.'

Valens grunted his thanks, but shook his head. 'It's nothing. A flux that lays me low for a few days. I fear the waters of the Padus did not agree with me.'

'They agreed with Otho less, I'd say.' Caecina was plainly enjoying his rival's discomfort. Ten years younger, he had handsome tanned features and an appealing nature that hid an ambition as great as his opinion of himself, which was enormous. Despite the setback at Placentia, where his desperation to outdo Valens had almost torn the heart out of his army, that opinion remained undiminished. Aulus Caecina Alienus was a young man on the rise. Vitellius had a suspicion he would not be satisfied with a consulship for long. He decided he'd feel more comfortable when the young general was on campaign, where his silver tongue could do less damage than among the marble columns of the Forum.

'You are . . .' Another rumble erupted in the Emperor's stomach, this time audible to the two men facing him. He struggled to suppress it, only to release an involuntary fart on a scale with his massive frame. Valens looked horrified and Caecina was about to say something more dangerous than clever, but thought better of it. Vitellius shifted uneasily in his seat.

'I apologize, consuls, but I too am feeling a little indisposed. However, I think we may continue.' He called to his secretary, Asiaticus, hovering attentively by the doorway, to bring a map of northern Italia. The tall Greek produced a scroll and pinned it to the large mahogany table that dominated this corner of the Emperor's personal quarters. 'Vespasian, that low-born mule driver, has challenged the authority vested in me by the Senate and people of Rome. The legions of Syria and Egypt have declared for him. They are far away, but of greater concern is the support of the traitors in Pannonia and Moesia who would have fought for Otho. You are my generals. Advise me.'

Valens blinked. Surely it was obvious. 'You must lead your army north at the first opportunity, Caesar. Whoever controls the Padus valley controls Italia, and by default the Empire. Choose your battlefield and draw the Balkan legions to you. They are Vespasian's elite; seasoned troops hardened by years of fighting on the Danuvius. Defeat them and you defeat him.'

Vitellius frowned. This talk of leading and choosing battlefields perplexed him. Wasn't that why he employed generals and showered honours upon them? He was no coward. A coward did not become Emperor of Rome. But he was prudent, and a prudent man knew his strengths. He studied the two soldiers. 'How long will it take to concentrate our forces and reach the Padus?'

Caecina looked away and Valens sniffed. 'Longer than it would have taken if we'd left the First Germanica with the Fifth and Twenty-first Rapax on the Padus as I suggested.' Vitellius frowned at the implied criticism of his decision to bring the majority of his legions south to take part in his triumphal entry into Rome. The spectacle had been a masterpiece of might and dignity, but the aftermath little short of a disaster. Thousands of troops full of themselves with victory spread through the city taking what they wanted, setting up camp where it suited them and polluting the streets and streams with their filth. With them they'd brought disease, which had spread rapidly, weakening the men and their units. These required replacements, who were already in short supply because he had been forced to replace much of the Praetorian Guard which had still been loyal to Otho's memory. The worst offenders had been the Batavian auxiliaries who had proved so ungovernable on Valens' march south. Vitellius had been forced to send them back to their homeland where they would undoubtedly cause problems for the governor of Germania. Still, none of that could be changed. He held the other man's stare until the legate continued: 'A week to bring the legions together west of the mountains.' Valens coughed. 'Another two to reach the Padus.'

Vitellius looked to Caecina, expecting him to disagree, but the younger man only smiled. 'I believe the general is correct in his dispositions, Caesar,' he said.

'Very well.' The Emperor nodded decisively, setting his great dewlap jowls wobbling. 'You, General Caecina, will rally our troops . . . here, at Narnia, before marching north to suitable positions in the Padus valley. You will also pick up whatever forces you can along the way.'

'The marines of the Ravenna fleet?' Valens suggested.

Caecina shrugged dismissively. 'Is that really necessary? We have four full legions and the substantial elements of another six. What use are a few wetbacks?'

'A few wetbacks of the First Adiutrix held the walls at Placentia.' The younger man bridled at Valens' unnecessary reminder of his failure. 'And they took the Twenty-first's eagle.'

'You must do as you see fit,' Vitellius said placatingly. 'In the meantime, you, General Valens . . .' Valens glared suspiciously and the Emperor hesitated, knowing there was no point in suggesting the old soldier take the rest he so patently needed, 'will ensure that whatever forces are available are ready to march north, and aid my brother Lucius in creating a cavalry force that will hold the south against insurrection.' He saw Valens' frown deepen and cut him off with a smile. 'Of course, you will complete your duties in time to re-join your legions before General Caecina departs from Narnia.'

Now it was Caecina's turn to speak out. 'So we are to fight as separate armies?'

'You will have joint command and you will cooperate, as you did at Bedriacum,' Vitellius answered smoothly. 'As you said, consul, you have more than sufficient forces to defeat our enemies. Choose your ground with care and the outcome is not in doubt.'

'And you, Caesar?'

Vitellius froze at Caecina's question. Did he detect insolence? Perhaps, but the young consul's smile seemed to rob his words of any slight. 'I will remain in Rome to run affairs of state and ensure that the Senate keeps my victorious generals well supplied.' He waved a plump hand towards the doorway to indicate the interview was over. 'We will discuss the details later, but you have your orders.'

The two generals walked down the marble corridor and past the gigantic gold-leafed marble statue of Nero that still dominated the entrance hall of the Domus Aurea. Caecina stopped to stare up at the head, with its spiked sun rays forming a halo around the dead Emperor's chubby features. He turned to face Valens. 'Did you ever serve with Vespasian in Britannia?'

'No. I was in Germania when Claudius invaded.'

'But he's a soldier, yes?'

'I believe so.'

Caecina shook his head in mock despair as he marched towards the doorway. 'And we follow a fat fool who will be counting wine barrels while we do the fighting and dying for him.'

Valens watched him go. He knew he should protest, would even be justified in shouting 'Traitor', but he was tired. In any case, Caecina was right.

V

Valerius woke to the distinctive bustle of a legion preparing for the march: the sound of centurions roaring at heavy-handed recruits as they struggled with the stakes that had protected the camp overnight, the flap of leather tents being dismantled in a light breeze, the clatter of cooking pots and spears piled for transport on the cohort's mules. He had seen the signs over the past few days. Instead of the customary exercises with *gladius* and *scutum* the men had been allowed to sit outside their tents sharpening their short swords, mending uniforms, polishing their armour and replacing the iron hobnails in *caligae*. A legionary's footwear was as important as his sword. He had to be able to march twenty miles a day and fight a battle at the end of it. A single nail out of place could leave the century a fighting man short, and they would need every man when they met Vitellius's legions.

Serpentius appeared in the doorway of the tent. 'It's happening,' the Spaniard confirmed with a shark's smile of anticipation. 'You've been called to a conference in the *principia* tent at the second hour.'

'Why didn't you wake me?' Valerius grumbled. He reached for the small leather bottle that was always within reach of his bedding and oiled the mottled purple stump of his right arm before slipping over it the cowhide socket that held his wooden fist. Serpentius watched as, with teeth and fingers made nimble from habit, he tightened and knotted the leather bindings that fixed it in place.

The former gladiator shrugged. 'I didn't reckon a few more minutes would make much difference. Full dress uniform.' He hefted the scuffed leather tribune's breastplate Primus had grudgingly provided and waited while Valerius drew his tunic over his head and belted it in place. Serpentius helped the younger man strap on the armour, then the belt with its apron of studded straps that was designed to protect his groin and upper legs. Over Valerius's left shoulder he draped the leather sling that would hold the decorated metal scabbard on his right hip, the sword ready to be cross-drawn. Only then did he slip into place the *gladius* he had spent an hour sharpening while the other man was asleep. Satisfied, he helped the one-handed Roman with the straps of his studded leather boots and finally handed him the polished iron helmet that had also belonged to the breastplate's previous owner, an over-enthusiastic young officer who had died on the end of a Dacian spear.

Serpentius stepped back and nodded approvingly. 'You'll do.'

'I specified full uniform.' Marcus Antonius Primus looked up from the document he had been studying as Valerius entered. All the other senior legionary commanders were already assembled. Aquila, legate of the Thirteenth Gemina, sniffed disapprovingly when he recognized the newcomer. Valerius nodded to Vipstanus Messalla, the only other military tribune to attend, a scarred veteran who had fought his way up through the ranks to become temporary commander of the famous Seventh Claudia Pia Fidelis. Messalla met his look with a sardonic half-smile that didn't bode well for the rest of the proceedings. A hollow-cheeked man at the far side of the table where Primus was seated nodded a greeting.

'Numisius Lupus, Eighth Augusta,' Primus grudgingly introduced his fellow commander. 'And this is Aurelius Fulvus, Third Gallica.' Fulvus needed no introduction. An old comrade, he had been one of Corbulo's commanders and Valerius remembered him as a steady, intelligent soldier steeped, like his men, in the traditions of the East.

'Arrius Varus, who commands our cavalry.' All the men apart from Messalla and Varus wore the scarlet cloaks that signified their general's rank. Those of Varus and Messalla were white and Valerius's should have been the same.

'I apologize, sir,' he said. 'If I'd realized I needed a cloak I would have had my servant steal one in time for the meeting.'

Messalla and Fulvus laughed. Primus's nostrils flared at the insubordination, but he waved Valerius to a chair at the far end of the table, picked up a pointer and turned to a map pinned to a frame beside him. 'When we are ready, gentlemen. Vespasian's spies report that the enemy legions have begun to gather, but they will take time to concentrate. At the moment only two legions and a few detachments occupy the Padus valley, which we are agreed must be the first step on our way to Rome. Two legions, and we can muster four at the moment and five within a few days.' He noted the look of concern that crossed Messalla's face. 'I am aware our leader has urged caution, tribune, but the Emperor is not here and cannot judge our situation. This is an opportunity that may not occur again. If we attack now, take Aquileia,' he pointed to a black dot at the head of the Mare Adriaticum, 'and open up the road to Cremona, we will be in a position to strike a decisive blow in this campaign while the enemy is still preparing for it. We—'

Valerius cleared his throat and every eye turned to him. Primus's face, already red from the sun, turned a more dangerous shade. 'You have something to add, tribune?'

'A question, sir, if I may be permitted?'

The legate threw his pointer on the table. 'Very well, and then you will no doubt give us the benefit of your knowledge, and perhaps the Emperor's too?' He surveyed the occupants of the tent and two of the men at the table laughed dutifully, but the lack of response from Fulvus, Messalla and Lupus told Valerius that Primus's command wasn't entirely united. That gave him encouragement to continue. He got to his feet.

'I only seek the identity of the two legions and the identity and size of the detachments.' He saw Primus's eyes narrow and sought to

40

explain. 'As you know, I have encountered several of Vitellius's legions in the recent past. General Aquila,' he bowed to the Thirteenth's commander, who exchanged a puzzled look with Primus, 'and I met them at Bedriacum and I am sure he would agree that, although they were victorious, they did not leave the battlefield undamaged. The Twenty-first suffered heavy casualties before Valens sent in his reserves . . .'

'Aye,' Aquila interrupted. 'And we made the Fifth Alaudae bleed for every inch of ground in that bastard maze of jungle on the north of the road.'

Valerius bowed again, acknowledging the general's support. He turned back to Primus. 'So the identity of the legions would give us a truer indication of the opposition facing us and help decide where and when to meet them.'

The interior of the tent went threateningly still. 'Do you question my right to make that decision?' Primus demanded.

'No, sir, but . . .'

'Perhaps you wish to add mutiny to your recent accomplishments? How many death sentences does it take to kill a man? Would you care to find out?'

Valerius bowed and resumed his seat, satisfied he had planted the seed and that whatever risk it had involved had been worthwhile. Aurelius Fulvus confirmed it.

'Nevertheless, I for one would be glad of the information. Better to know whether you are facing a bloodied and understrength Fifth Alaudae,' he bowed to Aquila, 'or a First Germanica fresh from their Rhenus stamping grounds and eager to emulate the success of their comrades against Otho.'

Primus gave a grunt of frustration. 'Very well. Varus?'

Varus, an intense young man with a long, doleful face and a horse soldier's stocky build, licked his lips, patently in awe of the other men in the tent. 'Our sources indicate the two legions at Cremona are indeed Fifth Alaudae and Twenty-first Rapax, that they have only recently returned to the camp outside the city and that they contain a substantial number of replacements.'

'Does that satisfy you?' Primus glared at the men around the table, but Varus carried on as if he hadn't heard his commander.

'In addition, elements of the Second and Twentieth legions, newly arrived from Britannia, are also billeted at Cremona, plus a detachment from the Ninth legion, which is currently garrisoning the city of Placentia.'

'And the strength of these elements?' Fulvus persisted.

'Each detachment is not less than three thousand men, general.'

Thank you,' the Third Gallica's commander said. 'So the equivalent of three full legions at Cremona, not two. You fought in Britannia, Verrens? What was your assessment of the units stationed there?'

Valerius glanced at Primus, and the army commander gave a reluctant nod.

'Well-trained, hard fighters, toughened by campaigning in difficult terrain against an enemy who never gives up,' he said. 'But they haven't fought a major battle since Suetonius Paulinus defeated the rebel queen Boudicca nine years ago. The Ninth had morale problems then, and if they've put them to guarding Placentia the situation may not have improved.'

Fulvus thanked him. Primus gave another grunt and returned to his map.

'So our enemy is split. An advance guard of two battered legions and three detachments in the north. Four others, or the major elements of them, currently making their way to the Padus, but still probably more than a week away.' He met the gaze of each of the generals in turn. 'A week.'

'As you say, the Emperor urged caution,' Lupus said warily. 'How long will it take Licinius Mucianus to reach us with his Syrian legions?'

It was a question designed to delay and give time to consider, because everyone knew the answer was at least a month.

'We have one chance.' Primus's voice grew in strength. 'One chance to smash Vitellius and present Titus Flavius Vespasian with the keys to Rome. A chance to make our names ring down through history, gentlemen. How many generals are given that opportunity?'

'Mainly dead ones.'

Primus greeted Messalla's interruption with a tight smile that said it was the last time he would be so forgiving. No matter what was said at this conference he had already made up his mind. Had made it up, Valerius reckoned, even before he'd marched the Seventh from Carnuntum to link up with Aquila. Now he outlined the detail of his plan.

'The town of Aquileia is the key that unlocks the door to Venetia, and if we take Venetia we have the gateway to the entire Padus valley in our hands.' He turned to his cavalry commander. 'Varus, you and your barbarians will test the enemy's strength and dispositions, and if possible clear him from our route. In the meantime, Thirteenth Gallica and Seventh Galbiana will take the van under the direct command of General Aquila and march on Aquileia at their best pace. Seventh Claudia and Third Gallica will follow, with Eighth Augusta acting as rearguard. I have already given the auxiliary cohorts their instructions. They will protect our right flank and secure the Alpine passes against any potential incursions from Noricum and Raetia. Are there any questions?'

'Supplies?' Fulvus asked.

'Another reason for acting with haste. We have sufficient rations for a week or ten days; when they are gone we will do what armies do. Live off the land.' They all knew what that meant. Starving peasants and grieving mothers. Farmers – Roman farmers – butchered trying to protect their stocks against the foraging troops. Primus shrugged. 'We are as well to go short on the march as stay here and go hungry.'

'And when we take Aquileia?' The question came from Messalla, who wore the resigned look of a man forced to choose between sharing a cage with a lion or a tiger. He had staked his future on Titus Flavius Vespasian and he wasn't certain whether the Emperor would approve of this impulsive advance. Success might take the edge off his displeasure, or it might not. Failure . . . ?

But Primus had no thought of failure. 'We will advance on Patavium and the rest of Venetia. But that is for the future. We will talk again and make a decision based on the dispositions of the enemy. Thank you, gentlemen. Verrens?' Valerius hung back as the other men filed

43

out to brief their officers and draft their orders for the advance. 'Fulvus tells me you were with Corbulo's cavalry.'

'Yes, sir,' Valerius said warily. He'd commanded ten thousand horse soldiers on campaign in Armenia, a force that played a crucial role in saving the Eastern Empire, defeated the Parthian King of Kings and ultimately sealed Corbulo's fate. While a single legion and a few auxiliary cohorts had held the Parthian Invincibles at the Cepha gap he'd led the cavalry on a night march through the mountains into the enemy rear. He remembered screams in the dark as men and horses took a single fatal step that hurled them into the void. The intoxicating relief of a bright new dawn. And the final terrible charge over grass the colour of gold that was soon stained with blood. Yet it was a battle with no heroes and no glory, because Nero had ordered it erased from the records.

'Then you may be of some use after all,' Primus sniffed. 'Varus is enthusiastic, but inexperienced for a command of this size. You will accompany him to assess the enemy's capabilities, and probe beyond Aquileia to discover if the country is clear. Varus will remain in nominal command, but I give you leave to act at your own discretion.' He smiled for the first time since Valerius had met him, but it was a shark's smile. 'Who knows, perhaps you will get yourself killed and give me peace of mind.'

He turned back to the map and Valerius knew he was dismissed, but he delayed as he heard the legate talking softly to himself. 'Valens or Caecina, which will it be?'

'You should hope it's Caecina,' Valerius dared answer the question he hadn't been asked.

Primus didn't turn round. 'And if it is Caecina, what will he do?'

Valerius remembered the countless dead and the desperate, ultimately futile attacks on the walls of Placentia. 'Whatever it is, right or wrong, the only certainty is that it will be what you least expect.'

VI

Valerius swatted at the black flies that swarmed around his head and heard Serpentius laugh at the futility of the gesture. It had been like this for the last five days: endless mountain trails hemmed in by scree-scattered slope and sweaty airless forest, and always accompanied by the maddening, relentless buzz of a million insects. But rank had its compensations and at least they'd been in the van of the column and spared the choking dust that coated the eight regiments of Varus's cavalry who followed. In the lead rode the Syrian archers of the First Augusta Ituraeorum: small, black-bearded men on light, sure-footed ponies, their green tunics and iron helmets now a uniform toneless brown. Behind them came two one-thousand-strong wings of wild, long-haired mounted spearmen from Germania of a type Valerius knew only too well from his adventures on the Rhenus a year earlier. Units from Hispania, Thrace and Gaul made up the rest. A strong force, but vulnerable until they were free of the mountain passes.

Valerius and Serpentius travelled with Varus's headquarters staff and the Roman quickly discovered he'd misjudged the young auxiliary commander's character. Varus might have been nervous when faced with four legionary generals, but in the field he proved the opposite: arrogant and opinionated, with seldom a good word to say about any-one but himself. He knew his business, though, sending out scouts ahead and on the flanking hillsides, with the column on constant alert and weapons always to hand. The reason for his professionalism became clear when Varus told the older man that he'd served with Gnaeus Domitius Corbulo in Armenia for three years.

'A fine general and a man with a reputation for discipline.' Valerius decided it was wiser not to reveal that he had led Corbulo's cavalry.

'I thought he was rather overrated as a commander,' Varus shrugged. 'Look at his record. Twelve years in the East and thousands of casualties and what did he have to show for it? Tiridates still on his throne in Artaxata, albeit with his wings clipped and his beard singed, and his brother with a mighty army at his disposal that still remains a threat to Syria and Judaea.'

'I thought his first campaign in Armenia had been hailed as a strategic triumph?'

Varus looked back irritably as the sound of a trumpet blared out over the rhythmic thud of hooves and clatter of metal equipment, urging a lagging squadron to close up. He rapped out an order to an aide before turning back to his companion. 'Oh, I'm not saying he wasn't a competent general.' A short laugh signalled the opposite. 'But sieges were more in his line than great battles. He was no Caesar, you see. Much too cautious. Not a man to take an opportunity in both hands, like our General Primus.'

Valerius had listened to the impugning of his late commander's reputation and record without reacting, but this fulsome praise for a man who had never witnessed a battle, never mind fought one, made him blink. He changed the subject, pointing to the flank guards on top of a nearby hill. 'It is wise to prepare for trouble, but do you think we will meet the enemy this far east?'

Varus shrugged. 'Not regular troops, but Vitellius's agents have been active among the local natives. The tribes of Pannonia are more or less civilized,' he said dismissively. 'They might steal a few horses or rob a single supply wagon, but normally they'd never risk attacking a column of this strength. Our greatest threat is from the Marcomanni and the Quadi, who may sniff an opportunity and decide to cross the river.' Valerius knew the Marcomanni were a tribe who ruled the endless pasturelands north of Noricum and the Danuvius, but he'd never heard of the Quadi. 'Their Sarmatian cousins,' the auxiliary explained. 'Newly arrived from the East and one of the reasons they need to expand their territory. I doubt it will happen, though. The Roxolani tried it in Moesia six months ago. Nine thousand warriors crossed the river, but the Third and the Eighth made sure not a single one got back. Word of that kind of defeat spreads.' He nodded to himself. 'Yes, we're in good company with the Third and the Eighth. They know how to fight.'

'They know how to fight barbarians,' Valerius pointed out. 'But do they know how to fight another legion?'

Varus frowned as if the thought had never occurred to him.

They broke free of the mountains next morning and reached the outskirts of Aquileia as the heat of the day reached its peak. Beyond the city the sapphire blue waters of the lagoons of the Mare Adriaticum had never appeared so welcoming, after a week sweating in the hills. Varus sent two regiments of his Syrian horse archers in a wide arc on the landward side to block any escape and advanced his remaining cavalry over the surrounding fields. As they approached, Valerius saw it was an extensive, thriving place filled with rich buildings, marble temples and terracotta-roofed tenements that shimmered in the afternoon heat. By the time Varus reached the scatter of houses on the outskirts a delegation of elders and merchants was already waiting behind a figure carrying the green branch that signalled his wish to discuss terms.

'Tribune, will you join me?' Varus slid from his horse, and Valerius did likewise, beating the dust from his clothes as they walked along the gravel road towards the group. 'What do you think?' Varus said quietly.

'If they wanted trouble, we'd already know about it.'

As they reached the group, the man with the green branch stepped forward and bowed, while the others stood back fidgeting nervously and trying not to look threatening.

'Marcus Annidius Ponticus, decurion of Aquileia's council of leading citizens, and local magistrate, greets you and welcomes you.'

The magistrate's toga hung on his narrow frame like a tent and he must have been eighty, with a wrinkled child's face and a shining dome of a head. His voice was strong enough, with the power of a man accustomed to speaking in public, but it held a brittle edge of fear. 'We have food and drink, and can provide entertainment for your men before . . . before they continue on their mission. If you wish to water your horses we have a fine stream on the far side of town, with a lush meadow for grazing close by.'

Varus stepped forward and knocked the branch from the decurion's hand, eliciting a gasp from the men behind and a frown of distaste from Valerius. 'I am Arrius Varus, prefect of cavalry, and I claim Aquileia for Titus Flavius Vespasian, rightful Emperor of Rome. Does any man here dispute that right?' His words sent a stir of unease through the gathering and Ponticus darted a desperate glance back towards the others. 'Do you deny me, old man?' Varus filled his voice with the promise of bloody swords and rampaging licentious soldiery. 'You will surrender this city or I will burn it to the ground and slaughter every living thing in it.'

A man in the tight-linked mail of an auxiliary officer advanced from the waiting group with his sword held across the palms of both hands in a gesture of surrender. He brushed past the old man and knelt before Varus. 'Oppius Lucanus, commanding First Alpinorum, pledges his sword and those of his cohort to the rightful Emperor, Titus Flavius Vespasian.'

'What is your strength?' Varus demanded.

'Four hundred and forty effectives, twenty-four sick.'

'Very well, I may have need of infantry. Have the fighting men ready and supplied with whatever rations they can carry. We leave at first light tomorrow.' He saw the momentary relief on the magistrate's face and swiftly disabused him of any notion that his city and its contents were being overlooked. 'They will be replaced by one of my cavalry cohorts. You will find stabling for their horses and provide food and drink for the men. From now on, all movement to and from the city, including from the port, will require the sanction of the commander. Is that clear?' Ponticus bowed his head. 'In addition, the people of

Aquileia will supply fodder for six thousand horses and three days' rations for the men of my column. Arrange it with my quartermasters. My officers will dine in the city tonight. Ensure that the hospitality and entertainment is the best Aquileia can offer.' The old man backed away and the delegation moved off towards the city, casting wary glances back at Varus and talking animatedly among themselves. Valerius reflected that Marcus Antonius Primus didn't seem to have passed on Vespasian's preferred strategy of making allies of those who accepted his rule. Fear was all very well, but experience had taught him that fear was a transitory emotion, and when it faded it was all too often replaced by hatred and defiance. Shame could be a great motivator for a man who had bent the knee unwillingly. At best, Varus had ensured there would be resentment in this city that held the key to his supply line; at worst . . .

But the auxiliary commander seemed happy with the outcome. He turned to Valerius with a satisfied smile. 'Well, that was simple enough.'

Later, Valerius and Serpentius stood on the city walls watching lines of carts rattle and squeak their way out towards the nearby auxiliary encampments, their beds forced low over the axles by the weight of fodder and provisions for the thousands of cavalry surrounding the city.

'Poor bastards,' the Spaniard grunted. 'They'll never see a bent *sestertius* for that, and there'll be empty bellies this winter.'

Valerius only shrugged. 'Aquileia got off lightly compared to some.' He remembered the burned-out settlements they'd encountered in Raetia on their mission to contact Vitellius, the victims of Aulus Caecina Alienus's terror policy.

'And now we wait for the legions to catch up?'

'Varus has orders to push ahead and scout towards the Padus.' A shout from below distracted Valerius. He looked down to see two drunken cavalrymen fighting over a woman, rolling in a gutter as she raised her skirts to piss in it. Varus had sent two squadrons into the town to add weight to his quartermasters' authority, but it appeared some of them had given their officers the slip. As the cries faded the scent of woodsmoke drifted in from the cooking fires that dotted the surrounding fields and they could hear some homesick auxiliary crooning a mournful ballad in his own tongue. 'My guess is that we'll probe along the Via Postumia until we either reach the river or come up against enemy cavalry. What I don't understand is why Valens or Caecina isn't already here. They're not fools. If they'd garrisoned Aquileia with even one legion they could keep Primus bottled up in Pannonia indefinitely. It would give them time to bring up the rest of their forces and provide a secure base that could be supplied by sea if need be. We'd be outnumbered, the troops would soon become disheartened and our generals would look like fools. Every day Vitellius sits in Rome acting like an Emperor his validity grows and it makes Vespasian look like the usurper. Vespasian must act quickly, yet Vitellius's generals aren't doing anything to slow him down. It doesn't make sense.'

They resumed their advance in the morning, the troops refreshed and resupplied, leaving a cohort of Syrian archers to hold Aquileia until Primus arrived with his main force. The column followed the Via Postumia west to the town of Opitergium, which declared for Vespasian as soon as they heard the sound of Varus's trumpets. By mid-afternoon they had reached Patavium, a substantial city between the Via Postumia and the sea, and their first major challenge. Here, the residents were as willing to talk as those of Aquileia, but there was no rush to surrender. The town had a substantial garrison of Gaulish auxiliaries who would make the attacking of it a costly affair, particularly for cavalry without supporting artillery. Varus, confident as ever in his own abilities, was certain he could lure the city council to the Flavian cause, but it would take time and he was keenly aware they still hadn't made contact with the armies of Vitellius. Valerius watched his growing impatience as the interminable negotiations continued at a requisitioned villa outside the city walls. He wasn't surprised when the young cavalry commander drew him aside during a lull in the talks.

'It is important that Patavium declares for Vespasian, but equally so that we discover the enemy's strength this side of the Padus,' Varus said with heavy emphasis.

'You do not have to be so coy with me, Arrius.' Valerius met the unsubtle hint with a wry smile. 'If you want me to take a patrol ahead while you bore the Patavians to death all you have to do is say so.'

'I just thought that Spanish wolf of yours needed some exercise,' the prefect grinned. 'I can let you have two *alae*, three if you think it necessary. That should be enough to make any opposing force you meet think twice before taking you on. If you make contact, don't get involved. Withdraw here and we'll wait for Primus to reinforce us.'

Valerius chose the spearmen of the First Cananefatium, a unit of heavy cavalry from the marshy wastelands of the Germania coast, and the First Hispanorum Aravacorum, recruited from the Arevaci, a warrior people of northern Hispania. These were *alae miliariae*, nominally a thousand strong, but in reality each cavalry wing could put fewer than eight hundred men in the saddle, so he bolstered his force with a wing of Thracian archers. They rode out in the early after-noon, skirting the mountains west of the city, and two hours later they approached Ateste, a *colonia* settled by retired veterans of Augustus's legions fifty years earlier. Valerius reined in and studied the road ahead. He and Serpentius rode at the head of the Cananefates, with the unit's red-bearded commander, Octavius. Valerius turned to the German. 'What do you make of that?'

The town was little more than a shimmering blur in the distance, but the twinkle of the sun on metal betrayed what might be a military presence. 'Could be trouble,' the German agreed in a Latin thick with the guttural intonation of his native dialect. 'We'll know soon enough.' Even as he spoke a scout galloped up and rattled out a report to his commander.

'Soldiers,' Octavius confirmed. 'Infantry – auxiliaries or militia he thinks, judging by their war gear – but without cavalry support. No more than three centuries,' he added, pre-empting Valerius's question, 'and they're not in defensive positions. Arminus here says it looks as if they're drawn up on parade.'

'Then perhaps we should go and inspect them,' Valerius suggested thoughtfully. 'But we'll send a couple of squadrons ready to flank them just in case they try anything foolish. I'll take the first *turma*, you follow with the rest of the column.'

As he and Serpentius rode ahead with the squadron's thirty-two troopers ranged warily behind them, the Spaniard produced a sour smile. 'The German swamp rats think you're an idiot who's going to get them killed. Maybe I hit you on the head one too many times?'

'Do you want to live for ever?' Valerius laughed. 'If I was baiting a trap, I wouldn't have three full centuries on parade by the side of the road. I'd have them lounging about looking unprepared and waiting to be slaughtered.' He gestured to the grape vines in the fields beside the road. 'You could hide an army in those bushes.'

Valerius felt the tension grow in the men behind them as they approached the town. By now he could clearly see the lines of helmeted men arrayed by the roadside, the points of their *pila* glistening dangerously in the sunlight. His eyes searched the ground to right and left looking for the threat that could kill him, but saw nothing but vines fluttering in the soft breeze, and beyond, on the slopes of the hill, ranks of dusty green olive trees.

With a hundred paces to go, he allowed his mount to drift back to the unit's commander. 'At the first sign of trouble,' he said softly, 'we ride straight through them and kill any of the bastards who get in the way. When we're clear, turn and join one of the flanking squadrons.' The man grinned with the cavalryman's time-honoured disdain for foot soldiers. His unit hadn't had a proper fight for almost a year and he'd as happily slaughter them as not.

But as they approached the silent ranks ahead, the only movement was from a single officer who stepped out briskly into the centre of the roadway and the accompanying ripple along the iron-clad ranks as the men came to attention. Valerius and the auxiliary approached warily and the man in the road slammed his fist into his breastplate in salute.

'Annius Cluvius Celer, *praefectus* of the Ateste cohort of *evocati*,' he announced. Valerius took a moment to study the man, who must have been in his fifties. Celer had a thick beard flecked with grey and the uniform he wore had been patched and mended. The combination brought to mind Falco, commander of the Colonia militia, which wasn't surprising, because that's exactly what these men were: legionary veterans who had been given a land grant to settle here. The *evocati* were soldiers who had completed their twenty-five years' service, but had volunteered to be ready for recall if the Empire needed them. Celer, their commander, was of equestrian rank, and his family probably originally came from the area. He would have invited the legionaries he served with to make their homes around the town when they retired. The men on parade looked well, still fit and hard, which told Valerius they weren't long out of the legions. They looked up for a fight. The only question was, who with? Celer answered that with his next words. 'The Ateste cohort of *evocati* declares for Titus Flavius Vespasian.'

Valerius relaxed and turned to the auxiliary officer. 'Send word to Octavius that Ateste is ours and to bring the men forward. They can water their horses in the stream.' He dismounted and walked with the prefect along the lines of men. 'They look impressive.'

'You mean they look impressive for militia.' Celer produced a great belly laugh. 'But don't be deceived, tribune. Not that long ago these men were the toughest soldiers in the Sixth Ferrata, the toughest legion in the Empire.' Valerius smiled at the boast. He knew it was no idle one. The Sixth Ferrata had been the rock on which Gnaeus Domitius Corbulo's Armenian campaigns had been built, and Corbulo never accepted less than the best.

'You know that the Sixth declared for Vespasian in Judaea?'

Celer nodded. 'We'd heard that. It was one of the reasons we decided Ateste should support him, but not the only one. In the spring, when we should have been planting our fields, Vitellius's bandits came this way, burning and looting, and killing anyone who didn't support their man. Ateste stayed loyal to Otho, the rightful Emperor. We managed to get most of the people from the outlying farms into town and we looked dangerous enough to keep the enemy out.' He spat. 'They were only cavalry, after all. But,' a shadow fell over his eyes, 'a few of the outlying estates didn't get word. I lost my son and his family. Many of these men lost people. All we want is the chance to avenge them.'

A muted rumble of agreement emerged from the throats of the men within hearing distance. 'Shut up, you useless shower,' Celer snarled. 'Have you forgotten what it is to be a soldier?'

'I'll make sure General Vespasian hears of your loyalty,' Valerius said.

The other man bowed his thanks. 'Just give us a chance to fight.'

'You'll get your chance,' Valerius assured him. 'But first you should stay here and hold the city for Vespasian until the Danuvius legions secure the territory. I'll leave word suggesting you be incorporated in Third Gallica.'

The Third had been another of Corbulo's legions until they'd been sent to Moesia. Valerius knew they were the Sixth's arch-rivals. Celer's smile broadened. 'They'll enjoy showing that useless bunch of raw recruits how a real soldier acts.'

Valerius waited with the prefect while Octavius approached at the head of the main force. 'Have you heard anything about troop movements in the Padus valley?'

Celer grimaced. 'I apologize, tribune; it should have been the first thing I reported. Word arrived this morning that soldiers have been seen this side of the Athesis river opposite Forum Alieni.'

'How far away is Forum Alieni?' Valerius frowned. 'Did your informant say how many?'

'Half a day's steady riding,' Celer said. 'As to numbers, I questioned him thoroughly, but he couldn't say for certain. He is a civilian, sir, just a travelling hawker. He saw men in armour guarding a bridge, and a few horses. There was no bridge at Forum Alieni a week ago, so they must have built it themselves. That would have taken a sizeable force.'

Valerius called up Octavius and passed on Celer's information. The big German cavalryman looked thoughtful. 'If they have constructed a bridge, it would seem they plan a crossing. The prudent thing to do would be to withdraw and link up with General Varus at Patavium.'

'That's true,' Valerius acknowledged. 'But it would also mean giving up all the ground between the Athesis and Patavium on the word of one man who isn't certain what he's seen. It's possible that the troops at Forum Alieni are only an advance guard sent to prepare the ground for a main force. We'd look like fools if we went back to Varus not knowing whether he was going to be facing four or five cohorts or four or five legions.'

Octavius could see the sense of that. 'A probe in force then, to gauge the enemy's numbers.'

Valerius grinned. 'And if those numbers are in our favour?'

The big German's yellowing teeth showed through his beard. 'We slaughter the bastards.'

VII

Serpentius slipped from the gloom beneath the olive trees as silent as any phantom, his face and clothing caked with mud the colour of a terracotta roof tile. 'Atticus,' he growled as he approached Valerius. Octavius and the ten-man patrol waiting in the fading light for his return relaxed in their saddles when they heard the watchword.

Valerius handed him a water skin and the Spaniard washed his mouth out and spat the residue to one side. 'The ground is as flat as a ten-year-old virgin's tits from here to the river,' he reported. 'But the olive groves and vines give plenty of cover until you're about two hundred paces away. It looks as if they've put all their effort into building the bridge, because a child could cross the ditches around their camp and you could spit through the palisade.'

'You got that close?'

Serpentius shrugged. 'There are drainage channels leading to the river, and the camp is between two of them.' He crouched and the other men huddled around him as he pulled out his knife and cleared a patch of sandy ground. There was just enough light to see the two lines he drew to represent the river, a further two to show the bridge, and a square on the ground to identify the camp. On either side of the camp a line extended to the Athesis at a slight diagonal, diverging as they approached the river bank. He met Valerius's eye.

'They have possibly two cohorts of infantry on this side of the bridge, and what looks like a third cohort and a cavalry squadron guarding the far side.'

Valerius felt a flare of exultation at the news that the enemy had split their forces. He tried to create an image of the fort, the bridge and the surrounding terrain. 'What about guards?'

'They were there, but they didn't see me. They didn't act like people who expect to meet opposition any time soon.'

'You're not two thousand men on horses,' Valerius pointed out.

Serpentius nodded, acknowledging the truth of it. 'But our Thracian archers should be able to take care of the guards. I can get them close enough, if they leave their horses behind.'

'They're holding the bridge until their main force comes up from the south.' Valerius mentally wove his way through the enemy strategy. 'That could be tomorrow, the next day, or next week, but if they do cross it gives them a tactical advantage over Primus. With enough men on this side of the river, they could push us back to Aquileia and bottle us up in the hills. If we attacked them it would be on ground they'd chosen and prepared for defence. We might still win, but it would cost a lot of blood.'

Octavius nodded, and his eyes glowed in the falling dusk as he realized what Valerius was thinking. 'But if we can throw them back across the river . . .'

'Burn the bridge and give Valens and Caecina something to think about . . .'

'We should hit them at dawn,' Serpentius advised, 'when they're taking their first piss of the day and thinking of lighting their cooking fires.' His face twisted into a scowl. 'But this isn't horse country. I don't know how close I can get your men before we're seen.'

Valerius turned to the cavalry officer. 'How will your men feel about fighting without their horses?'

Octavius grunted. 'How would you feel about fighting without your armour?' He sighed. 'But if it's the only way to kill them . . .'

Valerius slapped him on the shoulder. 'Officers' conference when we get back to camp. Serpentius will instruct your best scouts on the terrain. We'll hit them from both sides. They will be like sheep to our wolves.'

The German's eyes glittered. 'And like sheep they will be slaughtered.'

In Serpentius, Octavius's wolves were led by a hunting leopard. When they'd ridden as close as they dared, the Spaniard led the dismounted cavalrymen unerringly through the olive groves in the darkness. The last man in each *turma* of thirty men was linked to the first in the following *turma* by a rope, so even with two thousand men none was lost along the way. Despite the relative warmth of the night every trooper wore a cloak to dull the chinking of his armour. The silence wasn't perfect – Valerius cringed at the rattle of sword belts and the occasional muffled collision and whispered curses that signalled when a man fell or stumbled – but none was so loud that it carried to the Vitellian encampment four hundred paces away. They went three abreast, striding warily because in the pitch dark every step felt as if it would carry them into a ditch. Their eyes never left the shadowy silhouette of the man in front, and the rustle of movement to rear or flank was the only evidence they were part of a larger whole. Even for the veterans among them the still night held a constant threat that made the blood thunder in their ears and their hearts hammer against their ribs. They told themselves it wasn't fear, only the anticipation of battle, but few among them didn't pray to the gods of their homeland during the ordeal of that interminable journey. Eventually, a hissed command rippled down the line ordering the halt that confirmed they'd come to the most dangerous part of the march. Behind him, Valerius knew, the picked scouts of the Hispanorum Aravacorum would be leading their *turmae* east to the drainage ditch closest to the far side of the camp. The success of the attack depended on total concealment. If even one man gave away his position the enemy guards would alert the entire camp. A heart-stopping delay as Serpentius gave his fellow Spaniards of the *Aravacorum* time to reach their position, then the First was on the move again through the darkness. After a few moments Valerius heard a whispered command to the leading rank of the *turma*, and word came back that they'd reached the ditch and to take care. Valerius would have continued with them, but a hand came out of the darkness and drew him aside. A harsh voice whispered in his ear. 'Better that you're in the centre where you can control things.'

He waited, kneeling by Serpentius's side as the Spaniard counted the *turmae* through, warning each commander of the obstacle ahead. Once they were in the ditch they would make their way south towards the river, taking station opposite the temporary Vitellian fort. At a given moment Serpentius drew a junior officer aside from one of the units and told him to stay in position and inform the following cavalrymen about the ditch. When he was certain the man understood his duty he and Valerius joined the front rank of the man's *turma* and slipped down the bank until their feet sank into the shallow layer of stinking ooze at the bottom. Thick mud sucked at their sandals like a living thing and released a stench of rotting eggs to clog their nostrils. The channel was only chest deep, and to stay hidden they were forced to walk in a low crouch that quickly made Valerius's back ache and his calves burn as he wrestled to free his feet with every step. He was grateful when the man ahead stopped and he was able to sink back against the side of the trench to rest with his face to the sky.

His eyes picked out the brightest stars. When he was a child he had sometimes seen the faces of the gods in the stars, but at others they had formed images of sea monsters and ships. Now he could see that beyond the brightest stars there were many lesser ones, and beyond them a sense of still more, of great depth and untold numbers. The effect made him feel an unnatural sense of wonder and smallness. He shrugged off the sensation. Concentrate. Stars, but no moon, thank the gods. By now the men in the far ditch would also be in position.

Careful to remove his helmet to avoid creating a familiar silhouette, he risked a glance through the tangle of rushes and nettles on the lip of the ditch. Perhaps forty paces away a faint shadow was just visible against the luminosity of the night sky, and his mind visualized the raised bank topped by a palisade of stakes. That bank would be patrolled by sentries and fronted by at least two, possibly three ditches. In the enemy commander's position, Valerius would have dug those ditches deep and filled them with traps, but Serpentius said that wasn't the case, and Valerius had learned to trust the Spaniard with his life. Few men hated Romans as Serpentius did, but he was happy to serve Valerius because Valerius had saved him from certain death in the arena. The Spaniard had been taken in a reprisal raid after his Asturian mountain tribe had dared to raid one gold convoy too many. Romans like the men he marched with had killed his wife and son and he would never forget that, but revenge must wait until he had repaid his debt to the one who had given him his freedom and his life. A born warrior, and if he was to be believed a prince of his tribe, his fighting skills and preference for pitiless violence had made him an ideal recruit for the arena. Deadly with either sword or spear, his lightning speed and lethal precision soon earned him the name Serpentius – the Snake. Another man might eventually have won his freedom through his victories and popularity, but the Spaniard killed with a cold, murderous intensity that intimidated rather than entertained, and he never hid his contempt for the mob. Eventually, he would have been sacrificed, outnumbered and poorly armed, his death delivered to the crowd in a tawdry, blood-spattered spectacle. Valerius had found him just in time.

The Roman dropped back, doubt sending a shiver through him. Had he made the right decision, or should he have retreated towards Patavium? No. He'd done the only thing possible. If he could stop the Vitellians here it would give Primus time to bring his troops forward into the broad flatlands of Venetia. There, the general could choose his battleground and wait for Valens or Caecina to come to him. For the moment though, Valerius could do nothing but wait. In the surrounding darkness two thousand cavalrymen waited with him, every man alone with his thoughts, his hopes and his fears.

It wasn't dawn so much as the promise of dawn. The sky transformed in a moment from inky black to darkest blue and, in the next breath, to a slightly fainter shade that silhouetted the stakes of the palisaded parapet and the guards patrolling it against the dying night. A plaintive screech split the fading darkness as if a hunting owl was making its final pass over the grasses bordering the ditch. It was the last thing the sentries would ever hear.

Valerius had posted a hundred of his Thracian archers among the men in the ditch. By now they had already picked their targets among the dozen or so unsuspecting sentries. The moment the screech died in Serpentius's throat Valerius heard the familiar soft 'thrum' of bowstrings. It was followed by the unmistakable hiss of arrows carving the air, and a heartbeat later the smack as the iron-tipped shafts struck and the short-lived cries of men pinned by six or seven arrows apiece. In the same instant a single archer set the pitch-soaked cloth of a fire arrow to the bowl of glowing charcoal hidden beneath his cloak and sent the shaft curving through the sky like a shooting star.

Before the arrow fell to earth the men of the First had hauled themselves from the drainage ditch and were dashing silently towards the temporary fort. Valerius knew the death of the sentries wouldn't have gone unnoticed, but he gambled that the suddenness of it would cause a moment of confusion rather than an instant call to arms. His heart stuttered as the ground dropped away beneath his feet. The ditch. Mars' arse. He prayed Serpentius had been right about the ditch and the palisade. Fear gripped his guts like a closed fist. This was the moment. If the defences delayed them even for a few heartbeats the defenders would line the parapet above and their weighted javelins would lance down into the attackers. Those spears would easily punch through the light cavalry shields and the tight-knit auxiliary ring mail that would stop an edge, but not a point. Octavius and his men would be slaughtered and Valerius would be slaughtered with them.

He gritted his teeth and drove the fear aside; if he was going to die, let the fates decide. He was Gaius Valerius Verrens, Hero of Rome and the only survivor of the Temple of Claudius, and this was his attack. It was his plan that had brought these men here to this damp, misty field. Pride would haul him up the slope to die beneath the wooden palisade even if courage didn't. But Serpentius had been certain and he was proved right. The ditch should have been eight feet deep with a shallow slope on the outward side, to draw an attacker in, but a vertical face on the inner, topped by the earthen bank and the palisade. A virtually unscaleable obstacle the height of three men with defenders at the top. But the enemy had been lazy. The ditch was only half the proper depth, and the earth spoil had been heaped in a soft, easily mounted slope. Above him, Valerius could see gaps in the wooden palisade and already men had climbed to the top of the earthen bank and started to tear at the stakes and rip them free from the loose soil.

The first shouts of alarm rang out and he knew the men of the First Hispanorum Aravacorum would already be carrying their swords into the camp. From somewhere in the distance a trumpet sounded and a torch flared on the far side of the river. Valerius kicked at a four-foot post and squeezed through the gap, knowing Serpentius wouldn't be far from his side. Already hundreds of men were spilling down the rear of the earthen bank towards the neat rows of eight-man tents. He stepped over a dead man, noting the arrows that pierced his chest and throat. When he saw the dull glimmer of the man's armour he realized how fortunate he'd been. The sentries were all auxiliaries wearing chain link vests. If they'd been a regular legionary unit wearing the more protective plate, some would certainly have survived to raise the alarm. But they hadn't and now the killing could begin.

'Now,' he roared. 'Let the bastards hear you.' The Germans responded with the blood-curling wolf's howl that was their battle cry and threw themselves at the men spilling from the tents, attempting to fix straps and pull armour over their heads. The Vitellians were unprepared, and men who go into battle unprepared are ripe for the slaughter.

A bearded soldier wearing only a brown tunic appeared from the darkness to Valerius's left and tried to skewer him with a spear. Valerius swayed to allow the point to slip past his right shoulder and rammed forward with his sword, feeling it pierce soft flesh and solid muscle before the iron jarred against the soldier's spine. A sharp twist should have torn it from the dying body, but he'd struck too deep. Instead, he had to put his foot on his victim's chest to lever the blade free, thanking the gods no one was around to kill him for his stupidity.

He tried to gauge the course of the fight from the sounds around him. What he could hear was the noise of a rout. The sound of men exulting in the joy of battle in a guttural, formless tongue; the howls of the eviscerated and the shrieks of the dying; cries for mercy that would go unheard. It all seemed perfect, but something in the background made him uneasy. A headless torso lay nearby, the corpse wearing a set of *lorica segmentata* plate armour that told Valerius he wasn't facing only auxiliaries. Not that it made any difference to the German cavalrymen who whooped and laughed as they chased unarmed, half-clothed enemies through the tents. Valerius attempted to restore some order, roaring for Octavius to form a reserve, but the Flavians were driven beyond control by the taste of blood and the ease of the killing. Serpentius appeared at his side like a wraith from the Otherworld, a bloodied sword in his hand.

'The bastards had better enjoy it while they can,' the Spaniard said ominously.

'What?' Valerius struggled to hear him above the clamour of battle.

'To the west,' the former gladiator pointed with his sword. 'Some of them aren't running around like headless chickens, and if you don't do something about it we'll be the ones with our cocks on the butcher's block.'

VIII

Valerius ran in the direction of the river, cursing his stupidity for getting involved in the fight when he should have been directing it. He'd hoped the surprise attack would panic the Vitellians into either surrendering or retreating. Instead, somewhere among the rows of tents an officer had rallied his men and very soon the hunters would become the hunted.

'Stay here and try to round up as many Thracians as you can,' he called as he passed Serpentius. 'Tell them to conserve their arrows.'

Octavius was trying to form his men into some sort of line using the flat of his sword. 'I have a feeling that very soon this is going to be no place for a cavalryman,' the German shouted.

'Just get them formed up and follow me. Tell them we outnumber the bastards two to one and this is their chance to kill some Romans.'

The other man grinned and waved a reassuring hand.

On the west side of the camp, Valerius found a cleared space where the tents had been flattened and discarded equipment lay scattered all around. Here were the bloodied remnants of what had been the right flank of his attack on the camp. Six hundred strong and a mixture of Germans and Spaniards, they had lost all cohesion and stood shouting insults at the men on the other side of the open ground. The Roman stumbled to a halt, breathing hard, and a chill ran through him at the sight of an unbroken line of shields a few dozen paces in front of the bridge. The bridge was a temporary structure, made up of requisitioned boats and wooden planking, hastily roped together by men in a hurry to create a holding on the east side of the river.

As he felt the first rays of the rising sun on his neck Valerius realized his mistake had been not to take into account that the diverging ditches gave the attackers on this side of the camp a longer charge to reach the palisade. It meant the centurion commanding the legionary cohort had two or three seconds more to prepare, and that was enough. Unlike the auxiliaries who shared and had been responsible for building the temporary fort, he'd kept a full century on the alert in case of an emergency. Attacked from both flanks, they'd managed to hold off the assault and win time for their comrades to equip and arm themselves. Now something like four hundred battle-hardened legionaries formed two lines behind the big, brightly painted *scuta*, the shields' surfaces showing the golden lion symbol of the First Germanica.

But there was still hope. 'Form line!' Valerius roared the order as Octavius ran to his side followed by a few dozen of his troopers. The German and Spanish cavalrymen still outnumbered the depleted legionary cohort, and if they could hold firm long enough for the outer wings of their line to envelop the enemy they had a chance. But whatever the outcome, the centre of the line would be a horror of slaughtered auxiliaries. The centre of the line was where men would die, the outer flanks where men would win.

Valerius sheathed his sword long enough to pick up an abandoned legionary *scutum* and fix it to his wooden fist. He marched along the front of the ragged line of grim-faced auxiliaries. For all their training the dismounted cavalrymen Octavius led were little better than the barbarians the men opposite had spent years slaughtering in their thousands. But they were all he had. 'You fight here and win or you die here,' Valerius snarled. He didn't know whether they understood him, but he could hear Octavius shouting and hoped the German was translating his words. 'There is no going back. If you break, they will hunt you down like rats. So you will hold, and you will win.'

He forced his way into the centre of the line and a rumbling growl of defiance ran through the ranks. By now the enemy at the far end of the bridge should be thinking about reinforcing their comrades on the eastern bank, but he could see no threat. Where was Serpentius? It seemed unnatural not to have the Spaniard by his side, but even the thought of the feral, snarling features gave him comfort. He felt a fire ignite low in his guts, rise to fill his chest and surge into his brain, bringing with it an elixir that made the rest of the world seem slow and the men facing him nothing but victims: sacrifices for the long cavalry *spatha* he carried. In a fight he was the equal of any man – the equal of the gods. It didn't matter that he knew the reaction was illusory – a soldier's way of escaping the reality of battle – all that mattered was that it existed. He nodded to the man next to him and hefted his *scutum* to shoulder height. 'Keep your shield together with mine and hold. Any danger will come from your left. Aim for the eyes and the throat.' The soldier replied something Valerius didn't understand, but his reassuring grin was enough.

A barked order sent a thrill of dread and anticipation through him. The line of legionary shields opposite came up and the disciplined ranks moved towards him with the legionary's unhurried, seemingly unstoppable measured pace.

'Forward!' Valerius echoed the enemy order to advance and his cavalrymen, wishing more than anything they had their horses beneath them, took the first tentative steps towards the bobbing line of legionary shields opposite. They were less than fifty paces away now, and the Roman could hear the centurion in command barking at his men to keep their formation, to keep their shields up, to remember that a handspan of iron was enough to kill any man. Across the human detritus of the battleground the man met his gaze, his attention drawn by the legionary shield that marked Valerius out from the auxiliaries around him. Valerius raised his sword in salute, and the centurion grinned. It seemed madness that within the next thirty paces they would be trying to kill each other, especially now that Valerius could see his gamble had failed. For the survivors of the Vitellian auxiliary cohort had found a way to re-join their legionary comrades. Even as he watched, they took up station on the flanks, lengthening the line and ensuring there would be no envelopment and no victory. With a grunt of weary resignation Valerius hunched his shoulders and prepared for his last fight.

The sound, when it came, was almost lost in the clatter of armour and the thump of marching feet, but Valerius heard the faint slap and saw one of the men on the left of the legionary line fall backwards, creating a gap in the shield wall. In the next few moments more of the legionaries went down and now came the clatter of iron-tipped arrows hitting shield and armour. With his casualties mounting the enemy centurion had no option but to call a halt, ordering his men to shelter behind the big *scuta*. The archers' intervention had been as much of a surprise to Valerius as his opponent until he remembered his instruction to Serpentius to round up the scattered Thracians. He was tempted to order an all-out charge that might break the enemy line, but he knew the movement would only shield them from the arrows that were keeping them honest. Instead, he shouted at his men to hold their positions and wait. A growl of dissent went up from the ranks around him, and he stepped from the ranks to scream the order into their faces until the line stumbled to halt.

But the arrow storm was erratic, like a summer shower that came, and went, then came again, with no apparent rhythm. Experience told him there were not enough of the archers to keep the legionaries occupied indefinitely. Soon, he would have to throw his dismounted cavalrymen at the veterans across the way after all. Because, at last, he detected movement at the far side of the bridge. If he didn't push the two Vitellian lines backwards on to the wooden decked pontoons, the force facing them would be reinforced by another full cohort.

The arrow shower ceased and he opened his mouth to give the order to charge.

'Wait.'

Valerius froze at the harsh voice in his ear. 'Where—'

'Just wait.' Serpentius nodded towards the legionary line. Valerius watched with growing unease as the two ranks resumed their steady approach untroubled by the occasional arrow that thudded into their shields.

It had to be now. He tensed to give the order, but the Spaniard placed a hand on his arm. A heartbeat later he heard a hissing flutter of disturbed air followed by a sound like hail rattling on a tile roof. Hundreds of arrows arched into the legionary ranks from both flanks, seeking out throat and eye and groin and any gaps in armour. Valerius saw the centurion stagger, an arrow through his calf, but the man retained the presence of mind to give the order to form *testudo*. Harassed by three hundred Thracian archers Valerius had thought to hold in reserve, the survivors formed a carapace of shields and retreated steadily towards the bridge, leaving their dead lying in crumpled heaps.

With a last glare at his enemy, the wounded centurion shook his head in weary frustration and joined the *testudo* as it edged backwards. Valerius watched, relieved to see them go, then tensed as the formation halted.

'What are those bastards up to?'

Still flayed by the arrow storm, the *testudo* had stopped a few paces on to the makeshift bridge. Moments later they heard the sound of axes.

'Making sure we can't follow them.' Serpentius sounded almost admiring.

With a convulsive lurch the ropes holding the bridge parted and the entire structure swung downstream as if on a hinge, drawn round and bucking like a maddened horse in the strong current. Valerius heard a cry of terror as a legionary was pitched from the wooden boards to disappear with a splash into the dark waters, doomed by the armour that had saved his life moments earlier. Others were flung into the river when the bridge smashed against the far bank, dislodging boards along its length. Some of the men escaped to stumble into the shallows, but far fewer than had mounted the fragile structure. A half-hearted cheer went up from the German auxiliaries but most only stared. A man could kill another man on the battlefield and take satisfaction in his death; watching a brave man drown was different. Valerius prayed the enemy centurion still lived. Staring death in the face all he'd wanted to do was kill and kill again, but standing here with a gore-stained sword and a mouth so dry it hurt to swallow he felt all the emotion drain from him. These were Romans they were killing, brave Roman soldiers. The only difference was the men behind the First Germanica's shields chose to fight for an Emperor not worthy of the purple. He shook his head. Was that really true? Aulus Vitellius had a deserved reputation for sloth and greed, but Valerius remembered a mind as sharp as any philosopher's, a conscience he tried to keep hidden, and a heart as big as his gargantuan belly. Vespasian might be a fine general and the father of his friend Titus, but he'd cheerfully climbed the social ladder over the bodies of former friends – would he be any better? Yet Vitellius had tried to have Valerius killed, and after the defeat at Bedriacum and the horrors that followed there'd been no option but to join Vespasian. Only Vespasian's forces could carry him to Rome. And to Domitia Longina Corbulo.

Octavius appeared at his shoulder. 'A messenger just arrived from Patavium. Seventh Galbiana and Thirteenth Gallica joined Varus there last night, and General Primus has ordered them to march on Verona. You were right to fight here. If Vitellius's legions had been able to cross the Athesis they could have taken our people in the flank and destroyed them.' Valerius nodded absently, barely taking in the information. 'What now?' the German asked.

The Roman hesitated. 'Leave a strong screen of archers in case they try again. We'll bury the dead and take care of the wounded before we return to Patavium. The enemy dead too.' He felt the German stiffen. Many of Otho's casualties at Bedriacum had been mutilated after death and for all Valerius knew they still lay on the field where they fell. Octavius knew it too and he would have let the dead legionaries rot. Valerius couldn't explain his decision. He only knew that he must do what was right. Eventually the German strode away with a shrug, shouting orders to his surviving troops. Swaying on legs that would barely hold him, Valerius shaded his eyes and looked up at the sun.

'Less than an hour since dawn,' Serpentius confirmed. He laughed, short and bitter. 'I must be getting old. It feels as if it should be noon.'

They waited a moment longer, staring out over the surging waters. A few of the enemy legionaries had formed a human chain to try to rescue a comrade still floundering in the margins between the shallows and the deeper water. As they watched, the last man in the chain stretched out a despairing hand that must have been agonizingly close. Valerius willed him to succeed with a passion that surprised him, but the drowning soldier lifted an arm in what might have been a final farewell and slid from sight. The rescuers trudged back to the bank with their heads bowed and a few moments later the remains of the bridge parted from the far bank and floated away downriver. Within a few heartbeats it, and the men who had fallen from it, might never have existed.

IX

'They tell me you did well, Verrens.' The legate's voice contained a hint of puzzlement as if he couldn't quite believe what he was saying. Marcus Antonius Primus's nose twitched as he studied the tall figure who still stank of the alluvial mud clinging to his uniform and armour. Even the perfumed oil lamps that lit the dining room of the opulent villa didn't dispel the lingering scent of death. From an adjoining room, Valerius heard the soft murmur of the general's aides as they worked on the next phase of the campaign.

'Thank you, sir.' He hid his surprise at the warmth of the welcome. But he had enough experience of the other man's moods to know that a little praise didn't make them friends.

'You took a risk.' Primus nodded. 'But it was justified. If Caecina had crossed the Athesis in any force it would have placed us at a grave disadvantage.' The patrician frowned as he imagined the enemy's nine or ten legions formed up in their ranks on the flatlands between Patavium and the river. As it was, Gaius Valerius Verrens had presented him with the initiative and an opportunity. He turned to the map of northern Italia which was always near to hand. 'Instead, I am in a position where audacity and enterprise may win what caution would put at risk.' He hunched his shoulders and Valerius imagined a great weight bearing down on the figure brooding over the map. Only at that moment did he truly realize how much Primus had invested in this campaign.

'You mentioned Caecina, General. Not Valens, then?'

Primus looked up from beneath heavy brows, his dark hair flopping over a broad forehead creased with worry lines. 'We have received information from . . . sources . . . close to the enemy camp.' He didn't mention the letter which had accompanied the information. He'd yet to decide whether it was genuine or not – and if it was, whether the contents were to be trusted. 'Fabius Valens remains in Rome with the Emperor, sick or exhausted, our informant cannot decide which. Aulus Caecina Alienus is moving north to concentrate at Hostilia, on the Padus, a five-day march from Cremona. He commands four full legions, substantial cohort elements from three more and he has called the two British detachments south to join them. Only Fifth Alaudae and Twenty-first Rapax remain at Cremona, and three thousand men of the Ninth to hold Placentia.'

Curiosity drew Valerius to his commander's side. He traced the snaking line of the Padus east from Cremona until he found the tiny dot on the map that represented Hostilia. Primus saw his puzzlement. 'It is an insignificant place,' he agreed. 'A stopping place on the Via Claudia Augusta, nothing more.'

'This movement would make sense if he still held the crossing of the Athesis, but we are aware of his plan.' Valerius met his commander's gaze and shook his head. 'He can't ferry his legions over the river now for fear that we'll fall on them when they're divided. As it is, Hostilia has no strategic value. I don't understand it.'

'Unless he believes I am foolish enough to attack him with a weaker force?' Primus mused. 'That proposition might be attractive once we've been joined by Seventh Claudia and the Moesian legions.'

'If he stays where he is,' Valerius pointed out, 'he threatens Venetia and the eastern route that General Mucianus must take to join you. Perhaps,' he said warily, 'the Emperor-elect is right to urge caution.'

To his surprise, rather than exploding in rage, Primus laughed out loud; true, incredulity was mixed with the humour, but the laugh was genuine enough. 'By the gods, Verrens you do like to dangle your eggs over the fire. You urge restraint on me three days after you almost had your arse roasted using dismounted *cavalrymen* to take on a crack legionary cohort. If I didn't loathe your poxed lawyerly flesh, I might get to like you. You think I don't know the game you're playing?' The patrician face flushed red and it had nothing to do with the wine he was drinking. 'Keep him on the leash, that fornicating little mummy's boy Titus told you. Well, Marcus Antonius Primus doesn't react well to the leash. I was tempted to arrange a nasty accident for you, but I'm glad I didn't. You see, boy, you may think me a bully and a cheat who likes long odds and short races, but you're not the only one who's served. I'm soldier enough to respect courage and loyalty – even in a man who has done me a disservice – cleverness, too, although many would say that's not something to encourage in a military man. The way you used the ditches to get close enough to the fort to surprise the defenders. Then letting that cohort of the First think they were going to slaughter you so that they opened up to the archers on the flanks. A ruse worthy of Caesar himself.'

'I was responsible for neither,' Valerius said. 'The first was the suggestion of my freedman. The second was his way of stopping me getting myself killed.'

'So I understand.' Primus laughed. 'I've already had a complaint from the prefect of the Thracian cavalry demanding I send him the Spaniard's head on a plate. A barbarian of some resource and a danger-ous one at that, if I remember him rightly from the arena.' His face twisted into a sly smile. 'He's the other reason you didn't have a nasty accident. The man seems to have eyes in the back of his head.'

Valerius didn't react to the confirmation that Primus had planned to have him killed. 'I hope the general will reward rather than punish him.'

Primus nodded absently and picked up a wax tablet, inscribing it with short confident strokes of a metal stylus. He handed it to Valerius. 'Give this to my clerk on the way out and tell the Spaniard he's fortunate it's not an execution order. That's the problem with giving slaves their freedom, they get ideas above their station. Look at that bastard Tigellinus.' He scowled at the memory of Nero's freedman who'd risen to become commander of the Praetorian Guard. 'Asked for fifty thousand to guarantee a not guilty verdict. I told him to go and sodomise himself with a *spatha* and bribed the *quaestor* in charge of the count – much good it did me. I'd dance on the bastard's grave if I could find it.' Primus blinked, deciding he'd said more than was sensible. 'Anyway, tell the Spaniard to mind his manners. What was I saying?'

'That I was about to have a nasty accident.'

The general grinned. 'Courageous and loyal; honest too, I shouldn't wonder. I'm not myself, but I admire it in another man. Makes them easier to fleece. That's why you're here, because I know you won't stick a knife in my belly.' He turned back to the map. 'That and the fact that the army of Marcus Antonius Primus is not going to be cautious, whatever Vespasian and Mucianus may say. We will move up the Via Postumia to Verona, which is big enough and rich enough to resupply my legions, and if Caecina stays at Hostilia we'll march up the road and take Cremona before he can react.'

'And if he crosses the Athesis?'

'We'll still have time to about turn and crush him like a nut between the Pannonian legions here and the Moesian legions on their way from Noviodunum. You fought at Bedriacum, so you know the road and the terrain?' Valerius nodded, trying not to remember the blood-drenched earth, the severed limbs and the strings of blue-veined, fly-blown guts. A battle that should never have been fought and was lost from the moment the first trumpet blew. 'That's why I want you close, Gaius Valerius Verrens. Because you fought over that ground and may have to again.'

'Fought and lost,' Valerius pointed out.

'But you weren't fighting for Marcus Antonius Primus,' the other man said with the certainty of a man who knew he couldn't lose.

Aulus Vitellius Germanicus Augustus contemplated whether to call a slave or heave himself off the chair. It was becoming more difficult to get up every day and he wondered if, after all, a man could actually be too fat. He'd always looked upon his gluttony as a matter of pride.

At Tiberius's court, during the days when the old pederast had hidden himself away on Capri trying to play hide the sausage with young Gaius, or the sisters, Julia Livilla and the pretty one who'd died, it was a matter of pride to eat and drink more than any other man at the table. Tiberius, who loved excess the way a gambler loved a fixed race, had laughed uproariously and rewarded him with gold and jewels. He sighed. Happy days. Who would have predicted then that the man who would rather foul himself at the table than give way to another would be sitting here, in the great Golden House created to ensure Nero's immortality?

Eventually he pulled himself up with a groan, deciding it unbecoming for an Emperor to require the help of a servant just to get off his backside. It was almost an hour since he'd eaten, and he was already feeling the pangs, but he would starve himself for another few moments.

He walked carefully across to the great window where he could see over the sprawling parkland that stretched towards the Esquiline Hill. The Esquiline's red-tiled villas and temples looked down on the stinking rathole of the Subura the way that old snob Galba once looked down his long nose at everyone. To his left, he could just see the outstretched hand of the enormous gilded statue of Nero that towered over the Domus Aurea's entrance hall. Vitellius had already decided to replace the head with one of his own, but he was uncertain which expression it should wear. Noble, of course, but noble and what? Frowning with the cares of state? How did one portray wisdom? Or statesmanship? He must consult the Imperial sculptors already working on at least a hundred statues and busts that would fill the niches recently vacated by the head of young Otho.

But – and now he experienced a shudder of revulsion and fear – would that ever come to pass? Everything he looked upon from this window, every soul living out their little lives in their little houses, was his to command, but for how long?

It had started so well. Otho, defeated comprehensively on the field at Bedriacum, conveniently committed suicide to save further bloodshed and humiliation. His remaining troops had submitted meekly and took the oath to their new Emperor. Vitellius had wanted to ride into Rome at the head of his army, in a general's armour and carrying Julius Caesar's sword. Valens had cleverly pointed out that glorifying a victory in which tens of thousands of Roman citizens died might not be the wisest way to commence his reign. Instead, he'd worn the purple toga signifying his rank and spent a long, wearying day on foot, sustained only by the cheers of the crowds. Following him marched his officers, the eagles of four full legions and the banners of another seven, at the head of thirty thousand legionaries and auxiliaries. At the end, he'd taken his place on the Capitol and watched them march past before sacrificing to Jupiter, best and greatest. It was the most wonderful day of his life, but even then he knew the first stirrings of doubt.

In a matter of days word arrived that the eastern legions had hailed Titus Flavius Vespasian Emperor and Vitellius knew he was in a fight for his very life.

A comforting presence appeared at his side and he didn't have to look to know it was his wife.

'You will win, husband.'

Vitellius smiled. She'd sensed his mood. Galeria Fundana had always been able to read his mind. As small in stature as her husband was great, she wore her thick, dark hair tight bound to her head and her words could be as sharp as a wasp's sting. Her features were angular, almost mannish, and a large wart that disfigured the left side of her chin gave her a . . . yes, it had to be admitted . . . a rather startling presence. But he hadn't married Galeria for her looks. Money and power had been his objectives in negotiating the match with her father. Yet they had developed an unlikely affection based on shared cynicism and she'd borne him a son to be proud of and a daughter to be married off in her turn. If she had been with him in Germania, perhaps things would have turned out differently.

'Yes, I will win,' he agreed. 'Vespasian and his legions are far away in the East. His supporters plot and spy, but for the moment they have little influence.'

'You allow his brother, Sabinus, and that brat of his too much freedom,' his wife pointed out. She said it lightly enough, but Vitellius knew the words contained a suggestion that might be turned into action of a different, and potentially fatal, variety.

'Sabinus is the Flavian insurance policy,' he snorted. 'They hope he will bear fruit if Vespasian fails. If the brother had ambitions for the purple I would squash him like a fly in a wine press. Sabinus is an aristocrat, with respect and support in the Senate. In some ways he is more dangerous than the man who tries to replace me. What is Vespasian but a one-time dealer in mules, who once commanded a legion and believes it makes him the greatest soldier in Rome's history? Yet even now he cowers in Judaea and sends others against me. Should I fear him?'

'You should be wary of him. The legions of Pannonia and Moesia . . .'

'Are closer.' He nodded, sending the great jowls quivering. 'I understand that and have made my plans to oppose them. What are they, four legions, perhaps five? While the army of Vitellius will command the equivalent of eight full legions, twelve squadrons of cavalry and thirty auxiliary cohorts. Vespasian's commander is outnumbered two to one; he would be mad to take on such odds. His only hope is to maintain his position until reinforcements arrive from the East. If he does, he will give me the opportunity to hunt him down and destroy his army.'

It was sensible military thinking, confirmed by all his advisers. Victory was certain. But it had one flaw, understood by both.

'Yet you will not command them?'

Vitellius stiffened at the implied rebuke. 'You know I cannot leave Rome now. I have too much work to do here.' She bowed her head, but he sensed her mood. 'You were right,' he sighed. 'I should never have let Caecina go north without Valens. Together their ambitions cancel each other out. Apart . . . In any case he is young and impetuous and not half the soldier Valens is.'

'Not to be trusted, either.'

'What can I do?' He cursed the weakness in his voice.

'You are the Emperor. For now, you must rule. Perhaps later a decision will be required. We will know when the time comes.'

She reached up with her right hand to touch his face, but before he could say anything a bustling presence entered the room. As if by an unspoken agreement Aulus Vitellius Germanicus Augustus and his Empress turned together and met their son with a smile. Ten years old, slim and dark-eyed, with a restless spirit and boundless energy, the boy, called Lucius for his grandfather, opened his mouth to speak before remembering his manners. He bowed deeply at the waist. 'Stefanus says I have the finest philosophical mind since Seneca,' he grinned. 'We debated Aristotle's theory that the soul is independent of the body. I argued that the soul is part of the heart and ruled by it. At least mine is.'

'So you're in love again.' His mother shook her head in mock despair.

'And how many times did he have to beat you before he came to this conclusion?' his father asked.

'I just thought you should know, and now I must go.' The boy turned and ran from the room with a last shout across his shoulder. 'I have a wrestling lesson with Livius and I'm late.'

When he'd gone his parents turned to each other and Vitellius flinched as he recognized the terrible sadness in his wife's eyes.

'Whatever happens,' he promised, 'I will protect you and the children.'

X

'The situation has changed. I have a new mission for you.'

The solemnly spoken words of Marcus Antonius Primus came back to Valerius as he sat, death weary, studying the flat, marshy ground ahead. This was enemy territory. Every clump of trees or rustic farmstead could hold a threat. Yet the musical song of a soaring lark and the scent of fresh-mown grass made it seem as innocent as a stroll across the family estate. On the far horizon he could just make out the smoky haze that marked Aulus Caecina Alienus's camp at Hostilia.

He'd spent a long night in the saddle by the light of a liquid moon. An escort of mounted spearmen had accompanied him part of the way from the general's new base at Verona, but he'd been alone for the past five hours. Now an enormous mid-morning sky weighed on his shoulders as heavily as the burden of expectation Primus had placed there when he'd handed over the leather message pouch. An assignment so sensitive that even Serpentius couldn't be allowed to know of it. 'It must be delivered into his hands and his alone,' the general had emphasized. 'To do otherwise will lead only to death and disaster for yourself and this army.'

Valerius allowed the mare to drink her fill from a stream before using his heels to kick her forward, splashing through the clear water and climbing the steep bank. Of course, there was more. 'Succeed

in this mission and you can win it for us at a single stroke.' Valerius
had met the unlikely claim with the incredulity it deserved, but the
army commander was insistent. 'One man can change the fate of
thousands, perhaps tens of thousands, and that man will be Gaius
Valerius Verrens.' For a few moments Valerius wondered if he was in
a dream. It was as if he was living his life over. *Tell him I will pay off
his soldiers and his generals. I will do anything to save the Empire from
the terror and the bloodshed that rides hand in hand with civil war.* The
words Otho had used before sending him north to Vitellius echoed
in his brain. Fear had stalked him all the way through the mountains
and the trip down the Rhenus. Not fear of the hazards and perils of
the journey, which were real enough. Fear – the raw, terrible fear –
of failure. In the end he *had* failed and the fruits of that failure lay,
grinning empty skulls and grass-tangled ribcages, on the plain outside
Bedriacum. It was through no fault of Valerius's, but that did not
help now. Yet he knew that on this occasion his fears were irrational,
because it should be so simple.

Aulus Caecina Alienus wanted to change sides.

But why?

'Why is of no import,' Primus had insisted, his broad face red with
concentration. 'All that matters is that we take advantage. You will
carry letters from me accepting his terms and arrange the formalities
of the surrender.'

But here, as he rode with the rhythmic thump of the mare's hooves
in his ears and the heavy, bittersweet alluvial scent of the Padus
marshes in his nostrils, *Why* seemed to matter quite a lot. Why would
Caecina, victor of Bedriacum and newly appointed consul of Rome,
abandon everything he had won and throw himself on the mercy
of his enemies? Caecina had twice as many men as Primus's tired
legions. Could it be a trap? He thought back to his first encounter with
the enemy commander in the shadow of Placentia's walls. Caecina
had been dressed in all the finery of a Celtic nobleman, with only
the scarlet sash and sculpted breastplate to identify him as a Roman
officer. Valerius's first impression had been of a brightly crested
barnyard cockerel, ready to crow at every opportunity and bursting

with self-belief and ambition. But not a cockerel looking for a fight. Only the stubborn refusal of Placentia's irascible commander, Gaius Spurinna, to negotiate had forced the commander of the Fourth Macedonica to make his impulsive attack on the city. Otherwise, Valerius was certain, the younger man would have been happy to talk all day if it had meant a bloodless surrender. Caecina was not a natural warrior, but he was the commander of at least four legions all led by men who had pledged their oath to Vitellius. How likely was it that he could carry them with him? How wide was the conspiracy? One thing was certain: if Gaius Fabius Valens, who had led the second part of Vitellius's army from Germania, was with the army, Caecina would never have dared. Yet another aspect of Caecina's character must be considered. He smiled as he remembered Spurinna's opinion of the young general. *Aulus Caecina Alienus could sell a wooden leg to a four-legged dog, but at heart he's a backstabber.* Time would tell whether Caecina was stabbing his Emperor in the back, or playing some trick that would send a knife to the very heart of Primus's army. There was only one way to find out. Valerius must put his head in the noose once more.

His first problem was how to deliver the message directly into Caecina's hands. Primus had supplied Valerius with the yellow cloak of an Imperial courier, and a forged message purporting to come from the Palatium reinforced his credentials. His main issue was that the bronze plaque confirming the messenger's identity carried Galba's name. It wouldn't stand close scrutiny. Still, the courier guise seemed as likely as any to get him inside; once there he'd just have to bluff his way past Caecina's bodyguard. Imperial couriers tended to be arrogant young men, proud of their horsemanship and driven to reach their next destination as swiftly as their horses would allow. A little rudeness wouldn't be out of character. Naturally, he'd have to keep hidden the missing hand that identified him as clearly as a cohort standard, but he'd done it often enough before.

He gave his mount another dig in the ribs so they approached the massive camp at an appropriately urgent pace. Extensive marshes protected the flanks and the river provided a barrier to the rear. A single pontoon bridge allowed communication with more troops on the opposite side of the Padus. The sheer scale of the fort – it looked to Valerius about a hundred acres – was evidence of the presence of at least two legions, probably more. Deep triple ditches, filled with pointed stakes, and a substantial palisade surrounded the perimeter. He made for the gate that would lead to the Via Principalis and the heart of the camp.

'Message for General Alienus from the Emperor.' Valerius repeated the shouted refrain until he reached the gate, trying to look even more exhausted than he felt. Careful to keep the wooden fist beneath his distinctive yellow cloak, he used his left hand to wave the bronze plaque that confirmed him as a messenger even if the cloak was questioned. The sentries barely glanced at the token before opening the gate. 'The general's quarters?'

'With the Fourth, in the far compound.' The guard commander nodded him through and the relief was so intense he had to fight the urge to slump in the saddle. He'd crossed the first hurdle, but more dangers lay ahead.

The fort complex had been split into two major sections, each large enough to house a full legion. He took his time now, observing the familiar surroundings of the camp: the neat rows of tents, the granaries, horse lines, hospital and workshops, and the commanders' pavilions. If he had to get out fast he would use the rear gate and take his chances with the bridge guards. Of course, he knew that if he needed to get out fast it was probably all over in any case. Things had gone well so far, but experience told him that might change soon. As he suspected, the inner compound's sentries were much more alert and demanded to inspect the identification plaque. He saw them stiffen when they saw the Emperor's name.

Valerius produced a tired grin. 'What do you expect, the way they've been changing lately? There are thousands of us couriers.' He shrugged. 'I just got back from Thrace and they turned me round without replacing my plaque. They didn't worry about it in Ravenna; why should it be a problem here?'

If they'd been suspicious before, the innocent mention of Ravenna had them reaching for their swords. 'Sir!' The guard commander ran across from his tent at the man's shout. The sentry whispered something Valerius didn't catch and showed him the plaque.

'Get off the horse.'

Valerius shrugged and did as he was ordered.

'You have a message for the general?'

'That's right.'

'And you've come from Ravenna.'

Valerius nodded and the man smiled grimly.

'Then you can give it to me.'

Valerius shook his head. 'I have orders to place the message into the hands of General Aulus Caecina Alienus and no other.'

The sharp hiss of a *gladius* being drawn made Valerius tense. He made sure he kept his hand away from his own sword. Only a cool head was going to help him now. 'If you don't give it to me, I can always take it,' the decurion assured him.

'What's going on, soldier?' A young tribune marched from the direction of the command tents, drawn by the unmistakable colour of Valerius's cloak.

'This man claims to have a message for the general, but he doesn't have a current identity plaque, sir. And he's just come from Ravenna.'

The tribune looked Valerius up and down, taking in the tired eyes, the drawn features and the thin scar running down his cheek. 'A little old for courier work, aren't you?'

Valerius raised his chin and looked the man in the eyes. 'It's my life, sir. Born in the saddle.'

'Your message?' The tribune held out his hand.

'Into the hand of Aulus Caecina Alienus and no other, sir. I'm sorry.'

The tribune grimaced and the sentries tensed. The moment could have gone either way, but Valerius held the young man's gaze and eventually the officer grunted in frustration. He didn't have time for this. 'I'll take responsibility for this man, decurion. Give me one of your sentries and tell him if the insolent bastard tries anything to take his head off. The general is expecting a message from Rome and he doesn't like being kept waiting.'

Valerius followed the younger man through the tent lines towards the *principia*. He could feel the looming presence of the guard behind him and had no doubt that the soldier would follow his officer's order to the letter. The big headquarters tent was guarded, as always, by the legate's personal bodyguard and they eyed Valerius suspiciously. 'Return to your post,' the tribune told the sentry. He nodded to one of the guards. 'You come with me.'

Inside, Valerius was led to a small waiting area where he removed his helmet and placed it on a bench. 'Your weapons, too,' the tribune ordered. 'Slowly.' Valerius carefully used his left hand to draw his sword and place it on the floor of the tent, followed by the knife that hung at his belt. He saw the tribune's puzzlement at his reluctance to use his right hand. 'Take the cloak off.' Valerius complied and heard the intake of breath as the guard noticed the crudely carved oak fist.

The tribune frowned at the unexpected sight. He was a conscientious young man and he was tempted to tell this 'courier' to remove his strange ornament in case it could be used as a weapon. He was also wondering if he should take the now visible dispatch pouch by force. But something about the man's face made him hesitate; a challenge that let him know if he wanted the message he'd have to fight for it. His legate was waiting and Aulus Caecina Alienus had been oddly tense today. 'Watch him,' he ordered the guard tersely.

Valerius heard a soft muttering beyond the heavy canvas divisions of the tent.

'Bring him in.'

XI

The first thing Valerius noticed was that Aulus Caecina Alienus had dispensed with the exotic Batavian war gear that so endeared him to the German legions the previous spring. The young general wore a simple belted tunic and appeared to be reading a document on the campaign table in front of him, but Valerius sensed he was concentrating less on the words than on preparing himself for the meeting ahead. Cohort standards from the three legions Caecina and Valens defeated at Bedriacum lined the walls, and Valerius recognized the face of Aulus Vitellius on several of the pieces of statuary. On the far side of the tent hung a curtain that must conceal the entrance to the general's living quarters. The only other furniture was a pair of couches arranged by a low table.

Caecina looked up and Valerius instantly recognized the handsome, fine-boned features he'd last seen at Placentia. The only change was in the eyes. Six months ago they had been over-bright, like a man constantly on the brink of ecstasy; now they appeared hooded and wary. A year younger than the messenger standing before him, Caecina Alienus had been, in quick succession, a favourite of Emperor Galba, one of Rome's youngest legionary commanders, a disgraced embezzler of public funds, one of the two men who persuaded Vitellius to fight for the purple, and a victorious general and consul of Rome. Was he about to add 'betrayer' to the list for the second time?

'You have a message for me from Rome?'

Valerius reached for the pouch at his waist. He felt the guard behind him tense and his hand slowed as he unhooked the flap and retrieved the leather case with the message from Primus. A seal of red wax, so blurred as to be unidentifiable, proved it was unopened. He stepped forward and placed it on the table in front of Caecina. The general looked at it for a long moment. Valerius sensed that this was the moment of no return for the man behind the desk. Pick up the message and he was committed to whatever intrigue he had contrived with Primus. Of course, there was another option. Valerius went cold as he found himself the focus of the dark eyes. How much simpler, and perhaps safer, to leave things as they stood and rid himself of the evidence. Valerius saw the tip of the legate's tongue flick out to moisten his lips before he reached for the tube of dark leather. His decision made, Caecina confidently sliced through the soft wax with a knife and pulled back the leather fold. Valerius slowly released the breath he'd held since the other man's first words.

Caecina took his time over the document. It was in code, but it was *his* code, and long use brought familiarity. Of course, it couldn't be used again, because he'd revealed the fundamentals to Primus during the negotiations of the past few weeks. As he read, he felt his legs weaken and was glad he was sitting at his desk. He had it all. Do what he had committed to in the earlier letters and he would be treated with honour by his former enemies. And there would be greater rewards to come, he was certain. Could he do it? He'd done it before when he'd persuaded the legions of Germania Superior to revolt against Galba in those terrible days after word arrived that Caecina was to be stripped of his command. Yes, he could do it. His mother once told him he could charm the birds from the trees and the clouds from the sky. He would charm these rough plebeian soldiers. The key was the centurions and junior commanders in direct contact with their men. Most of them would do anything as long as it could be portrayed, however implausibly, as patriotism. Convince them that their . . .

that Rome's best interests lay in ousting the fat man in the Golden House, promise them a suitable donative and they would follow him into Vespasian's arms. The senior officers would be more difficult to persuade, of course – they held their own loyalties – but presented with a situation beyond reversal they would have no option but to comply. Or die. The two legions at Cremona, Twenty-first and Fifth Alaudae, were another matter, but he must harden his heart. They would join him or be crushed.

He read on and the name Valens leapt out, sending a chill through him.

By the gods, how he hated the man. All the glory of Bedriacum, the heroism and the blood and the victory, tainted by that malevolent, skeletal presence forever whispering in the Emperor's ear. It had all seemed so simple with the fat man on the throne and the promise of a broad-striped consul's toga. Then the whispers started to trickle down to him. *Caecina couldn't have won without Valens. He was in trouble until the old soldier pulled his eggs from the fire. Valens is a fighter, the true hero of Bedriacum. Caecina looked good, but he didn't have the stomach for a real fight.* He'd seen the way Valens looked at him. It was only a matter of time before one of them had to go. Caecina understood he was outmatched by the man who had personally cut the head from Gaius Fonteius Capito. When the news arrived that Vespasian had been hailed Emperor by the legions of the East it had come almost as a blessed relief. He had a choice. He could choose the perilous path that might lead to life, or certain death. He chose life.

For the moment, though, Valens didn't feature in his calculations. That would continue to be the case if he acted swiftly.

'General Valens is still indisposed and will be unable to join us for another few weeks.' The lie came easily and he accompanied it with his most charming smile. By the look on the tribune's face the news would be around the whole camp within the hour. Caecina turned to Valerius. 'This says that you also have an oral message for me?'

Valerius bowed. 'For your ears only, lord.'

'You may leave us.' Caecina directed the order at the other two men. 'I must consider my reply. A one-handed man is no threat to me in my own camp.' The tribune hesitated and the young general smiled. 'Your concern for my well-being is admirable, Aurelius, but unnecessary. He is unarmed and your swords are only a shout away. Clear the area apart from my personal guard. I don't want any slaves tittle-tattling about my business.'

When they were alone, Caecina fixed Valerius with the unyielding stare of a python studying a trapped rabbit. The Roman had noticed him darting occasional glances towards the curtain that separated the main tent from his living quarters. Now the reason swayed into the room and her slanted, gold-flecked eyes never left Valerius. She stopped and tilted her head as if she needed to see him from a different angle.

'I recognize you.' Valerius heard Caecina's intake of breath. 'He was at Placentia,' she continued. 'The negotiations when that odious little general was so rude to you.'

Salonina Julia was even more beautiful than Valerius remembered, with the face of an Egyptian queen and a body that moved with the natural fluidity of a cat. The last time they'd met those slanting eyes had been full of promise, despite the situation. Now all they held was suspicion.

'The hand,' Caecina exclaimed. 'Now I remember. But why would I forget such a face?' He smiled. 'You have lost weight, I believe.'

'Defeat does that to a man, as you may discover to your cost.'

'You should cut his throat.' Salonina said it as if she was telling a servant to snip the head from a wilting rose. 'But first give him to me for an hour and we will see if that clever tongue has any more to offer.'

The look that accompanied the words sent a shiver through Valerius, but Caecina rose from his seat and frowned. 'You don't think I was defeated at Placentia?'

Valerius shrugged and tried to ignore Salonina's stare. 'You walked away from a fight you couldn't win without unacceptable casualties. You won the battle you needed to win and with it you won the war.'

The legate grinned at his wife. 'A proper soldier. I like him.'

'I still think you should cut his throat,' she said sourly, taking a seat on one of the couches.

'Why didn't I take Placentia?' Caecina asked. 'I had enough men.'

'General Spurinna's defences were too strong for a direct attack on the walls. You might have had a chance if you'd battered the gates with your heavy catapults.'

'But you burned them in the amphitheatre as I remember. That was very clever. And you destroyed my battering ram. I was annoyed.'

'A soldier does what he must to win.'

'And at Bedriacum I won.' Caecina smiled at the memory. 'You were at Bedriacum? I'm curious. Where were you in the battle line?'

Salonina sniffed to let her husband know she was bored with this military talk. Caecina ignored her and Valerius gave him his answer. 'I commanded the gladiator detachment in the second rank of the Adiutrix.'

The other man's dark eyes widened a fraction. 'Where the Twenty-first lost its eagle.'

Valerius nodded, not caring to elaborate on the memory of that glorious but ultimately futile action.

'And I ordered that all the gladiators should die. And they did.' Caecina's gaze drifted away as he sought some lost memory. 'All but one, a dangerous savage who slaughtered everyone who faced him. I remember it now. A man with a wooden hand butchered on the bloody sands in the arena at Cremona. The Emperor was most put out. In his cups he would bemoan the death of a friend. What was the name he used? A martial name, I think. Yes. Valerius.' The general fixed the one-handed Roman with that same python's stare. 'I saw you die.'

'Not every gladiator who bleeds on the sands of the arena is a dead gladiator.' Valerius quoted his friend, the deadly fighter Serpentius.

'So,' Caecina's face broke into an unexpected grin, 'the man I could not kill.'

Salonina laughed. 'There is still time.'

But Valerius understood that a decision had been taken and control had shifted. He turned to meet her dark eyes and for the first time she saw something in the scarred soldier that sent a thrill of fear through her breast. 'The question is can your husband deliver what he has offered?'

XII

'His message is that if you give him three days he will convince every man at Hostilia to join Vespasian's cause.'

Valerius saw Marcus Antonius Primus's dark eyes gleam as the general listened to the report of his meeting with Caecina. After two days in the saddle Valerius had trouble staying upright. His face was a mask of shadows and stubble, dust caked his clothing and he stank of the acrid reek of hard-ridden horse. But exhilaration blinded Primus to the weariness of his messenger. Clearly, all he saw was a vision of himself riding into Rome at the head of ten legions and the craven Vitellius kneeling before him in supplication.

Valerius closed his eyes and continued in a voice that rose and fell with the waves of exhaustion that threatened to overwhelm him. 'He can make no such promises for the two legions at Cremona, but his gift to you is the information that they are lacking replacements and short on artillery. With your forces combined he believes the commanders have no alternative but to surrender Placentia and Cremona to you. The road to Rome will be open.'

'Does this upstart provincial truly believe he can betray an Emperor and then ride beside me at the head of my troops?' Primus shook his great head in disbelief. 'He's fortunate to be given his life and the promise that I will ask Vespasian to consider allowing him to keep his estates. How did his mood seem to you?'

Valerius struggled with the interview's sudden change of direction. It all seemed so long ago. 'Nervous.' He shrugged. 'Perhaps even excited.'

'No shame or remorse?' Primus laughed. 'Not that it makes him any less of a man. He did not tell you about the Ravenna fleet?'

'No.'

Primus realized for the first time how tired his messenger was. 'Sit, man, before you fall down.' He waited until Valerius slumped on to a couch. 'They declared for Vespasian four days ago. If he'd marched against us he would have had to leave behind a sizeable force to guard against an attack on his supply lines. That must have focused his mind if nothing else did.'

'It would explain why his guards reacted the way they did when I said I'd handed over a message at Ravenna,' Valerius admitted. 'They thought someone had sent me to assassinate Caecina. It may have made him nervous, but I think the information is known only to his personal staff.' He remembered the confident certainty in Salonina's face as he had left the tent at Hostilia. 'Experience tells him Vitellius hasn't the strength or the will to defeat Vespasian, but, more important, he fears Valens, and perhaps that's why Valens isn't here.'

Primus nodded thoughtfully. 'In either case we can't afford to trust him. If he wanted to desert Vitellius all he needed was to gather a few personal guards, ride out from the camp and head east. Why put his neck on the line by trying to bring his legions with him? Mars' arse, even I know he would probably have given us a whipping if he could combine his forces. I'd hoped to surprise him, but now . . .'

'Now he is our ally.' Valerius unconsciously echoed the army commander's thoughts. 'But do we think he'll keep his word?'

'No.' He felt Primus's eyes on him. 'And that is why we will not wait to join forces with Caecina's army. I will march on Cremona at first light and either my legions will force the surrender of Twenty-first Rapax and Fifth Alaudae or we will destroy them. Then let the bastard change his mind. Glico!' An aide appeared in the doorway. 'Send word for my legionary commanders.' The man disappeared and

Primus stared at the map of northern Italia that dominated one wall of the room. His tone changed to one almost of concerned comradeship. 'Get some rest, Valerius. I need you close and sharp in the morning.' He hesitated, his eyes homing in on the ground between Bedriacum and Cremona. 'It was the gods' will that I did not have you killed, Gaius Valerius Verrens, and it is fate that has brought you to my side. You will guide me over the ground that consumed Otho and together we will share in the fruits of victory. Whatever happened between us is in the past, do you understand? All debts are paid.' He turned, but Valerius was already fast asleep on the couch, his eyes closed, his scarred face relaxed and almost boyish. For a moment, Marcus Antonius Primus felt an unlikely affection for the man who had ruined his career and sent him into exile, but he quickly pushed it aside. He was a soldier. A commander. In the days ahead he might have to sacrifice Gaius Valerius Verrens and a thousand more in the name of victory and he could not afford to hesitate. If he succeeded, Vespasian would award him the triumphal regalia, if not more. He would be the governor of somewhere that would make him a fortune, not the dusty little shithole up on the Danuvius that Galba had handed him. Later, perhaps quite soon, he would wear a consul's toga.

He shuffled through the papers on his desk until he found the one he'd been reading before Valerius had returned from his encounter with Caecina. *Titus Flavius Caesar Vespasianus Augustus greets his loyal friend and comrade Marcus Antonius Primus* . . . Primus smiled at the method of address which, for all its fulsomeness, contained a none too gentle reminder of the Emperor-elect's authority and his own subservience. Several lines of outright flattery followed, hanging like ribbons on a thorn tree; pretty decorations, but they didn't take away the sting. He read down to the passage that was the letter's true purpose.

'Your Emperor exhorts you to hold the strategic outpost at Aquileia and there maintain your position until the arrival of the legions commanded by our faithful friend and comrade Gaius Licinius Mucianus. This disposition and the steadfast defence of the city

will deny our enemies the opportunity to meet our Pannonian and Moesian legions from a position of strength. Our command of the Egyptian corn reserves and the wealth of the East places the armies of Vitellius at a grave disadvantage. In time, his troops must be forced to capitulate for want of pay and provisions and in the face of the overwhelming combined forces at our disposal. Your Emperor understands that, in war, it is sometimes sweeter to advance in pursuit of glory than to take the road of prudence, but he is certain that you will accept his advice that the latter is the more fitting, and the most sensible, strategic option. In paying heed to this advice you will help bring about a great victory, one shorn of the usual accompaniment of blood, tears and penury, and you will have the thanks of Rome, its people and the Empire, and, of course, your Emperor, Titus Flavius Caesar Vespasianus Augustus.

Advice? Primus almost laughed aloud. He was soldier enough to know an order when he read one. But he was already beyond Aquileia and the agreement with Caecina had placed him in a position of paramount strength. One more effort and he would win the war before Vespasian was even aware it had been fought. Something wriggled its way across the inside of his skull and his euphoria faded. Were the gods reminding him of the price of defeat? But he would not be defeated. Before they marched he would sacrifice a white bull to Mars and ensure that the omens for victory were favourable in the extreme. He glanced at the map fixed to the wall. Three days' easy marching and he would reach Cremona with a force of five legions against the city's defence of two. When they heard that their commander had pledged his oath to Vespasian, the legates of Twenty-first Rapax and Fifth Alaudae would have no option but to surrender.

The rugged plebeian features of the Emperor swam into his vision; the face of a provincial butcher, but for the rather handsome aquiline nose. A quick victory and all would be forgiven. Defeat was unthinkable. Primus smiled. He had nothing to fear.

Because Aulus Caecina Alienus had placed victory in his hands as if it were ordained by the gods.

‎*

'Wake up.' Valerius felt a hand on his shoulder, but he decided he'd sleep for another hour. He deserved it after all those hours in the saddle. It was only when the hand shook harder that he sensed the motion beneath him and realized he was back on a horse. He opened his eyes and squinted into a low sun that shone from his left flank. 'The general's called a conference,' Serpentius said quietly. 'And you're wanted.'

The Spaniard handed his friend a water skin. Valerius splashed a handful of the lukewarm liquid on his face and wheeled the mare back down the column to where Primus's staff were setting up his command tent. Gradually, the details of the morning came back to him. The legions had worked through the night to be ready for a dawn departure. Their supplies and heavy weapons were part of a precisely structured train that crammed thirty miles of the Via Postumia. It had taken a gargantuan effort and the troops didn't hide their bewilderment when a cohort from each legion was told to gather for the sacrifice of a white bull that would cost at least another hour. Primus, on the other hand, counted it time well spent when the wonderful omens for the coming battle filtered back to their parent units.

From the position of the sun Valerius estimated they must have been on the march for less than four hours. What would make Primus call a halt so soon, after all the urgency to get started?

He had his answer the moment he entered the tent, when Primus's senior aide drew him to one side.

'One of our patrols captured a courier on the way from Hostilia to Rome. At dawn this morning Aulus Caecina Alienus was arrested for treason. The legions at Hostilia are breaking camp and marching for Cremona. If they link up with Twenty-first Rapax and Fifth Alaudae they'll outnumber us more than two to one.'

XIII

Hostilia, the previous night

'You are the backbone of my legions. The sword blade that runs through the cohorts and centuries of this great army.' Aulus Caecina Alienus addressed the hundred senior centurions he had invited to gather in the *principia* of the Fourth Macedonica's temporary camp. They were mainly men from the Rhenus legions he had led from Germania to win the Empire for Vitellius; men he had rewarded personally with crowns of grass and gold, torcs, *phalerae*, and other honours. They were also the greatest recipients of plunder from Placentia, when it had eventually fallen into Vitellian hands, and the other towns they had won along the way. Yet despite their allegiance to the man who now sat in the Golden House in Rome, they too had their grievances, for anything they won had been lost when Vitellius had announced his reforms to the army. Now the honorariums from selling leave tickets and dispensations from work details they had counted on to augment their pay were no more. Many of them had expected these extras to pay for the houses and land they planned to buy for their retirement, and were relying on another campaign to recoup their losses. Unfortunately, they had discovered that a civil war was a sad disappointment for a soldier when he fought on the side of the state. He'd plied them with substantial amounts of unwatered wine from his best vintages and they were ready to listen to anything he had to say.

'We officers give commands,' Caecina continued with his flattery, 'but you are the guarantee that those commands are obeyed. You have fought well, given more than any man can be expected to give, and now I expect you to give more.' He heard the muffled groans, interspersed with demands for silence, and took strength from them. 'The legions of Germania are rightly hailed as the elite of the Empire' – in the theatrical pause that followed the words were greeted with broad grins and shouts of hurrah – 'and soon you must prove it again. The legions we will face in the coming days – Roman legions – are the Pannonian and Moesian legions who have held the line of the Danuvius for a generation. Only six months ago they destroyed the might of the Roxolani, leaving not one man alive to return to his homeland. For a generation they held back the Dacians and the Quadi, the Cotini and the Marcomanni. They too believe they are the elite of the Empire.'

'Only five legions,' a voice came from somewhere in the pack, 'and some of them have marched six hundred miles.'

'Who won at Bedriacum?' another demanded.

Caecina raised a hand for silence.

'You won at Bedriacum, and deserved your triumph,' he paused again to let them bask in the glory of their victory, 'but we fought only two legions. And yes, now we face only five legions when we number many more. But think on it, comrades: how many of your legions are at full strength? How many of you have been asking for replacements for months, but not received them? How many of your best soldiers now serve with the Praetorian Guard, your centuries and your cohorts weakened at the behest of the Emperor who now demands victory of you?' He allowed the self-evident truths to make their mark and sensed the rumblings of discontent running through them. 'Can that be right? Of course, we will win, but how many more must die because of the failings and jealousies of others? And when we defeat the five legions of Pannonia and Moesia, when the battle is over and we count our wounded and our dead comrades in the thousands and the tens of thousands, what then? Will your Emperor send you on leave to enjoy the fruits of victory or into retirement to reap the rewards of your long service? No. He will keep you in arms, because Titus Flavius Vespasian has already dispatched more legions to oppose us, the legions of Syria and Egypt and Cappadocia, the legions of Corbulo. Even that will not be the end, for Hispania and Lusitania and Gaul also stand against us.'

It was a blatant lie, but Caecina rationalized that if he prevailed it would become truth and no longer matter. He shook his head. 'None of this would signify if we were led by a Caesar, or an Augustus. But we are not. The man who calls himself your Emperor sits in Rome counting the money that you, the legions of Rome, won for him, and feasting on the plenty that you, the legions of Rome, cannot enjoy. It is with a heavy heart, my friends, that I now tell you that the Ravenna fleet, which controls the seas to our rear and the supply convoys that use them, has pledged its allegiance to Titus Flavius Vespasian.' There had been rumours of the defection; now he watched the shock of their confirmation ripple through them like a summer breeze on ripe corn. 'Who knows how long our dwindling supplies last before we go hungry? What will we do once our javelins are spent and our *ballista* bolts fired? The man who now marches against us . . .'

'I thought he was still in Alexandria?' It was the same voice from the back. Caecina smiled as three or four of his supporters closed in on the potential troublemaker.

'Yes,' he nodded regretfully as if a favourite uncle had stolen the last piece of duck at a family dinner, 'but that is only because he has pledged not to shed the blood of one Roman in his name. He wishes only to further the cause of the Empire.' He sought them out with his gaze, the dark soulful eyes roving across the hardened soldiers arrayed in front of him. 'Because he does not believe the man we follow is worthy of the name Emperor. Because he feels that Aulus Vitellius has undermined his legions and betrayed his soldiers. I ask you a question. Does any man here believe that if his legion is under threat, Aulus Vitellius will come to his aid?'

'Only if I can't finish my rations.'

Caecina waited until the laughter died down. 'We have fought

97

together and shed blood together. We have seen our friends die; or, worse, seen them live with wounds that no mortal man should be asked to bear. We have seen farms burned and families impoverished. Your homeland has been ravaged by civil war until it has nothing more to give. Who among you would ask it to suffer more if an alternative could be found?'

One man, a centurion on the brink of retirement, stood up and asked a question that had been carefully rehearsed hours earlier. 'But what is the alternative, legate? What must we do to avoid more bloodshed and sacrifice?'

Caecina studied the speaker with a face lined by torment, while inside his heart soared at the perfectly choreographed opportunity he had created. He began softly, and like a true actor allowed his voice to rise with every word. 'It grieves me to say, but I do it for my soldiers, and my people, and for the Empire which I hold so dear. Say it I must. We can ask ourselves who is more worthy of our trust. The man who has abandoned us, or the man who is coming to save Rome? The man who can barely hold a sword, or the man who carried his blade against the traitors of Britannia and Judaea? The man who has taken your money, or the man who has pledged to give fifteen thousand sesterces to every legionary who lays down his weapons in the cause of healing the wounds of the Empire?' He saw instantly that he had them. 'It is my sad duty, my friends, to tell you that Aulus Vitellius has proved unworthy of Rome. We must place our trust in Titus Flavius Vespasian to ensure that the Empire has a future.'

The room erupted as he reached his climax and he heard a startled yelp as the dissenter at the back was pounced upon and dragged through the curtained doorway. Centurions from the Fourth, carefully salted through the crowd, shouted 'Down with Vitellius! Down with the traitor to the Empire!' and matched their words with action, toppling the statues and emblems of the Emperor that lined the walls of the tent.

Caecina watched for a while, revelling in his power and wondering at the ease with which men could be manipulated, even strong men like these. Eventually, he raised his arms for silence. 'Return to your legions, and relay my words and their import to your men. Supplies are low and the Ravenna fleet will no longer support us. Your commander believes it is in their best interests to pledge our oath to Vespasian and fifteen thousand sesterces to every man.'

Accompanied by growls of assent the men filed out and Aulus Caecina Alienus retired to his private quarters. He was tempted to slump on one of the couches until the shaking in his legs died down, but he knew he must inform Primus of his success, so he took his place dutifully at the desk.

Salonina glided through the curtained doorway to the sleeping area and their eyes met as she swayed towards him. He felt an over-whelming rush of desire that was multiplied as she approached and kissed him on the lips.

'You were masterful, husband,' she whispered, the front of her gown gaping to expose her breasts as she leaned towards him. He reached out to brush his hand against them. Tempted. She smiled, but her look said 'Later' and he returned to the letter. The sounds of the outer camp came to him, seemingly magnified by the blood rushing like lava through his veins. A moment of utter silence as if the man and woman in the tented room were the only people in the world, followed by a roar. He had won.

In the hour before dawn, Caecina was still working on the letter and Salonina emerged from the curtain to greet her husband with a kiss. As their lips met a disturbance erupted outside the tent, followed by a sharp cry much closer. They stared at each other, both mirroring the other's puzzlement. Caecina leapt to his feet and motioned his wife to leave. Before she could move, the door flaps were thrown back and the tent filled with fully armoured legionaries, their short swords bared and glinting in the light of the oil lamps. Aulus Caecina Alienus slowly subsided into his seat.

He sat frozen as a tall man in the scarlet sash of a legionary legate pushed through the troops towards him. Caecina's heart sank as he recognized Fabius Fabullus, the legate who had served him so well at Bedriacum and should have been with Fifth Alaudae at Cremona.

Fabullus's eyes bulged and his purple face was twisted into a grimace of almost apoplectic fury.

'General.' Caecina made to rise, but rough hands held him down. Fabullus stood two paces in front of the desk as if to advance any further would drive him to physical violence.

'Aulus Caecina Alienus, you are hereby placed under arrest on charges of treason and inciting treason. When the time is right you will be taken before your Emperor to receive the justice you deserve. Think yourself fortunate that I do not stand back and allow my men to tear you apart as was their intention.'

Caecina wondered that his heart didn't explode in his chest. How could he possibly bear it? To have been so close and have it snatched away like this . . . Two men hustled forward and he closed his eyes as he heard the rattle of chains. The cold iron against his skin made him flinch and he had to force himself not to cry out as the fetters closed painfully on his flesh.

'Were you really so deluded as to believe you could buy and sell your soldiers like slaves and present them to our enemy? Did you think the honour of the Rhenus legions had fallen as low as your own? These men,' Fabullus indicated the soldiers who'd accompanied him, 'fought and their comrades died at Bedriacum to place Aulus Vitellius Germanicus Augustus on the throne of Rome. They will not abandon him without taking a wound. We have already defeated the legions the usurper Vespasian arrays against us. They know us and they fear us, which is why we will defeat them again when we meet. The sounds you hear are the sounds of the camp breaking. At first light we will march to Cremona to link up with Twenty-first Rapax and Fifth Alaudae. Then we will see whether that dog Primus has any fight in him.' The jailers finished their work and stood back. 'Take him away.'

They pulled Aulus Caecina Alienus to his feet and as the former commander of the armies of Vitellius was hustled out his eyes met those of his wife. His last thought before she disappeared was that he had gone from glory to defeat and despair in the time it took to exchange a kiss.

XIV

The mood was sombre when Valerius gathered with the army's legionary commanders in the headquarters tent hastily set up by the Via Postumia. Sweating in their thick cloaks and leather breastplates the officers stood disconsolately around the general's campaign table debating the consequences of the grave news from Hostilia. As the legates argued, their soldiers waited on the road in that resigned, wary, but thankful of the opportunity to rest way that soldiers do.

'We should withdraw to Aquileia and form a defensive perimeter.' Numisius Lupus, legate of the Eighth Augusta, spoke with a quiet intensity, and his words were greeted with a murmur of approval. 'We cannot hope to prevail against a force of forty thousand and probably more.'

'There is no disgrace in a tactical withdrawal.' Agreement came from Vipstanus Messalla, the most experienced soldier among them. He looked to his commander for some reaction, but Primus continued to stare at the map spread across the scarred oak surface of the table. The tribune belatedly tried to remove the taint of defeat from his words. 'Your original strategy was sound, but circumstances have changed. If the enemy combines then our whole enterprise is placed in jeopardy.'

Valerius looked to his old friend Fulvus, who commanded Third Gallica, but the other man answered with a shrug. The dark-jawed features of Vedius Aquila, the legate who two months earlier had been so keen to execute Valerius, twisted into an expression of almost pained frustration. He opened his mouth to speak before clamping it shut again as if he believed his words might condemn him. As the tense silence in the tent lengthened the only sound was a loose flap fluttering in the wind and the faint buzz of insects making the most of a late-blooming oleander.

Eventually, Primus looked up from the map. 'This changes nothing.'

'But . . .' Lupus looked as if he'd been struck. Messalla stared at Primus as if he wasn't certain what madness was coming next. Aquila's only reaction was a tiny involuntary groan. Aurelius Fulvus met Valerius's look of dismay with a grim smile.

'It changes nothing,' Primus repeated, his eyes roving from each man to the next and filled with challenge. 'There are still only two legions at Cremona,' he continued. 'The legions at Hostilia are between three and four days' march away, and that over poor roads or rough ground. We have the advantage by a day and a half and the Via Postumia provides good marching all the way. It is my intention to defeat the Twenty-first Rapax and Fifth Alaudae at Cremona and swing round to await the arrival of the Hostilia legions in a strong defensive position, here,' he pointed to a spot on the map midway between Cremona and Hostilia, 'at Ad Castores.'

'Even so,' Lupus persisted. 'There is no guarantee we can reach Cremona first.'

'Then let us ensure it,' Primus growled. 'Gentlemen, we will abandon our baggage train and our heavy weapons here, to follow us as they can. Issue your men with three days' rations and tell them they will soon be feasting from the storehouses of Cremona. We will force the pace, use every minute of daylight and meet the enemy while his forces are still divided. You have your orders.'

There could be no doubt of his determination, but Valerius sensed the hesitation before the legionary commanders saluted and saw that Primus felt it too. After a moment's thought, the tension faded from the general's face as he decided this was a time for explanation not confrontation. 'The men are fractious and starting at shadows,' he said quietly. 'You saw what happened at Verona when the picket guards of the Seventh Galbiana mistook our own cavalry for the enemy's. Cries of betrayal and a near mutiny. The Moesian legions would have torn Governor Saturninus apart if I had not ordered him back to Naissus, and all because he was slow to join them. They are up for a fight and they need a fight. If I turn back now what message would that send? That their commander is cautious? That he fears the enemy?' Once more he met each eye in turn. 'The sacrifice was good. The gods have spoken. We will fight and we will win.'

Valerius remembered Titus Vespasian's entreaty to rein in Primus's rashness, but as he opened his mouth to speak he felt a hand on his arm and a voice whispered in his ear. 'You would be wasting your breath. He will not be moved on this.'

Aurelius Fulvus pulled Valerius aside as they left the tent with the general's headquarters staff already dismantling the table and rolling up his maps. They walked to where the horses waited. 'Our commander is very decisive.' The legate of Third Gallica smiled. 'Some might say impetuous. We may go a little hungry, but with the gods' will we could yet win a great victory.'

'I remember another general who was in a hurry to meet the enemy,' Valerius pointed out as he heaved himself into the saddle. 'And it didn't end well.'

Fulvus frowned at the reminder of Otho's defeat at Bedriacum. 'Well, we must hope that whoever has taken command of Caecina's legions is less prone to impulse than the general. He appears to have forgotten that the enemy is just as able to abandon his baggage and heavy artillery as we are. All it would take is two days of forced marches and Valens to appear . . .'

Valerius had a vision of air misted with blood, and his mind's ears filled with the sound of clashing swords and screaming men. If what Fulvus spoke of happened, the five legions of Marcus Antonius Primus would be walking into an ambush by troops who outnumbered them two to one and were commanded by a general who had learned his business on the Rhenus frontier. It would be a disaster.

The question was: where was Valens?

Gaius Fabius Valens hunched low in the saddle and cursed the bastard pain eating into his guts, the bastard Emperor who'd roused him from his sickbed in a fit of panic, and above all the fornicating whoreson bastard Aulus Caecina Alienus who had caused that panic. Of course, it would take a one-eyed halfwit offspring of a donkey and a sheep to have ever trusted the whoreson in the first instance, but Aulus Vitellius Germanicus Augustus had done just that. He'd given Caecina *his* legions – the legions Valens had led all the way down the Sauconna and the Rhodanus; the legions whose might ensured that the people of Gaul would have no doubt who their true Emperor was; the legions he'd led to overwhelming victory at Bedriacum. *All* his legions, even his beloved First Germanica, of which he was, and let no man deny it, still legate. Aulus Vitellius had trusted the whoreson Caecina with every fighting man east of Hispania and west of Pannonia, and the whoreson Caecina had faithfully promised not to move from Narnia until Gaius Fabius Valens rose from his sickbed and travelled north to take joint command.

But here Valens was in Narnia and the legionary camps outside the garrison town on the Via Flaminia north-west of Rome were empty. The best information he could get said the whoreson was already two hundred miles away, either at Cremona or Hostilia.

Another gripe of searing pain tore through his lower stomach and he suddenly felt very old. What to do? The only force available was the three cohorts of auxiliaries and a cavalry squadron Vitellius had reluctantly agreed to give him as escort. As an attacking force it was worse than useless. Too large to hide and too small to fight, even if their morale was any good. Yet what choice did he have? Vitellius, for all his failings – and he had many – had placed his trust in him.

'We go on,' he told the senior prefect of auxiliaries. 'Perhaps there will be more intelligence of our comrades when we reach Fanum Fortunae.'

It took three days to cross the spine of the Apennine mountains and wind their way through the foothills to the flatlands by the coast. By the time they reached the busy port of Fanum, Fabius Valens was exhausted to the point of delirium. As if his words had been prophetic, there was indeed intelligence. But not the kind he wanted.

'Word came yesterday that the Ravenna fleet has declared for Vespasian.' The young tribune commanding the city sounded wary as he briefed Valens while he recovered from the journey. 'The prefect, Lucilius Bassus, can field at least one full legion of marines, possibly more. It is likely that he has already cut the Via Aemilia to the north.'

'What word of Caecina?' Valens demanded.

'The last we heard he was still at Hostilia, but that was a week ago. Since then, nothing.'

Valens released an audible groan. He needed up-to-date information, not rumours.

'There is more.' The tribune saw the general wince but continued remorselessly. 'A cargo ship arrived this morning claiming to have escaped from Aquileia. The captain told anyone who'd listen that Primus passed through with his legions a week ago and would even now be crossing the Padus.'

'The man is clearly spreading sedition,' Valens snapped, trying to gather his thoughts. 'Where is he now?'

'I was of a similar opinion, legate. I had him arrested. An Illyrian trader out of Spalatum, a man long suspected of being a pirate. We executed him as a spy and his crew is on the way to the slave pens at Ariminium.'

'Wouldn't it be better to have silenced them all permanently?'

'I am responsible for the security of this city, sir, but I am not a murderer . . .'

'You are a soft fool.'

'. . . and in any case they know that if one of them speaks out of turn all six of them will have their tongues cut out.'

Valens had a moment to change his opinion of the young officer before his world seemed to turn upside down. He would have fallen if the man hadn't caught him. 'Slave,' the tribune called. 'Watered wine for the legate. You should sit, sir.'

'No time,' Valens muttered, his mind drifting as if he was on the edge of sleep. 'Must make a decision. Send me my aides.'

But when the legate opened his eyes again it was already dark and he was lying on a soft bed. Another day lost, he raged inwardly. A servant came into the room with fresh water and he snapped, 'Why did you not wake me?'

'We tried, sir,' the servant said nervously. 'They . . . they thought you were dead.'

'Get me your master, and tell him to bring my officers.'

He heaved himself out of the bed and waited until they had gathered under his acid stare, the trusted members of his staff in their fresh uniforms and the auxiliary commander's leathery features locked in a scowl as if someone had stolen his breakfast. It had come to Valens as he lay asleep. No chance of reaching Caecina by the direct route now. The fool must fight his own battles for the moment.

He turned first to the auxiliary prefect. 'You will advance your men as far as Ariminium and reinforce the garrison against any attack from the north. The Ala Petriana' – the commander of the cavalry squadron bowed – 'will act as your eyes and ears and warn of any incursions by the marines of the Ravenna fleet.'

'You will wait here and send for reinforcements from the Guard?' The tribune's voice didn't hide his concern. 'Surely the Emp—'

'I will re-cross the mountains with my headquarters and either take the coast road north or make for the port of Pisae, depending on the enemy's dispositions. We will outflank the Flavians or, if necessary, sail north and land at Genua. From there it is only two or three days to Cremona. With the gods' help we will reach Aulus Caecina Alienus before it is too late.'

He closed his eyes and listened to them filing past him towards the door. If he had kept them open he would have seen the doubt on their troubled faces.

Marcus Antonius Primus studied the men repairing and rebuilding the earth defences of the camps originally created by Otho's army at Bedriacum six months earlier. He wiped dust from his mouth and spat. 'Good,' he said. 'This will do as a base for the attack. You disagree with my decision to continue, Verrens?'

Valerius shifted uncomfortably in his saddle. 'It's not for a soldier to agree or disagree, but to obey.'

The careful words drew a grin from the legate. 'That is not what your friend Titus would say. He and his father would urge caution as always. But when did caution ever win a man glory?' His eyes drifted to the road leading west. 'We are, what? Fourteen miles from Cremona? Very well, I intend to lead a cavalry reconnaissance in force towards the city while our auxiliaries forage among the farms and villages to the north. The farmers have been supplying the Vitellians for long enough; now they can feed us.'

Valerius reckoned it unlikely Twenty-first Rapax and Fifth Alaudae would leave much to forage, but he kept the thought to himself. 'You seem to enjoy placing your life in danger. Don't you think the legions at Cremona will respond to your reconnaissance?'

Primus shrugged, but his smile was almost companionable. 'Life without danger is a life only half lived. You of all people should know that. I will be safe enough, Gaius Valerius Verrens,' the big moon face split into a grin, 'for you will ride at my side and advise me, after which your insubordination may make you expendable and I'll give you the opportunity for a glorious end.' When Valerius didn't rise to the bait he continued: 'How far to the battlefield?'

'Perhaps half a day's ride. Closer to Cremona than to Bedriacum. The fighting spread across a wide area on both sides of the road.'

'When we reach the site you will tell me exactly how it happened.'

Primus's reconnaissance in force consisted of four cavalry cohorts. Two cohorts rode in columns of fours on the Via Postumia while the others took up positions on the flanks, providing outriders and scouts. Every trooper was protected by a vest of chain link armour that hung to the waist, over a leather shirt and woollen tunic, and wore an iron helm of the style traditionally favoured by his tribe. Unlike the legionaries', their legs were covered by trews, for that was the preference of the northern tribes. They carried seven-foot iron-tipped spears and the heavy *spatha*, the standard weapon of the auxiliary cavalry.

Riding at the centre of a cavalry column produced a mesmerizing effect, even in the midst of a war zone. The constant movement of the horse and the familiar jingle of brass and harness competed with the scuff of hooves on the gravel surface of the road to lull the brain. Occasionally a trumpet sounded in the distance and heads would come up, but there was no sense of urgency. Valerius preferred to be up ahead where Arrius Varus had nominal command of the expedition and he could see the horizon. Instead, Primus had insisted they ride in the centre of the column with his headquarters staff. The one-handed Roman found himself hemmed in by the bodyguard section and unit standard-bearers, their brightly coloured banners twitching with each step. They passed through a village with a small shrine to the twins Castor and Pollux.

Valerius moved to the general's side and explained how Otho's senior commander, Suetonius Paulinus, had wasted the opportunity to gain a decisive victory against Caecina. 'You spoke of Ad Castores? I was not present during the fighting, but the way it was told Paulinus had the Vitellians surrounded. If he'd used his reserves he could have annihilated them. Instead, they were allowed to retreat back to Cremona at their own pace. If Paulinus had attacked, Caecina would never have ventured from Cremona, your Pannonian and Moesian legions would have reached Otho in time and the whole outcome would have been different.'

'So Paulinus was too cautious,' Primus said pointedly.

Valerius nodded. 'Otho thought so.'

'You liked him?'

Valerius felt a twinge of regret as he remembered how Otho had changed in a few short months from a young man tortured by ambition to a wise one wearing the purple. 'He was certain of his right to rule. A man who didn't fear difficult decisions. But he didn't have the heart for this.' Valerius waved a hand to his right, where columns of smoke from burning farms dissected the horizon. 'I think if he'd known how much blood would be spilled in his name he would have handed the throne to Vitellius and gone into exile.'

Primus shot him a look of amused disbelief that any man, let alone a Roman patrician, would give up power out of conscience.

From Bedriacum to Cremona the Via Postumia ran arrow-straight on a raised causeway over land that had been a swampy quagmire until the Gallic ancestors of the region's inhabitants drained it for agriculture. Now it was rich and fertile, and provided the people with a good living – until the armies came. Armies had been coming this way for centuries. The Carthaginian Hannibal, with his elephants, from the west. Wild Raetian hillmen from their mountain fastnesses in the northern Alps. And, in the distant past, the forefathers of the Pannonian and Moesian auxiliaries who accompanied Primus had raided far into Italia along this very route. As Valerius surveyed the road ahead he experienced a moment of revelation, as if part of him had separated and was looking down upon his own body from above. Broad ditches flanked the road and he pulled his horse to the left, down the slope and up the slight incline on the far side. When he reached the rough fields he drew up and looked back to where Primus was staring at him with a look of bewilderment.

'You wanted to know about the battle?' he shouted. 'This is the best position from which to see the field.'

The general kicked his horse into a trot and rode to join the younger man. Serpentius and a bodyguard squadron of cavalry followed, but Primus ordered the decurion in charge of the escort to take his men out on the left flank towards the grey line of distant trees that marked the Padus. Serpentius ignored the order and rode up to take station at Valerius's shoulder, but the general didn't object.

Valerius studied the terrain ahead. Directly to his front, perhaps eight miles distant, lay Cremona, and he couldn't understand why the column's scouts hadn't yet clashed with patrols from the city. The bulk of Primus's gaudily clad auxiliary cavalry were massed on the Via Postumia's hard-packed gravel surface, their ability to manoeuvre constrained by the ditches. On the road's southern flank, where Valerius and his companions rested their horses, a flat expanse of fields stretched into the distance. Valerius pointed to where the escort cavalry were galloping along the line of the Padus.

'Between here and Cremona a maximum of four miles separates the river from the road,' he informed Primus. 'You can't see them, but these fields are cut by streams and man-made irrigation channels.

The land to the north of the road is much the same, except it's also covered in olive trees strung with grape vines. Marcus Salvius Otho's greatest mistake,' Valerius's voice contained a cold edge that told of the dark memories this place held, 'was to put his generals in a position where they were forced to fight three separate battles, and only one of them with any room for manoeuvre. On the right, Aquila and the Thirteenth faced the elite of Fifth Alaudae, but could make no use of their artillery. It was less a battle than a mass brawl and the officers lost control of their men among the trees. In that kind of fight every soldier must be his own general, but for legionaries trained to instant obedience it was the worst kind of nightmare.' He directed Primus to the causeway. 'In the centre, six Praetorian cohorts softened by garrison duty in Rome met the entire First Italica. Only the stronger would prevail because their movements were restricted by the ditches.'

He nudged his mount through the long grass and the spindly growth of plants and weeds that no farmer should ever have allowed to flourish in this rich earth. The reason became clear to him a few moments later. These fields weren't harvested because the local people feared the spirits who inhabited them. Marcus Salvius Otho's defeated legionaries still lay where they had fallen. Shattered skulls grinned ghostly pale out of the red earth and bones, thousands of them, littered the flat ground. Grass and weeds sprouted through the bleached ribcages of man and mount alike. Valerius guided his horse through the carpet of white and green. Let Primus make what he would of the First Adiutrix's battle. Here they had stood and died. He noticed a pile of bones that seemed larger than most, the head missing. Was this Juva, the giant Nubian, *optio* of the first century, Fifth cohort, the man who had broken the ring of spears to take a legion's eagle? He lay somewhere out here, along with the crew of the *Wavedancer* who had volunteered to serve Otho. And old Marcus, the *lanista* who had taught Valerius to fight like a gladiator. Did he not deserve a better memorial than a bunch of stinging nettles? They sat there for a moment, Valerius lost in his own memories and Primus pensive and thoughtful. The only sounds were the wind whistling through the grass and the distant cry of a soaring buzzard.

Serpentius finally broke the silence. 'They're among friends and they died with a sword in their hand. What more could a man ask?' He looked up sharply, disturbed by something carried invisibly on the breeze. 'Like as not we'll be joining them soon enough.'

A moment later Valerius and Primus noticed a dust cloud in the far distance and the tiny figure of an auxiliary messenger driving his horse up the flank of the cavalry column. Without a word, Primus kicked his mount back towards his headquarters in the centre of the four cohorts. The enemy was coming, and, in his eagerness for action, Marcus Antonius Primus had become separated from his army.

XV

'Auxiliary cavalry approaching fast, sir, on the open ground south of the causeway.'

Valerius heard the rushed conversation between the scout and Primus as he urged his horse to the legate's side.

'Numbers?' the general demanded.

'Only two cohorts visible,' the man frowned as if he wasn't certain of his information, 'but my commander believes their aggression indicates they expect to be reinforced.'

'You should return to the safety of the camp, general.'

Primus's square jaw came up at Valerius's suggestion, but he saw the expressions on the faces of his staff officers and reluctantly conceded. 'Very well,' he snapped, 'but we will withdraw with the bulk of the cavalry and not before.' He turned to a junior tribune. 'Order Aquila and Messalla to bring their legions forward in battle formation as we discussed. We will brush these irritants aside and continue the march on Cremona.' As the officer rode off Primus turned to Valerius. 'Inform Varus that he is to take a single wing and make a display that will slow the enemy. He is not to engage, but to delay them and follow at his best pace.'

The one-handed Roman saluted and turned to go, but a shout from one of the other aides froze him in place. 'What's he doing?'

Valerius looked towards the front of the column. A flurry of movement indicated where Arrius Varus, commander of Primus's cavalry, had sent his leading squadrons galloping to the left of the road. As he watched, the young prefect formed line with half of his thousand-strong unit and set off directly for the approaching Vitellian cavalry. Valerius waited for the auxiliary prefect to wheel his troopers to right or left and threaten a flank attack, but gradually it became clear this was no demonstration.

'Verrens,' the legate's voice was a full octave higher than normal. 'My orders to the prefect remain the same, but you will take the rest of his wing to cover his withdrawal if he has not already ordered that. Do you understand?'

'Sir!' Valerius was already on his way. He heard another horse close behind him and glanced across his shoulder. 'Get back, you fool,' he rasped. 'A cavalry charge is no place for a gladiator, especially one as old as you.'

Serpentius's face twisted into a wry grin. 'You didn't say that at the Cepha gap when I kept the Parthians from skewering your liver.' His expression turned sober. 'Let's face it. This cavalry charge is no place for any man who likes the fit of his own skin. There are thousands of the bastards out there.'

They galloped along the left flank of the remaining squadrons of auxiliaries until they reached the leading ranks. A confused decurion watched the diminishing backs of his comrades with an expression close to panic. His face changed to relief when he recognized Valerius's white cloak.

'I was given no orders, tribune. I . . .' He slapped his fist against his chest in salute. 'Tiberius Simplex at your command.'

Valerius studied the dark line on the horizon that marked the Vitellian cavalry and made his decision. 'Squadrons to form line three deep south of the road. We will follow your prefect at the canter. Be ready to wheel left at my command.'

'Sir!' The officer saluted and rode off shouting his orders.

Serpentius continued to gaze at the five hundred men bearing down on a force four times their number. 'Is he trying to commit suicide?'

Valerius rode out into the open ground towards the river with the Spaniard at his side. 'He's gambling that the commander of those men will think he's the bait in a trap and hesitate before attacking him.' The movement of the horse made talking awkward and his words came in bursts driven from his chest. 'That would give Varus the chance to escape without a fight like the little boy who tweaks a chained bear's nose and runs away.'

'So he'll have the glory without the pain.' The Spaniard nodded approvingly.

'But what he doesn't know,' Valerius continued, 'because he was too impulsive to wait for the scout's information, is that those two cohorts of cavalry are just the vanguard and they're probably about to be joined by at least the same number again.'

'And that will make their commander a lot braver.'

Valerius turned in the saddle to check the twelve squadrons of cavalry moving into formation behind him. 'He won't be worried about the trap, because he knows reinforcements are on the way, and he'll be able to gobble up the bait before any trap could close.'

'Only there's no trap. Only us.'

'That's right. Sound the advance.' Valerius snapped the order to the young signaller who had just arrived at his side. The familiar blast rang out from the curved *lituus* the auxiliary carried, and five hundred horses moved to the walk, then the trot. Valerius gentled his mount into a steady, unhurried stride and tried to calculate the distances between the forces. Arrius Varus was already more than five hundred paces ahead, with the Vitellian cavalry something like a mile beyond, advancing at the trot in their familiar open squares. Surely Varus must realize by now that the enemy wasn't going to stop. But the Flavian commander showed no sign of hesitation. Valerius considered his options as the gap remorselessly closed. A messenger would never reach Varus in time. If it came to a fight their only hope was to reach the point of collision soon enough to support the auxiliaries before they were swamped. On the other hand, Valerius couldn't afford to push his horses too hard or the enemy would ride them down during the retreat. If they ever got the chance to retreat.

He shouted to the trooper with the *lituus*. 'What's your name?'

'Julius Felicio.' The words were just audible above the thunder of hooves on the heavy round. 'Trumpeter, tenth squadron, Second Thracum Augusta, sir.'

'Stay close to me, Julius. I don't want you more than a sword's length from my side even if we're in the middle of a fight.' The advice was accompanied by a savage smile and he saw the boy's face go pale. 'And don't worry about getting killed because you'll be in good company. If you die, boy, we all die. So stay close.'

Serpentius moved into position on the trumpeter's right side and Valerius knew that whatever happened he could do no more to protect him. The Spaniard was as deadly in the saddle as on foot. He'd fought on horseback for Nero's spectacles in the Circus Maximus when whole squadrons of gladiators would clash for the entertainment of the Emperor and his friends. Valerius had seen him in battle against Batavian wolf men and Parthian Invincibles and neither could match his skills with sword or spear, or the little Scythian throwing axes he kept at his belt.

The gap between the two formations grew smaller with every passing second. *Turn, you fool. Turn.* He felt Felicio's eyes on him and realized he'd spoken aloud. If Varus turned even now, Valerius could wheel his squadrons left to threaten the Vitellian right flank. It might not hold the enemy in place, but with Fortuna's aid it would cause enough confusion for the two divisions of the Second Thracum to win free and join up with the main force as it retreated towards Bedriacum.

But it was already too late.

Only four hundred paces separated the two lines now and the bellow of Varus's trumpeter sounding the charge scraped across the inside of Valerius's skull like a sword point. Each individual *turma* in the attacking formation contained forty men, ranged in ranks four deep. Charging shoulder to shoulder the ten men in the front ranks shared an attack frontage of fifteen paces, with five paces separating each *turma*. But few horses, even trained cavalry mounts, would charge home against an unbroken line. Another short blast of the trumpet and Valerius saw daylight as the individual units obediently changed formation to open order and the line rippled out, increasing its length, but still only two thirds the span of the enemy's front.

'Wheel quarter left,' he shouted.

'Now we're for it.' Valerius barely registered Serpentius's doom-laden prediction before the two lines struck with a tumultuous clatter of iron, shrieks of mortal agony and the squeals of dying horses. Splintered lances twisted through the air and he saw at least one horse somersault over the heads of the first line and smash into the rear ranks of the enemy.

'Sound the charge!' Valerius accompanied the order with a primeval scream that combined anger and fear and frustration at Varus for getting him killed. His long sword was already in his left hand, drawn without its owner's volition. The urgent repeated trumpet call turned the ranks behind into a wall of roaring, shrieking madmen. The Second Thracum was made up of hard men born to the saddle, the third or fourth generation of their line to serve the Roman cause. They were instinctive warriors, of an ancient lineage that had learned the killing trade on the flatlands where the Danuvius flowed into the Pontus Euxinus. Valerius had calculated that to follow Varus directly into the centre of the Vitellian line would do as much harm as good. Instead, he had carefully angled his attack to come at the outer right fringe of the attacking line. But his orders were to get Varus clear, and the only way to do that was to ride directly into the heart of the carnage.

'With me, boy. Not a sword's length away.' He cut across the signaller and made for the seething mass of men who were hacking and jabbing at each other in the centre. Behind him, the crashing collision between two walls of horse soldiers was repeated, but he only had eyes for the men ahead and finding Varus's standard.

'There.' At his side, Serpentius pointed to a red and yellow banner that weaved and dipped in the midst of the struggling men. 'Silly bastard's got himself caught in the middle of it.'

'Jupiter!' Valerius roared the watchword, praying the enemy hadn't chosen the same one. It would be foolish to die on the point of a friend's spear after escaping the headsman's sword. A trooper careered across his front, intent on spearing a wounded man on a horse with Thracian trappings. Valerius automatically swung his sword at the unfamiliar helmet and cursed as the cut clattered against metal, jarring his arm to the elbow. The half-stunned enemy cavalryman turned his spear to meet the threat, but Serpentius was already inside the point and the air sprayed scarlet as the former gladiator's *spatha* took out his throat. Valerius saw Felicio's eyes widen in astonishment at the speed of the Spaniard's attack. 'With me,' he urged the boy. 'Stay with me. Jupiter!'

He focused on the bobbing flash of red and yellow as he forced his way through a bustling herd of mounted men hacking at each other with long swords. In the whirling mass of soldiers and horses the distinction between enemy and friend became blurred. A hand clawed at his leg and he chopped downward, drawing a gurgling scream of agony. Bile rose in his throat as he realized he'd just sliced the lower jaw from a Flavian cavalryman, who fell back with blood spurting from his shattered face. 'Jupiter. Vespasian. Varus?'

Somehow they reached the Flavian cavalry commander as he exchanged blows with the enemy in an unseeing cloud of rage and battle madness. His signaller was down, felled by a backhand cut across the eyes that left him groping blindly among the flying hooves. A bloodied standard-bearer was screaming at him to disengage, but Arrius Varus was lost in an Otherworld that only soldiers know, his heart soaring on the death cries of his enemies.

'Varus?' Valerius pushed his mount between the standard-bearer and his commander, grabbing roughly at the cavalry prefect's reins and hauling the horse away from the enemy blades. Varus's sword came round like a striking snake, but the Roman's *spatha* flicked out to knock the blade away and the cavalryman froze at the feel of cold iron against his throat. The blood-crazed glow in his eyes faded.

He shook his head. 'You? How dare—'

'General's orders, prefect,' Valerius said with a formality that seemed out of place amongst the butchery. 'You're to withdraw and join the main force.'

'Are you a fool?' Varus spat. 'This is my victory. Look at them.

They're running like rabbits. If Primus reinforces me we can chase them all the way back to Cremona.'

Valerius had been concentrating so hard on finding his quarry that he'd lost sight of what was happening on the rest of the field. Now he looked, and he realized Varus was correct. The enemy had faded away, beaten in the centre and the right, inexplicably followed by the men on the left who had not struck a blow in a fight that had lasted barely three minutes. Varus's troops jeered at the retreating backs and cut down the few dismounted men attempting to surrender.

'We should go back,' Valerius persisted.

Varus shook his head like a man in a fog. 'My victory.'

'You're welcome to it then,' Serpentius snorted dismissively. He took Valerius's reins and hauled his horse round. Cursing, Valerius tried to pull them back, but the former gladiator shook him off and nodded to where the defeated Vitellian cavalry had regathered. Valerius felt his heart freeze at the sight that greeted him less than a mile away. Line after line of glittering spear points marked the arrival of the Vitellian reinforcements; a solid, invincible mass of man, metal and horseflesh four or five times the number of the blown and battered survivors of the Flavian charge. 'Do you want to die with him?' the Spaniard demanded.

Valerius turned to Felicio, who hadn't moved a sword's length from him during the entire battle. 'Sound the retreat,' he said wearily.

XVI

It was a horse race and in its initial stages it seemed there could only be one winner. The Thracian mounts had been ridden twelve miles, taken part in a full cavalry charge and found themselves at the centre of an intense, fear-crazed, blood-scented battle. Serpentius looked back over his shoulder as they galloped over the open fields, leaping the occasional ditch, the causeway to their left. 'They're gaining,' he grunted breathlessly. 'But not as much as I thought. Maybe they're scared of us.'

Valerius shook his head. 'Their horses are almost as blown as ours.' He saw the puzzlement in the Spaniard's eyes. 'The two cohorts Varus attacked would have been attached to the garrison at Cremona. The cavalry who are chasing us now must have come from their main force at Hostilia.'

'That means the legions won't be far behind them.'

'I don't think we need worry about that for the moment.' Valerius glanced back. 'Because they may not be gaining fast, but they are gaining.'

They concentrated on getting the most from their mounts, the grass flashing beneath the flying hooves. By now, the retreating squadrons of Varus's Second Thracum Augusta were spread out over the length and breadth of two cavalry parade grounds. Small pockets of riders formed round the wounded who reeled in the saddle leaking blood, but as their pursuers closed the maimed were reluctantly abandoned to fend for themselves. Survival was all that mattered.

In the centre of the retreating Thracians, Valerius saw Varus away to their right. Beside him rode his standard-bearer and Felicio, whom the cavalry commander had demanded as a replacement for his dead signaller. At first it seemed all was well. Men grinned at each other, congratulating themselves on their escape or their prowess. Yet the thunder of hooves from the rear increased with every length and in a heartbeat the euphoria of survival turned to panic. Suddenly men who had been encouraging each other to safety cursed and fought for the swiftest course. Comrades competed for gaps in the field boundaries and priority at the easiest crossing points of streams and ditches. Their hard-ridden mounts sensed the fear of their riders and snapped at their neighbours, breath snorting from their nostrils and the foam thick on their flanks. Soon the first screams announced the moment the weakest became prey for their pursuers' spears.

Valerius looked up to see a shadow across the fields and the causeway. A surge of relief washed through him. Primus had withdrawn to the legions, but he'd left his cavalry to act as rearguard. Ahead waited three thousand hardened fighters, more than enough to give the enemy pause and save the bulk of Varus's fleeing men. Whoever commanded them had disposed his troops to create a gap fifty paces wide in the centre. It was a risky formation for the defenders, but one that made sense with hundreds of cavalrymen galloping to seek refuge in their midst. Better to leave a gap in the line that would allow a route to safety and could be closed at need, than hundreds of men and horses trying to claw their way through the tight-packed formations.

Valerius risked another glance towards Varus's banner and was puzzled to see the cavalry commander without his trumpeter. He searched for Felicio in the group around the prefect and began to edge in their direction. A surge of panicked men blocked his progress, but a sharp cry alerted him and he groaned as he realized what had happened. The young signaller's horse had snapped a foreleg and now it was limping along as the rearguard of the Second Thracum thundered past. Felicio looked round in despair towards the massed ranks bearing down on him.

'We can't . . .' Serpentius began. But Valerius had already turned his mount and the Spaniard followed with a curse and a prayer. They swerved their way through troopers blinded by fear and past riderless horses wide-eyed with terror, trailing flecks of foam from their sweat-slick sides. Felicio was still three hundred paces away, diagonally across the enemy's front. Valerius dug his heels into his horse's ribs, desperately trying to ignore the fast-approaching wall of steel-tipped death. The young signaller raised his head and Valerius saw hope flare briefly in his eyes before the crippled horse collapsed, pitching him from the saddle.

'Run,' Valerius screamed. 'Run.'

They were so close now that Felicio heard the cry and looked up. He hauled himself to his feet and began to fly across the rough ground to meet his rescuers. With less than fifty paces separating them the Roman saw the boy's face relax as he raised his hands ready to be plucked to safety. In the same instant a dark shadow appeared at the edge of Valerius's vision and with almost supernatural swiftness the trumpeter was gone, swept away in a welter of shattered bone and exposed viscera by the sword of a Vitellian cavalrymen.

With a cry of despair Valerius turned to follow the killer, but Serpentius drove his horse across his friend's path. 'That won't help,' the Spaniard snarled. 'If you want to avenge him, do it without getting yourself butchered.'

With a last glance at the remains of the young signaller, Valerius reluctantly followed Serpentius through the chaos of retreating men. The vanguard of the Vitellian auxiliaries tore at the fleeing Thracians like wolves in a sheep pen, whooping their war cries with every kill. Valerius and Serpentius found shelter with a more or less organized group and Valerius found himself riding at the shoulder of Tiberius Simplex. The decurion's face was a mask of defeat, but he acknowledged their arrival with a weary salute. Valerius pointed ahead. 'Gather what men you can, form column and ride for the gap.' Simplex looked. up and his eyes came alive as he saw the breach in the cavalry line and the possibility of survival. His jaw hardened and he galloped ahead shouting instructions to his men.

Barely two hundred paces to Valerius's right, Varus rode in a fog of confusion. He could see his standard-bearer's mouth opening and closing, but the words made no sense. Orders? How could he give orders when his signaller had abandoned him? This was no fault of his. He was certain he had done everything he could. Now it was up to every man to save himself. The trooper was screaming something about a gap, but Arrius Varus's whirlpool of a mind recognized no gap. All he could see was a long line of cavalry squadrons waiting to provide sanctuary. Narrow avenues showed between the individual units that might give access to two or three riders. He shut out the terrible sounds around him and set his mount for the closest break in the line.

A galloping horse will take less than a minute to cover half a mile. Already the bulk of Varus's men were bearing down on the sanctuary of the Flavian cavalry line. Most had maintained their discipline; a few, like their commander, were consumed by panic. The one thing they had in common was a determination to survive. Behind and among them rode the great mass of enemy cavalry who had chased them from the field. Savage thrusts of their spear points pierced chain armour, rib and spine to the accompaniment of the shrill death cries of their victims. Their blood was up and they barely noticed the static line of mounted men ahead.

Valerius had seen it before. Panic is like the disease that spreads through a camp on swampy airs, carrying rashes and lung rot and showing no mercy or discrimination for rank or quality. A wave breaking on a beach inundating every shell and grain of sand until its energy is spent. Now it leapt from the Thracian riders to those they had elected their saviours.

'Stay together!' Valerius roared the order at Simplex. 'Whatever happens aim for the gap and stay together.'

Three hundred paces. Ahead, the long line of cavalry seemed to ripple as they realized what was approaching. They could see the enemy's standards mixed with their own in the confused mass rushing

122

towards them, and beyond, the solid formations of the trailing Vitellian cohorts. They'd been told to expect an orderly retreat and disciplined columns who would take advantage of the gap in their centre. Instead, they faced a tidal wave of terrified men and horses that would break their carefully prepared defence lines and wreak havoc with sword and spear. When the first man turned his horse his decurion tried to push him back into line. By then it was too late. He was followed by first one then another of his comrades, and within a dozen heartbeats the whole line began to disintegrate.

Valerius watched it happen with a sinking heart, but his course never deviated from the gap in the line where the officers still exerted some semblance of discipline. Stern, determined faces flashed past to right and left and he was through and safe. The men Tiberius Simplex had gathered remained with him and he knew their first instinct would be to lower their guard, but he couldn't allow that to happen. He roared above the thunder of hooves, 'Stay together. Stay in formation.'

Serpentius had never left his side and he heard the Spaniard curse. 'Mars' sacred arse, what a fucking shambles.'

Valerius looked about him and was reminded of the mountain avalanche that had almost killed him the previous year. It had roared down the slope absorbing everything in its path, be it rock or snow, or tree – or man. The Flavian defensive line had absorbed the fleeing cavalry and taken on its momentum, careering blindly back towards Bedriacum. Thousands of men and horses thundering east in a confused rabble without form or discipline: a commander's worst nightmare.

Marcus Antonius Primus had overseen the formation of his legions and was returning to join his cavalry when he saw the disorganized horde sweeping down the Via Postumia. For an instant the same panic that drove them threatened to overwhelm him. Yet the fear he felt was nothing to the realization of the humiliation he would suffer if he was defeated. Better to die on this field than see his name a laughing stock.

Twenty paces ahead a narrow stream with steep banks cut across the line of the road, spanned by a wooden bridge. He turned to the prefect in charge of his personal guard. 'Tear it down and form a line on this side of the stream. This is where we make our stand. Not one step backwards.'

The men set to work and as more officers arrived from Bedriacum he ordered them to extend the holding line along the eastern bank of the stream. 'Kill the leaders if you must,' he instructed, 'but stop the rout at all costs. They will be slowed by the gully. Stop them and turn them round to face the enemy.'

Then he waited.

The first fugitives were those who had fled fastest, their horses foaming and close to spent, but they ignored their general's entreaties to stop and fight and galloped on. In desperation, Primus seized a spear from the closest of his escorts. The next man to cross the stream and top the bank was a standard-bearer, still clutching the red banner with his unit's symbol of a rearing horse. His eyes were glazed with fear and he didn't even hear his commander's order to halt. Primus thrust forward and the impact almost broke his wrists as the spear took the man square in the breast and pitched him out of the saddle. An aide swiftly stepped forward to pick up the banner and set it on the bank of the stream.

Primus dismounted to heave the spear free from the dead man's still twitching flesh. A shadow loomed threateningly over him, a tall, mounted figure silhouetted against the sun, and he turned with the point ready.

'Well,' he said savagely. 'Will you fight or do I have to kill you too?'

Gaius Valerius Verrens rapped his wooden fist against his chest in salute. 'One tribune and a hundred and fifty men at your service and ready to fight, general.'

'This is not a defeat.' Marcus Antonius Primus spat the word as if it was poison on his tongue. 'It is a setback, and a setback that we will turn into a victory. Do you understand? There will be no turning back. We will fight here and we will die here, if necessary.'

'Your orders?' Valerius asked.

For a moment Primus looked slightly bemused, as if, despite his fiery words, he hadn't expected to be able to do anything tangible to stem the tide. He shook his head to clear it and the orders flowed as a plan took shape. 'Form your men into five squadrons and place them to the south of the road about a hundred paces out. That will be the centre of our line and this stream and the men behind it will be our only defence. Spread your junior officers on either flank to help gather everyone who can fight and order them to kill anyone who refuses. They will collect them into squadrons and add them to the line.'

'And the road?'

'I will hold the road. You must hold the rest.'

It felt like the end of something, but it was only the beginning.

The makeshift line of cavalry behind the gully firmed up thanks to Valerius's decurions and *optiones* and their willingness to use a blade when required. Their efforts slowed the flow of fleeing men and created a dam of Thracians on the far bank of the stream. Those on the fringes of the cowering mob suffered terribly from the swords and spears of the pursuing Vitellians, but as Primus said: 'If they hadn't run they wouldn't be dying now.'

Eventually, the flow of friendly troops slowed to a trickle of wounded and shocked survivors and the leading enemy formations became visible, strong and unbloodied. If they'd followed up their advantage they might have broken through, but their horses were winded and the men felt they'd already won a victory. That was enough for now. Besides, in the far distance towards Bedriacum, they could see the banners of Primus's legions marching to reinforce the battered and demoralized cavalry units. The sound of trumpets echoed across the flat, churned-up fields and Valerius watched as they wheeled about and trotted unhurriedly back to Cremona.

When the Vitellian units had vanished into the distant haze, Primus rode along the line of the stream calling encouragement and taking stock of his exhausted cavalry. They were still nervous, but the fact that they had fought off the Vitellians, however belatedly, had raised their spirits. Valerius was glad their commander showed enough wisdom not to reverse that situation.

'We will have words about this,' Primus promised his officers. 'But at the right time. When the legions come up we will camp on this side of the stream and maintain strict vigilance until morning. For now, we will rest.'

But there was to be no rest.

XVII

'My men refuse to take up defensive positions.' The look on Vedius Aquila's lined features reflected an anxiety that seemed to exceed the news he imparted. 'Their blood is up and they demand to continue on to Cremona. They believe the withdrawal of the enemy shows a lack of fight.'

'Then have the dissenters whipped in front of their comrades,' Marcus Antonius Primus said dismissively. 'And have them sleep outside the perimeter,' he added with a grim smile. 'The enemy is welcome to a few mavericks who do not obey orders.'

'*All* of my men,' Aquila persisted. 'Every last century and cohort.'

The smile froze on Primus's face.

'The Eighth also has disciplinary problems,' Numisius Lupus admitted gloomily. 'They can see the smoke of Cremona's cooking fires while they dine on rough porridge. They mutter that we promised them they would be feasting on the city's food stores and they are but an hour's march away.'

Primus turned his attention to the campaign map for a few moments, but Valerius knew by the set of his shoulders that he was attempting to control his rage. They'd gathered in the commander's headquarters pavilion at the place where an hour earlier Primus had turned the tide of Vitellian cavalry by sheer force of will. Now he faced an even greater challenge: mutiny in his own army. Everything won might be lost in the next few moments if he made the wrong decision. The general might be impetuous, and he understood that any decision was better than no decision at all, but that didn't mean he was ready to blunder headlong into a battle. Eventually, he addressed the respected commander of the Seventh Claudia. 'And you, Messalla?'

'The bastards will do what I tell them,' the veteran tribune said. 'But they want to fight. They know only two legions defend Cremona and that it's there for the taking.' He shrugged and Valerius saw he agreed with his soldiers. 'Our supplies are low. We can't afford to get involved in a protracted siege. Why delay when they could have another five or six legions here tomorrow?'

'But our heavy weapons won't be here for another two days,' Primus pointed out. 'And a night action?' His expression said it was absurd.

'If we move now it could be all over by nightfall.' Messalla kept his tone respectful, but failed to hide an edge of impatience. 'If not, we've fought night battles before. Cohesion is the key. Make sure every man knows the watchword, keep your formations tight and kill everything that gets in your way.'

Valerius's dismay grew with every word he heard. The discussion reminded him of the conference before Otho's army marched down this very road. Then, it had been clear the Emperor had lost the faith of his generals and the result was a disaster that cost forty thousand lives. Primus still had his commanders' respect, but they had lost control of their soldiers. That was the problem when fighting a civil war. Every man had a stake in the result. He wasn't just fighting for victory and plunder, he was fighting for the future of his family and the Empire. And he was a Roman citizen, with a Roman citizen's rights and privileges, and sometimes he believed that gave him licence to dispute a commander's decision. A lull in the conversation broke his train of thought. He realized that Primus had asked him a question.

'I said you and Aquila have fought over this ground. He has given his opinion. What is yours?'

Valerius took time to gather his thoughts. 'To carry on risks being caught in a battle you can't control, against an enemy whose numbers you can only guess. Setting up camp here allows us to rest and consolidate our forces, with only a short march to Cremona at dawn and the opportunity to choose our own ground. Yes,' he cut off Aquila's interruption, 'it also risks allowing the legions from Hostilia time to reach Cremona, but that risk exists in any case. I say do not be caught in the trap that ensnared Otho. Fight the battle you choose, not the one the enemy wants you to fight.'

Primus nodded thoughtfully and made his decision. 'I will talk to the legions,' he said. The moon face twisted into a sarcastic smile and the slightest hint of contempt edged his voice as he surveyed his commanders. 'Are there any other complaints I must deal with for you?'

'The Thirteenth blames the city of Cremona for what happened at Bedriacum,' Aquila said carefully. 'Its people supported Vitellius from the start and gave shelter and supplies to his legions. My soldiers believe it should be made to pay.'

'And mine,' Lupus reinforced the point.

Primus frowned. 'It is Vespasian's policy that civilians should not suffer for the mistakes of their political leaders. I cannot be seen to allow such behaviour, nor to condone it.' He met the eyes of each legate in turn to ensure every man understood exactly what his words meant. 'However.... in war who knows what happens when a general's attention is drawn elsewhere?'

Valerius felt the unnatural silence that followed as the occupants of the tent digested the reality of what they had just been told – or not told.

With a verbal shrug of the shoulders Cremona's fate was sealed.

'The centurions are running things now,' Serpentius confirmed dolefully. They were returning to their tent past a *valetudinarium* where the army's surgeons were working on the day's wounded. A terrible scream rent the air and the Spaniard visibly paled at the rasping sound of a bone saw on an arm or a leg. Valerius felt a twinge in his right hand, but he smiled at the thought of Serpentius being squeamish about a doctor's work. The Spaniard swallowed and spat before he continued his theme. 'The centurions smell loot and when a centurion smells loot you'd best not get in his way. Their men are ready to follow them.'

He was right, Valerius knew. The sixty veterans who led a legion's centuries were a hundred times more respected and feared than the tribunes who had nominal command. Experienced, often avaricious men, they used their seniority to milk their soldiers of bribes for allocations of leave or to be given light duties. A man's centurion could make his existence a living nightmare

Primus did as he'd promised and spoke to the men of his five legions. Valerius listened as the general stood at the centre of the massed square formed by Eighth Augusta. He reasserted his right to command and highlighted the perils that would face them if they continued: the lack of supplies and artillery, the strength of the enemy position, the possibility of ambushes. But they wouldn't be swayed. They had the scent of plunder in their nostrils and his reputation for audacity told against him. When he spoke of caution, they heard something entirely different. He'd spent the last week telling them of the need to strike quickly. What had changed? In the end he had no choice but to resume the order of march.

They set out as the light began to fade, joined by three ragged cohorts of Praetorian Guards disbanded by Vitellius who marched in from the swamps south of Mediolanum. But the vanguard had been on the road for less than an hour when a blare of trumpets from the head of the column announced they'd inexplicably halted.

Primus was with his staff at the centre of the second legion, the Seventh Galbiana, and Valerius heard him complain to his aides, 'I did not order this.' Valerius exchanged glances with Serpentius and they simultaneously checked the column's flanks. The land around them was flat as a table top, but far to the north the mighty Alps shimmered like silver wraiths in the fading light. To the south the lamps of an occasional unsuspecting homestead shimmered beyond the river. Neither appeared to show any sign of a threat.

'Perhaps the Twenty-first and the Fifth have decided to contest the road?' a tribune suggested. 'If so, it's a decision they will come to regret. Let me send a galloper to find out.'

'Better that I see for myself.' Primus smiled grimly. 'But pass word to my generals that they should prepare to deploy. If the Vitellians believe they can defy Marcus Antonius Primus with two legions and a few auxiliary cavalry it will be my pleasure to disabuse them.'

He twitched his mount to the left, down the slope, and galloped up the flank of the column accompanied by his staff and personal escort. When they reached the leading legion, Valerius saw Vipstanus Messalla questioning the commander of a cavalry patrol which had ridden up with two prisoners. The men were bearded cavalrymen from some eastern auxiliary unit, bound and bloodied, but surprisingly defiant.

'It is impossible,' Messalla barked, his weathered, hook-nosed features a mask of consternation. 'Ask them again.'

'What is impossible?' Primus demanded.

Messalla turned in surprise and hastily saluted the general. 'The patrol commander claims to have seen the insignia of at least five legions on the road from Cremona.'

'Why should that be a matter of concern?' Primus said calmly. 'We know Twenty-first Rapax and Fifth Alaudae are supported by small detachments from another three legions.'

'But these are not the banners of the Ninth, Second and Twentieth, lord,' the cavalry prefect interrupted. 'My men identified the Twenty-second Primigenia, Fourth Macedonica and First Italica.'

Primus's aides shuffled in their saddles and Valerius could tell from the man's voice that the information he carried frightened him. The general's face froze. When he spoke his voice had lost its certainty. 'A few outriders . . .'

'No, lord.' The trooper indicated the two prisoners. 'These men confirm it. The legions at Hostilia broke camp immediately after the arrest of General Caecina Alienus. First Italica alone covered thirty miles yesterday. They marched into Cremona, resupplied and were on the road again within the hour.'

Expectation filled the air and the aides tensed, ready for the in-evitable order that would send them scurrying back to their units and another night of chaos as they reversed course to retreat to Bedriacum. Valerius knew the calculations that would be going through Primus's mind. He faced five full legions instead of only two, and those legions were just the vanguard of Vitellius's army. If he attacked, they'd pin him in place on ground of their choosing and eventually destroy him by sheer weight of numbers. If he retreated, they'd chase him all the way out of Italy. The morale of his men might never recover, but at least his army would survive. However, for a man like Marcus Antonius Primus there could only be one answer to that dilemma, and it wasn't the one his officers expected.

'We fight. Vedius?' Primus searched the ring of startled faces for the legate of the Thirteenth, but Aquila was with his legion almost two miles back up the road. The general's face twitched with irritation until his eyes fell on Valerius. 'Verrens? You have fought over this ground. I need a position where we can hold the enemy and hurt them.'

Valerius struggled to recall Otho's conference and the detailed map his generals had studied. Nothing would be gained by retiring to the position where Primus had earlier stopped the Vitellian cavalry. The runnel where they'd made their stand was flanked to the north of the road by row upon row of olive trees strung with the vines which had so hampered Thirteenth Gemina in the first battle. In any case, the bulk of the army would be well past now. Every mile closer to Cremona, the better the ground became. An image entered his head – a certain set of contours; a winding stream that followed the Via Postumia before curving south across the line of march; a crossroads nearby where a slightly elevated farm track dissected the raised causeway of the main road. He hurriedly explained the position to the general.

'How far?'

'Perhaps a thousand paces ahead,' Valerius estimated. 'If we push on now we can form a defensive line before the enemy reach it.'

True to his nature, Primus didn't hesitate. 'Messalla? You will force-march Seventh Claudia and wheel to form our left flank on the banks of the stream. Galbiana will follow. Verrens will command in my absence.' He read Valerius's disbelieving glance. 'I will conduct the battle from the centre, with the Thirteenth, but you will be responsible for the tactical dispositions of your legion. Do you think yourself incapable?'

Valerius drew himself up to his full height in the saddle. 'No, general, but—'

'Then carry on. Your warrant will follow.' Valerius was forgotten as Primus turned back to the aides frantically scratching out his orders on the wax tablets strapped to their saddles. 'Third Gallica will form the right flank, with Eighth Augusta defending the boundary of the track . . .'

When Valerius rode back to where the eagle of the Seventh glittered above the column, auxiliary cavalry units were already streaming to the front and flanks. He prayed they would carry enough threat to make the advancing Vitellians pause, because if the enemy caught Primus's legions on the march the inevitable result would be carnage, chaos and defeat. Valerius Verrens didn't intend to allow that to happen.

Because a man who wanted him dead had given him the Seventh Galbiana. The Seventh was his legion and Gaius Valerius Verrens' legion would fight and it would win.

XVIII

'Gaius Valerius Verrens, appointed commander of Legio VII Galbiana on the orders of Marcus Antonius Primus.' Valerius struggled to keep the raw edge from his voice. 'And with the full authority of Titus Flavius Vespasian.'

He saw the conflicting emotions flicker across the face of the fresh-faced military tribune who was the Seventh's second in command. First disappointment, because the young man had his pride and his bloodline. That bloodline dictated he was born to command and his pride told him he should want it. But it was swiftly replaced by relief, because a battle was imminent and he was as inexperienced in battle as the young Spaniards who made up the legion's ranks. The Seventh had been formed less than a year before by the prospective Emperor Servius Sulpicius Galba. Its ranks were filled by Roman citizens, mainly farmers, from his province of Hispania Tarraconensis, stiffened with a backbone of centurions from other legions. The legion had escorted Galba to Italia and taken part in his blood-spattered entry to Rome. They'd stayed only long enough to see him formally proclaimed Emperor before being dispatched to the Danuvius frontier to learn their trade under Marcus Antonius Primus. Since then, they'd trained and they'd patrolled, but they'd never had to fight. Only a handful of the men now under Valerius's command had ever stood in a shield line or hurled a *pilum* in anger. What he needed to know was their mettle and their temper. He waited patiently as the tribune twitched under the unforgiving dark eyes and took in the white scar that disfigured his new commander's face from eyelid to lip. Valerius flicked back his cloak to reveal the carved wooden fist on his right arm and the young man's eyes widened.

'C-Claudius Julius Ferox, at your service, sir.'

Valerius nodded. 'I don't have time for pleasantries, tribune,' he said. 'We leave the instant the legion is formed up, so you may introduce me to your officers on the march. For the moment I need to know our supply situation and ration strength.'

'We resupplied at Bedriacum with rations for three days.'

'Water?'

'Skins filled during the halt.'

'Numbers?'

Ferox frowned. 'We have the usual sicknesses and men on furlough. The only major loss has been a few dozen men from the fifth cohort we had to leave with the heavy weapons.'

A nervous smiled flickered across his face as he sought some acknowledgement. Valerius turned to look over the ranks forming up behind them. 'I didn't ask you for an estimate, tribune.' He kept his voice audible only to the young man, but it took on a force that pinned the smile in place. 'I asked you for numbers. If you don't have them find out from someone who does.'

The tribune rode off, shouting for his camp prefect. As he waited, Valerius found himself the focus of a grinning face peering out from beneath the savage mask of the bear's pelt that hung over its owner's wide shoulders. Big, worker's hands clutched the pole of the legion's eagle standard. It came to him that the last time he'd seen that face he was being marched to his execution on a dusty field in Moesia, found guilty of cowardice and deserting his comrades. Somehow he managed to keep his face straight.

'The Seventh must have been short of proper soldiers if they made you *aquilifer*, Atilius Verus. You probably need an assistant just to carry that shiny new bauble.'

'The legate must have felt sorry for me, I reckon, sir.' The grin broadened. 'Glad you've overcome your, er, difficulties, if you don't mind me venturing.'

Valerius laughed. 'Who's your *primus pilus*?'

'Our first file would be Gaius Brocchus, sir. Twenty-year man and a proper . . . soldier.'

'Proper bastard, you mean?'

'Proper clever, ugly bastard.'

'Up to any little tricks, is he? Naughty games with the rations or the leave tickets?'

Verus's face went blank. 'I wouldn't know about anything like that, sir.'

'No.' Valerius raised an eyebrow. 'Well, I think I'll have a little chat with him anyway.' His face split into a smile. 'Glad you're with us, *aquila*.'

'You too, sir. They're young, but keen, sir,' the standard-bearer blurted. 'A bit raw, but you can depend on them in a fight, especially now they're well led. The Seventh won't let you down, sir.'

Valerius nodded, but for a moment the breath caught in his chest. He remembered another young legion, raw, but keen, who'd torn the heart out of a force of German veterans, taken their eagle, and then been ground to bloody ruin. He hoped it wasn't an omen.

Serpentius had kept well back from the conversation. Valerius called him forward and together they walked their mounts towards the head of the column where the First cohort had pride of place. 'Did you want me for something specific?' the Spaniard asked. 'Or am I just along for local colour?'

Valerius kept his face straight. 'Just do what you do best.'

The cohort was the tactical fighting unit of a legion, and each normal cohort consisted of six centuries containing eighty men each. The First were the elite of the legion, shock troops who would be called upon to break the enemy line. Each of their five centuries was double the size of a regular unit, giving the cohort a total of eight hundred men. Officers apart, the rank and file of the Seventh Galbiana contained no veterans, so the First cohort was where Marcus

Antonius Primus had placed his biggest and toughest troops. Brocchus, the cohort's commander, was the exception. He was short enough to be dwarfed by the soldiers around him, but appeared as broad in the shoulders as he was tall. The scars of old battles criss-crossed his sour features like lines on a gaming board and someone had chopped off the end of his nose. But it was his mouth that made him truly fearsome. As Valerius approached, the centurion's lips parted in a gruesome smile of welcome. The centre teeth in his upper and lower jaws had been knocked out, and the remainder filed to sharp points to give him the ferocious gaping maw of a monster from Hades. Valerius had seen Iceni warriors snapping at Roman throats with their teeth and he had a feeling Gaius Brocchus would know the taste of another man's flesh.

'And you thought I was handsome,' Serpentius muttered under his breath.

Brocchus looked from Valerius to the Spaniard and back again, the smile never leaving his face. Word had evidently filtered down the column faster than the mounted men, and belatedly the centurion slammed his fist into his armoured chest in salute. 'Sir.'

Valerius acknowledged the perfectly timed not-quite-insolence and studied the ranks of bright-helmeted legionaries standing behind their painted shields. 'Your men look good, First, but how good are they?'

The compliment brought a murmur of pride from the massed ranks. Brocchus whipped round with his vine stick and rammed it into the chest of the nearest man. 'Quiet, you noisy bastards. The officer was talking to me.' His deep-set black eyes searched the front files for any sign of dissent before he turned back to Valerius. 'They're Spaniards, so their brains are between their legs,' he leered. 'But the only things they like better than fighting are wine and women and we don't mind that in a soldier, do we, sir?'

Serpentius went very still and Valerius knew he was trying to work out whether the centurion had been complimenting or insulting his race. Before he could decide Valerius slipped from the saddle and threw him his reins. He walked along the ranks, inspecting the men and their equipment. Brocchus had no option but to escort him, barking minor complaints to the men. Clearly he regarded this as his domain and Valerius – legionary commander or not – as a temporary inconvenience.

The whispered words that accompanied the inspection confirmed that view. 'No need to bring your pet killer with you, sir.' The centurion darted a contemptuous glance at Serpentius. 'Old Brocchus is too long in the tooth to be frightened by a broken-down sword juggler.' He looked down at Valerius's wooden hand and grinned. 'I've heard all about you and from what I hear that's not all you're missing. But it doesn't matter to me whether you ran from the rebels or not. We should be friends, you and I. All you have to do is mind your business and leave the dirty work to me and we'll get along just fine.'

The one-handed Roman decided to ignore the implied insult. Every *primus pilus* protected his authority like Cerberus guarding the gates to the abyss. It wasn't unknown for them to make this clear to a new legate, but he'd never heard of it done quite so blatantly. He guessed word of his dispute with Marcus Antonius Primus had spread and Brocchus believed it gave him some leeway to mark his territory. He halted in front of a dark-featured young legionary. 'Name and length of service, soldier?'

'Marcus Ulpius, second rank, first century,' the man said in heavily accented Latin. 'Ten months, three weeks and four days, sir.'

Valerius looked the legionary up and down. He noted the *lorica segmentata* plate armour was entirely free of rust, which was unusual, because it took an enormous amount of effort to keep it that way. Each set consisted of thirty-four separate pieces of body-hugging, polished iron bands; breastplates, back plates, rib protectors, shoulder-guard plates, collar plates, hinges and buckles, and every one prone to tarnish at the first hint of damp. Brocchus obviously kept his men busy.

'Sword.' Ulpius's expression didn't change as he reached across his body to draw the twenty-two-inch blade of the *gladius* free from its scabbard. Again, the iron was spotless and the triangular point honed needle sharp. He nodded, and the legionary replaced the weapon. Valerius could almost feel the glow of Brocchus's pride. But now he turned to the reason for his choice of this particular legionary. The shade of Ulpius's tunic of tight-woven wool was still close to the deep red it had been when he'd purchased it from the stores in place of a previous garment.

'Your tunic has been replaced recently. Tell me,' he said casually, 'how much does a new one cost these days?'

Ulpius shot him a look of dismay. 'Sir?'

'You must know how much it cost, soldier,' Valerius said reasonably. 'When I was in Britannia, it was as much as four *denarii*, a lot for an ordinary ranker. I'm curious to know if it has increased.' He had gambled that Brocchus would have added a premium to the cost of a new tunic – which would go directly into his pocket – in return for ignoring the extra punishments he could inflict on the unlucky soldier. Ulpius's reaction confirmed his suspicion.

The young man's mouth opened and closed and he looked wide-eyed past Valerius's shoulder to where Brocchus twitched and spluttered. 'I . . .'

'Or perhaps we could talk about leave entitlement?'

'If the legate doesn't mind,' Brocchus said hastily, 'this man is a little confused. A fine soldier, but . . . kicked by a mule . . . proper bang on the head.'

Valerius nodded to the legionary. 'A fine turnout, Ulpius. You're a credit to your unit. As for you . . .' he turned his attention to the centurion, bringing his face close and lowering his voice, 'I know all your little tricks and dodges, Brocchus, and they stop now. I will not have my legionaries fleeced of their pay and I don't want them going into battle worried about losing a knife or a cooking pot.'

'You can't touch me, tribune.' Brocchus shrugged, undismayed by the threat and certain of his leverage with the army commander. 'I have friends with influence.'

'You think you're above military law just because you have twenty years and a vine stick?' Valerius laughed. 'From the moment Marcus Antonius Primus seals the warrant that gives me command of the Seventh Galbiana, I am the law in this legion. You will obey my orders or be back digging ditches with your pension in the legion's hardship fund. Tonight or tomorrow we'll be going into battle. This is a fighting legion now, not a knocking shop where legionaries get screwed for the pleasure of Gaius Brocchus. Do you understand, *primus pilus?*'

Brocchus snorted so hard that snot sprayed from the ragged remains of his nose, but he smashed his fist into his chest. 'Sir.'

Valerius laughed. 'You may think my back needs to be making closer acquaintance with the point of a javelin, centurion. Just remember that when you're lining me up you'll need someone watching your own back. Because my pet sword juggler will be watching mine and he's much, much quicker than you. Now get this legion on the road and I want to hear them singing.'

Brocchus shot him a look of pure murder as he re-joined Serpentius by the side of the road to watch the red-clad formations pass. 'What was that all about?' the Spaniard demanded.

Valerius remounted and looked out over the never-ending tide of legionaries as the familiar strains of the March of Marius was struck up by the First cohort. 'I just wanted to make sure they knew there was more than one proper bastard in charge of this legion now, one worth fighting for.'

Serpentius noted the grinning faces as word spread along the column of Brocchus's humiliation, and looked up at the darkening sky. 'They know that, but it's going to be nightfall soon. If some fool decides to fight in the dark, pretty boy up there is going to be less interested in fighting than in making sure the new legate of the Seventh doesn't survive his first battle.'

Valerius clapped him on the shoulder. 'Well, you'll just have to make sure he fails.'

He had made a new enemy, but his whole being was filled with pure, heart-pumping joy. Gaius Valerius Verrens had his legion, and he had his eagle, and he was taking them to war.

XIX

'Mars' arse, I wish we had some of those shield-splitters that did such a good job at the Cepha gap,' Serpentius complained. In the gathering gloom, Valerius agreed with him, but kept his counsel in front of Ferox and his other aides. Shield-splitter was the name the men gave the wheeled *scorpio* artillery that fired five-foot arrows capable of ripping through a *scutum* as if it were silk. The *scorpio* was a giant bow mounted on a heavy wooden platform; it took two or three men to turn the ratchet to draw back the string – a twisted leather cord an inch in diameter. Shield-splitters had broken the back of the enemy charges when Corbulo defeated the Parthians at Cepha, a narrow valley north of the Tigris. Seventh Galbiana's complement of ten *scorpiones* for every cohort, plus a *ballista*, had been left behind to speed up the march to Cremona. Valerius's only consolation was that the Vitellian legions hurrying from Hostilia were likely to be equally unencumbered. Twenty-first Rapax or Fifth Alaudae were the only enemy units close enough to bring up their *ballistae* and *scorpiones*.

Primus had stationed the men of the Seventh Galbiana on the southern side of the Via Postumia with the Seventh Claudia, under Messalla, on their left flank. Aquila's Thirteenth Gemina held the road in a tight column just three centuries wide and twenty deep, a solid backbone through the centre of the Flavian position. On their right stood the veterans of the Eighth Augusta and, holding the far right flank, the bronzed warriors of the Third Gallica in their outlandish Syrian cloaks. The general had stationed his auxiliaries on both wings, knowing they were out-muscled by the Vitellian legions. Valerius prayed the gamble paid off, because if the enemy commander used *his* auxiliaries to hold the centre and hammered the flanks with his legions there'd be only one outcome. Primus's sole reserve was the host of three thousand disbanded Praetorians, who made up in enthusiasm and hatred for the enemy what they lacked in organization. Arrius Varus, surprisingly, retained his general's confidence, scouting ahead with his cavalry to give warning of the enemy's approach. In battle his squadrons would take up position on either side of the army. From there they could harass the Vitellian flanks, exploit an enemy retreat, or – and all Valerius's experience told him it was a much more likely event – cover their own.

Valerius studied the western horizon, where the faintest of ochre glows marked the dying of another day. It must be now, or the chance would be lost. He'd borrowed a fine white stallion from one of his aides, the better to be seen as the light faded. Heaving himself into the saddle he rode along the front ranks of the First cohort, which held the position of honour on the right of the legionary line.

He saw Brocchus spit surreptitiously and he had no doubt the *primus pilus* accompanied it with a muttered curse. Atilius, the legion's *aquilifer*, standing to the centurion's left in his bearskin and gleaming breastplate, met Valerius's nod with a grin. Behind them the legionaries stood in long silent lines, resting their arms on their heavy curved shields. An army of faceless strangers, their features hidden in the shadow of their helmet brims.

The first time Valerius heard a legionary commander rallying his troops had been on the crest of a gentle slope that would soon be slick with the blood of Boudicca's rebels. He'd never thought to be in this position. Yet, when it came to it, he found the words flowed easily. Less than six months ago he'd stood on these damp fields with brave men at his side. Then the trampled crops had been new planted, the green shoots struggling through the dark earth into the spring sunshine.

Now it was the stubble of the autumn harvest – for these were fields not yet haunted by the ghosts of battle – that prickled the feet of the men in their hobnailed sandals.

'Do you fear the enemy?' His voice sounded loud in his own ears, but he knew it wouldn't carry to five thousand men. To ensure his message was heard every centurion had orders to relay his words strongly enough to carry to the next century.

'No!' The shouted reply rippled through the ranks after a short puzzled silence.

'Do you fear the darkness?'

'No!'

'Then you are either liars or fools.' He paused and after a moment they laughed as he'd hoped they would. 'For together they may combine to destroy us. Our enemy is confusion. Our friend is discipline. The watchword for tonight is Tolosa.' The Gallic city was Primus's birthplace and an unlikely word for the Vitellian commander to choose for that reason alone. 'Your *tesserarius* will remind you, but etch it on your soul. Remember it. Trust the men beside you and in front of you, and stay in contact. In the darkness, cohesion is your friend. Division is your enemy. You are a young legion; you have never fought the legions of Vitellius. That is no shame, and no fault of yours. An emperor gave you your eagle, but he was foolish enough to send you away, and paid the price. Another called for your aid, but that call came too late. Now is your chance to show your quality. Atilius?' The standard-bearer marched forward, led by a soldier with a torch. He held the eagle aloft on its wooden pole and the spread wings glittered in the flickering golden light as if it were a living thing. Valerius could almost feel the legion hold its collective breath at the sight of their sacred charge. He waited until the *aquilifer* reached his side. 'I promised a dying man I would save his legion's eagle or die in the attempt.' He allowed the image to make its impact. 'I failed him. I . . . will . . . not . . . lose . . . another.' The words emerged as if from a slingshot, hurled by the strength of his emotion, and the legionaries caught his mood and roared their approval.

'Galbiana! Galbiana! Galbiana!' A great swelling storm of defiance hung over the battlefield like a banner.

Valerius raised his hand for quiet and waited for the hubbub to cease. 'That eagle belonged to a young legion too,' he continued. 'And I watched that legion charge to glory. I watched it tear the enemy ranks apart. I watched Juva, of the *Waverider*, *optio* of the first century of the Fifth cohort, destroy an enemy square and rip an eagle from the dying grasp of its *aquilifer*. I watched him carry it to his legate and I watched him promoted to centurion and become a Hero of Rome.' He paused again, his mouth dry with the memory. In the silence he sensed the waves of emotion ripple through the long ranks of armoured men behind the brightly painted *scuta*. Battle madness, they called it, the madness that would carry a man through a shield wall to the gates of Hades. It was an elusive quality, unreliable, often untrustworthy and rare as a phoenix egg. Yet in the right hands it could be as fearsome a weapon as was ever forged in an armourer's fire. The night air seemed to throb with its power, and Valerius marvelled that he, and he alone, had called it up. He smiled, and would have been surprised if he could have seen the elemental savagery etched in the lines of his face. 'I was wrong.' His voice shook with the passion that welled inside him. 'You need not fear the enemy, because the enemy is a leaderless rabble and fodder for your swords. You need not fear the night because the spirit of Juva is with you, and Mars and Jupiter watch over you. If you forget the name Tolosa, then let Juva be the unit watchword of the Seventh Galbiana.' This time it was the big Nubian's name they roared, and again he raised his hands for silence. 'We will fight on the defensive, a wall of iron that kills anyone who dares come against us. But if an opportunity arises, we must be ready to exploit it. Be ready for the command and do not hesitate. Now,' he bowed his head, exhausted by emotions he struggled to keep under control, 'make your peace with your gods.'

In the hush that followed, Ferox walked his horse forward to Valerius's side, pride shining in his eyes. 'The Senate has lost a great politician by your presence here,' the second in command said quietly. 'But I for one am glad of it.'

Valerius felt as drained as if he'd already fought the battle, but he shrugged off the feeling and clapped his deputy on the shoulder.

'Who would have thought it, Claudius? An orator. Cicero reborn.' He lowered his head, so no other man heard. 'Can I count on you?'

The tribune raised his chin. 'To the death.'

'I never doubted it. Make sure our best men are with the eagle. Take no argument from Brocchus if you have to put his placemen back in the ranks.'

Ferox nodded and rode off, to be replaced by Serpentius. 'When you were telling them about Juva's heroics you forgot to mention watching him being chopped into little pieces along with the rest of First Adiutrix.'

'Sometimes a speech is as much about what you leave out as what you put in.' The Spaniard heard the smile in Valerius's voice before the tone changed. 'If they attack in the night it's going to be bloody and confused. Noise and distraction on every side, *pila* coming out of the darkness and no way of knowing whose hand threw them. If the Seventh stays together we'll be safe enough, but if they break . . . At the start, I want you to stay by me and listen.'

'Listen?'

Valerius nodded. 'This fight will be won by the man who under-stands what is going on around him. You will be my eyes and ears. Listen for the enemy's watchword.' He felt Serpentius stiffen with interest. 'When we're certain we have it, put together a reserve from my personal bodyguard to deal with any breakthrough' – a thought struck him – 'and collect the enemy shields.' The Spaniard produced a leopard growl of a laugh as he guessed Valerius's purpose. 'It will probably be a wasted effort, but who knows? They might come in useful.'

On the far side of the raised causeway, the mounts of Marcus Antonius Primus's aides skittered nervously at the muffled roar from the legion on their right.

'Stop flapping around like a flock of headless capons,' Primus barked. 'Don't you fools know the difference between a legion that's in a fight and a legion that's spoiling for one? Is there any more news from Varus?' The answer was negative, the situation the same as before. Legionary-sized formations were on the march from Cremona, but they could be anywhere between one and three miles away. The general didn't know the exact numbers, and with full dark imminent he wasn't going to. Worse, their dispositions and intentions were hidden from him. Even now they could be flanking him, readying for an attack that would roll up his line. He shuddered at the thought and fought the snake of panic that squirmed in his belly. His horse sensed his mood, dancing nervously on its hooves, and he hauled at the reins to curb it, muttering: 'Stay still, you brainless bastard.'

He must keep his faith in Varus and his cavalry out there prowling the darkness. Still, he cursed the weakness that had made him concede to those bastard mutineers who demanded to be led straight to battle. Caesar would have butchered one in every ten, and, if that hadn't convinced them, butchered one in every ten more. Instead he had given in, and now he was going to have to fight in the pitch dark. It would be like orchestrating his funeral from his own tomb. Would they attack? He had to assume so. Otherwise why leave a perfectly good defensive position at Cremona, with supplies of food and weapons close to hand and the support of heavy weapons from the walls?

He turned his thoughts momentarily from the enemy to his own position. His defences ran from south to north across the gravel of the Via Postumia. The stream or ditch Valerius Verrens had identified defined the line in the south, while the northern sector was marked by the slightly raised country track that dissected the main road. Naturally, his legions had protected themselves with all the ingenuity of their years of service. Pits and hidden stakes, a ditch such as could be thrown up in the time available. Not enough, but it would have to suffice. Third Gallica and Eighth Augusta defended the northern flank. Thirteenth Gemina stood like a compact bulwark three centuries wide and twenty deep in the centre, eager to avenge the humiliation of their defeat at Bedriacum. A new roar from the south interrupted his thoughts and he smiled. He was glad he'd allowed logic to triumph over emotion and handed command of Seventh Galbiana to the man who had been his enemy. Gaius Valerius Verrens might be an irritating combination of equestrian disdain for the pursuit of power and wealth and a man of boringly predictable honesty, but he was a soldier to his very bones. And Primus needed a soldier in charge of Galbiana today. The legion held the most exposed position in the line, in front of the raised roadway but unprotected by the stream which ran almost due east before taking a propitious dogleg across the neighbouring Seventh Claudia's front. As the sky darkened tiny pinpoints of light begin to appear, not bright enough to lighten his mood. He hunched in the saddle, neck sunk into his shoulders as if the weight of his predicament was physical.

'Sir!'

'Look.' A shout from one of his aides alerted Valerius as he talked with Vipstanus Messalla, who had ridden across from the Seventh Claudia to discuss tactics. First one, then two, then a dozen bright streaks split the sky to his front as fire arrows released by Varus's scouts announced the imminent arrival of the Vitellians.

Messalla's face set in a tight smile. 'So.'

'May Fortuna favour you, tribune.'

'And you, boy. I've placed a cavalry wing between your left flank and my right and they should alert us to any infiltration, but . . .' He shrugged. Both men understood what would happen if the enemy broke through. 'Death or glory.'

Messalla rode off and Valerius took a deep breath to steady the nerves that no man could entirely escape. 'Cornicen? Sound: prepare to receive enemy.'

The strident call rang out along the Flavian line, followed by the distinctive metallic ripple as thousands of men checked their equipment one last time. Valerius tugged at the straps on his helmet, making certain they were secure, but he resisted the urge to draw his sword. He was the legion's legate, not a common solider. His job was not to fight, but to command and to lead. But how did you lead men you couldn't see against an all but invisible enemy?

'I will not lose another eagle.'

He didn't realize he'd turned the thought into words until Serpentius's rasping voice echoed them.

'Neither will I.'

147

XX

Waiting. The waiting was always the most difficult part. In the hour before battle the spirits of the dead came to taunt you with the thousand ends that awaited a soldier. They whispered in your ear like the slave in an Emperor's chariot during a triumph, intoning *You are only mortal*. Mortality was a treasured amulet hanging from the neck on a worn leather cord, a coin that had proved its luck in a game of chance, or the memory of a pretty girl in a distant town. Every man understood that the gods could snatch it away at any time of their choosing. In daylight, a legionary might look to his right or left and find reassurance in a smile or a word, but the darkness was like a physical barrier separating each individual.

Before the warning arrows landed a thousand pinpricks of light appeared like twinkling fireflies along the Roman front. Valerius knew they'd be the torches held by enemy engineers leading the individual cohorts and centuries to their pre-planned positions. Valens, or whoever led these men now that Caecina had been caught in his betrayal, would have his own scouts. Even as Valerius had addressed his legion those wily countrymen would have crept up close, trying to identify the exact placing of the Flavian units. Once the cohorts were in position and certain of their angle of attack, the torches would be extinguished and the enemy would be as blind as Valerius. Would they attack? He knew the question must have been haunting Primus since darkness fell less than an hour earlier. Why else march almost five miles from Cremona to a field chosen by their enemy when they could have rested and resupplied and attacked fresh in the morning? As he studied the twinkling lights, Valerius's greatest concern was that the Vitellian commander would hesitate and Primus would lose patience and order an attack of his own. Unity, cohesion and discipline would win this fight, if there was a winner. He'd heard of night battles of such chaos and confusion that neither side knew who'd won before they retired. In such circumstances, the attacker was at much greater risk of losing his cohesion, stumbling into the darkness over rough ground like a blindfolded boxer. In his enemy's position Valerius would bring his men in close and launch a lightning, all-out attack. A single flight of *pila* then five thousand men screaming like banshees over the last twenty paces. An explosive combination of power and surprise calculated to dismay men who'd spent the night waiting in fear of what was to come. But who was his enemy?

'Send word that I need a prisoner,' he said quietly to Serpentius. 'I need to know who I'm fighting.'

The Spaniard disappeared into the darkness and Valerius dismounted, handing his mount's reins to an aide, and walked through the ranks whispering encouragement as he went. When he reached the front he found Brocchus and his standard-bearers still standing ahead of the main line. He tapped Atilius on the shoulder and ordered him to retire to the centre of the legion. When Atilius was gone he joined the *primus pilus*.

'First.'

He could almost feel the man bristle with resentment at his interference. Brocchus didn't acknowledge the greeting. His eyes never left his front where the lights of the enemy engineers still hovered in the darkness. 'What's taking them so long?' His voice betrayed no fear, only curiosity.

Valerius had been pondering the same question and now he studied the faraway lights all the harder. A silent presence appeared at his right shoulder. Serpentius. 'Do you see it?'

Valerius swept the darkness until his eyes began to sting from the effort. There. Just for the faintest moment a group of lights in the centre vanished and then reappeared. Vanished again. 'The clever bastard,' he whispered, half in admiration.

'The lights are a feint,' the Spaniard guessed. 'They're on poles so that nothing will be silhouetted against them. There must be a slight rise in the ground and every time a century passes over it the lights go out for a moment.'

'How far?'

Serpentius hesitated only for a moment. 'A hundred and fifty paces.'

'Wait till they're at thirty.'

He turned to Brocchus and whispered his orders. 'Pass the word. *Pila*. Both front ranks. One single cast. The signal will be the screech of a night owl.' For once there was no hesitation and the centurion marched off into the darkness.

Valerius retreated through the lines of silent armoured figures. Tension made the men shuffle in their places. Sweating left hands shifted on shield grips to get the best hold, and each man measured the familiar weight of the *pilum* in his right. Somewhere a legionary was reciting a prayer in a muffled whisper, while his comrades cursed him to be quiet lest he attract the attention of an officer. A soft whinny and the jingle of harness from the south announced that Messalla had been true to his word and auxiliary cavalry were moving into place on Valerius's left.

He had arrayed the legion in the standard defensive formation of four cohorts in three close order lines, each composed of seven hundred and fifty men. Since every man required a fighting space of just over three feet, it meant the Seventh's front was almost three quarters of a mile wide. Ten paces behind the battle lines, a further three cohorts made up a reserve line which would feed men into the battle as casualties were replaced. A further fifty paces back stood the legion's strategic reserve of three more cohorts, still in their squares. When the time came – *if* the time came – Valerius would use these men to capitalize on any enemy weakness or, as seemed more likely, to stem moments of crisis. It was a tidy formation, strong where it needed to be, but flexible enough to react to opportunity or emergency. As he reached Claudius Ferox and the rest of his headquarters staff, the aide returned his reins and helped boost him into the saddle. They were in the gap in front of the reserve cohorts, compact squares twenty men wide and twenty-plus deep. The *signiferi*, the standard-bearers for the individual cohorts, would be ranged along the rear of the main defence line, with Atilius and his eagle in the centre, surrounded by his hand-picked group of eight bodyguards. How can you direct a battle in the dark? Valerius closed his eyes and opened them again, but it made no difference. His only point of reference was the twinkling lights to the east, and he cursed their attraction when his useless eyes should be probing elsewhere. His ears strained for the faintest noise. Five thousand men couldn't get within fifty or sixty paces of the line without making a sound. But all he heard was the rasp of his own breathing and the thunder of his heartbeat. 'You can't command,' Messalla had said. 'So no point in trying. It's difficult enough to know what's happening in a normal battle; at night you have to trust your centurions to follow your orders and stay in formation. What you can do is lead. Lead by example. Let them know you're where the fighting is hardest; they like that. It might only directly affect thirty or forty men, but word will spread. And let them hear you, even if it's only so they know you're alive.' Where was that fornicating owl? Surely they must be close enough by now. But of course they would be just as wary as the men who waited for them. Did all commanders suffer this sense of impotence? Was this how Corbulo felt during that long day watching his men dying before the Parthian King of Kings finally overstepped himself and threw in his Invincibles? Valerius had considered a volley of fire arrows, but discarded the plan because it would illuminate the defenders as well as the attackers. It must only be seconds now, surely? His horse danced under him, sensing its rider's frustration. Come on.

'Keeeeeeyick. Keeeeeeyik.'

At first the only sound was the soft flutter as two thousand missiles carved through the night air, but before Valerius had reached the count of three the arrhythmic, staccato clatter of metal on metal filled the night. Within moments screams and agonized groans accompanied

151

the familiar sound as the weighted points of the heavy *pila* found gaps between armour and below helmets. A momentary hesitation followed that was broken by the strident blast of horns and the screams of *'Percutite!'* as the attacking commander ordered a charge. The enemy's roar split the darkness as the unique sound of another hail of javelins landing amongst armoured men announced their reply. More men were screaming, but now they were his.

Valerius had no need to order his legionaries to prepare to receive the enemy charge. They'd drawn their short swords the moment each had launched his single *pilum*. Now the big shields would be fixed edge to edge in a single unbroken wall. Valerius had never felt so helpless. This was the moment. They must weather the first terrible surge like a breakwater holding back a giant wave. If even one man failed the line would be broken and slaughter would follow. Nothing he did would shape what was to come. The breath seemed to solidify in his chest as he waited. His heart jumped as a crash like thunder began on his far left and rippled all the way along the line in a series of thundering collisions. His horse bucked beneath him and he curbed its antics, fighting the urge to go forward and try to influence what was happening. This was a time for patience. A time for listening and attempting to tease order from the insane clamour of war. Serpentius still hadn't returned to his side, but how would anyone make out the watchword in this cacophony? It was like being at the centre of a giant bell hammered by demented circus performers. A great roar off to his right announced the clash of two more formations, one of them certainly Aquila's Thirteenth Gemina. Closer still, on his flank, Messalla's men would already be fighting, but he concentrated on events immediately around him.

Tension, frustration, fear and anxiety, that was the world of the men in the reserve formations. Not for them the snarling, bitter, animalistic fight for survival of the front line, stabbing at the darkened faces beyond the big *scuta* and only knowing the enemy by the power of his shield and the quickness of his blade. They must stand and be thankful that, for the moment, they weren't the ones emitting the screams that announced success and failure alike. In the darkness, a man's only notion of personal victory came in the unique feel of a sword trapped in living flesh, or the shriek as the point found eye or throat. Yet even that meant little. When one opponent fell away he'd be replaced by another, and the deadly game of blindfold combat would begin again. A soldier could only fight on, knowing that in time his arms would tire, his blade slow and his shield falter. Eventually his defeat would be signalled by the glint of a *gladius* point, a moment of bowel-draining terror, a searing flash of agony as cold iron sliced through cringing flesh – and the scent of his own blood.

'I need a man here.'

'Close the gaps. Get forward there. Quick now.'

The orders rang out in the dark, the centurions urging their reserves forward. Valerius imagined the blood-soaked, mutilated men crawling towards him with their jaws hacked off, their throats slashed or their eyes jabbed out. Even a fine helmet, with its protective cheek pieces and low brow, didn't entirely protect an armoured man's face. They'd come with their fingers chopped off, perhaps even the sword hand, because a swordsman must risk exposing his hand. He winced, remembering the moment of exquisite agony and a right hand lost in the ashes of some burned-out British villa. The smell of the blood was tangible now, along with the sewer stink of pierced intestines. Darkness seemed to have made his nose more sensitive, as if it were trying to make amends for his lack of sight.

'I need men here.' The centurion's voice, shriller now, the need more urgent. Valerius's head whipped round and he tried to gauge from which flank it had come. Should he act? No. They held. For now the Seventh Galbiana was still the effective fighting unit that Marcus Antonius Primus had forged. Valerius must trust centurions he barely knew to make the right judgements. Men like Brocchus, a man of no honour and little integrity, would win this battle or lose it. All he could do was support them. A new clatter of javelins landing among the front rank. More screams and more shouts for reserves. Did that mean that whoever was commanding the enemy had brought up his own reserve cohorts? No, not yet. The battle couldn't be more than a few moments old.

A rustle in the darkness and he felt the men of his bodyguard stiffen. 'Tolosa.'

He relaxed at the whispered password. Serpentius. The Spaniard rode out of the darkness. Valerius made out a struggling figure held against his horse's flank by the collar of his tunic, choking as if he was on the end of a rope. A legionary's shield lay across the former gladiator's saddle. 'He says he's from the Fifteenth, but I wouldn't know.' He dropped the squirming man and brought the shield close so Valerius recognized the symbol on its face, a jagged star around the boss.

'The wheel of Fortuna. He's telling the truth. What else does he have to tell us?'

Serpentius leapt from his mount and dragged the cowering legionary to his feet, a wicked curved knife appearing in his hand with the blade at the soldier's throat. 'I'm only going to ask once, friend. Who's in command?'

Valerius heard the pitiless menace in Serpentius's voice and almost felt sorry for his prisoner. The man swallowed. 'My legate is the honourable Munius Lupercus. Fabius Fabullus of Fifth Alaudae commands the army of Vitellius.'

'Not Valens?' Valerius asked.

'No, lord. Some men wanted to wait at Hostilia for Valens, but General Fabullus insisted we march for Cremona. They say we covered a hundred miles in three days. I know we did thirty this day past. The men are exhausted. They just want this over.'

'What word of Vitellius?'

The legionary's face turned sombre and he shrugged.

'Very well.' Valerius turned to his bodyguard. 'Take him to the rear.'

When the prisoner was gone Serpentius remounted. Valerius beckoned him close. 'How did it seem to you?'

'From what I heard we're holding them. At least in the centre.' The Spaniard shrugged. 'As for the rest . . .'

Valerius nodded. No Valens, but Fabius Fabullus was an unknown quantity. He had driven his men hard from Hostilia to Cremona, but was he too eager for battle? The one-handed Roman felt like a blind man groping his way along a cliff path. He could hear the wind and the waves, but what good was that if there was nothing but fresh air where his foot was about to fall? Five thousand lives depended on his next decision and all he had was his intuition. He called to Ferox.

'Send an aide to check the reserve line. I need to know if it's time to feed in another cohort from the squares.'

The guard tensed again as a legionary loomed out of the darkness calling the watchword and dumped something on the ground nearby. 'What's that?' Valerius demanded.

'You asked for shields,' Serpentius pointed out. 'So they're bringing you shields.'

'Of course.' Valerius remembered now. Why had he wanted shields? He had no idea. Still, things seemed to be going remarkably well . . . Even as the thought formed he froze in the saddle at a great howl from his right flank.

'What . . .'

'Flank attack.' Claudius Ferox's voice betrayed his fear.

Valerius reacted instantly. 'Take the Ninth and Tenth cohorts and do what you can to stop them. Send a runner once you have an idea of their strength.'

Ferox galloped to the reserves, already shouting orders, and Valerius spent the next long nerve-grating moments in a turmoil of frustration before the runner returned.

'Tribune Ferox reports that he is facing an entire new legion and begs for further reinforcements.'

'Which legion?'

'Fifth Alaudae, lord.'

Valerius closed his eyes. Otho's bane at Bedriacum, and now they were coming for him.

XXI

Valerius sensed the balance of the contest changing.

The front ranks of Seventh Galbiana were under pressure, but they were holding. From the right, where the First and Ferox's two reserve cohorts were struggling to hold what might be the entire Fifth legion, he could almost feel the panic amidst the cacophony of a battle being fought to the death. A sense of enormous pressure accompanied it, as if in the darkness a great physical mass was pressing against his legion's flank. In the past few moments he'd been informed the enemy had taken at least two cohort standards. The next order would be crucial, not just for the Seventh, but for the battle and Titus Flavius Vespasian's bid for the purple.

Only one aide remained, the others missing, sucked into the shadowy maelstrom around them; dead, wounded or just lost in the darkness. 'Find General Primus and tell him we are sore pressed on two fronts. Beg him to send reinforcements,' he instructed the soldier, the youngest of the legion's tribunes. 'Serpentius?' He muttered a curse as he realized the Spaniard had disappeared, and rode to where the last of his reserves waited. A single cohort held by the iron discipline of their trade as their comrades fought and died out there in the darkness. Atilius would be at its centre with the legion's eagle standard, his face a stony mask of resolve beneath the bear's yellow-toothed hood.

Valerius hesitated, searching the clamour for a sign that would save him from giving the order. The desperate cries of men struggling for their lives told him that if he didn't use the last of his reserves now he might not get another chance. He would not lose another eagle? The words of less than an hour earlier sounded hollow in his ears. What a vain, comical boast it had proved; nothing less than an invitation to the gods to prove him false. Sometimes an eagle must be risked. If he did not risk the eagle, he would certainly lose his legion and Primus his battle. So he'd risk the eagle, and if it was lost, make sure he didn't live to suffer the terrible emptiness that followed, and the pain worse than defeat.

'Aquilifer,' he shouted, 'to me.' The standard-bearer marched from the centre of the cohort with the flickering torches of his bodyguard creating a circle of light that revealed his burden to every man.

Valerius dismounted and met the soldier's eyes. 'You know what you must do?' he said quietly. 'Our comrades are pressed hard and they are wavering. They fight for their lives, but sometimes a man needs something more important to fight for.' He saw the white flash of Atilius's teeth and the glint as he raised the eagle standard a little higher. 'Eighth cohort?' Close to five hundred men came to attention at the shout. 'I know you hoped your services wouldn't be needed tonight,' he heard a laugh from the ranks that raised his spirits, 'but our enemy has decided otherwise. They have honoured the Seventh with the attentions of not one but two legions, and who can blame them? Your tentmates in the Ninth and Tenth cohorts are the anvil that holds them. The Eighth will be the hammer that destroys them.'

Serpentius appeared from the darkness on foot. 'You were right.' His voice was just loud enough for Valerius to hear. 'They flanked us. We have one chance. Ferox and his two cohorts are holding firm and as long as they keep their attention we might be able to surprise them. But we have to be quick.'

Valerius ordered the eagle's guards to extinguish their torches, but keep them ready in case of need. With the six close-ranked centuries on their heels he and Serpentius led the way across the uneven farmland; first north, then west. They found themselves in an almost uncanny peace between battles. If Valerius had calculated correctly, their parent legion, the Seventh, lay a hundred paces to their left front, fighting for its very existence. The Thirteenth were the same distance away on the right, apparently holding their own. The gap between should have been held by one of the Thirteenth's auxiliary cohorts, but they'd either been forced back or joined in the fight. Serpentius stopped and Valerius's order to halt was passed back in an urgent whisper. 'Thirty paces,' the Spaniard whispered. Valerius could make nothing of what was ahead thanks to the chaos of sound that filled the darkness, but he trusted the freedman's instincts. If he was right, they would be on the left flank of the legion that had punched into the Seventh, if not . . . But battles weren't won by ifs.

Valerius turned back to the ranks of legionaries, praying that none of the centuries had lost contact during the heart-pounding dash. 'They don't know you're here.' He spoke loud enough for the closest century to hear, aware of the risk but reckoning it worth taking. 'So hit them fast and hit them hard. One cast and we will come screaming from the night like the *daemones* of Erebus. Form cohort wedge, let your eagle be your rallying point. Your watchword is Tolosa, the reply is Juva. Just get in amongst them and kill everything that isn't screaming it at you. Slaughter the bastards.'

He advanced another five paces to be certain. 'Now!'

The right arms that drew back had been straining for action all night and now the frustration of hours of inactivity was released in a single burst of energy. The *pila* curved into the darkness in an unerring arc, six feet of iron-tipped ash, with a weighted pyramid point designed to penetrate shields and chain armour. In daylight, a legionary facing a *pila* attack raised his big curve-edge *scutum* to protect himself. If it stuck, the missile might encumber him for the rest of the fight, but his odds of escaping injury were good. At night, in a surprise flank attack, it was different. The first the men of Legio V Alaudae knew of the danger was when ears long attuned to danger detected a soft rushing sound behind the raucous symphony of battle. A heartbeat later, the heavy javelins punched into helmet, neck and shoulder. Even protected by a stout iron helm and *lorica segmentata* plate armour, a direct hit would instantly stun the wearer, if the impact didn't break bone or find the fatal, fleshy gap between helmet and armour. Before they recovered, the shocked legionaries found themselves the target of an unseen armoured battering ram that slammed into their unprotected left. The Boar's Head. Valerius had first seen it used in Boudicca's last battle when General Suetonius Paulinus had crushed an army of seventy thousand rebels to dust between his arrow-shaped wedges. Valerius had used it himself, to smash the Vitellian line, when Juva had taken the eagle of the Twenty-first Rapax.

A cohort wedge consisted of a 'point' of a single century, formed eight men wide and ten deep, followed by two further centuries, and finally three more, to complete the arrowhead. Valerius was at the very heart of the formation in the gap between the second and third centuries, with Serpentius, Atilius and the eagle's eight-man guard. He'd considered a mass charge into the enemy's unsuspecting flank that would have caused instant and widespread confusion, but that wasn't the legions' way. Instead, the Boar's Head lanced into the attacking enemy formations and broke the assault's momentum. He might be charging as many as five thousand men with fewer than five hundred. The greater cohesion of the men in the wedge would keep them in the fight for longer, rather than wasting them in bloody single combat. Despite the odds, Valerius could feel the battle joy growing inside, that insane confusion of invincibility and power, speed and strength. Yet at his very core was the same emptiness he'd felt as he'd approached the executioner. With the gods' aid they would survive, but only if Primus hurried to reinforce the Seventh Galbiana – and there was no guarantee he would.

The legionaries of the Eighth cohort had practised the manoeuvre a thousand times, and the six centuries drew swords and charged the moment they hurled their spears. Valerius, their precious eagle and his little pocket of men were carried with them. He felt the lurch as the shields of the first century smashed into the flank of the Seventh's attackers, the momentary hesitation and the cries of confusion and pain. Then the man-weight of the wedge carried it deep into a formation whose entire being was focused on its front. It pierced the unguarded flank like a knife blade entering a living body, plunging ever deeper. But it would not last. Inevitably, it must be slowed by the mass ahead until it was finally forced to a halt. Valerius didn't hesitate.

'Form square, three ranks,' he roared.

Never give an order you know won't be obeyed, boy. Wise counsel from the camp prefect of Valerius's first legion more than a decade earlier. So why was he giving an order he knew *couldn't* be obeyed, at least not to the letter? Because a battle is like a living thing, a pulsating beast whose power surges and wanes, ebbs and flows, where strength can change to weakness, or victory to defeat, in a moment. It was like being at the heart of a nightmare. A thunderous, whirling vortex that blinded your eyes and battered your senses with howls of mortal agony, screams of terror, shouts for aid and cries for an unlikely mercy, all to the accompaniment of metal hammering on wood, metal clashing with metal and the butcher's block thud of a bladed instrument meeting flesh. All around legionaries fought for their lives, snarling defiance as they wrestled shield to shield with the man in front of them. At the centre of the maelstrom, Valerius imagined the beast in his head, its jaws clamped on the cohort like a wolf tearing at a deer carcass. But the pressure from the wolf's jaws was not uniform. The beast's greatest weakness was in the hinge, at the point of the wedge, where the fewest enemy would be in contact. In contrast, the most dangerous threat came from the northern flank. Here, along the length of the wedge, the entire weight of the rear portion of the initial Vitellian attack would be attempting to claw their way forward. Instinct told him opportunity lay to the south, where the enemy centuries must be torn between carrying on the original attack and defending themselves against the shocking assault happening in their rear. This was where confusion would be greatest. By ordering square Valerius had gambled that he could force the southern jaw back, allowing the men of the three rear centuries of the wedge to take their places in the defensive formation that must stand – stand or die. Success depended on his officers' ability to envisage the situation as he saw it, but he had faith that something like it was possible. Not a square, by any means; a ragged misshapen perimeter, but one that might be held. But for how long?

Because already men were dying.

Not many. Not yet. They were hard to kill because they fought from behind their big shields and their helmets and armour protected all but the eyes and throat, or a carelessly exposed armpit. But they were outnumbered. In the darkness, every man was faced by two, three and more battle-crazed faces, and those attackers were just as well armed and just as capable. If a legionary of the Fifth was brave enough to throw down his sword and tear a shield aside with his hands, he would open the way for his comrades. So Valerius's men fell where they stood and their bodies lay to hinder the enemy. As the fighting raged around him, he attempted to judge where his precious reinforcements were needed most. Serpentius and Atilius stood at his side, the *aquilifer* bellowing encouragement to his tentmates, reminding them of their oath to the Emperor and to Jupiter Optimus Maximus. Pride swelled in Valerius's chest. He knew these men would stand to the last, eagle or no eagle. His legion . . . Realization scored the inside of his skull like a knife point. Fool that he was to lose concentration in the middle of a battle. He alone hadn't picked up a *scutum*. Before he had the chance to act on the thought something hammered into his chest and he was down, staring bewildered at the stars. Claw-like fingers took his wrist and hauled him to his feet. Serpentius shoved a shield at him and Valerius fixed it to the oak fist the Spaniard had personally carved. 'Spears.' The gladiator hefted his own *scutum* to protect Valerius's head. He nodded to the still twitching figure of one of Atilius's guards on the ground nearby, with the shaft of a *pilum* through his right eye. 'I wondered when they'd get round to it.'

No time to mourn. Valerius sensed a growing pressure on the centuries of the northern flank where they faced the full weight of the Vitellian attack. Should he reinforce it with every third man from the south? As his mind scrabbled for an answer a hoarse yell of triumph cut through the other sounds of battle like an executioner's axe. From the corner of his eye he saw men thrown aside as a group of the enemy smashed their way into the square.

'Hold your ranks and fill the gap,' Valerius roared. 'Serpentius.'

The Spaniard threw his shield aside and in four strides was on the

161

closest of the infiltrators. The man had been charged with guarding the backs of his comrades while they attacked the interior ranks of the already crumbling square. Serpentius ignored the darting *gladius* and in a single flowing movement slid into a forward roll that carried him beneath the enemy shield to bring his sword up into the other man's groin.

'Close the gap,' Valerius screamed. 'Close the gap.' By now a stream of men were pouring into the square and he launched himself at them, praying that the eagle's guards were still with him. One of the first attackers hesitated to find his bearings in the confusion. The momentary pause allowed Valerius to smash his shield into the legionary with all his weight behind it. Momentum forced the soldier back into the gap, but he recovered with incredible speed. Valerius reeled as the point of the infiltrator's *gladius* flicked out to slice the flesh beside his eye. Blinded by the searing pain, he tried desperately to defend himself as his opponent hacked at his shield. Blow after blow smashed the *scutum* from his wooden fist, and only the thick leather of the cow-hide stock saved him from more serious injury. For a fatal instant, the one-handed Roman was defenceless, and his exultant adversary raised his sword for the killer blow. Valerius had all but resigned himself to death when something swooped out of the darkness to smash the man backwards, spitting teeth and spewing gore. An anonymous legionary stepped from the rear rank of the first century and dispatched the fallen man with a *gladius* thrust before wordlessly returning to his position. Blood spurted like liquid obsidian in the darkness.

Still dazed, Valerius looked up to find himself the focus of a grinning shadow creature that turned out to be Atilius. The *aquilifer's* grin faded as he inspected his eagle, which had one wing bent back at an angle to the body from the impact on the enemy's jaw.

'Don't worry, Atilius,' Valerius assured the crestfallen soldier with a shaky smile. 'I won't take it out of your pay.'

They barely had time to draw breath before a new rush of intruders threatened to overwhelm them. The eagle's guard, now reduced to five, fought like demons to protect the sacred symbol, but for all their valour Valerius sensed they were weakening. Not in spirit, which was unvanquished, but in strength, their sword arms numbed by what seemed hours of fighting. As they fought, the numbers facing them grew with every passing second. The perimeter was long gone and he cursed himself for losing control of the cohort. No possibility of retreat now, if there ever had been. A great mass brawl surrounded him, with men screaming 'Tolosa' and 'Juva' to identify themselves to their comrades. Men fought not for victory, but to stay alive for a few more precious seconds. A lean silhouette appeared silently from his right and he turned to meet the new threat. Serpentius placed a hand on his sword arm. 'Save your strength, because you're going to need it.'

And he was right. Out of the darkness roared a new stream of enemies and the little group of men around the eagle was almost engulfed. Valerius fought with Serpentius at his right side, the Spaniard's sword spinning a deadly pattern that kept all but the bravest at bay. He heard a scream to his left, and in the gloom saw Atilius swinging the eagle like a giant axe. A man grabbed for the sacred emblem of the Seventh Galbiana, only for one of the surviving guards to cut his hand off at the wrist. Another ducked below the whirling staff and stabbed upwards, but Atilius stepped forward and kicked him in the face with an iron-shod sandal.

'Fight for your eagle,' Valerius roared. 'Remember your oath.'

Men heard the rallying cry and broke away from individual combats to hack at the men threatening the legion's cherished standard. The counter-attack won a few moments' respite – a lull in the almost endless ebb and flow of violence – but Valerius knew it couldn't last. The next concerted assault would overwhelm them. He stood there fighting for breath, barely able to raise his sword arm, his chest filled with fire.

Serpentius sensed his despair. 'Did you want to die in your bed?' he snarled.

Valerius shook his head wearily. 'What does it matter? We failed. I threw away these men's lives for nothing.'

The whites of the former gladiator's eyes shone like ivory in the darkness and trickles of blood – Valerius couldn't tell whose – turned

Serpentius's already savage features into a nightmare vision from Hades. 'They're legionaries,' he spat, wiping gore from his sword blade with the skirt of his tunic. 'Dying's all they're good for. Every man in the Eighth cohort knew it might end like this, but they followed you anyway, didn't they? Because they trusted you. And they were right. If you hadn't checked the bastards here, you'd have lost the whole legion.'

'Maybe. I—'

'Tolosa! Vespasian!' The cry from thousands of throats drowned out every other sound on the battlefield and was followed by an enormous clash of arms from the north. Valerius exchanged a startled glance at the Spaniard and Serpentius cocked his ear like a hunting dog.

'They're running. The bastards are running.'

'Tolosa! Vespasian!' The men around them took up the cry as their opponents faded away into the deeper darkness. To the north, the battle continued.

'Eighth cohort?' Valerius roared. 'Rally to the eagle. Atilius? Give voice. Let them hear you.'

'The *aquilifer* is down, tribune. That last attack . . .'

'Someone fetch a torch.' Valerius rushed to where he'd last seen the standard-bearer. With the click of metal on flint a light flared startlingly bright to illuminate a circle of ground scattered with bodies and parts of bodies. At its centre Atilius Verus knelt, head bowed, his torso supported by the sacred emblem he'd protected with his life, hands still clutching the pole with the battered eagle glittering defiantly above him. Valerius reached forward to touch his shoulder but the *aquilifer* toppled sideways, forcing him to grab for the falling standard. A dark pool on the ground showed where Atilius's lifeblood had poured out from a gaping wound in his groin.

Still holding the precious eagle, Valerius surveyed the ring of grief-warped, savage faces in the flickering shadows cast by the torch. They had all seen men die, but some losses leave a void that is impossible to fill. 'Atilius Verus died a soldier's death,' he reminded them. 'An honourable death and a good death. He defended his eagle to his last breath and fulfilled his oath to the end.' He paused to let them reflect on a towering comrade with a great heart. 'Who will replace him? Who will accept this sacred burden?'

After a heartbeat's hesitation one man stepped forward to a murmur of approval, one of the eagle's surviving bodyguards, blood-spattered and limping. 'I, Drusus Rufio, will take on this sacred task,' he declared, 'if my commander sees fit to honour me with it.' Valerius nodded, and with a desolate glance at his predecessor Rufio accepted the staff and lifted his eyes to the eagle.

In an age-old ritual that went back to Gaius Marius, founder of the legions, Rufio recited the sacred oath in a voice shaking with emotion. 'In the name of Jupiter Optimus Maximus I accept this eagle, this sacred symbol of my Emperor's faith, into my keeping and that of Legio VII Galbiana, and I pledge on behalf of my comrades that we will defend it to our last spear and our last breath or may the god strike us down. For Rome.'

'For Rome.' The survivors of the Eighth cohort echoed his words in a shout that could be heard in the capital.

Valerius closed his eyes as a wave of exhaustion and relief threatened to consume him. He had defended the Seventh Galbiana's eagle and kept it safe. But even as the thought formed the gods must have been laughing at him. Because from the darkness to the north came the sound of rushing feet and the unmistakable metallic clatter of armoured men approaching at the run.

XXII

The torchbearer dropped his brand and stamped on it, plunging them into darkness.

'Tolosa!' Valerius shouted the watchword and held his breath as he waited for the reply. His reeling mind tried to work out the hour, but he had no idea how long the fight had lasted. All he knew was that he was exhausted beyond caring. The surviving centurions silently ushered the men into line and they waited expectantly, their weary arms holding shields shoulder high and swords at the ready. The distant clamour of battle still rang clear, but the sound of men running in armour faded.

'Tolosa!' Valerius repeated the call, his body tensed for the storm of javelins that might accompany the reply.

'Who are you?' a querulous voice demanded from the gloom.

'The watchword is Tolosa.'

'I know that, but by now so does everybody on the battlefield. So answer the fucking question.'

Valerius hesitated.

'You have to the count of five,' the voice threatened.

'Gaius Valerius Verrens, acting legate, Seventh Galbiana.'

'*Merda.*'

Serpentius laughed as the whispered obscenity reached them. 'Your reputation goes before you, tribune.'

'Tolosa!' The cry began opposite Valerius and was taken up all along the line. A torch flared and a group of shadowy figures marched towards the survivors of the Eighth cohort. The one-handed Roman relaxed as he recognized the grizzled figure in the centre.

'My apologies, tribune.' Annius Cluvius Celer, prefect of the Ateste cohort of *evocati*, removed his helmet and wiped a sheen of sweat from his brow. The old soldier's face was as grey as his hair and his hand shook. 'Even the bravest are apt to become a little nervous when they don't know who they're fighting.'

'Nervous or not, my friend, you have never been more welcome,' Valerius assured him. 'I take it we have you to thank for the withdrawal of the Fifth.'

'The Fifth?' Celer's face mirrored his puzzlement. 'We've taken prisoners from Twenty-first Rapax and Fifteenth Primigenia, but none from the Fifth that I know of. But yes, we beat the buggers. That is, us and the Praetorians. We were in reserve behind the Thirteenth when we had word to reinforce your right flank. General Primus sent a wet-behind-the-ears tribune to take command and a scout who led us blundering about in the dark. Eventually we found some Thracian auxiliaries who pointed us in this direction and when we came across some fighting the tribune decided we might as well join in. Fortunately, it seems we attacked the enemy.'

Valerius suppressed a shiver at the realization that the survival of his legion had been decided by a blind throw of the dice. But that was past now.

'Can you put out a picket to allow us to regroup and care for our wounded? Our little battle may be over, but there's still plenty of fighting and I wouldn't like to be surprised by some cohort that's got lost and is looking for a fight.'

Celer nodded and issued an order to one of his officers. Valerius had already sent a runner to Claudius Ferox asking for a detailed report on the Seventh's status, but his instinct told him that they would be able to hold their own now that the pressure had been removed from their flank. He asked Celer for news of what was happening in the centre and on the left, and the old man responded with a cackle of bitter laughter.

'Only the gods and the owls have the answer to that question. Annius Cluvius Celer cannot see in the dark, and neither can Marcus Antonius Primus. I can give you my impressions, for all they are worth.' With a shrug he bent and stabbed his bloodied *gladius* into the earth to clean the blade. 'Two blindfolded bears meet in the forest. They roar. They push. They test each other's strength. They back away. Push again. Eventually they must decide whether to wrestle or to run. Only when they properly come to grips will they know who is stronger, and even then greater cunning or Fortuna's aid may still decide the outcome.' Celer's face split into a surprised smile, as if he'd only just realized that he'd survived. 'As I understand it, our strongest defences are on the right, with two legions to hold them. I know of no crisis before we received our orders, though what the position is now I cannot guess. Primus has confidence in the Thirteenth and they are defending the narrowest of fronts on the causeway itself. It would take Achilles and all his Heroes to shift them. They were faced by the Fifth Alaudae and I'd hazard the flank attack you faced was as much a probe to feel out their width as a genuine attempt to destroy you.'

Serpentius sniffed and spat. 'I can assure you it seemed genuine enough at the time,' Valerius said. 'You mentioned Praetorians?'

'The ragged fellows we picked up on the road,' Celer explained. 'Vitellius butchered their centurions and stripped the rest of their position and their rank. Three cohorts strong and they fight as hard as they hate, which is hard indeed. They charged off into the murk, but I thought it best to obey our original order and reinforce the Seventh.'

'You did right.' Valerius gripped the other man's arm and Celer winced. 'We're still hard pressed, and the Eighth cohort is out on its feet and has lost half its strength. Form your men up and we will re-join the legion.'

The militia veteran smiled wearily. 'It will—' A surging rush rent the air to the north, followed almost instantly by an enormous crash that seemed to shake the very ground they stood on. Then the screaming began, a different kind of screaming that made the normal battlefield sounds almost commonplace. The kind of screams men utter when they have been visited by some nameless, faceless horror.

'What in the name of Mars was that?' Celer found his tongue.

Valerius exchanged a glance of recognition with Serpentius. They'd heard that sound before and could imagine the results. The screams came from the ranks of the Thirteenth Gemina, the backbone of Primus's battle formation, packed three centuries wide and twenty deep on the narrow causeway and the ditches beside it. Celer had said that not even Achilles and all his Heroes could shift them.

But they weren't facing Achilles and all his Heroes. They were facing Cyclops.

The engineers of the Twenty-first Rapax called it Cyclops because it was huge and instead of only one eye it had a single arm. The Vitellian legions who force-marched from Hostilia to meet Marcus Antonius Primus's attack had left their artillery to make its own plodding way in their wake. But the Twenty-first had been at Cremona for months and their camp east of the city walls was defended by all that centuries of Roman ingenuity in the art of war could provide: palisades, ditches, stake-filled pits, towers – and artillery. Their 'shield-splitters' and *onagri* catapults had been manhandled from their positions and accompanied the bulk of the legions, but their value on the damp ground and in the dark was limited. Cyclops was different. A dozen oxen had taken three hours to haul the great siege catapult the four miles from Cremona. It had cost another two to peg and rope the structure into place so it wouldn't be hurled into the air by the earth-shaking power that kicked through the wooden frame during a launch. It had an arm as long as three tall men ranged top to toe, and could throw a boulder the weight of a small ox six or seven hundred paces. Valerius went through the calculations in his head. Even now the engineers would be straining at the levers to pull the arm and sling back into place, ready for the next release. Cyclops was designed to destroy walls and buildings; its effect on flesh and blood could be truly awesome. Corbulo had used

169

catapults against the massed ranks of the Parthian host at the battle of the Cepha gap and the giant missiles had broken the King of Kings' resolve. They were notoriously inaccurate, but that didn't matter against a target directly ahead and half a mile deep. From somewhere to their right front came the distinctive thump of the great oak beam hitting a barrier of straw-filled leather sacks. A rush of displaced air and the almighty crash as the boulder landed. Valerius winced at the thought of the giant rock, the size of a large cauldron, landing among the close-packed ranks of a century. Men utterly destroyed in an instant, their flesh pulped and their splintered bones turned to deadly shrapnel. The first bounce tearing through rank after rank, to be followed by a second and as many as three or four more. Each bound killing and maiming and spreading terror and despair. A single catapult could cost Marcus Antonius Primus his battle.

'We have to stop it.' Valerius knew he had no choice. He called for axes to be brought forward, but Serpentius laid a hand on his arm.

'Times have changed, Valerius.' The Spaniard kept his voice low. 'You have a legion to command. Your job is to lead, not to go crawling around in the dark getting yourself killed.'

Valerius would have shrugged him off, but it was like being gripped by an eagle's claw. Besides, he knew the former gladiator was right. Almost five thousand men depended on him for direction and leadership. The bulk were less than two hundred paces away, bewildered, hungry, exhausted and still fighting to stay alive in the darkness. They would hold their positions as long as they could wield a sword and keep their shields high. To desert them, even for so vital a mission, would be a betrayal.

He nodded reluctantly. 'How many men will you need?'

'Twenty should do it,' Serpentius said. 'Enough to take care of the engineers and the guards, form a perimeter and keep two or three of us alive long enough to disable the beast.'

'All right. The first century is as good as any for this kind of work. Choose your men from the survivors.'

'With respect, tribune.' The voice was Celer's. 'Your men have been fighting all night, and you said yourself that they're exhausted. We, on the other hand, are relatively fresh. Do me the honour of allowing me to lead the escort and choose them from amongst my men.'

Valerius hesitated. These were old men – no, not old, not quite, but worn by time and hard service. Yet every one was a veteran, with a life-time of campaigning behind him. And the Colonia militia had taught him not to underestimate the value of experience. They might strug-gle to march twenty miles in a day, but they were fighters. He walked along the line of soldiers. Their eyes glittered in the torchlight and not one flinched when he met their gaze. 'Very well, prefect. Choose your men. But Serpentius leads. This is the kind of work he was born for.'

A legionary appeared out of the dark and laid a bundle of long-handled iron-headed axes at Valerius's feet. Serpentius bent to pick one up, weighing it in his hands. 'Four should be about right.' He turned to Celer, and Valerius was surprised at the respect in his voice. 'You'll know your men best, sir.'

'Crispinus, Lucco, Julius.' Three broad-shouldered legionaries stepped forward as the prefect chose his axe men. He rattled out a list of names and sixteen others formed line beside them.

'You'll do,' Serpentius ran a challenging eye over the old soldiers. 'But if any of you don't fancy taking orders from a former slave and hired killer, now's the time to say so.' He waited, but not one of them spoke out and he grinned. 'Don't worry about making a noise, because we'll all be carrying these.' He picked up a fallen enemy shield. 'We'll be going in as fast as you're able. Leave me to do the talking if someone challenges us. If you get separated, the enemy watchword is Ajax and the reply Agamemnon. Watch the man in front, because when we get closer that'll be the time to become slow and silent. Prefect?' Celer nodded, flinching as a new rushing sound signalled the latest missile arcing towards the Thirteenth's ranks. 'Once we pinpoint the catapult you stop and regroup. I'll be up ahead checking the positions of the guard. We hit them once we know how many and where they stand. With luck they'll be so busy watching the show they won't notice us until we're cutting their throats.' They smiled at that, but Valerius saw little humour in it, and no wonder. These men would have to traverse the battlefield in the pitch dark, find the catapult, defeat its defenders and destroy it. The enemy weren't fools. They were as aware of the machine's importance as Primus. For all Serpentius's brave words this was a dangerous, possibly suicidal venture, with only a limited chance of success. But it had to be attempted. He felt the Spaniard studying him. 'No time like the present.' Serpentius nodded and hefted the shield. Twenty men followed his example. 'We should be back by first light.'

Valerius went to Cluvius Celer and took him by the arm. 'Don't take any chances, prefect. Trust this brute, do the job and get your men out. Succeed and you'll be worth another legion to Primus.'

Celer nodded and took his place beside the Spaniard. Together they led the nineteen men of the Ateste cohort of the *evocati* out into the darkness. Valerius watched them go before ordering the torch to be extinguished. When the light died he had a gut-twisting premonition that something else had died with it.

XXIII

In the starlit darkness, Serpentius set a steady pace over fields flattened by the march and counter-march of thousands of legionaries. This was when the Spaniard came truly alive, when he felt the blood surging through his veins and an almost god-like belief in his ability to move unseen and unheard through the landscape. Without the clumsy militia men he would already have been halfway to his destination, but he couldn't destroy the catapult on his own. He hissed a warning to Celer as he was about to plunge into a narrow drainage ditch and the prefect passed the alert on to the men behind. On the way, Serpentius picked up a fallen legionary's helmet. With the big shield it gave him a silhouette familiar to the men of either side. He kept his *spatha* sheathed and carried the long-handled axe comfortably in his right hand. Somewhere out there in the darkness lay the big catapult. He had no doubt he could lead these men to it. The question was which route to take.

The causeway of the Via Postumia was perhaps two hundred paces to the left and would provide the most direct passage. To reach it they would have to pass through the rear ranks of the legion whose swords the Spaniard could hear beating against the shields of the as yet unyielding Thirteenth Gemina. There was also the possibility of bumping into small groups of survivors from the attack against the

173

Seventh Galbiana's right flank. So far there'd been no sign of the Praetorians Celer had mentioned and Serpentius guessed they'd overcome the enthusiasm of the first flush of victory and prudently retired to the Flavian line. Visualizing this section of the battlefield he realized just how fortunate Marcus Antonius Primus had been. With a little more luck the Vitellian flank attack would have found the gap between the Thirteenth and the Seventh and carried on to rampage in his rear. It seemed clear that in the dark the attackers had no idea just how narrow a front the Thirteenth defended. When they struck the Seventh Galbiana they'd probably thought they were fighting Aquila's legion. It all proved how chaotic a battlefield was in the night.

Serpentius intended to take full opportunity of that chaos. The enemy commander's first probes would have convinced him Primus intended to defend the road in depth and he'd have to alter his tactics accordingly. The Spaniard recalled First Adiutrix's dispositions at Bedriacum. Four cohorts in the front line, followed by two banks of three cohorts: a formation three hundred and fifty paces deep. So a narrower front might mean a further hundred or hundred and fifty paces. Valerius had reckoned the catapult's maximum range at seven hundred paces, which put its likely position, at most, a third of a mile behind the enemy front line. Did that mean it could be sited among the three reserve cohorts in the rear? The possibility triggered a mental shrug. If it did he would just have to meet that obstacle when he reached it.

'Ajax.'

Serpentius felt his companions freeze at the authoritative voice from the darkness. 'Agamemnon,' he replied with equal arrogance. 'Headquarters section carrying our injured tribune back to the *medicus.*'

He heard a disapproving sniff. 'The legate won't be too happy with that. First win the battle then deal with the wounded, that was the order. Even officers.'

'Well this tribune is connected.' The Spaniard kept his head low. He could just make out the mounted shadows away to their left. He prayed it wasn't some officious legionary officer who'd turn them round. 'Very well connected, if you see what I mean. But we might be a bit off course?'

A long hesitation while the other man pondered his decision. Serpentius envisaged an unseen shrug of the shoulders. 'Not just a bit,' the voice resumed, 'but that's hardly surprising in this shithole. It's hard to know who you're supposed to be fighting. Keep going and you'll find the road. Follow it back and the Fifth's *medicus* has set up just beyond the big rock thrower.'

Serpentius muttered his thanks. 'Move, you bastards, or he'll be bled white by the time we get there.'

He led the militia men in a diagonal across the horsemen's front, then stopped for a moment to listen, moving only when he heard the thud of hooves fading into the distance. For a time they marched through a steady stream of wounded, walking, staggering or crawling back from the fighting line. Many were badly hacked about and one or two pleaded pitifully for aid or water, but Serpentius maintained the steady pace of a soldier with an important task on his hands. When they reached the road he abandoned his shield and axe and told the men to crouch down in the ditch where they wouldn't be seen. The road sat perhaps seven or eight feet above the ditch. 'If anybody challenges you, you're just back from the front line waiting for orders and the return of your tribune.' Without another word he was gone, leaving Celer and his men sitting nervously in the darkness.

Night was Serpentius's element and he crept along the muddy bottom of the ditch as silently as the reptile he was named for. Missile launches had punctuated the trek across the darkened fields, but had become so commonplace as to go almost unnoticed. Now, as the rocks passed directly overhead, he was reminded again of their terrifying power. At regular intervals he heard the sound of iron-soled boots crunching on the road above as reinforcements were fed into the slaughterhouse of the front line.

The former gladiator felt no compassion for these men who might be marching to their deaths. Rome had taken his family and his soul; all that was left was emptiness. Romans had cheered as he was forced to kill friends in the arena. They were a people without pity;

they deserved none. Let them kill each other as long as they had the strength. It must be twenty years since they'd burned his village and taken him for a slave in retaliation for the tribe's raids on Roman gold trains. His wife and baby son had burned together in their hut. The boy would have been full grown now, and on lonely nights the Spaniard tortured himself imagining the man he might have become.

The only Roman he could call friend was the one-handed soldier who saved him from certain death in the arena. Valerius had given him his freedom – he wore the little bronze manumission plaque in a leather bag at his throat – but he would not walk away until the debt was paid. A glow in the darkness brought him to a halt. Of course, they would need light to work the machine and to load it. The lamps must be masked in some way to ensure their glow couldn't be seen from much more than a hundred paces. He slithered closer, more careful even than before. When he could hear voices he climbed to the top of the bank and risked a glance, ducking back as the great catapult sent another missile through the air above his head.

The incredible power of the machine was evident in the way it leapt against its restraints like a living thing. He took advantage of the empty road to have another look. The catapult took up most of the roadway. Serpentius knew it would be pegged down with metal pins reaching deep into the ground. As he watched, the crew threw themselves at wheels and levers on either side of the machine. The throwing arm moved slowly backwards, drawn by two ropes almost four inches thick. He tried to identify other important elements of the huge weapon, but it seemed to him that the ropes and the levers were the most vulnerable. The Spaniard chewed his lip as his mind turned to the thickness of the ropes and the axes they'd brought. Twelve men working the machine that he could see: eight whose job it was to reset the beast's arm and then load the reinforced leather sling that held the missile, two to check and reseat the pegs after every launch, and two whose only task was to watch the proceedings. Four guards, one to each corner of the structure, but where there were four there would undoubtedly be more, probably resting in one of the tents he could see nearby.

A half-cohort of legionaries appeared behind the machine and one of the watching men directed them into the ditch on the far side of the road. Serpentius squirmed backwards to the mud-slick base, but he didn't return immediately to Celer and his men. Instead, he waited patiently, counting the seconds as he'd done with every passing unit. There seemed to be a set pattern that amounted to a count of about three hundred between each detachment. It would have to do.

'The odds are about even, but we have the advantage of surprise.' Cluvius Celer had been listening intently for the Spaniard's return and almost had a seizure when the voice whispered in his ear. He hadn't heard even the flutter of a moth until the man spoke. Serpentius had been away so long the militia commander had begun to despair and the cold had seeped into his bones, stiffening his limbs. Now, with the prospect of action, he felt instantly invigorated.

'Cover your shield fronts and your faces with mud.' The Spaniard picked up his axe. 'Now is the time to vanish, only to reappear like ravening wolves, but silent wolves, because everything depends on surprise.' The men gathered round in the darkness and he raised his voice slightly, deliberately downplaying the risks. 'The crew are intent on their duties; you will be on them before they know it. The guards and the two supervisors must be dealt with simultaneously. I will take the two on the far side of the road. Prefect, you and Crispinus must deal with the two on this side. Lucco, Julius? You have the watchers. Timing is everything. We strike the moment the machine is fired. While we are killing the guards the others will slaughter the workers. No pity and no mercy. A moment's hesitation and we are all dead, got that?' He sensed the nods in the darkness. 'When it's done, four men to destroy the machine's vital parts.' He explained about the ropes and levers. 'Twelve to form a perimeter and four at the tent to deal with any reaction. We do the job and then we disappear.'

A murmur of assent, but Celer's voice came from close to his ear. 'Two guards in the same second? How is that possible? At least allow me to . . .' His words trailed away as Serpentius turned and their eyes met from a distance of less than a handspan. Cluvius Celer would remember that look for the rest of his life.

The Spaniard led them to within a hundred paces of the lights. Celer touched his shoulder as he counted the seconds to the next formation. 'May Fortuna be with you,' he whispered. Normally Serpentius would have snorted his disdain at the possibility that he required luck to keep him alive, but something in Celer's voice stopped him and he nodded. I must be getting soft, he thought. When the unit was past and only a blur in the darkness, Serpentius sprinted across the road and slipped into the far ditch.

As he slithered towards the catapult, uncharacteristic doubts began to assail him. Could they do it? They seemed steady enough, but they were old and slow. In other circumstances he would have laughed. Old? Some of them might be younger than him. No, Romans they might be, but they had proved their worth and he had to trust them. Just as he must trust that the workmen and guards were arranged exactly as he'd left them and that the units marched that vital count of three hundred apart. Fifty to allow the formation to pass out of sight. Twenty of silent killing. A hundred and eighty to do what they'd come to do. That gave them fifty to escape into the darkness before the next formation arrived. A strong man with an axe and an appetite for destruction could do a great deal of damage in a count of two hundred. Serpentius banked on the sound of the axes being similar to the sound of the pegs being hammered into place. He'd leave the oil lamps lit, because to extinguish them might alert someone to a change of circumstances. Just outside the circle of light thrown by the lamps he left the ditch for the empty field to his right. And waited.

By now his mind automatically recorded the passing of the units and the interval between. When he had reached two hundred and eighty a new group appeared to be ushered into the ditch. He watched the men clamber down, bypass the big catapult and then climb back to the road, grumbling as they went. When they were gone he slipped back into the mud and crept along until he reached the shadows below the closer of the two guards. He laid the axe aside. Would the others be in position yet? The huge boulder must be in its sling by now. He heard the arm whip forward with an enormous *whuuuppp* of released energy and the machine bucked as the oak beam slammed into the straw-filled sacks. Curiously, so close to the weapon there was no characteristic rush of disturbed air. But he had no time to think about that.

A suspicion of movement in the ditch alerted the furthermost of the guards to potential danger. His racing mind registered a whirling circle of light, but before his brain could turn instinct into reaction the little Scythian axe Serpentius had thrown was already embedded in his throat. As the nearer guard turned at the soft *thunk* of the axe striking its target, Serpentius whipped the feet from under him. Too surprised even to call out, the guard died silently as the Spaniard's knife sliced through his windpipe and the big arteries on either side. Serpentius ignored the blood on his clothing and hands, picked up the axe and scrambled up the bank. He was conscious of a disturbance on the far side of the road. With satisfaction he heard the sound of bodies falling and the little grunts and mews of agony that were the noise of a man being killed quietly by an expert. No time for congratulation. Some instinct told him they were already a count of twenty behind schedule. In the lamplight he saw Celer ushering his men into a defensive perimeter and four making their way silently towards the tents.

'Forget the levers,' he hissed to the three men climbing on to the machine. 'Two men to a rope. Crispinus? With me. Lucco and Julius, you take the other.' The throwing arm was still in position against the padded buffer from the last shot. Two ropes of plaited leather ran taut to a wooden roller between a pair of ingenious wheels that somehow contrived to haul the arm back and hold it in place until its own tension could be released. Serpentius stood over the point where rope met roller and brought his axe down in a measured arc, allowing the power to flow through the handle to the honed edge. '*Merda!*' He heard Lucco's curse even as his own axe bounced off the plaited leather, barely marking it. Crispinus looked at him in consternation. 'Chop, you bastard,' he snarled. 'Did you think it was going to be easy?'

They swung like demons, cursing and muttering, but no amount of curses would more than fray the edges of the rope. A few feet away Lucco and Julius were making even less progress. Serpentius looked

179

round desperately for an easier target. 'Smash the levers and wheels,' he hissed. 'Anything that looks important.' A soft breeze tickled the bristle on his cheek and a flicker caught his eye. Fool, he thought. Valerius would have seen it at once. He threw the axe aside and ran to a pole holding one of the eight or nine oil lamps illuminating the machine. Without thinking he reached up, cursing as his fingers touched the ceramic lamp and the tips were instantly turned into balls of agony by the heat.

'Here.' Celer held out a bloodstained cloak torn from one of the bodies scattered around the machine. Serpentius wrapped his hands in the thick woollen cloth and unhooked the lamp from the pole. He dashed back to the catapult and poured half the burning oil over the wooden roller and leather rope then smashed the pot into the pit below so the flames leapt up and singed his eyebrows. Crispinus stepped back with a cry of fear, but quickly overcame it to resume his attack on the rope. Serpentius recovered his axe and joined him, only to pause as Celer appeared at his side, another smoking lamp in his hand. 'Wait,' the Spaniard said. 'Better to spread the damage.'

Bewilderment replaced the wild look in the militia prefect's eyes.

'The arm.' Serpentius pointed to a reinforced block in the centre of the catapult. 'The base of the throwing arm is where the greatest stress must be. Weaken that and the generals can whistle for their rocks. Use splinters from the damaged parts to kindle the fire. Quickly now. We don't have much time.'

His words were prophetic. At last the sound of axe on wood brought the bleary-eyed remnant of the guard charging half-dressed from their tent, only to be cut down by Celer's militia veterans. One, barely a boy but agile as a cat, evaded the searching blades and darted back into the tent. A heartbeat later Serpentius cringed at the strident cry of a *cornu*.

'Will somebody kill that bastard,' the Spaniard raged.

Two of Celer's militia charged inside the leather tent and the trumpet call was cut off in mid-note, but already cries of alarm echoed through the night. Celer called a warning as men began to stream out of the darkness towards the catapult.

'Hold them,' Serpentius shouted. 'We have to let the fire weaken the throwing arm.' Someone had thrown another lamp at the base of the oak beam. Flames licked up the roughly planed surface, but the Spaniard knew the damage would still only be superficial. Celer had to buy them time, and the tortured shriek of a man dying with a sword in his belly told him the prefect knew his duty. He concentrated on the blackened surface of the leather rope, alternating blows with bull-shouldered Crispinus and ignoring the flames that licked at his face and arms. They were making an impression now. More than an impression. The leather strands began to fray and come apart. With one final blow the rope snapped, the end whipping up to smash into Serpentius's face and knock him off his feet. Spitting blood he clawed himself upright and turned towards the second rope, but one glance told him they didn't have time. By now the perimeter was hard pressed, with shadowy figures struggling in the flickering light of the flames. He saw that two of Celer's men were already down. The time for thought was past.

Roaring the ancient war cry of his tribe the former gladiator leapt from the catapult, whirling the axe. A man sprinted towards him with a bucket in his hand and no regard for his own safety. Serpentius repaid his bravery by sinking the axe head in his belly. As his victim shuddered with the awful effects of the blow the Spaniard hauled at the weapon and cursed as he realized it was beyond recovery. Danger was everywhere. Someone ran past screaming but Serpentius never discovered whether he was friend or foe. The respite gave him time to draw his long sword and he turned to face the next attack. It was a heavy weapon, designed for mounted troops, with a lethal double edge that cavalrymen used to bludgeon their enemies into oblivion. On foot, few men had the skill to use it effectively. Serpentius was one. The former gladiator who had survived a hundred fights. Master of his trade, and a born killer.

As he fought, he screamed his defiance and contempt for the cowards who faced him. But another part of his mind knew time was running out. So far the opposition had been piecemeal, disorganized; a few men at a time rushing out of the darkness. Suddenly, above the cries of the maimed and the dying, came the familiar sound of iron-shod feet, and they were coming at the run.

A hand touched his shoulder and he dispatched another man and turned with a snarl.

'You must get him away,' Crispinus shouted. 'The prefect. You must get him away.'

Serpentius looked from the hunched figure of Clovius Celer to the darkened road where perhaps three or four hundred men were advancing at the trot.

'We will buy you time,' the militia man assured him. The mud- and soot-stained face shone with pride. 'Your job is done. Save the prefect.' Beyond Crispinus, Lucca nodded, and Serpentius saw the resolve mirrored in the eyes of the dozen survivors of Celer's band of veterans. Emotion was unfamiliar to Serpentius of Avala, unless that emotion was hatred, but for a moment he found his vision clouded.

'I will take him, but hear me: you will be remembered. Wherever soldiers gather they will talk of the deeds of the Ateste cohort of the *evocati*.' With a last nod he shouldered Celer to his feet and half carried, half dragged him away into the relative sanctuary of the darkness.

When he was a hundred paces from the road, he lowered the prefect to the ground and felt the man's body shudder as waves of pain racked him. With practised fingers Serpentius checked for the rent in the chain armour. He grimaced at what he found. A stomach wound, and the familiar stink told him the bowels had been torn. A death wound. He reached for the knife at his belt. Better to . . .

'You must leave me,' Celer groaned. 'No point in us both dying. Leave me and get back to Valerius where you belong.'

The Spaniard slipped the knife back into its leather sheath. 'I said I'd stay with you.'

'Pah.' It was almost a laugh. 'What good . . .'

Serpentius placed a hand over the old man's mouth. On the causeway the last of Clovius Celer's men were dead or dying. The Vitellians would be spreading out from the road looking for anyone who had escaped the massacre. He could hear the sound of men shouting encouragement to each other in the darkness.

Celer stifled a cry as Serpentius heaved him on to his back and stumbled further away from the road. After a moment, the Spaniard paused, and coming to a decision turned west, deeper into enemy territory. When he judged they were safe, he sat with the militia commander and listened to his spirit fade. At first Celer was lucid, talking of his farm on the plain outside Ateste, the son he'd raised and the rich dark earth and vines that grew as if at his command. But gradually his mind returned him to the rocky highlands of Armenia and the days when he had followed a general he had revered as a god.

'He should have been Emperor, you know.'

Serpentius blinked, because for the first time in an hour the voice sounded rational, but they were the last words Clovius Celer uttered. As the first faint pink glow that heralded dawn appeared in the eastern sky Serpentius sensed he was alone. He sat for a while considering his options, most of which seemed to end up lying in a cold grave. Eventually, he nodded to himself. One chance. Another hour and he would be trapped in the midst of his enemies in broad daylight. He cut a diagonal that would take him beyond any searchers and followed the causeway west until he saw lights and his nose told him he was close. Keeping to the darkness he reached his goal at last. When he was certain he was alone, he stripped off armour, sword belt and tunic . . .

XXIV

Valerius only understood he'd survived the longest night of his life when there was enough light to make out the features of the man next to him. Claudius Ferox seemed to have aged ten years. The tribune's aristocratic features were the colour of whey and the texture of parchment, and the deep lines on his cheeks hadn't existed when the sun went down. From beneath the rim of his helmet, sunken, red-rimmed eyes studied the plain where the enemy waited. Valerius knew he looked no better. He'd never been so exhausted. Did he last sleep thirty-six hours ago, or was it forty-eight? His stomach screamed for food, but he'd shared the last of his bread with a *contubernalis* from the second cohort hours earlier. He slipped the water skin from the pommel of his leather saddle and handed it to the younger man. Ferox took it eagerly, drawing the tepid liquid through his salt-caked lips until he realized how little remained.

'My apologies, legate.' The words emerged almost as a sob as he handed the skin back. Valerius patted him on the shoulder and drank what remained, the barely discernible moisture as welcome as any nectar. He closed his eyes. By the gods, he'd never felt so old. Old enough to be Claudius Ferox's father.

During that long night the men of Seventh Galbiana had fought their Vitellian opponents to a standstill. They'd stood shoulder to shoulder behind their big shields, rotating in and out of the front rank only when their blood stained the earth or their sword arms tired. Some men stood shield to shield with the enemy seven or eight times in that front line. Many would never leave it, lying in everlasting embrace with the men who died under their swords. While they fought, Valerius walked the lines, handing out food and water and giving quiet encouragement, accompanied by Drusus Rufio and the eagle standard. They repulsed attack after attack and always the enemy kept coming. Yet in the sixth hour of the night, shortly after the catapult missiles stopped falling on the Thirteenth's positions, Valerius had sensed a weakening of resolve. They still fought. Still howled their hatred and their scorn, but the men of the Fifteenth Primigenia no longer believed they would prevail. When he realized it, he deliberately weakened his centre and placed his strongest cohorts on the flanks. When next they came the centre cohorts fell back, drawing the enemy on, then halted them with a devastating javelin shower. In the same instant he launched the flank attacks that would have destroyed the entire legion had they not retreated for the last time. None fought better than the First cohort. Yet, as he'd walked the lines in the darkness, his mind on the far side of the field where a few brave men were fighting and dying to save Primus's campaign, Valerius would swear he heard a soft voice. *One thrust and it would be over, my proud peacock. One thrust and the Seventh legion would be under the command of a proper soldier.* At the time he wondered if he had imagined it, but now Brocchus's face swam into his mind and the sneer on his lips said it was true. Why hadn't he struck? With Serpentius gone, there would never be a better opportunity. But too many men were aware of the enmity between the legion's *primus pilus* and his commander. His absence would have been noticed and questions asked. Brocchus might have survived or he might not. Those odds weren't good enough for a man like him.

Valerius remembered the flames consuming the enemy's catapult and exulting in Serpentius's success. But, as the hours passed, the certainty grew that it had been bought at a terrible price. One part of him said he should have ignored the Spaniard's words and gone

185

himself, though he knew that would only have meant sacrificing the one for the other. Perhaps he should have let the Thirteenth deal with their own problems. Could he have sent Celer and his men without the gladiator? He knew he would have been sacrificing them for no purpose. Of course, with a man like Serpentius there was always hope, but . . . He shivered and wrapped his cloak tighter about him. At Colonia he'd lost his right hand, but in the grey, doom-filled light of this blood-soaked dawn it felt as if he had been robbed of something much more important.

A little later he noticed movement on the right where the three Praetorian cohorts had filled the gap left by the Thirteenth's auxiliaries. Marcus Antonius Primus, in gleaming armour and sitting tall on a black stallion, rode into their ranks with an escort of twenty cavalry. The guards formed square and fleetingly Valerius heard the sound of shouted words on the wind, followed by a muted cheer.

'Take one man in every three out of the line and have them prepare to receive the commander,' he ordered Ferox. 'And make sure they know to enjoy his speech.'

'Perhaps if it was accompanied by some breakfast.' The tribune smiled wearily.

'And keep them on the alert, Claudius. It would be embarrassing if the general was killed during a visit to the Seventh Galbiana. History would never forgive us.'

By the time Primus approached, the legionaries had already formed a three-sided square to receive him. Valerius advanced to greet the general, who returned his salute with a tired smile. The one-handed Roman remarked inwardly how like Otho the man was; difficult to really know, but hard not to like.

'Your men did well last night,' Primus said quietly. 'They – and you – have my thanks.'

Valerius bowed in the saddle. 'They all did.'

The general nodded thoughtfully. 'Though it was a close-run thing. Whether by accident or design, whoever destroyed the machine that was flaying the Thirteenth tipped the scales in our favour.' He saw the mixture of pride and sadness on Valerius's face. 'Your people?'

'Annius Cluvius Celer, prefect commanding the Ateste cohort of *evocati*,' the general's eyebrows went up as Valerius drew a wax block from his tunic, 'and nineteen of his men. Serpentius was with them.'

'The Spaniard?'

Valerius nodded.

'Then their deeds shall be known and Vespasian will hear of your part in it.'

As the sun rose above the eastern horizon to capture the ranks of the Seventh in a halo of misty gold an enormous roar erupted from the far end of the Flavian line. Immediately cries of 'Mucianus!' went up, accompanied by shouts for silence and the rattle of the centurions' vine sticks against helmet and armour.

Primus smiled. 'The sun worshippers of Third Gallica,' he said, referring to the legion that held the right of his line, 'who some would say spent too long in the East, but it won't do any harm to let our men think Mucianus is close.' He kicked his mount forward into the centre of the square. 'You did well last night, my fiery Spaniards,' he told them. 'You held the line, and but for the foot-racing prowess of your opponents you might well have added Victrix to your legion's title.' The flattery brought a cheer, as he intended it to. 'You are tired,' he continued, 'as we all are, and hungry, but the enemy is more so. I have one more task for you. Drive them back and take Cremona. Drive them back and win the throne for Titus Flavius Vespasian. Did I hear that my friend General Mucianus and his African legions are close? Are we going to allow these latecomers to take all the glory and the loot?'

'No!' the shout went up.

'Of course not. When your rations come up you will eat your fill and then you will drive the enemy from this field, drive them back on Cremona, where you will destroy them. This is where the war will be won, and the Seventh Galbiana will win it. Destroy them here and all the riches of Cremona will be yours.'

They cheered the general from the field and Valerius escorted him halfway to the Seventh Claudia.

'You really think they are beaten?'

'Oh, yes.' Primus nodded emphatically. 'They've pulled back to draw breath, but we won't allow them that freedom. They are leaderless. They attacked piecemeal and in poor order when their commander should have concentrated against a single part of the line. If he had done that it might have been this army on the retreat. We will march in battle order and the Thirteenth will be our battering ram. Straight up the road, Valerius. Four miles to Cremona. Four miles to wipe away the stain of the defeat at Bedriacum. Four miles to victory.'

Valerius watched him go and marvelled at the man's self-assurance. The legions he commanded had marched sixty miles in two days and gone forty-eight hours without sleep. Now he expected more of them? Well, only time would tell. They were still outnumbered, and though Primus's light artillery had finally caught up with them, the heavy siege artillery needed to take Cremona was still somewhere down the road. But he must put all that to the back of his mind. The Seventh Galbiana and Gaius Valerius Verrens had another battle to fight.

And this time he would have to do it without Serpentius.

Not many battles go exactly to plan, but the final stage of the battle of the Cremona road happened exactly as Primus predicted. Thirteenth Gemina pushed the Vitellian centre before it, causing the enemy legions to north and south to retire in step to preserve their defensive line. In all, Primus's five worn-out legions faced six full legions and substantial elements of at least four others, but, for the moment at least, it appeared the enemy commanders had lost heart, and their soldiers their taste for a civil war which had its own unique definitions of tragedy.

Valerius advanced his men across a field scattered with the bodies of dead and dying men from the previous night. As they went, the legionaries stooped to strip the dead of what spoils they could. He saw one young man suddenly fall to his knees beside a corpse and heard a wail that voiced more anguish than any sound he'd heard during that terrible night. A centurion immediately began screaming at the legionary and beating him with his stick. 'Find out what's happening,' Valerius ordered an aide.

He came back within a few moments. 'Tiberius Mansuetas of the second century Third cohort.' The young man hesitated. 'The dead legionary is his father. He was with Twenty-first Rapax.'

For a moment Valerius felt as if all the horrors of all his battles were bearing down on him in a tidal wave of darkness. Bile welled up in his throat and he had to spit the foulness out. The philosophers spoke of civil war being brother against brother and father against son, but how many had experienced its indescribable reality? 'Tell his centurion the boy is to fall out and do his duty to his father. He will re-join us when he is done.'

Before the soldier had returned, Primus's advancing legions cornered the retreating Fifteenth against its own baggage train as soldiers and camp followers fought for a place on the road to Cremona. Two casts of the javelin turned the retreat into a rout. Valerius saw that all along the line the Vitellian soldiers were making their way back to the sanctuary of the city by any means they could, utterly leaderless and all discipline gone.

Vipstanus Messalla, commander of Galbiana's sister legion the Seventh Claudia, rode over from his position on the left. He greeted Valerius without ceremony. 'It's like herding sheep,' he said. 'Primus should order a general advance and we'd slaughter them before they got anywhere near the city. Once they're in their camp it'll be a different story.'

'He wants to maintain the line,' Valerius pointed out, 'so they don't have the opportunity to counter-attack. Maybe this is the end?'

'No.' The veteran tribune shook his head, his face grim. 'They'll fight, and it'll be all the bloodier when they're behind walls and we're not.'

Not far away the Thirteenth's advance guard toppled the charred remains of the great catapult into the ditch to allow free passage for the centuries that followed. The blackened skeleton lay on its side, partially intact, and the two men went to inspect the burned timbers.

'This could have been the difference,' Messalla said. 'You did well to burn it.'

'I hope so.' Valerius attempted to disguise the break in his voice. 'It was an expensive victory.'

Patches of drying blood stained the gravel where the catapult had been pegged. Valerius looked for the bodies of the men who had defended the machine or those who sacrificed so much to destroy it, but could see no sign. Messalla made his farewells and rode off towards his legion. Left alone with his personal guard, Valerius allowed his mount to make its own way through the scattered debris and wrecked tents of a Vitellian camp beside the road. The horse shied nervously as they approached a cloth pavilion that had been left more or less untouched. It was only when Valerius dismounted and looked inside that he understood why. A hospital tent, a temporary *valetudinarium*, and the *medici* who served it had either fled or been slaughtered as they worked, along with the wounded in their care. His nose wrinkled at the scent of freshly shed blood in the confined space. Some morbid fascination took him to inspect the rear of the tent and he felt a stab of pain in the stump of his right arm when he recognized the pile of amputated limbs. Beyond the severed arms and legs a large hole had been dug in the damp earth, perhaps fifteen paces across. Valerius warily approached it, knowing what he would find, but steeling himself to look anyway. The death pit.

The butchered lay where they'd been thrown, stripped of all clothing, possessions and dignity, piled haphazardly this way and that, their faces in repose or in the rictus of agony, depending on the method of their passing. These were the men who had been wounded on the field and were felt capable of recovery. Once they'd reached the *medicus* they'd either died in any case, or succumbed under his instruments. Valerius was used to death, had seen it in many forms and more often than he liked. However, this casual discarding of what a few hours earlier had been living, breathing human beings always disturbed him. His heart fluttered as he searched for a familiar face among the top layers – and froze. The man might have been sleeping, but for the fact that his eyes were half shut and would never see again. His only consolation was that despite the awfulness of the wound in his abdomen, it appeared the suffering of Annius Cluvius Celer had been over long before he died. Valerius sent up a prayer to Jupiter for Celer's onward passage to the Otherworld and vowed to make a sacrifice in his memory, and that of . . . He turned away, sickened. He'd had his fill of death.

He'd walked five paces when at the very edge of his consciousness he registered a conversation between his guards. 'Look, it's moving.' The words were Milo's, reliable and never jumpy, but now patently shaken by what he saw.

'Maggots,' came the dismissive reply from Julius, the decurion. 'You always get maggots in a pit, stands to reason. All those flies.'

'No,' Milo insisted. 'It's moving. Fuck . . .'

Valerius only reacted when he heard the whispered song of a sword clearing its scabbard. He spun, reaching for the *gladius* on his right hip. And froze. The sight that confronted him sent a spear point of superstitious dread down his spine and he almost cried out. A bloodied arm reached up from between a pair of corpses. A scarlet dome of a head broke from the surface of the pit, as if Hades was giving birth to some single-headed spawn of Cerberus. For a moment, the head stayed motionless as if considering its new surroundings, then it shook and growled like a dog, snorted to catch its first breath and let out an enormous roar that transformed the dog into a lion.

Julius stood by the edge of the pit, his face white as parchment and his sword raised. Milo had a *pilum* in his big fist ready to throw.

'No!' Valerius cannoned into the legionary just as the javelin left his hand, flying wide to impale a body less than a foot from its target, who had somehow managed to force himself waist high in the sea of bodies. The would-be corpse's eyes bulged like duck eggs in the gore-stained mask of his face and his body shook with fury. 'If that fornicating spear had found its mark, Roman, my shade would have haunted your dreams for all eternity and a bit fucking longer. As it is, I will be your living nightmare unless you help me out of this offal.'

The threat was directed at Milo and the man in the pit blinked as he noticed Valerius for the first time. Bizarrely, he raised his free hand to his chest in salute. 'Serpentius of Avala, headquarters section of the Seventh, reporting for duty, tribune.'

Valerius wondered that he didn't die of shock. 'Don't just stand there gaping like idiots, get something to pull him out.' He ran to the edge of the pit, grinning like a moonstruck schoolboy, his heart soaring at the sight of the bloodied figure. He shook his head. 'What kind of fool spends the night in a mass grave?'

Serpentius struggled to suppress a grin of his own. 'The kind of fool who volunteers for a suicide mission and gets his skinny Spanish arse trapped behind enemy lines with the promise of a spear up it if he's caught.' He snorted and spat a gob of something red. 'When I first went in I was only under one body, but they kept putting more of the bastards on top and I could barely move. I thought I might not get out before they got round to filling the pit in.'

Valerius shuddered at the image. But he had to ask. 'What was it like?'

'Cold,' the Spaniard admitted. 'But sometimes the company of the dead is preferable to the company of the living.'

XXV

They caught up with the leading elements of the Seventh Galbiana three miles from Cremona. The terrain became more accommodating the closer they came to the city, and the men of the Seventh marched over firm ground to avoid the chaos on the road. Wreckage from enemy baggage trains, abandoned weapons and the discarded belongings of camp followers obstructed the causeway. Valerius noticed a new spirit of confidence in his legionaries. Already exhilarated by the fumes of what had seemed an unlikely victory, the sight of their foes' retreating backs gave new energy to weary legs. They knew they'd achieved something remarkable and they sensed that one last effort would bring them ultimate victory and never to be forgotten glory. They were eager to finish the job.

Marcus Antonius Primus halted his army just short of the city. In the commander's headquarters tent Valerius struggled to keep his eyes open as the other legates gathered. For him, battle had always been a place where danger and proximity to death seemed to multiply the living essence. Sometimes when he fought, Valerius swore he could have called Mars kin, but he had a feeling this battle had taken a toll like no other; a diminishing of self as if an inner fire was dying. Primus was as tired as any of his soldiers, the very flesh seeming to hang wearily from the bones of his face. Yet despite days in the saddle, the general's eyes radiated a messianic zeal that no amount of exhaustion could extinguish.

'Our scouts report the enemy has strengthened his defences immeasurably in the past few weeks.' Primus addressed the legates of his five legions around a hastily fashioned sand table modelled to produce a crude likeness of Cremona and its surroundings. 'They have expanded the ring of camps around the city, added lines of palisades and ditches here, here and here,' he leaned across and pointed to a series of scores to the east of the city, 'and filled them with the usual horrors. Sixteen towers dominate the most vulnerable stretches, armed alternately with *scorpiones* and *onagri*, and sited to provide crossing fire. We will undoubtedly face heavy catapults of the kind the Seventh' – Valerius acknowledged his bow – 'dealt with so efficiently, but they will be more difficult to reach.' For a moment the general's voice faltered and he looked to each of the men in the tent as if trying to draw strength from them. Eventually, he shook his head and found the will to continue. 'Altogether a formidable obstacle, gentlemen. True, these entrenchments will be filled by legions who have been thinned by our efforts, but they will fight, and it is clear we must oblige them. The question is how?'

'My men are exhausted.' Every eye turned to Numisius Lupus, commander of Eighth Augusta. 'I do not say that they cannot fight,' he explained hastily. 'They see their enemy and itch to be at him so I must struggle to control their enthusiasm.' His words were greeted with a murmur of accord from commanders who had experienced the same eagerness. 'My doubt is whether they have the strength, or the will, to entrench a camp of our own, and create suitable defences against an enemy capable of sortieing from Cremona to destroy us while we dig.'

'You think we should besiege the city?' Primus asked quietly.

Lupus's eyes showed consternation. 'Do we have any other choice?'

'Certainly we have choices,' Vedius Aquila interjected impatiently, 'unpalatable though they be. We could withdraw to Bedriacum and recover our strength while we await reinforcements from Syria.'

'And throw away everything we have won?' Primus's tone was mild enough, but the Thirteenth's legate bridled defensively at the implication of defeatism.

'I am speaking hypothetically, of course,' he growled. 'A mere listing of the options. But what is the alternative to siege or withdrawal? It would be folly to attack Cremona with exhausted troops. We would need every man to assault these walls, with not even a few thousand ragged Praetorians in reserve.'

'Folly perhaps,' Primus conceded. 'But I believe it is our *only* option.'

The tent went very still, and Valerius was reminded of the depthless silence of an African night.

Primus turned to him. 'You think me impulsive, Gaius Valerius Verrens? No,' he raised a hand, 'do not deny it.' A smile flickered on his thin lips. 'It is true that my impetuousness has brought us here, to the brink of victory or defeat, depending on your point of view. But my belief is based not on *my* desire to close with the enemy, but on the facts as I see them.' He frowned and bowed his head as if he were considering those facts; lining them up, then repositioning them like a carpenter contemplating the best way to approach a complex piece of work. Eventually, he had them where he wanted them and he looked up to meet his subordinates' doubting eyes. 'Time is running short, but I will outline my reasoning. We cannot starve the defenders without starving ourselves. Our foraging parties range far and wide between the mountains and the sea and still return empty-handed, because our enemy has prudently stripped the countryside to provision the city. To eat, we must first fight. You say your soldiers are exhausted, Numisius? I agree. They are approaching the very limits of their endurance. Yet their howls for the blood of the Vitellians remain undiminished. My question is not can we fight but can we afford *not* to fight? It is they – our soldiers – even more than I, who have driven us here. It is you, the legates of my legions, who have lost control of them. If I ordered these men to return to Bedriacum they would like as not cry "traitor" and kill me, and you too, Aquila.' He shook his head. 'It would be folly to attack at these odds? No, it would be folly to waste their precious energy digging ditches. They have one last fight in them. We must make the best use of it. My message to your soldiers is this: you are hungry? Cremona is our granary. Take Cremona and you will eat your fill – aye, and a surfeit of loot and women too. You are sick of civil war? Then finish it. Here and now. One cast of the dice. One final effort. For Rome and Vespasian.'

'For Rome and Vespasian!' The four legates echoed his words and Valerius was astonished at the change Primus had wrought since they entered the tent. Then, they had looked like defeated men despite their recent victory, cowed by the odds facing them and the seemingly insurmountable logistical problems that plagued their legions. Yet in one brief piece of genius their commander had negated their concerns. The facts remained unchanged, but the situation was entirely different. He had shown them that only a single course of action was open to them. The decision was no longer theirs. The men wanted to be at their enemy and nothing would change their minds. If they wanted to fight they must be given their wish.

'Your orders, general?'

Primus smiled grimly. 'We will pause only long enough to allow the artillery to come up, and to furnish the engineers with sufficient siege equipment to make the assault practicable. Aquila? Your eager Thirteenth are furthest forward as always. When you are ready, array them before the Brixia gate and tempt them with what lies within. Fulvus and Verrens? Third Gallica and Seventh Galbiana will concentrate on the eastern defences to the south of the causeway. Eighth Augusta and Seventh Claudia will invest the walls on the northern side. Varus?' He called his cavalry commander forward. 'Take ten squadrons and five cohorts of *auxilia* and come at them from the west. It is a feint, no more, but you must *appear* dangerous enough to keep their attention. Do you understand?' Varus nodded, the knowledge that he still had much to prove written plain on his face.

The commanders filed out, but Valerius held back. Primus looked up from the sand table. 'You still have concerns, Verrens?'

Valerius hesitated. 'You outlined the situation admirably, general. Win, or die trying. What could be clearer? The kind of simple command a soldier likes.' Primus's eyes took on a dangerous look: was he being mocked? But Valerius ignored the threat. 'My concern is with

Cremona. It was my impression that the Emperor's express wish was that no harm should come to the populace unless they took up arms directly against him.' He pointed to the table. 'It appears the defence of Cremona is entirely in the hands of Vitellian legions who gave the people of the city no chance to flee.'

'And I am encouraging my soldiers to treat them as enemies?'

'It is . . .'

The colour rose in Primus's cheeks. 'You are wearing your lawyer's cloak again, or perhaps your friend Titus is using you as a mouthpiece. Is that it? I could dismiss your concerns with a single lawyerly word: semantics. The people of Cremona supported Aulus Vitellius from the first. They fed, armed and aided his soldiers. Have they taken up arms *directly* against the forces of Titus Flavius Vespasian? I do not know. But I also do not know they have not.' He sighed, and his voice lost its certainty. 'But that is not the issue here. Not even the fate of thousands of . . .' a shrug of what, impatience? Regret? 'Very well, let us call them innocents. The issue is victory and saving perhaps hundreds of thousands of lives by ending this war *now*. My legions are tired, Valerius. Yes, they have one last fight in them. If I thought they did not I would not attempt this whether their blood was up or no. But strength and will can only take them so far. They need something more tangible than a cause to fight for. Something real. The storehouses of Cremona and the hunger in their bellies are real. The answer to everything lies beyond those ramparts and palisades and walls, and they will take them or die in the attempt. If they succeed have I the right to snatch the fruits of victory away from them?' He met Valerius's eye. 'I promise you that if there is another option, I will take it. That must be enough for you. Cremona is the tethered goat to attract the wolf, Valerius, and the truth is that without that lure I fear my legions may not be strong enough to take the city.'

He turned back to the mound of papers on his campaign desk and Valerius saluted, knowing there was nothing else to say. Cremona was the goat to attract the wolf? Serpentius would tell him that things seldom turned out well for the goat.

XXVI

'Caecina Alienus is a traitor to Rome.' Aulus Vitellius Germanicus Augustus's powerful voice echoed from the walls of the Senate House and he accompanied his words with a contemptuous wave of the hand that won cheers from the packed benches. 'He is a betrayer and a coward. By his actions he has threatened the stability of the Empire.'

Looking down on his senators from his golden throne, Vitellius acknowledged inwardly that the Empire's stability at the time of Caecina's gross betrayal was questionable at the very least. Still, he didn't let the thought alter the expression on his pendulous, sweating countenance.

'I applaud the decisive action taken by our loyal officers of Fifth Alaudae. The betrayer is made captive and will be held until he can be brought before this house, tried for his perfidious crimes and put to death in a manner fit for a traitor.'

More cheers and a few gruesome suggestions as to the technical details of that death, including some from senators Vitellius would gladly see sacrificed in Caecina's place. He'd long suspected Caecina's weakness, his ambition and his want of loyalty, but this? A full-scale attempt to defect to the enemy with the legions under his command? Was the man mad? Vitellius had made Caecina a consul of Rome. When the war was won, Caecina might rightfully have expected to be handed a province that he could pluck like a plum. A province that would enrich his family for generations. Of course, he would never be heir; Valens would not stand for it. In any case, he'd made it plain the Empire would go to his son when he was ready. But surely that was not enough to cause Caecina's defection? Why had he given it all up? The question had plagued Vitellius since news of the betrayal arrived. Now the possible answer turned the glistening beads of sweat on his forehead into a stream that dripped from his cheeks to soak into the folds of his toga. Did Caecina know something that Vitellius did not? Was the enemy so strong he was certain he could not win? No, he would not accept that. Valens insisted the legions in the field outnumbered those of Marcus Antonius Primus by two to one. Victory was certain as long as those legions were commanded by the right man. But Valens was struck down by illness and Vitellius had had no choice but to send Caecina. He'd issued strict orders to the young general to delay until Valens joined him. Instead, the deceitful bastard had taken the army north. Yet a further contradiction now perplexed him. Caecina had placed his legions in a position of strength, at Hostilia, where they threatened Primus's flanks. With one swift move across the river he would have forced the arrogant swindler to run back to Pannonia with his tail between his legs. So why, on the very brink of victory and eternal fame, did he turn against those who elevated him? Vitellius could only think it was some want of character; a genuine cowardice or a lack of self-confidence in a man who appeared confident to the point of caricature. And then there was the wife, Salonina. Galeria Fundana had identified her as a scheming, conniving bitch on their first meeting. He pictured the slim, lithe figure lying naked in bed whispering into the traitor's ear. Well, he would have her head as well.

He realized belatedly that he was the focus of an expectant hush, and, with the glare of a man who'd been contemplating his adversary's awful death, resumed his onslaught. 'We have taken steps to ensure the renegade's absence will have no effect on our campaign against the misguided rabble sent to their deaths by the arch-traitor Vespasian. Our faithful and honourable subject, the ever-victorious General Gaius Fabius Valens, is even now on his way to take command of our

Army of the North. With ten legions – yes, I say *ten* legions – he will crush Vespasian's rabble to dust.' He saw some concerned looks and knew they were asking themselves why it required ten legions to defeat a 'misguided rabble'. To explain might be seen as a sign of indecision, but a moment of enlightenment dawned. 'Once they have stamped out the rebellion on Rome's soil they will move into Pannonia and Moesia and restore our authority in those provinces. They will provide a base to advance on to Syria, Egypt and Africa and wipe out the stain on Rome's honour that is Titus Flavius Vespasian.'

It was a masterstroke. If there was one thing the venal, corrupt and arrogant occupants of the cushioned marble benches of the Senate understood it was ambition and revenge. The applause almost lifted the roof off that venerable building. For the first time, more so even than on his triumphant, nervous entry into the city, Aulus Vitellius Germanicus Augustus truly felt like the Emperor of Rome. They followed him into the street and cheered him through the Forum, and the mob who had congregated on the steps of the basilicas and temples joined them. But by the time Vitellius was carried by his bearers to the steps of the Golden House the familiar emptiness had returned. Not emptiness of spirit, emptiness of stomach. Success was clearly good for the appetite. He visualized the banquet he would order his cooks to prepare and a groan of pure pleasure began in his stomach and sang from his throat. Which left only one decision: what delicacy would fill the time until the first course arrived?

He frowned as he passed in the shadow of the enormous statue depicting the man he still considered his predecessor – Galba and Otho hardly counted, did they? He really must make a decision. A martial expression, certainly. A victor's expression. He would have the head removed tomorrow.

When the guards escorted him through the doors to his private apartments his heart almost skipped. How proud she would be. His secretary would already have conveyed news of his triumph in the Senate. Nothing could spoil his day.

The look on Galeria's face brought him up as if he'd collided with a buffalo. For a moment he thought his heart had stopped. 'Lucius?'

Mutely, she shook her head, pointing to the corner of the room, where a grey-faced messenger wrung his hands in terror.

'A . . . A . . .'

'Speak!' Vitellius flinched at the threat of violence that contaminated the word. I am a gentle man, he thought. What is happening to me? 'Please,' he said more soothingly, 'speak. Take your time, boy.'

The messenger swallowed and eventually found the words he sought. 'A rebellion, Caesar. Rebellion in the north.'

Vitellius laughed incredulously and looked to his wife. 'Rebellion? Of course there is a rebellion, but even now our armies are taking steps to crush the usurper Titus Flavius Vespasian.'

'Not that rebellion.' Galeria's voice had a frightening, haunted quality. 'Rebellion on the Germania frontier. That one-eyed monster Civilis has incited the Batavians to rise against the legions. Fire consumes the Rhenus frontier and the barbarians east of the river flock to join him.'

XXVII

Carnage.

'Send in the fifth century to support the attack.'

Valerius watched from a raised earth platform as the eighty men of the fifth century of the Third cohort trotted towards the fiendish combination of ditches, palisades and blind entries the defenders of Cremona had created to confound any assault. Once within range of the fort's archers, slingers and carefully sited *onagri* and *scorpiones*, the century formed a protective *testudo*. Maintaining their steady pace, they crossed the first ditch unscathed. Good, they'd chosen their line well, meeting the obstacle exactly where the Seventh Galbiana's engineers had bridged it with bundles of branches.

'The palisade on the bank beyond was demolished by the first attack, so it shouldn't delay them too much.' Claudius Ferox's dutiful optimism was welcome, but didn't quite succeed.

Valerius's eyes never left the compact shell of shields. Who was leading them? Of course, Geminus. He'd promoted him to centurion after the battle by the causeway.

'No trouble crossing the second ditch.' Serpentius's harsh bray injected a note of reality. 'Not with it being packed with all those bodies.'

Valerius shot him a venomous glance, which the Spaniard ignored, and turned back to the attack. Would they manage to keep their formation? Yes. He tried to still the exultation that rose in his breast. If anyone could take the position, it was Geminus. The *testudo* topped the next rise, the banks thick with hundreds of Valerius's men sheltering from the hail of javelins and slingshot that had thwarted every attack so far. As he watched, a boulder from one of the flanking Vitellian *onagri* glanced off the armoured carapace and bounced away to decapitate a legionary who'd raised his head to watch. One more earth wall. One more palisade. The sheltering centuries began to combine, ready to exploit the success of the *testudo*. He saw the moment Geminus and his men hit the slope, still protected by that impenetrable wall of shields. Waited for the inevitable storm of missiles. Nothing. But Valerius's elation faded as the palisade opened. The genius of the *testudo* was that anything thrown or launched at it would bounce off the impregnable wall of shields, but it had one weakness. The big round boulders the defenders pushed from the top of the slope weren't thrown, they were rolled. He saw them gather pace to smash into the exposed legs of the *testudo*'s unsuspecting occupants. He imagined the snap of breaking bones and winced as he watched the formation disintegrate, the whole splintering into a dozen smaller fragments comprising four or five men whose legs still pumped as they fought their way up the slope. A roar erupted from hundreds of throats as the sheltering centuries launched themselves from the second bank to join the attack. There was still a chance. Valerius clenched his fist so hard the knuckles turned white as exposed bone. Could they do it?

Serpentius spat in the dusty earth. Valerius remembered willing the attackers upward on to his sword as he stood on the wall at Placentia. Waiting until the man on the ladder was perfectly placed and . . .

'Merda.'

A horn sounded and a storm of missiles from the flanking towers ripped into the attacking formations, tearing gaps through the charging men. In the same instant a cloud of spears arced from the parapet and a dozen attackers fell, writhing and clawing at their bodies as they rolled back into the ditch. Still the survivors fought their way up the slope and Valerius knew without doubt that the man at the very tip of the attack was young Geminus. A big man, with powerful shoulders and the invincibility of youth; he remembered the pride in the tall Calabrian's eyes as he'd presented him with the crest and his vine stick of office. Watching the charging figure, he imagined the determination on the broad peasant face as he led his men forward. Saw the shield thrown aside as he tore at the stakes of the palisade. The dart of a spear and the moment Geminus's hands flew up to his throat and the centurion fell backwards.

His death signalled the failure of the attack. The few legionaries who reached the crest were met by javelin or sword. Accompanied by the jeers of the defenders, the rest fell back to their original positions, where they could shelter from the deadly missile fire. The dead were left where they fell and the wounded to make their own way. Throwing in another century would only have the same result. He must try something different.

'Brocchus?' Valerius snarled.

'Sir?' Somehow the Seventh's *primus pilus* managed to turn the word into an insult.

'Cohort attack on the wall at the base of the south tower. Wait for the signal.'

'Sir! Don't you worry, the First cohort will get in there for you. Skirt for all and the best wine kept for the legate, my word on it.' Valerius didn't look up, but he could imagine the leering gap-toothed grin. Still, an assault close to the base of the tower would save them from the pair of shield-splitters the defenders had placed overlooking the ditches. A heart-warming vision of the *primus pilus* spitted on one of the five-foot arrows flicked into his head, but he dismissed it as unworthy.

'Claudius? A runner to General Fulvus. Seventh Galbiana will launch a cohort attack on the south tower at the sixth hour. Tell him I hope it will draw the defenders away from the gate and I suggest Third Gallica might be able to exploit the opportunity.' He grinned at the image of Fulvus's face as he realized he was being advised how to fight a battle. Better to be here than the messenger who delivered it. 'A *cornu* will signal the assault.' It was a risk that had to be taken. The sound might alert the enemy to the attack, but they were alert enough anyway. At best, Brocchus and his men would breach the walls and carry their swords into the fort. At worst they would provide the Third Gallica with a breathing space to attack a weakened defence. He paused, trying to gauge the battle by the sounds he could hear. Cohorts would be probing all along the line as Primus had ordered. Would it have been better to combine the legions for an all-out assault on one section of the walls? Perhaps, but the casualties would be just as heavy and the chances of success as variable. He couldn't criticize the general's tactics. A commander had to take a decision and be judged by it afterwards, right or wrong.

'Cornicen?' He looked from the trumpeter to where Brocchus was organizing his cohort into wedge formation. At least the ugly bastard knew his business. 'On my signal you will sound the attack.'

He waited to allow Fulvus to get the Third's cohorts into position before giving the word.

'Now.'

At the blaring signal from the cornicen, eight hundred legionaries moved off in tight-packed wedge formation. The First cohort consisted of five double-strength centuries and they trotted towards the defences with two in the van and three behind. Such a mass of men made an inviting target. Somewhere inside the fort an officer would be scream-ing at the crew of one of the big siege catapults to adjust their aim. But that took time. Valerius had gambled that Brocchus and his soldiers would be able to reach the shelter of the entrenchments before the enemy found his range. As they approached the first barrier each of the cohort's individual elements formed *testudo*.

From his elevated position Valerius tried to stay dispassionate as his men closed on their objective, one of a pair of thirty-foot towers to his left. Claudius Ferox gasped as a rock from the one of the defenders' *onagri* smashed off the locked *scuta* of the leading century, splinter-ing one of the shields. At this distance the missiles looked harmless enough, but inside the sweating hell of the *testudo* men would be in agony from the pain of wrists broken by the shattering impact of the boulders. Shield-splitters were more effective – a perfect strike would punch through a shield and impale the man holding it – but they took longer to reload. In any case they were too few to trouble an attack of this size. Not that it would matter soon, because when the cohort reached the shadow of the tower the angle would be against the machines. Valerius's heart beat a little faster as the attacking cohort flowed over the defensive ditches and through the first and second palisades.

As he had planned, four of the First's centuries concentrated on the main defences while the other angled towards the base of the tower. Now Brocchus proved his worth and it was a joy to see the precision with which each double-strength century moved seamlessly to form four normal half-centuries. The final ditch had been dug with the defenders' side almost vertical, to trap the attackers where they could be cut down at leisure. But it had one disadvantage. It required the defenders to expose themselves not only to the legionaries' spears, but to sling and arrow fire. Valerius had positioned three centuries of auxiliary archers to support the attack. Now they peppered the palisade overlooking Brocchus's cohort, their well-aimed shafts striking down any spearman foolish enough to show himself. Trapped in the ditch, another attacker's resolve might have been tested, but these were Roman legionaries, trained to a brutal effectiveness in tactics honed by centuries of war.

'I hate the bastards, but you can't deny they're good,' Serpentius muttered with grudging approval. They watched the lead half-century form a ramp of shields and a second leap up to create a new *testudo* on top. The manoeuvre allowed the front rank of the elevated formation to tear at the palisade or drag careless enemy defenders into the ditch to be butchered. Satisfied with their progress, Valerius focused his attention on the attack against the tower.

Here also, a lower tier of legionaries supported an upper unit on their shields, but with a different purpose. This century had carried a cauldron of glowing coals in their midst. Now they used the contents to try to set the supporting pillars of the tower ablaze, while the defenders above tried equally hard to stop them. One of the garrison appeared at the parapet and leaned out to pour water on the men below. Valerius saw him straighten, pierced by countless unseen arrows, and topple to plunge into the ditch. Flames began to lick at the uprights and if they caught hold it was only a matter of time before the tower must be abandoned. But the Vitellian defenders had other ideas. Valerius watched as they braved the arrow storm and began to tear the wooden parapet apart.

'Bastards,' Serpentius muttered.

'What are they up to?' Ferox demanded.

Valerius's heart sank as he realized what was about to happen. A dozen defenders bodily heaved one of their now useless *onagri* over the wreckage of the wall so it plunged on to the attackers below. The powerful machines were constructed of massive baulks of wood and enormously heavy. Even at this distance he heard the shrill screams as the catapult smashed through the carapace of shields as if it didn't exist, to crush the helpless legionaries beneath. Both *testudines* disintegrated and the shattered survivors retreated to re-form and renew their attack, taking the injured with them.

'It's ready, sir.'

Valerius turned, ready to snap at the messenger before he realized what the information meant.

'Very well. Tell them to target the tower when they're ready. Claudius, send a runner to the commander of the third century to abandon the assault on the tower and reinforce the main attack.'

Primus had been able to bring forward only two of the big siege catapults in time for the attack and they'd been assigned to the northern sectors. Valerius was promised the support of the next to arrive. He ignored the attack for the moment and looked to his rear. In the far distance, he could see the long arm of the machine being pulled back. Experience told him there was little hope of a direct hit, but the psychological power of the huge missiles landing amongst the defenders would keep their heads down. With a tiny flutter of unease Valerius checked the angle between catapult and tower and realized he was in direct line of shot. He tried not to think what would happen if the cursed thing fired short. His fears vanished when the first giant boulder made the familiar whooshing sound as it flew overhead to crash into the centre of the Vitellian camp. A second throw fell almost two hundred paces to the left, making Serpentius hoot in disdain.

Valerius shook his head and concentrated on the attack, calling up a new century of archers to cover Brocchus's flanks, which were coming under increasing pressure. The rush of air directly overhead made him duck. He looked up just in time to see the lower part of the tower disintegrate, sending its occupants tumbling screaming into the ditch below as the upper section toppled to smash the defensive rampart. Pure luck, but the gap was like an open invitation. If he were quick, he might exploit the breakthrough before the defenders had time to recover.

He turned to Claudius. 'Fifth cohort is the reserve. Tell—'

A mighty roar cut off his words and he turned to see the defenders on the ramparts looking over their shoulders before they disappeared altogether. A few moments later a tiny figure appeared at the south gate waving what looked like a cohort standard and soon a messenger rode up to Valerius's position.

'My legate's compliments,' the man grinned. 'The Third Gallica has breached the gates and he invites you to join him.'

Valerius looked back towards the broken palisade where Brocchus's men were pouring through in their hundreds as the panicked defenders fled. 'I believe we already have.' He matched the man's grin. 'Cornicen? Sound the general advance.' He stayed long enough to watch the legion's remaining cohorts set out in the First's wake. He should have been elated, but at its heart – its very core – victory seemed very much like defeat. His body felt drained of everything but a weary emptiness. Those were Romans being slaughtered among the tents of the enemy camp. Roman soldiers who had fought bravely for their Emperor and their Empire. He could take no joy from their deaths. The only consolation was that this victory would tear the heart out of Vitellius's army. It might not be the end, but it was certainly the beginning of the end. It could be only a matter of time before his old friend must concede defeat, and what then for an Emperor without a throne or an army?

'I give you joy of the victory, sir.' Ferox beamed, as well he might, because the fall of Cremona would be a stepping stone towards a command of his own. 'Will you enter the city?'

'No, Claudius.' Valerius managed a weary smile. 'I think I can trust you to look after the rest of it. But remind the centurions that we're to take prisoners. The men we faced today could soon be fighting at our side and one of those legions could be yours.'

The young man's grin grew wider and he was laughing as he rode off at the head of the headquarters staff. Valerius felt Serpentius's eyes on him. 'What?'

'Everything will be gone by the time we get there.'

He was talking about loot, but Valerius didn't have the energy to object. 'Go then, with my blessing.'

'Do you want me to look for anything in particular?' Valerius shook his head and yawned. The Spaniard turned towards his horse.

'Oh, there is one thing,' Valerius said.

'What?'

'Wake me up before sunset and I may have to kill you.'

XXVIII

'Valerius!'

The urgent voice seemed to come from very far away, much too far away to bother answering. Better to stay drowned in this tranquil pool where the shadows of past failure caused you no pain. 'Valerius, you must come.' More insistent now, and accompanied by an uncomfortable feeling of responsibility that made the pool shimmer and the shadows withdraw. With the greatest reluctance, he swam upwards, towards the mirror surface, and opened his eyes.

'How long have I been sleeping?'

'Long enough,' Serpentius snapped.

'I told you . . .'

'They're burning Cremona.'

'What?' He rolled off the cot as the Spaniard reached for his sculpted breastplate. 'No time for that.' He picked up his sash of office. 'Just help me with this and strap on my sword.' He waited impatiently until Serpentius had carried out his instructions. 'Is my horse ready?'

'The groom is saddling it now. I—'

Valerius was already on the way out. 'Bring my cloak and you can tell me on the way.'

He emerged from the tent to see black smoke hanging over the city like a funeral pall. Bright pricks of flame and bursts of sparks erupted from burning buildings inside the walls. They set off at a gallop and reined in outside the shattered south gate of the entrenchment to be met by a visibly shaken Claudius Ferox.

The young tribune pointed towards the scattered corpses of friend and foe lying in small huddles around the entrance. 'After the Third took the gate we had the usual slaughter, but when the Vitellians started to throw down their swords our lads seemed happy enough to let them surrender.'

Valerius nodded. Serpentius had given him the details on the way. How the trouble started when a few men had retreated to the city and closed the gates and a few of the braver townsfolk thought they were safe to shout insults from the walls. They'd been cleared away by a flight of arrows before Primus took the surrender of the city and all the units in the Padus valley. 'What I don't understand is how in the name of the gods it could lead to this.' He swept a hand towards the great tower of smoke hanging over Cremona.

'It was the Thirteenth, sir,' Ferox looked sheepish, 'and I'm afraid a few of ours got involved too. They were searching the tents for any loot that was hidden inside, digging up below the hearths in case someone had used them to hide his gold. You remember the Thirteenth thought they'd been badly treated after the surrender at Bedriacum?' Valerius grunted acknowledgement. During his trial for cowardice and treason, Aquila had tormented him with the stories of the indignities that his legion had suffered. 'The worst of it was a centurion who roared and wept, snarling at the townsfolk about some women – the Thirteenth's women – who'd been rounded up and locked in a barn then burned to death. Well, his tent-mates weren't having that. They were hungry and they'd have their fill of what Cremona could offer, aye, and the rest. General Primus was gone by now, and their officers didn't dare stop them . . .'

'So they went on a looting spree,' Valerius predicted as they walked their horses through the lanes of flattened tents, past dead bodies and parts of bodies. The sickly-sweet scent of early putrescence was familiar enough, but Valerius would never become accustomed to it. In the distance his ears detected a low murmur punctuated by howls of delight and high-pitched screams. 'That's all in the past. I need to know what's happening now,' he persisted.

Ferox shifted uneasily in the saddle. 'As soon as they charged inside, the rest followed them, including ours, and even some of the Vitellians they'd been fighting. At first all they wanted was food and drink, but you know how these things escalate, sir; soon food wasn't enough.'

Valerius could imagine it all too well. A wine shop, its door battered in and the contents poured down the throats of men who hadn't had a wine ration for a week. Some poor bastard trying to protect his property or his women. The next thing he's lying weeping amongst the blue-veined coils of his own guts and his women are naked and on their backs. Oh, and just for good measure we'll burn his house down for his insolence.

After the tents they came to ramshackle houses of the city suburbs that had been served the same way, contents spread on the streets, doors and shutters ripped off. They were close enough now to hear the crackle of burning timber and the roar of flames fanned by the brisk breeze. Thick black smoke billowed and rolled above the city walls. A few men of the Seventh stood uneasily by the gate or slumped against the wall staring into the distance. Valerius dismounted and handed his reins to Ferox. 'Round up any stragglers from the Seventh, Claudius, and send them back to camp. All plunder to be kept in a common fund. We'll decide what happens to it later.' The young tribune nodded, and Valerius turned to Serpentius. 'Well, what are we waiting for?' With the Spaniard in the lead, they walked through the gate, prepared for a scene worthy of the deepest pit in Hades.

It was quiet enough close to the entrance, and they soon discovered why. The houses had been spared the torch, but their occupants hadn't been offered the same mercy. They lay in the streets, or half in and half out of their homes, blood spilling from cut throats and smashed skulls to run in scarlet streams to the central drain. Men, women and children; none had been spared. Their lifeless bodies were surrounded by shards of shattered red-glazed pottery that sparkled like rubies in the sunlight. The two men passed a house where a couch hung haphazardly from an upstairs window with the corpse of a grey-haired woman draped head down beside it. A little further ahead, they came upon a group of legionaries drinking outside a burning shop. The soldiers seemed oblivious of the bodies scattered around them, and ignored the little dark-haired girl tugging at her dead mother's *stola*. A few eyes were drawn briefly to the sash signalling Valerius's rank, but none of the men acknowledged either it or its owner.

Serpentius was silent as they marched through the carnage, but Valerius sensed the pent-up frustration in the Spaniard. Eventually the former gladiator turned to him. 'Why are we here if we aren't trying to stop this?'

'I can't bring the dead back to life,' the Roman said wearily. 'But I need to understand what happened here and why. If we get the opportunity to intervene without getting our throats cut, we will, but leave the decision to me.'

Serpentius answered with a grunt that might have been acquiescence and might not. By now, whole streets were in flames and choking smoke filled the air. Broken tiles fell from a building up ahead and by tacit agreement they turned up a narrow side street. It seemed to have been left unscathed and Valerius thought it might eventually lead them to the Forum. Even here intermittent gusts of heat hit them from openings between the buildings. Halfway along a prancing blood-soaked figure staggered from a doorway waving a *pilum* with something spitted on the point. Valerius's gorge rose as he recognized the corpse of a small baby, the tiny arms and legs flapping lifelessly as the drunken legionary swung the spear in circles. He took a step towards the man, but Serpentius was already past him. Without a word the Spaniard kicked the soldier between the legs and grabbed him by the ear flaps of his helm to smash his head against the red brick wall. As his victim collapsed, Serpentius retained his grip. He hammered again and again, making the brass helmet ring like a bell until the crown was crumpled metal and blood poured from the legionary's ears and nose. With a grunt of disgust he dropped the body on to the cobbles.

He turned to Valerius. 'I knew what your decision was going to be before you did.' He walked to where the spear lay and tugged it free from the tiny corpse. With surprising tenderness he picked up the child's body and carried it into the nearest house. When the Spaniard re-emerged Valerius glanced back the way they'd come. He thought he saw something jerk back from the entrance to the street. The sight stirred some memory, but he dismissed it.

'I think we should get out of here.' The soldier was still alive, but Valerius doubted he would be for long. Short breaths bubbled from his bloody nose and his eyes were rolled back in his head. They stepped over the body. 'This place makes me feel dirty.'

Closer to the centre, where the inhabitants had been driven like cattle, more houses were burning and screams and cries for mercy came from every direction. A naked woman, tall and heavy-breasted, ran round a corner fifty paces in front of them. Long dark hair flowed over her shoulders and blood covered her thighs. A heartbeat later a jeering crowd of a dozen legionaries appeared. The terrified woman was blind to anything but escape. As they watched she caught her foot on the corpse of a bearded elder who lay in her path with his skull smashed. She fell with a shriek a few paces from Valerius and he instinctively went to her aid, freeing his cloak with his left hand. She cowered away, shaking with terror. 'Please,' he said. 'I can help you.' The suspicion remained, and confusion and fear filled her eyes, but she stayed still and he was able to wrap the cloak around her.

'Yes,' he heard Serpentius say. 'Try it. There's nothing I'd like better.'

Valerius looked up to see the woman's pursuers lined up across the road, eyes wild and breathing hard. They looked like a herd of racing antelope halted by the sight of a leopard. Serpentius faced them down, his long sword in his hand and death in his eyes. Valerius waited, ready for the inevitable confrontation, but the men looked at each other and then at the Spaniard. A moment of decision was reached and all the threat faded from them.

Valerius rose to his feet. 'If you want her, come and get her.' His voice was as much of a challenge as Serpentius's sword. 'But she won't come cheap.' Among the men a pair of eyes widened at the sight of the wooden fist and the sash that marked the commander of the Seventh Galbiana. Valerius choked back his anger as he recognized their owner, but his voice remained as cold as a Silurian's heart. 'Genialis, second rank first century, First cohort, isn't it? What are you doing here, boy? We have work to do back at camp. Tomorrow we will march on Rome. Rome, do you hear? Not this provincial backwater.' He looked from Genialis to the woman at his feet and shook his head. 'What are you doing here, boy?' he repeated.

They stared at him shamefaced and he recognized more of them, all from the First cohort. 'Yes, your legate is here. But he struggles to recognize the men he led into battle this morning.' Anger and frustration filled him to overflowing and his voice shook with fury. 'Men? Not men: vagabonds and thieves, defilers of women. Have you no sisters? Mothers? Is there no discipline in my legion? Where is your centurion? Where is your *primus pilus*? You are not a legion, you are a rabble. Gather up your comrades and go back to the lines. This is done, do you hear me? As long as Seventh Galbiana is my legion you will be warriors. Warriors, not murderers. Soldiers, not civilian street rats driven mad by the first sniff of a woman. Fools. Today you won eternal glory, but with this act you condemn your legion to eternal shame. Are you killers of soldiers, or killers of innocents? Now is the time to decide. Genialis? March these men back to the camp and collect as many more as you can. Make sure your actions from now on reflect the honour you won this morning and not the shame of the last hour. Now get out of my sight!'

When they were gone, he felt utterly drained. Serpentius helped the sobbing woman to the nearest intact house and told her to stay inside until the soldiers had gone.

'Is this what it's come to?' Valerius asked wearily when he returned.

The Spaniard turned to him with a bark of bitter laughter. 'Have you been blind all these years, Valerius? Have you not seen what I have seen? This *is* Rome. When Rome marches into your town or your village this is what it brings. Slaughter and fire and rape. Rome first enslaves you, then it strips you bare with its little lists that calculate your wealth down to the last egg and its bland, pitiless tax collectors who leave you with just enough not to starve. And when you say *Enough*, as any man of honour must, they send you.' His eyes burned with a passion Valerius had never witnessed, even in battle. The Roman remembered weeping Catuvellauni wives and smouldering African villages and felt ashamed. Serpentius sensed it. The feral features hardened and he nodded his scarred head. 'Yes, you, Valerius, you and Genialis and animals like Brocchus. It does not matter if one man, or even ten, feels the slightest compassion for those they enslave and they rob, because you are part of a legion – like a small cog in the wheel that turns a baker's millstone – and a legion is merciless. This troubles you because it is Roman killing and raping Roman. It troubled you less when it was Roman killing the Helvetii or the Armenians who stole our horses on the way to the Cepha gap. No Roman mourned the family of Serpentius when Avala ran with blood.'

Valerius looked anew at the man who had shared a thousand dangers with him. He'd become so used to having Serpentius at his side that he sometimes forgot he wasn't a Roman. In that moment he wanted to apologize for every death caused by a legionary sword and every innocent led away in chains. But fine words would change nothing. 'A long speech for someone who is normally reluctant even to confirm his name.' He said it lightly, seeking refuge in jest.

'It cannot be unsaid.'

'I would not wish it unsaid.' Valerius shook his head. 'You are right. I have been blind.'

'Then let us leave the city now,' the Spaniard urged. 'There's nothing else we can do here.'

'No.' Valerius's tone cemented the decision. 'I can be blind no longer. I must see the rest.'

If anything, the rest was worse.

With every step closer to Cremona's centre, the smoke clogging their throats thickened and the bodies carpeting the streets became more numerous. Individual legionaries fought each other for gold looted from shops and temples. A crucified tavern keeper hung limp from the shutters of his smouldering crossroads inn, his throat mercifully cut after he'd revealed the location of his savings. They met groups of soldiers carrying bundles of plunder wrapped in blankets or whatever came to hand. A few laughed and joked among themselves, but most had the thoughtful, confused look of men in a trance. Valerius exchanged glances with Serpentius and the Spaniard shrugged. It was a sign of how unmanageable they'd become that not one took notice of the senior officer who walked among them. Why became clear when the two men finally entered Cremona's forum. This was where the bulk of the townsfolk had fled. And where they'd died. They lay in their hundreds, bodies piled high on the marble paving where they'd once stood to listen to the councillors of the *ordo*, men of consequence and power who now lay cheek to cheek with night soil carriers and harlots and the shopkeepers they'd despised. Streaks of blood on the white marble steps showed where they'd been dragged from their hiding places in the colonnaded temples.

Those temples, now wreathed in flame and billowing smoke, had been put to the torch, but not before they'd been plundered. The city's treasures had been gathered on the far side of the Forum, close to the steps of the blazing basilica. Statuary, carvings, fine furniture and wooden chests that Valerius knew must contain the temple gold all lay in orderly piles. He noted that they were guarded by a wary group of legionaries very different from those who staggered drunkenly among the burning buildings. Every man was a member of Marcus Antonius Primus's personal bodyguard.

'I've seen enough.'

They walked back through the blood-spattered streets, each wrapped in his own thoughts. 'What happens now?' Serpentius asked eventually.

Valerius considered for a moment before replying. 'We rest and re-supply, I suppose. Then Rome.'

The Spaniard looked to his right, where another of Cremona's countless corpses hung from the window of what had once been his home. 'Will it be like this when we get there?'

Valerius turned sharply to the Spaniard, his eyes bleak. 'Do you think I would allow this to happen to Rome?'

XXIX

Rome

'The tide flows inexorably against him.'

'Perhaps,' a smooth voice she didn't recognize acknowledged, 'but tides have an obstinate habit of ebbing as well as flowing.'

Domitia Longina Corbulo told herself she wasn't eavesdropping as she stood in the garden outside the low balcony. She'd escaped the cloying confines of the great house and the constant attentions of Domitianus to walk in the gardens. Pure chance had brought her below this window where she could hear the conversation as clearly as if she was in the room between the two men. She drew her cloak closer against a chill wind that threatened more rain.

'My dear Saturninus.' This time the unmistakable cultured tones were those of Titus Flavius Sabinus, Prefect of Rome. 'Your knowledge of the natural world is enviable, but it is your knowledge of the political one that interests me more. Surely you won't deny that my brother would bring the kind of stability the current occupant of that glittering monstrosity across the valley cannot and will not command?'

'True.' She heard a smile in the other man's voice as if he needed to show evidence he took no offence at the mild rebuke. 'But the current occupant sits on an Emperor's throne and wears an Emperor's purple.

He also has substantial forces in the field, forces which currently outnumber those of your brother, we are told, by two to one . . .'

Sabinus laughed, but the laugh had a forced quality. Domitia imagined him wearing the terribly sincere but patently dishonest mask he donned whenever he was trying to convince someone that lie was truth. 'When the armies of Syria and Africa take the field . . .'

'But prefect,' the other man said reasonably, 'those armies are still six hundred miles beyond the borders of Italia. Our understanding is that Marcus Antonius Primus is determined to bring the enemy to battle the instant he is in a position to do so. Why, the battle might already have been fought . . . and won, of course.'

'Vespasian would never have countenanced it.' Sabinus sounded horrified. 'He advised caution. A consolidation of Primus's position until Mucianus could bring the Syrian legions forward . . .'

'Perhaps if your brother were with his army?' the other man suggested.

'He has made his position clear.' To Domitia's ears Sabinus sounded overly defensive. 'The legions hailed him Emperor. It is for the legions to make him Emperor. Until the Senate and people of Rome proclaim him so he cannot move from his position in Judaea. The beginning of his stewardship must not be associated with bloodshed. That is why Primus must wait for Mucianus and his legions. When they combine they will form a force so great that the enemy must bow to the inevitable and surrender.'

'A commendable strategy,' the other man's voice held little conviction, 'but one which depends on many assumptions. Let us understand each other, Sabinus. I can persuade the Senate to declare for Vespasian, but only when his armies are at the very gates of Rome and we can see his banners on the Via Flaminia. Even that is dependent on your assurance that the urban cohorts will arm to protect the Senate. Perhaps the tide does not favour Vitellius, but he can be eloquent and persuasive. Look at the speech he made condemning that fraud Caecina. He still has the support of the mob, and the mob will not take kindly to our opposition to an Emperor who, after all, has been declared so by the Senate and *people* of Rome. We must consider our own safety. What is the point of acting too quickly if it invites Vitellius to help himself to our heads?'

'Perhaps I'd receive more spirited support from Trebellius Maximus,' Sabinus said sulkily. 'He too has asked for an appointment, you know.'

The man called Saturninus laughed. 'Only because the Emperor despises him and he seeks a new sponsor. What kind of support would you get from a man who was thrown out of his province by his own troops? I know Trebellius of old, Sabinus. He will tell you he can supply the support of five hundred senators and you can divide that figure by ten, yes, and ten again, and only then will you have the truth of it. Come, let us not part in bad odour. We need do nothing for the moment, and you may be correct in your assertion that Vitellius's time is coming to an end. Certainly, the current events in Germania do not favour him.'

'What have you heard?'

'Civilis and his barbarian allies run riot from one end of the Rhenus to the other while the legions of Rome stagger around like headless chickens. Vetera gone, the entire Rhenus fleet lost, Moguntiacum, Novaesium and Colonia besieged, our troops demoralized and old Flaccus dithering as usual . . .'

The voices faded as the two men moved away from the window and Domitia allowed herself to breathe for the first time in minutes. Her hands trembled and she had to clasp them together to still the shaking. She had been listening to treason.

She walked towards her quarters with her head spinning, her own perilous situation within reach of Domitianus's clutching fingers driven from her mind. What did it mean, and what should she do about it? The first was the easier question to answer. Sabinus was planning to take Rome and hand it to Vespasian when circumstances were favourable. He had the support, at least in principle – though it seemed hardly enthusiastic – of certain powerful members of the Senate. Saturninus. She remembered the name, though she couldn't place it for now. But when would circumstances be favourable? She was her father's daughter, and she couldn't help but take an unwomanly interest in military matters. She knew the Emperor still commanded the support of at least ten legions. If, as she'd just heard, the Flavians were only capable of fielding five, the matter should be beyond doubt. Of course, that might change when Mucianus – she remembered the name with distaste from her time in Syria – arrived with his legions. Still, Saturninus had been quite insistent that he would not act until Vespasian's army was at the gates. But what did it mean for her? Titus Flavius Vespasian had been her father's friend and had supported her after he'd been murdered. He'd helped her return to Rome and had a hand in arranging a respectable if unappealing marriage. She enjoyed Sabinus's protection, for what it was worth. As a man, she owed Aulus Vitellius nothing, but Domitia Longina Corbulo was blessed with a very old-fashioned notion of loyalty, and Aulus Vitellius was her Emperor. She remembered her father's words. *A Corbulo does not have the luxury of choice, only duty.* But what was her duty? Her head dropped and she blinked away a tear.

'You seem perplexed, lady.'

Domitia felt her heart stutter. How long had he been watching? She turned, willing her face to smile. Whatever happened she must not alienate Domitianus further; the future of Rome might depend on it. 'I was thinking of my father,' she said truthfully. 'I miss him very much.'

'Your father, not your husband?' Domitianus's laugh and his thoughtless, uncaring appropriation of a sensitive subject for his own ends irritated her almost beyond control. She clenched her teeth and somehow maintained her composure. 'My husband sends word that he is well and thanks your uncle for my safekeeping,' she replied.

'What kind of husband would go off to his province and leave a wife such as you unprotected in the first place?' Domitianus demanded. He stood closer than was necessary, as always; so close the pockmarks in his sallow skin were clearly visible. She forced herself not to step away from the piercing, overbright eyes. A head taller than Domitia, with a thin, elongated neck, Titus Flavius Vespasian's younger son was a man who considered low cunning a more admirable trait than honesty. 'I would never abandon a wife such as you.'

Domitia turned, elegant as a dancer, and slipped away. He followed as she walked towards the viewpoint that looked out towards the Domus

Aurea, the great golden palace built by Nero and now inhabited by the Emperor Vitellius. 'Your uncle has had visitors.'

Domitianus frowned at the change of subject. 'My uncle has many visitors.' He sounded bored and she felt a surge of relief. His words suggested her fears that he'd seen her listening below the window were unfounded.

'This one looked very distinguished.'

'Oh, Volusius Saturninus.' His lips twisted in a sneer that was mirrored by his tone. 'A pompous old fart from the Senate. He came to consult my uncle about some land dispute.'

Of course, now she remembered. Quintus Volusius Saturninus served as consul in Nero's time and still had great influence. Deep in thought, she would have missed his next words but for the almost comic intensity of the passion that accompanied them.

'You dismiss me because you think I am young and of little consequence.' He shook his head. 'You are wrong. When my father is Emperor I will have power and wealth, and some day I may follow him. Divorce your husband and you will never regret it.'

So it had come to this? She almost laughed aloud at his arrogance. Emperor? This unformed puppy? Did he think her a fool? If Vespasian's forces triumphed, Titus would be his father's heir and Domitianus would be what he'd always been: a nobody clinging to the skirts of power. Yet the suggestion had been made. She must not simply dismiss it, because that risked becoming his enemy. She could not afford that now.

'I am not blind, Domitianus. I know you are attracted to me.' She said the words, though they almost choked her. 'I will think on it, but I must have time.' She nodded and turned away, so he didn't see the look of disgust on her face.

If only Valerius was here to guide her.

XXX

They were passing the city's bath house when Valerius heard a high-pitched scream of the utmost terror. He searched the area to look for the source, but Serpentius urged him to continue. 'Haven't we done enough?' the Spaniard demanded.

'Where did it come from?'

'Over there.' Serpentius pointed to a burning building on the corner of a street of *insulae* apartments. 'There's nothing we can do,' he insisted.

But Valerius was already racing towards the smoke and flames vomiting from the lower windows. At street level the building was occupied by small shops, the frontage covered by a wooden awning to shelter their displays. The awning stretched the entire breadth of the arcade and by the time they reached it the structure was well alight.

'I told you, there's nothing we can do,' the Spaniard repeated. 'We should—'

A second shriek split the air, this time the unmistakable cry of a terrified child.

'*Merda*,' Serpentius cursed.

Valerius paused when he felt the blast of heat from the blazing awning. At first glance it looked impossible to get into the building. Flames ate at the wooden posts supporting the roof of the structure.

But when he studied it more closely he saw that the door and the stairway beyond were still relatively clear. 'We can do it,' he insisted. 'It will hold long for enough for us to reach whoever's inside.'

Serpentius studied the burning awning doubtfully. 'You don't know what it's like in there. If that comes down we'll be trapped with our arses on a roasting plate.'

'Then let's get it done before it does.' Crouching low, Valerius made a dash for the doorway. With a muttered curse, Serpentius followed him.

As they sprinted upwards through the darkened stairwell a stumpy figure walked warily across the street towards the burning building. Gaius Brocchus had had a good day. He'd survived the assault on Cremona, made more than a few Vitellians pay, and found a goldsmith who had helpfully guided him to the location of his buried stock, thanks to the incentive of a *gladius* point in his rectum. He carried the most portable slice of the proceeds in the bag across his shoulder, but there was more, much more. He'd come back for the rest in a couple of hours, when it was dark. Brocchus had seen Valerius in the alleyway by pure chance, but the encounter had been enough to make him follow the two men. Gaius Valerius Verrens had insulted him in front of his men and undermined his authority. As far as Brocchus was concerned his new legate was nothing but trouble and not really a proper legate at all. He studied the doorway where they'd disappeared, the smoke now billowing from the second-storey windows and flames licking at the shutters. But it was the awning he found of greatest interest. With a grin he put his boot to the support nearest the doorway, so that it shuddered and sparks fell from above. Once. Twice. With the third kick the structure gave way, bringing the burning roof crashing down with it. Jumping away from the glowing cinders, Brocchus studied what he'd accomplished with satisfaction. Where the door had been was nothing but an inferno of flaming timbers.

Whoever was inside wasn't coming back out again.

Valerius heard the crash below and a blast of heat surged up the narrow stairway of the apartment block.

'*Merda!*' Serpentius repeated, the *I told you so* left unsaid.

'Keep going,' the Roman shouted. 'The scream came from one of the top rooms.'

'That's comforting,' the Spaniard coughed. 'We'll be able to offer them the choice of being incinerated or trying to fly five floors without the benefit of wings.'

'You'll breathe less smoke if you keep your mouth shut,' Valerius rapped.

On the first landing the maze of corridors and curtained doorways was already well alight, but the stairs were clear. Valerius launched himself at the next set, taking them three at a time to escape being scorched. A distinctive scent caught his attention and the stink of roasting flesh reminded him of the day poor Messor had burned to death nailed to the doorway of the Temple of Claudius. Already the heat seared his bare legs and he could feel it through the soles of his iron-shod sandals.

It was a similar story on the second landing and they continued upwards without pause. Halfway up the body of an old man lay face down on the stairs, the blood from his cut throat staining the worn concrete. They leapt past with barely a glance. Valerius noticed that although the lower floors of the *insula* had been brick built, up here it was different. The stair corridor was constructed of tinder-dry wood, added by a greedy landlord who'd somehow circumvented the fire regulations. When the flames reached this level the entire building would probably go up like a torch soaked in pitch. Up here there was no water supply, but a two-storey light well looked on to a small paved courtyard where the residents could safely cook food in shared ovens.

'Is anybody there?' Valerius shouted breathlessly.

'What now?' Serpentius demanded when there was no response from the curtained doorways surrounding the courtyard.

'If you were trying to escape a fire and hiding from killers, where would *you* go?'

The Spaniard's eyes immediately went to the top floor. They headed for the stairs, only to be halted by a crash that shook the whole building. A new cloud of sparks and smoke exploded from the lower stairwell. 'There's no going back whether we wanted to or not,' Serpentius grunted. 'I hope you're working on a way to get us out of here.'

'Just one last look,' the Roman insisted.

This time they split up, making a cursory search of each apartment. Valerius was just about to give up when he heard what might have been a sob, instantly drowned out by another thunderous crash and a great flare of yellow that illuminated the sparsely furnished room.

'Valerius!' Serpentius shouted. 'We have to get out of here.'

But another sound confirmed Valerius's suspicions. He hauled back the curtain on to the apartment's narrow balcony and found himself the focus of several terrified sets of eyes. Two children, a boy and a girl of about five and seven, a babe in swaddling clothes, and two couples, one of the women heavily pregnant, all huddled together and struck mute by fear.

'Come,' he said urgently. 'We are here to help.'

'Valerius!'

'Please. You must come with me or we will all die.'

Without a word the older of the two women picked up the baby and took the little girl by the hand. Their father followed with the boy and finally the younger man and the pregnant woman. Valerius led them to where the inner balcony overlooked the central courtyard. A shrill cry of terror greeted the sight that met them. The base of the light well was already an inferno that belched flame and smoke. It meant the rooms directly below must already be partly consumed and the only surprise was that the whole building hadn't collapsed.

Valerius turned to the father, knowing the answer before he spoke. 'Is there another way out?'

The man shook his head and held his son closer, hopelessness filling his pale eyes.

'The roof,' Serpentius coughed. 'It's our only chance.'

'The women . . . ?'

'Women can climb too. Give me your belt.'

Without hesitation Valerius unhooked his leather belt and handed it to the Spaniard, who had already freed his own. The red-tiled roof sloped into the well about seven or eight feet above, supported by pillars on the edge of the balcony. Serpentius took hold of one of the pillars and sprang up on to the narrow rail that guarded the two storey drop. The platform just allowed him to reach the roof. Perched above the inferno, the Spaniard stretched up and tested the red clay tiles with his free hand. When he was satisfied they were firm enough to support him he turned to Valerius with a grim half-smile. 'Do or die, eh?'

Without a glance at the flames below, Serpentius placed the belts between his teeth and reached up to take the roof in both hands. His arm muscles bulged and the sinews stood out like writhing snakes as he hauled himself up so his head and shoulders disappeared from those below. At first it seemed he must be stranded halfway, but with an acrobatic flip of the hips he somehow found the purchase to swing himself up. A second later the fearsome head reappeared.

'Hand me the boy.'

Valerius held out his left hand, but the child clung tighter to his father and stared in nervous fascination at the wooden fist of the right.

'We don't have time for this.' Valerius met the man's terrified eyes as the building shuddered and another crash sent a fountain of sparks up from below. 'What is his name?'

'Gaius.'

'Come,' Valerius encouraged. 'My name is Gaius too.'

The man bent and whispered something in his son's ear. Whatever he said, the words had their effect, because Gaius frowned, his chin came up and he took Valerius's hand.

'You are very brave,' the Roman said, picking him up, 'and I'm sure your sister will be too. Now hang on tight until I tell you to let go.' Small hands wrapped round his neck and he was able to clamber up and balance on the rail using the pillar for support. Smoke billowed past them through the opening in the roof and he felt the boy flinch at the heat from the flames. 'Now,' he said. 'Don't look down. I'll lift you and you must reach up with both hands. Do you understand?' Gaius's dark eyes turned serious and he nodded. Valerius freed his hand from the pillar, took a deep breath and raised the slight figure. The wooden fist made holding his burden awkward, but somehow he managed, and as Gaius raised his arms Serpentius snatched him to the temporary safety of the roof. Unbalanced by the sudden loss of weight Valerius felt a thrill of terror as he teetered over the drop until Gaius's father stepped forward to steady him. Breathing hard, he nodded his thanks and steadied himself.

'Now the girl,' came the voice from above.

The girl, Julia, was less reluctant. With a word of assurance from her mother she came into Valerius's arms and he was able to repeat the exercise with less peril. Serpentius helped her up to the spine of the roof and sat her down beside her brother with orders not to move a finger.

'Best get the mother up next.'

'My baby?' the woman whimpered.

'You won't be apart for long,' Valerius promised.

She handed the wriggling bundle to the pregnant girl and stepped forward without any further urging from Valerius. A slim woman, he could see she was terrified, but utterly determined to join her children. Her husband helped her up on to the rail, where she held fast to the pillar trying not to look down at the flames.

One end of the knotted sword belts flipped down from above. 'Tie this round your wrist.'

With Valerius's help the woman did as she was instructed. 'Now,' Valerius said, 'your dignity may suffer a little, but you will soon be with your children. I will hand the baby up next.'

Her husband hovered protectively below and Valerius had an idea. 'Get up on the other side of the pillar, put your arms around it and make a sling of your hands. Understand?' The man nodded and climbed gingerly on to the rail.

Valerius turned back to the woman. 'When I boost you up, use your husband's hands as a foot rest and raise yourself as high as you can, with your hands in the air. Don't worry about falling, I'll steady you and Serpentius will lift you. Are you ready?' She nodded and he saw that in her terror she'd bitten her lip so hard it bled. He placed his hands round her waist. 'Now!' He lifted her, straining to keep his balance on the rail, felt the moment she pushed with her foot and the burden lightened as Serpentius gripped her hands. Even the Spaniard's great strength was tested by the weight and the awkwardness of his position. Somehow he managed to wrestle her up and with a cry the kicking legs disappeared from view. As they'd been working, Valerius had been conscious of the increasing heat from below. On the far side of the space he could see the flames licking at the bottom of the same level where they were perched. The floorboards beneath his feet creaked and smoke filtered through the cracks. He had a moment of mind-tearing panic that faded as the pregnant girl stepped forward and handed him the baby. Serpentius had the belts ready and Valerius held the child while the father made a sling and tied it firmly round the whimpering infant's armpits. Serpentius pulled on the belts and Valerius guided the baby until the Spaniard could lift the cloth-wrapped bundle.

With the baby gone, the pregnant girl stepped forward willingly, her face set in an expression of utter determination. Valerius and the older man were able to repeat the technique they'd used with the mother. The two men went next, leaving Valerius alone on the balcony. By now the flames were licking at the rail and he reached above, praying that Serpentius still had the strength to lift him. Hands like a pair of iron bands closed on his wrist and the cowhide stock of the wooden hand and he felt himself suspended in mid-air. With one convulsive heave the Spaniard dragged him over the edge of the tiles.

For a moment they lay side by side in a daze of physical and mental exhaustion. The Spaniard's eyes were closed and he breathed like a man who'd just swum the Strait of Messana.

Valerius moved first. 'This is no time to be lying around, unless you want know what a roasted chicken feels like,' he said. Serpentius grunted and they hauled themselves to their feet and edged their way to the ridge to join the family. The wide eyes of the adults reflected not only the peril of their situation, but the horror done to their city. In every direction the smoke from a thousand fires smeared the sky, and they winced at the crackle and crash of burning buildings. Valerius had always known a price would be exacted for Cremona's unflinching support for Vitellius, but he had never expected this. It

229

was as if Primus's legionaries wanted to wipe the city from the map.

He dragged his eyes away from the destruction and surveyed their position. The *insula* occupied a corner site joined to the buildings around it. Behind them, the red tiles stretched away at the same height, but no route back to the ground presented itself. Billowing smoke confirmed the shops and apartments below were also well ablaze. The way to his left seemed to offer more opportunity. Here also the buildings were on fire, but the roof fell away in a succession of steps until perhaps two hundred paces away it was only two storeys high. In a courtyard behind the *insulae* he could see the upper branches of a large tree which might provide their escape.

He made his decision. 'This way,' he said. 'And stay together.' He picked up Gaius and Serpentius took the girl by the hand, and they led the little group to the edge of the roof. It was a drop of twice the height of a man to the lower roof and would have been much more dangerous if Serpentius hadn't retained the sword belts. The Spaniard went first and Valerius used the thin strip of leather to lower the boy, repeating the exercise with Julia. When he'd helped the adults descend, with the pregnant girl last, Valerius lowered himself and dropped like a cat on to the tiles below.

Step by wary step they made their way to the next drop in the roofs, climbed down, and repeated the manoeuvre on to the lowest level. By the time Valerius followed, the others were already well ahead. It was only then that he realized the roof was shimmering with heat. As he walked forward he could feel it on his legs and through the soles of his sandals. The temperature was so high that some of the roof tiles had cracked. As he pressed cautiously forward he could hear others snapping and noticed small wisps of smoke seeping through gaps. He could only imagine what was happening beneath his feet.

'Hurry,' he called to Serpentius. The Spaniard was four-fifths of the way across, leading little Julia, and he raised his free hand to show he'd heard. Behind him came the father with Gaius in his arms, then Gaius's mother with her baby. The pregnant girl walked hand in hand with her husband, but she'd slowed and they were clearly in difficulty. Valerius hurried forward to help them. Four paces from the couple he heard a loud crack, instantly followed by a moment when the world seemed to freeze. He watched in disbelief as the tiles fell away and, still clutching each other, the two young people dropped into a sea of fire. Valerius recoiled from the furnace blast of heat that erupted from the gaping fissure and stared at the place where they'd disappeared.

'Valerius!' The urgency in Serpentius's voice brought him back to the present. The Spaniard had sent the rest of the refugee family away to the far end of the roof where they stood in a weeping huddle.

'I . . .'

'You must jump, now. Delay even a moment and it will be too late.'

Valerius contemplated the glowing barrier and shook his head at the impossibility of what the Spaniard was asking. He searched desperately for an alternative. Surely there must be another way?

'Do or die, Valerius.' Serpentius's eyes met his and Valerius felt as if the Spaniard had read his mind.

Before another negative thought could fix itself in his head, he backed up four paces and launched himself at the gap. How far was it? Four paces? Five? What if he lost his footing? He would burn to death in an instant. Better to have tried to climb down and broken his neck in the attempt. Too late. He fixed Domitia's face in his head. Do or die. He picked a spot a pace back from the edge. When his front foot hit the mark, he threw his body forward and upwards, feeling the heat singe his lower body. He tried not to think about what was below as he stretched his legs in front of him. Was he going to make it? He was so close. A scream of frustration escaped him as he realized that though his feet were going to hit the first row of tiles he didn't have the momentum to carry his body with them. *Great Mars save me.* His boots touched with a clatter of breaking tile and he tried to throw his torso forward. For a moment he hung in space before his weight inevitably pulled him back into the inferno. From nowhere a hand shot out and snatched the front of his tunic. Very carefully, Serpentius pulled him to safety.

'Next time you decide to rescue somebody, please do it yourself.'

'Very well,' Valerius released a long groan of relief. 'But can we get away from here? My backside appears to be on fire.'

XXXI

'Where in the name of Hades have you been?' Marcus Antonius Primus contemplated the scorched, soot-stained figure who had just walked into the tent. 'I expect my legates to be available when I need them, not gallivanting about collecting plunder. You have a staff who can do that for you.' Valerius tensed and Primus looked up to see the dangerous light in his eye. The general waved a placating hand. 'In any case, it is of no matter. I—'

'It is of matter when Roman citizens are being slaughtered in your name,' the younger man interrupted coldly. 'Perhaps you did not notice, but the glow that allows you to write your reports without an oil lamp is the city of Cremona burning.'

'An unfortunate accident,' Primus said dismissively. 'As to your so-called slaughter, there are bound to be a few casualties when a city declines to surrender immediately, especially one which treated its enemies so badly after defeat.'

'A few?' Valerius sounded incredulous. 'Have you even been in the city? Hundreds, probably thousands of corpses lie in the streets of Cremona, or roasting in their burning houses. A tribute to the victorious Marcus Antonius Primus, whose name will come to be spoken alongside Nero's as the great incendiary of his age.'

Primus stiffened and his eyes went as cold as an executioner's heart.

His fingers twitched and Valerius knew they were itching for the dagger that hung on the tent post to his right. 'You are very free with your words for a man who is still under sentence of death.'

'A man under sentence of death has little to lose. I saw too many unwarranted deaths today to fear one more, even if it is my own.'

'I never wanted it to be this way.'

'You sanctioned it.'

'Not this. I thought they would do a little looting, kill a few people who would probably have died anyway when we began to root out the biggest traitors.'

'It has gone far beyond that.'

Primus threw his stylus aside and called for his clerk. 'A guard on all the gates of Cremona immediately,' he ordered. 'The looting and the burning stops now. No captives to be sold into slavery. Any legionary still inside the walls in the morning to be screened and the ringleaders apprehended.' He shook his head wearily. 'The great incendiary of his age . . .'

'You—'

'No, what is done cannot be undone.' A bitter laugh escaped the general's lips and he picked up a roll of parchment from the desk. 'The latest missive from Vespasian. He believes I've over-extended myself. He rebukes me for "over-enthusiasm" and wishes me to hold my position, which he thinks is still at Aquileia. He sees the possibility for the war to be ended with no more civilian casualties.' His eyes rose to meet Valerius's. 'You see my difficulty? Delicate negotiations are under way. Nothing further to be gained by forcing battle on the enemy. Mars' arse, you'd think the man had never held a command. What does he think soldiers do? If you don't let them fight the enemy they will fight each other, aye and kill their commanders, too, for their *cowardice* or lack of enthusiasm. What choice did I have?'

'You have your victory, despite all this,' Valerius pointed out.

'It is not enough *because* of all this,' Primus insisted. He threw the scroll carelessly back on to the desk. Without warning his tone hardened. 'There is only one answer. I must finish the war before Mucianus arrives and that means marching on Rome. But there will be no more massacres. I plan to send the defeated legions to Moesia under new legates. Messalla will be one. Vespasian has decided he cannot endorse his permanent appointment despite being one of my best fighting generals, but at least I can give him another temporary command. He will be replaced as legate of the Seventh Claudia by Lucius Plotius Grypus, a nephew of Mucianus, and no doubt one of his spies. I also intend to resume personal command of Seventh Galbiana.' The general's voice contained a certain sympathy, but Valerius felt as if he'd been kicked in the stomach. It had been foolish to think it would last, but he thought of the Seventh as his legion. 'This does not reflect on your command of the legion, which has been exemplary, but releases you for a mission which may be even more important given my future plans. Vitellius is finished, we are agreed on that?'

Valerius nodded warily. His old friend's position was desperate and could only worsen. 'It is only a matter of time now that you have destroyed the core of his army,' he agreed. 'The Batavian rebellion pins his reserve legions on the Rhine. He can hope for no more troops from Britannia. Hispania and Gaul have nothing to offer. Caecina is taken and is in custody in Verona. Valens is still missing. Sooner or later Vitellius must surrender or flee.'

'Then I would be a fool to spurn this opportunity.' Primus waved Valerius over to where his campaign map was pinned to its wooden frame. 'Nothing but small garrisons between here and the Apennines.' His finger swept down the coast from the Padus to Fanum Fortunae. 'When they hear of Cremona's fall and the army's surrender, they will have no choice but to do likewise. The only substantial force between us and the capital is a detachment of the Praetorian Guard, here, at Narnia, perhaps equivalent to an understrength legion. Caecina tells me their commander's faith in Vitellius is shaken and he may be favourable to an accommodation.' Valerius listened with growing dismay. Experience told him where this was leading. Primus's next words confirmed it.

'I plan to negotiate with this Praetorian directly and from a position of strength. To do so, I need an emissary well versed in these arts.

Nero recognized your talents in this direction, as did Galba and Otho; it would be unwise of Marcus Antonius Primus to ignore them. When we reach Fanum you will ride ahead and make contact carrying an offer similar to that which netted us Caecina. If he can persuade his forces to lay down their arms he will have his life, his liberty and an honoured position when Vespasian is formally declared Emperor.' He must have seen the lack of enthusiasm in Valerius's face, because the flow of words died. 'You doubt your ability, Verrens? You feel that this mission is beyond your capacity?'

Valerius had slept less than two hours in the last forty-eight. More than anything, he doubted his ability to stay on his feet for much longer. He was certain he could reach Narnia, and quite possibly make contact with the Praetorian commander. What happened then was much less certain. Who was to say the situation would not have changed when he reached the city? Turncoats were, by their very nature, fickle. Officers could be enthusiastic for one course of action and their men for another. For the negotiator – or, he could not deny it, the spy – caught in between, the outcome might be perilous indeed. The truth was that he was weary of intrigue. Weary of war. But if he concluded the negotiations successfully Narnia would fall without a life being lost. And if Narnia fell, the way would be open to Rome, and Domitia Longina Corbulo. He managed a tired smile.

'It would be a poor sort of man who came here to rebuke you about what happened in Cremona and then refused your request to try to stop the same thing occurring again. A decent night's sleep and some food and I will be at your service.'

Primus nodded, and accepted Valerius's salute. When the one-armed tribune had left he continued to stare at the doorway. A strange character. All that honour and duty tearing at the inner man: it seemed unlikely he would survive the war. A pity.

The army that headed south on the Via Aemilia was very different from the one that had marched on Cremona with so much confidence. True to his word, Primus dispatched three of the Vitellian legions to Pannonia and Moesia to combat a growing threat from beyond the

Danuvius. He also freed captured Vitellian officers and sent them to carry word of his victory to Germania, Britannia, Gaul and Hispania. Yet the aftermath of Cremona had created a rift between Primus and his legates. The commanders of the three legions which hadn't been involved in the massacre were incensed at being tainted by the stench of burned flesh, rapine and looting that would for ever be linked with the victory. Aquila of the Thirteenth felt ashamed because he knew he should have done more to stop it. The result was that Primus's authority was dangerously undermined and the commanders' trust in their general, and his in them, badly eroded. Valerius witnessed the outcome when Primus sent substantial elements of the legions back to rest at Verona, along with their convalescent wounded. The cohorts and centuries he retained were all led by men in whom he had personal trust or interest. The legionaries understood what was happening and why. It was a moody and disunited force that formed up in order of march beside the Temple of Mephitis, the only building of any substance in Cremona left unscathed.

The situation wasn't improved with the arrival, when the column reached Bononia, of Plotius Grypus, the new legate of Seventh Claudia. An arrogant, opinionated patrician in his mid-thirties, Grypus used his connections to the full to further undermine Primus, who fumed, but could do little about it. Meanwhile, his army marched through a damp, often flooded landscape only recently ravaged by war. Primus had hoped to end the conflict without further bloodshed, but no one had informed his lately acquired allies, the marines of the Ravenna fleet. They had marched and countermarched across the flat coastal plain destroying Vitellian outposts and reserve units, including three cohorts of auxiliaries said to have accompanied Fabius Valens from Rome. Of Valens himself there was no sign. Primus's greatest fear was that the victor of First Bedriacum might reach Gaul or Germania, but, for the moment, he could only concentrate on his current campaign.

Primus incorporated the marines into his force and his cause was further boosted by the arrival of a new legion, the Eleventh Claudia, from Dalmatia. One by one, the towns of the Via Aemilia pledged their allegiance with little or no opposition. Only Fanum Fortunae put up much resistance, but the city's defenders agreed to surrender after a week.

With success, the general could have been forgiven for displaying his natural vanity, but whenever Valerius saw him the heavy brow was invariably lined with concern and the dark eyes troubled. Much of this was due to the stream of letters he received from Licinius Mucianus, a sign his successor was both not far away and very well informed. Fulvus, who still commanded the Third Gallica, revealed that they alternated between demands for more speed to take advantage before winter, and equally strident recommendations to delay so as not to out-run his supplies. The uncertainty made Primus uncharacteristically indecisive and was compounded by the conflicting advice he received from his legates, led by the smirking Grypus. The result was another week's delay at Fanum. Meanwhile, Valerius could only polish his sword and conceal his frustration as he waited for word of his mission. It was a relief when he finally received the summons from Primus. He ordered Serpentius to prepare their horses and see to supplies so they could leave without delay.

But when the guards showed him into the *praetorium*, the general looked up from his papers and said: 'I have decided to change your orders.'

Valerius barely had time to take in the general's words before he noticed a third man standing in the corner of the tent. He was dressed in a heavy cloak against the damp and his legs were spattered with mud as if he'd just completed a long ride. Primus's ever-present campaign map had drawn his eye and he had his back to Valerius, but the thick dark hair and stocky build stirred a memory.

'Quintus Petilius Cerialis brings news from Rome,' Primus con-tinued, and Cerialis turned with a grave nod, which Valerius returned.

How long had it been? Nine years, now, since they'd stood in a tent just like this on a hillside in Britannia. It wasn't an occasion Valerius cared to remind the newcomer of. Then, Cerialis had worn a legate's sculpted breastplate and looked what he was: a man who had just lost half a legion. His face had been clouded by the shadow of defeat and the possibility of execution. Now, though dressed in a motley collection of armour and with an auxiliary's cavalry *spatha* at his belt, he fidgeted with nervous energy. The dark hair was shot with grey and the waist a little thicker, but otherwise he seemed physically unchanged. He was Vespasian's son-in-law, married to Titus's sister.

'The commander at Narnia has been replaced,' Primus explained, 'and the Praetorians reinforced with a further nine cohorts, including auxiliaries, and an unknown number of cavalry. Therefore I judge your negotiations unlikely to succeed . . .'

'I agree,' Cerialis interrupted, prompting a glance of irritation only a student of human nature would have noticed. Clearly, despite the affable introduction the general was not completely comfortable with his highly placed visitor. 'The new prefects are loyal to Vitellius. You would be placing your head on the executioner's block.'

Primus resumed. 'Cerialis escaped from the city three weeks ago, and put together an irregular cohort of cavalry, former legionary officers for the most part. He has been doing what he can to advance his father-in-law's cause. He came over the pass this morning.'

Valerius looked up sharply. Cerialis had come from Rome. Domitia Longina Corbulo was in Rome. Could it be that Fortuna was favouring them?

'You will travel to Rome.' His heart beat like thunder in his chest as Primus confirmed his hopes. 'Alone or with your servant, whichever is your preference. The situation in the capital is complicated, but we believe it has the potential to be exploited . . .'

'When I left the city,' Cerialis interrupted his host again, 'Vitellius was discomfited by his generals' lack of aggressive spirit. Only the strength of his wife Galeria and the ruthlessness of his brother Lucius keep his shaking hands on the reins of the Empire. By now he knows about the Batavian revolt on the Rhenus and, if he hasn't already, he will soon hear of his legions' defeat at Cremona. His world is crumbling. Only by giving up the purple can he save himself.'

'And his family,' Primus pointed out helpfully.

'That is not the Flavian way,' Cerialis sniffed. 'His advisers – particularly his brother – will urge him to fight on while he still has hope, however unlikely, of a favourable outcome. We believe he is open to other possibilities. My kinsman, Titus Flavius Sabinus, retains his position as urban prefect and has already made approaches through an intermediary . . .'

'These are the delicate negotiations of which Vespasian writes,' Primus interjected. 'But there is a question of trust. Put baldly, Vitellius would not trust Sabinus to clear out the city sewers.'

Cerialis smiled at the irony of this man preaching about trust and Primus had the grace to look embarrassed. 'Naturally, Vitellius would prefer not to have Sabinus as urban prefect with the *vigiles* and urban cohorts at his command, but he cannot afford to alienate my kinsman's allies. He has given Sabinus every opportunity to leave the city and is suspicious of his motives for staying. The truth is that Sabinus is frightened to take the risk, but Vitellius would never believe that of a man who has led a legion. Whatever promises Vespasian makes are immediately viewed with suspicion because of their source. If, however, the same approaches were made by a man in whom Vitellius has trust, a man of patent honesty and integrity, perhaps even a friend, the result might be very different.'

Valerius felt the intense gaze of the two men on his back as he walked to the campaign map. He traced his finger from Fanum Fortunae, across the Apennines and down through the rugged valleys on the western side. All the way to Rome. 'Vitellius once tried to have me killed. What makes you think I can convince him?'

Cerialis opened his mouth to speak, but the voice was that of Marcus Antonius Primus. 'Because you are probably the only friend he has left.'

Valerius looked from one man to the other. He knew Primus was right, but he still had suspicions about his motives. 'Very well,' he said eventually. 'But first you must convince me that Aulus Vitellius can trust Vespasian.' He allowed his voice to harden. 'I will not be duped into betraying him.'

Cerialis recoiled at the implied insult to his family, but Primus didn't even blink.

'My friend Cerialis has discussed the Emperor-in-waiting's terms with Sabinus,' he insisted. 'Vitellius and his family will go into exile somewhere suitably remote, probably on the island of Sicilia. They will be treated not as criminals but as "guests of the Emperor", free to come and go on the island as they please. Guaranteed their safety as long as Vitellius pledges to have nothing to do with politics. When he reaches the proper age, Vitellius's son will embark on the *cursus honorum* with Vespasian's support and protection.'

A hundred million sesterces would be available for the family's upkeep, Cerialis laughed; even Vitellius was unlikely to be able to squander such a sum. In return, all Vitellius had to do was surrender himself and his family to Sabinus and the city prefect would ensure his safety until Primus arrived to garrison Rome. No reprisals would be carried out against any Roman citizen who had supported Vitellius, unless those citizens were found to have broken the Empire's laws. No soldier would be hurt as long as they laid down their arms before the Flavian forces supporting Vespasian entered the city.

'Antonius tells me you have met my father-in law?' Cerialis asked.

'In Alexandria two years ago,' Valerius confirmed.

'Then you know he is a man of integrity and honour,' the patrician said earnestly. 'He will not break his word.'

As he nodded his final agreement, Valerius felt as if a great burden had been lifted from his shoulders. He had done what he could to protect his old friend, but he couldn't deceive himself. He would have agreed to carry whatever terms Vespasian dictated. Because he was going to Rome, and in Rome a condemned man would find Domitia Longina Corbulo and make his offer.

XXXII

When Aulus Vitellius Germanicus Augustus returned to the Domus
Aurea from his villa south of the Tiber, the paralysing shock of the
Batavian revolt had faded. In truth, once he had considered the odds
– the main elements of five elite legions against a rabble of barbarian
mercenaries – his initial panic had seemed foolish. Yes, there may
have been setbacks, but Flaccus had sent word of new advances and
a concentration of forces that would bring ultimate victory. Even if
the Rhenus legions could only hold Civilis in check, Vitellius would
soon be able to free one or two legions from Cremona. He intended
their march north to herald such a reckoning that the Batavians
would remember his name and tremble for twenty generations. The
thought pleased him so much he decided to share it with Galeria. By
now Valens would be with the army and he had great trust in Valens.
With the enormous force under his command he might have already
pushed the rebel forces of Marcus Antonius Primus back past Aquileia.

He waddled along the corridor with his curious short-legged gait.
When he reached his private apartments two of his personal guards
opened the doors, though he'd become so used to their presence that
he barely registered them. His freedman Asiaticus came running as he
flopped on to a padded couch. 'Send for my lady Galeria,' he ordered.
Was it his imagination or did the Greek look paler than usual?

'My lady is visiting her sister, lord. She was unaware of your return, or . . .'

'No matter,' Vitellius said dismissively. 'Arrange a banquet for tonight. A whole boar, I think, for a centre piece, a pair of haunches of venison, the usual birds, an assortment of fish,' something rumbled in his stomach and he frowned, 'but no catfish or moray eel. I have had a surfeit of catfish and eel of late and I find they loosen me. Invite Saturninus and Trebellius and make sure they and their wives are seated together. It's always entertaining to see two men who despise each other trying to make small talk. And Sabinus . . .' Vitellius hesitated. Should he invite Sabinus? His informers had been hearing ever more interesting and disturbing rumours about Sabinus. It would be of use to make a few polite enquiries face to face, perhaps drop a few hints, but, no, the danger of provoking an outburst, whether a denial or some kind of stand, was too great. A crisis must be avoided. When Valens had won his victory, that was the time to deal with Sabinus. 'No, not Sabinus. Send a note to old Senator Corvinus instead; he always appreciates a free meal . . . Have you eaten a bad oyster, Asiaticus?'

'No, lord. It is . . .'

'What, man?'

Asiaticus closed his eyes and the words tumbled out. 'There is a person, a soldier I believe . . . he has been here several times seeking an interview but the lady refused him entry. He is ragged and much wounded.' The Greek swallowed. 'He says he has come from Cremona.'

All the breath seemed to be driven from Vitellius's lungs at the word Cremona. What should he do? If Galeria had turned the petitioner away she must have had good reason. Yet the man persisted. A soldier, wounded and from Cremona – perhaps seeking an early pension, or an Imperial grant? But if that were his aim could he not have found another route? At worst he would have nothing of value to tell. At best, some news of Valens' manoeuvrings. And if Vitellius refused, he knew he would only be plagued by doubts. 'Very well,' he decided. 'I will see him in the receiving room, but make sure it is well guarded. And first bring me a brace of roast quail and a flask of the best Caecuban.'

Normally, he would have relished the thought of a juicy, well-flavoured quail, but something had taken the edge off his appetite.

An hour later he sat on the padded cushions of the great golden throne as a small, almost shambling figure limped through the doors, dwarfed by the vast scale of the receiving room. Generally, this space would be filled with nervous, expectant faces – senators, traders, ambassadors, praetors and *quaestores* from all over the Empire, every one seeking advancement or enrichment – but he'd suspended the usual mass audiences during the crisis. Half a century of his guard lined the walls, each with a hand on the hilt of his *gladius*. Two more stood protectively at the base of the steps with their swords already drawn. The petitioner advanced towards the throne, and Vitellius stifled a giggle of – yes, almost hysterical – laughter. All this for one little man in a torn military tunic. A little man attempting to march despite his trailing leg. A little man stooped with pain and with bloodstained bandages on his head and right arm. Yet a little man who still managed to exude a certain wounded – that giggle again – dignity.

'Who seeks an audience with his Emperor?' Vitellius demanded when the bandaged soldier stood below him.

'Julius Agrestis,' the voice was a hoarse croak, but still managed to exude pride as its owner recited his lineage, 'of the Horatia voting tribe, centurion of the fourth century, Second cohort, Legio XXI Rapax, twenty years' service, come from Cremona with urgent news and a plea for his Emperor.'

'Your Emperor welcomes a soldier who has served so long and so diligently.' Vitellius managed a benign smile despite the fact that his heart was thundering fit to crack his ribs. Urgent? What news could be so important that he hadn't already heard it from his own generals? 'What is this *urgent* news from Cremona where my legions wait, poised and ready to do battle with the pawns of the rebel Vespasian?'

The other man's head came up and from his perch above Vitellius saw Julius Agrestis's eyes widen. 'You have not heard?' the centurion whispered. 'The battle is already fought . . . fought and lost.'

The smile froze on Vitellius's face. 'A local engagement. A minor setback.'

Agrestis shook his head. 'Not a setback. A defeat. Thousands, tens of thousands, dead. The city burns.'

'Liar!' The scream that echoed from the walls froze every man in place as Galeria Fundana swept through the great double doors, her face pale with fury and her diminutive frame visibly shaking. 'Liar!' she repeated more loudly still.

Julius Agrestis flinched at the charge, but when he turned back to Vitellius he drew himself up to his full height despite the obvious pain of his wounds. 'It is no lie, Aulus Vitellius Germanicus Augustus. I fought for you at Bedriacum and I fought for you again at Cremona. My century took a cohort standard in the battle for the Via Postumia when the bodies of our comrades lay as thick on the ground as walnuts in October. I suffered these wounds as we stood on the rampart at Cremona and held off the First cohort of the Seventh Galbiana until the defence collapsed elsewhere. I . . .'

He flinched at the click of tiny feet marching across the marble floor. 'Why are you listening to him, husband?' Galeria howled. 'Arrest this traitor.'

Vitellius had listened with horrified fascination as the litany of defeat froze something inside him. Could it be? He held up his hand to silence his wife. 'When did this happen?' he asked, surprised at the calmness of his own voice.

'Ten days ago, lord.'

Ten days? The Emperor shook his head and the great jowl quivered. 'But surely I must have heard before now. Why would my commanders not send me word?'

'Your commanders are either dead by their own hand,' Agrestis's voice shook, 'or marching to Moesia and Pannonia with their legions, subject to the orders of Titus Flavius Vespasian.' He swayed and might have fallen, but no one moved so much as a finger to aid him. Somehow, by a huge effort of will, he managed to stay upright. 'On the second day of our captivity I managed to escape. I rode through night and day until my strength gave out on the road near Falerii. While I recovered, I sent four messengers with word of our defeat . . .'

'Spies and traitors and I will serve you as I served them.' The maniacal screech froze Agrestis in mid-sentence and Vitellius flinched at the violence in his wife's voice.

'You kept them from me?'

Galeria's narrow features took on a look of murderous certainty. 'You should not have to deal with spies, traitors, liars and madmen.' With the last word she shot a poisonous glance at the wounded centurion.

'Lies?' Julius Agrestis responded incredulously. 'Why do you think I have come here?'

'It is the enemy's policy to plague the populace and their Emperor with disinformation,' Vitellius said gently, wondering at the strange haze that seemed to have cloaked his mind. What had happened to his wife? She had always been strong-willed, but to his certain knowledge she would not harm a house spider. Yet he didn't doubt that she'd had these messengers killed to keep them from him. He groped in his mind for the full implication of what Agrestis had said, but it eluded him. He noticed that Galeria's eyes shone bright as diamonds and he saw something he had never thought to see there. In that instant he knew he must support his wife or send her beyond the brink of irrecoverable madness.

A cry of outrage penetrated his thoughts. 'I saw them surrender. I saw the fire and heard the screams as Cremona burned.' Agrestis was raving now and in his detached state Vitellius pondered that Galeria was not the only inhabitant of the room on the edge of insanity. 'I saw the Fifth Alaudae march away to far-off Pannonia,' the centurion shouted, froth dripping from his lower lip. 'You want the truth?' He hauled one-handed at the bandage on his head to reveal a terrible sword cut that must have almost penetrated bone, then attacked the stained cloth at his shoulder to show where the point of a *pilum* had pierced muscle. 'My wounds are my truth, Aulus Vitellius Germanicus Augustus, and this is the truth.' In the same instant, Vitellius heard the swords of his guard hiss from their scabbards and Galeria scream 'Why was he not searched?', and saw the glint of the knife Julius Agrestis had drawn from his tunic. The two guards at the base of the stairs moved forward, the swords coming up. Too late. Julius Agrestis, centurion of the fourth century, Second cohort, Legio XXI Rapax, plunged the knife point into his breast and toppled forward with a shriek on to the marble floor. Vitellius sat unmoving as a great lake of blood slowly oozed across the polished marble tiles. Galeria was still howling obscenities he had never heard from her lips as the *optio* in charge of the guard shouted an order and four soldiers rushed forward to pick up the still twitching body and carry it from the room.

Gradually, Galeria's screams faded. Vitellius closed his eyes and cradled his head in his hands. When he'd recovered his composure, he whispered an order and the guard formed up nervously and marched out, their iron-studded sandals clattering rhythmically on the tiles, leaving him alone with his wife.

He made his way cautiously down the steps. 'Come, my dear.' Galeria shivered like a trapped deer as he put his great arm gently round her shoulder. 'I know you did what you thought best, but you must always remember that I am Emperor. Do you understand?'

A single convulsive sob escaped her, but he felt her nod. With a heart as heavy as the great head of the golden statue in the atrium he led her towards the doorway, his feet carefully avoiding the splashes of Julius Agrestis's blood.

XXXIII

Gaius Fabius Valens held his cloak tighter about him as a white-capped wave crashed into the bow and washed the length of the deck of the slim Liburnian galley. The rough conditions didn't concern him. He'd always been a good sailor, and the ship's captain assured him the storm would soon blow out. Oddly, he felt an unlikely confidence. Unlikely, because only ten men were still with him, all that remained of the staff and escort provided by the Emperor. Despite the lack of numbers he was certain he could form the nucleus of an army among Vitellius's loyal allies in Narbonnensis. If he could reach Massilia the legions of Gaul would flock to the banner of the true Emperor.

Valens had sailed north from Pisa hoping to outflank the Flavian forces of Marcus Antonius Primus and re-join his legions in the Padus valley by way of Liguria. But when he'd reached Portus Herculis on the Ligurian coast his old friend Maturus, procurator of the region, had urged caution. It was here he heard the news that Caecina had turned traitor and the battle for Cremona had already been fought and lost. Within an hour of the awful revelation the stomach gripes had returned and he was forced to take to his bed, unable even to think. Two days later he had recovered enough to be able to eat with his host, and reached his decision. He would travel on to Narbonnensis and put together a force strong enough to take the offensive, perhaps with reinforcements from Germania. When he was ready, he would retrace his steps of the previous spring. With good fortune and some resolve from the Emperor, Primus's doubtless exhausted and short-handed legions would be crushed between two armies of fresh troops.

Maturus had tried to dissuade him, suggesting instead that he travel immediately to Germania, where the loyalty of the legions was not in doubt. The suggestion was tempting, but Valens knew that he was too weak to undertake such a journey. There was too great a risk that he would be trapped in Germania by winter and in no state to dictate events in Italia. No, it must be Massilia.

'The Stoichades.' The captain pointed to a faint green blur towards the coast of Gaul. 'We will be in Massilia before nightfall, general.'

The motion of the ship made Valens stagger, but he kept his balance and a wave of relief flowed through him. The game was not over yet, with Fortuna's aid . . .

'Two sails coming up fast in our wake, captain.' The shout from the lookout sent a ripple of ice running down Valens' spine.

'Your orders, sir?'

Gaius Fabius Valens couldn't meet the captain's eyes. 'You must do what you think best.' He did not even trouble to look back.

A week later he lay in the damp chill of a half-autumn, half-winter morning and hugged the salt-stained cloak tight about his body. Alerted by the noise of approaching footsteps, he waited for the plate that would hold his daily meal of thin porridge. But when the cell door opened there was no plate. He looked up, his eyes straining against the low sun of a new dawn.

'How glad I am to meet you at last,' his visitor said. 'There is a duty I must ask of you.'

Valerius sensed the eyes of his companion studying him as he looked out across the mist-shrouded peaks of the Apennine hills that still barred his way to Rome. He turned in the saddle to meet the gaze of Quintus Petilius Cerialis.

'This is where we must part.' The aristocrat reached across to touch the wooden hand. 'I would ride south with you, but, good as they are, a few hundred worn-out old soldiers on horseback are no match for true cavalry. May the gods look favourably on your mission.' He hesitated. 'I also thank you for not bringing up our previous meeting. Yes,' he smiled at the other man, 'I recall it well, Gaius Valerius Verrens, Hero of Rome, but it is not a time I remember with any joy. If the gods will it, we will meet again in more auspicious circumstances, and perhaps I will have erased that particular stain. In Rome.'

Valerius couldn't resist the man's infectious enthusiasm. 'In Rome,' he agreed.

Serpentius rode to Valerius's side as Cerialis and his escort took the western fork in the trail and began to wind their way down the mountain. 'What do you think?'

'I think we're putting our heads back between the lion's jaws.'

'Then what are we waiting for?' The Spaniard grinned and put his heels to his mount's ribs. 'Hades is full of old friends who are looking forward to seeing us.' Valerius followed down the winding path with the former gladiator's laughter ringing in his ears.

They travelled in civilian clothes, as master and servant, their swords hidden but close to hand, and with everything they needed for the journey in cloth bags tied to their saddles. The road was familiar and Serpentius knew all its perils and advantages, but circumstances had changed since they'd ridden north to find Vitellius all those months ago. It seemed every farm and hamlet they passed had been devastated by the war. At first, the destruction puzzled Valerius. This was Vitellian territory and his supporters farmed these slopes: why burn them out? Serpentius supplied the answer an hour later when he drew the horses aside into the shelter of the trees and they watched from hiding as a little column of foot soldiers stumbled past weighed down with plunder.

'Auxiliaries.' Valerius identified the men by their chain vests and exotic headgear.

'Not now.' His companion sounded unusually thoughtful. 'No officers and no discipline. They're bandits and deserters. All they're after is enough loot to see them home, wherever home is.' He sniffed the air. 'We'll see the evidence soon, I reckon.' A burned-out farmstead a mile up the track confirmed his prediction. It was one of many they'd passed, but Valerius turned his eyes away from the sight of the still-smouldering, blackened corpses nailed to the doors. Would it never end?

They bypassed Iguvium without trouble, but just before darkness fell the Spaniard reined in at the top of a ridge and pointed to the valley below. Valerius looked though the branches and saw the black soil of new-dug ditches and piled earth banks that were the unmistakable signs of an encamped army. That night they stayed alert in their forest hide, but when the sun came up Serpentius announced the camp was empty and the threat past. Relieved, they broke their fast on bread and water before inspecting the temporary fortifications stretching across the valley mouth.

'A place this size would have accommodated two legions,' Valerius estimated. Every legionary marching camp was built to a standard design and he could read the signs as easily as any piece of parchment. 'I wonder why they left? This would have been a perfect place to stop Primus.' He pointed to the narrow cut where the Via Flaminia emerged from the hills. 'They could have bottled him up in the pass for a month and given him the option of retreating or freezing to death when the snows came.' He shook his head. 'I can't understand why they're not still here.' A discarded piece of horse brass caught his eye and he chewed his lip as he studied the distinctive emblem of the Praetorian cavalry. 'Only a fool would abandon a position like this.'

'Or a traitor,' Serpentius suggested. 'Maybe Vitellius doesn't have as many friends as he thinks.'

Still puzzled by the conundrum they rode on, warily following the muddy trail left by thousands of marching soldiers and always on the lookout for cavalry patrols. Bypassing Spoletium, they climbed into the hills through a narrow, winding passage in the tree-lined slopes. Around mid-afternoon Serpentius left the road without warning and led the way into a grove of trees beside it. He signalled Valerius to dismount and beckoned him to a raised outcrop.

'See?' Serpentius nodded to the other side of the valley, but Valerius could see nothing but trees. 'There, under the big oak halfway up the slope.' Slowly the image came into focus. The glint of a spear point. Two men on horseback – no, three . . . 'And more in the trees behind them,' the Spaniard forestalled his question.

'We can't kill them all.' Valerius waited for Serpentius to respond. In a straight fight it was always the one-handed tribune who led, but in a situation like this he would be a fool not to defer to the Spaniard's experience.

'I'll go ahead on foot. See what we're up against,' Serpentius said. 'We might be able to find a way past without troubling them.'

Two hours later he returned, sweat staining his tunic and mud on his face. They crouched in the lee of the outcrop where he'd left Valerius. The Roman handed his friend a water skin and Serpentius drank deeply. When he'd had his fill he belched and reported what he'd seen in a harsh whisper. 'We're here.' He drew two lines to indicate the valley and planted a twig in their approximate position. 'Where the valley opens out there's a town – I presume it must be Narnia – perched on a hilltop on the far side of the plain. You can see from the cooking fires that there's a big military encampment in front of it and the ground between is crawling with auxiliary cavalry.'

'Our friends from yesterday?'

'At least a full legion,' the Spaniard acknowledged. 'And this time it looks as if they're here to stay.'

'We could try to trick our way through. It worked before,' Valerius suggested, but his voice lacked conviction.

Serpentius shook his head. 'They're alert as cats. There's an outpost by the road with an officer questioning everybody going in or out of the valley.' He hesitated. 'If we wait till dark I think I might be able to get us past.'

They rested until the sun went down, but kept the horses saddled in case a patrol stumbled on their hideout. Both mounts were cavalry trained to stay silent, but Serpentius wrapped a cloth around their jaws just to be sure. The Spaniard took off his hobnailed sandals and Valerius followed suit, stuffing them into the bag tied to his saddle. When they were ready, Serpentius set off, leading his horse by the reins. Valerius took hold of the front horse's tail and followed suit.

The darkness was unnerving to man and beast alike, but Serpentius kept up a constant whispered monologue that calmed his mount and her mood transmitted itself to Valerius's horse. Somehow, he seemed to have memorized every rut and pothole. At one point they heard the murmur of voices and Valerius held his breath, as if the act would make him invisible as they passed the resting cavalry scouts. After what seemed like an eternity the looming blackness of the tree canopy faded and they emerged thankfully into a less oppressive darkness. Valerius sensed the horse in front angle to the left and, after a few steps, the compact firmness of the paved road changed to mud. 'You can put your shoes on now,' a voice whispered from the gloom.

A little later Valerius noticed the dull glow away to their right that must be the encampment the Spaniard had pinpointed earlier. He remembered the horse brass with the Praetorian symbol. Not a legion, but enough Praetorian cohorts to form a force of a similar size. Normally, the Guard seldom left Rome, and then only to protect the Emperor on campaign, but the times were not normal. Vitellius had replaced Otho's supporters with his own officers and men from the German legions. They would be veteran soldiers, not the posing peacocks who once strutted around Rome in their black and silver finery.

Keeping close to the foot of the mountains, the two men skirted a substantial town before returning to the saddle. Twice the Spaniard halted where a soft flicker in the darkness marked a campfire not quite damped and twice he led them unerringly away from danger. 'One more pass,' he whispered. One more pass. Valerius knew what he meant. One more pass and they were clear.

At dawn they re-joined the road, happy that the worst was behind them and protected by their guise of merchant and servant. They passed military units marching north while yellow-cloaked Imperial messengers galloped back and forth with dispatches. But the country-side around was peaceful, as yet untouched by war. A few miles ahead Valerius paused at a crossroads where he recognized the silhouette of a familiar whaleback hill. He nodded to himself and, despite Serpentius's objections, insisted on turning off. They crossed the Tiber at one of the few fords and soon joined the Via Salaria, the old salt route that approached Rome from the east.

'Perhaps the fates have given me this one last opportunity to make my peace with Olivia.' Valerius tried to explain his decision. 'Just because we get into Rome doesn't mean we will get back out again.' Serpentius let him ride a little way ahead so his friend couldn't see him cross his fingers to make the sign against evil.

Another few hours brought them to the gates of a large estate where twin pillars of golden sandstone were topped by a pair of Mycenaean lions. Valerius wondered idly who occupied the grand villa now. It had once belonged to his old mentor, the philosopher Seneca, but on Seneca's death Nero had given the estate to Offonius Tigellinus, his torturer in chief. Tigellinus, in turn, had reaped a less welcome reward, forced to commit suicide on the orders of Marcus Salvius Otho. An unlucky place. They continued down the salt road to a much less imposing gateway. In fact, Valerius barely recognized the entrance to the family estate at Fidenae. Someone had put up a brush fence along the boundary of the Verrens' land and a rough barrier blocked the space beneath the crumbling stone arch.

'It seems we are in for a warm welcome.' Serpentius's curled lip said it all.

But the precautions stirred a memory and Valerius laughed as he dismounted to haul back the flimsy barrier. He noted a flash of movement in the olive grove to the left of the gate and nodded appreciatively. 'Tell me what you see,' he asked the Spaniard as they rode on. 'But for the gods' sake keep your hand away from your sword.'

Serpentius grunted what might have been agreement or a mortal insult, but his eyes surreptitiously scanned the tree-lined hills beside the worn track. 'Four or five men with bows in a camouflaged earth redoubt amongst the trees to our right,' he murmured. 'Another to the left twenty paces ahead. An ambush. They must have known we were coming long before the first runner we saw.'

Valerius nodded. He didn't have the Spaniard's unfailing eye for a potential threat, but he'd hoped they would be there. He guessed a third position would be sited somewhere close that even Serpentius hadn't been able to detect, and he grinned at the thought.

'What's so funny?' the former gladiator growled.

Valerius slapped him on the shoulder. 'It's good to be home.'

As they turned the corner he felt the breath catch in his throat as he recognized the long, low outline of the villa, a sprawling single-storey range around a central courtyard. The emotion had its roots in childhood days spent among the dusty vines and olive trees, chasing sparrows and pulling weeds; a contentment linked not only to the land, but the living things in it, and on it. It was the familiar sensation of the warm air against his cheeks and the soft eternal buzz of insects in his ears.

This was home.

But home, it seemed, was not as he remembered it.

When they entered the courtyard a stocky man in a brown home-spun tunic stepped out from the shadows holding a spear. Serpentius automatically went for his sword, but Valerius laid his hand on the Spaniard's arm. In the same moment perhaps twenty more men appeared, armed with whatever weapons they'd been able to find: short sickles, knives, a few spears, even one or two swords that had seen better days. Valerius studied them, seemingly unconcerned. Slaves and servants for the most part, with a few contracted labourers and the estate's craftsmen. Their faces wore a uniform look of determination, but one or two shifted uneasily in the silence.

'We had thought to impress you,' a female voice said lightly.

Laughing with delight, Valerius turned to the villa doorway. 'And I am impressed,' he lied. His sister Olivia looked more beautiful than ever. A few years ago she'd been struck down by some wasting disease and for months her life had hung in the balance. Now she was pink-cheeked and cheerful, with an aura of rustic good health. She'd put on weight, beneath the *stola* . . . His eyes widened a little and she tilted her head and smiled.

'Yes, Valerius.' Her hands went protectively to the slight bulge in her stomach as she confirmed his suspicion and her eyes went to the stocky figure with the spear.

For a moment he wasn't certain how he should react. His father would have been outraged: how could she have done this to him? But Lucius had been dead these seven years, and Valerius had scorned the old man's straight-backed patrician certainty, which would have him bristling with offended dignity at the first opportunity. Yet in the final year of his life his father had embraced the outlawed sect led by Petrus, the so-called Rock of Christus. Undoubtedly, a man could change.

With a nod of reassurance to Serpentius, he dismounted and marched purposefully towards the spearman. The man's knuckles whitened as his grip on the shaft tightened and the point rose a fraction so it would take only the slightest adjustment to send it through Valerius's throat.

'It seems I must congratulate you, Lupergos.' He said it gravely, struggling to suppress a smile. 'The estate has not looked so fine since my father was in the Senate and Granta and Cronus ran the place.' Granta and Cronus were his father's ancient freedmen, no doubt hovering nervously somewhere out of sight. Lupergos, son of an Etruscan farmer, acted as the estate manager, and, Olivia had let him know on his last visit, her husband in all but name. The spear point dropped, the challenge faded from the dark eyes and his broad peasant face cracked into a shy grin.

'It is a fine estate.'

'More fertile than when I last visited, certainly.' The laughter started low in his belly and soon Lupergos joined in as the slaves and servants looked on with shy smiles.

'Enough of this foolishness,' Olivia scolded from the steps. 'Valerius, you must be hungry; you look as thin as one of Granta's chickens. Come, I have new-baked bread, and Lupergos trapped a pair of hares in the far meadow yesterday. Serpentius, will you join us?'

'Perhaps later, lady.' The Spaniard bowed in the saddle. 'First I will see if your protectors can actually use these pointed sticks and farm implements in earnest, or if they're just for show.'

Valerius smiled at the disconcerted faces as Serpentius slipped from the saddle and gestured for the men to follow him. 'I fear they are in for a more exacting and much less pleasant hour than I am,' he said.

'A fine display, Lupergos, but you should never show all your strength.'

'Ah,' the Etruscan said with a chuckle. 'But you didn't see the ten archers hidden in the trees with arrows aimed at your back.'

'We always have two slaves watching the road.' Lupergos tugged at his ear as he explained the reception Valerius had received while they ate. 'It is their responsibility to warn of soldiers or armed gangs, but they also have a special instruction to look out for a one-armed man.'

'You took my advice, I see?'

'Three fortresses on the track to the villa,' the Etruscan agreed with a wry smile. Valerius was pleased to hear no evidence of complacency in his voice. It seemed Lupergos was perfectly aware of the limitations of his little force, which could only be to the good. 'They're sited as you suggested with fields of fire to attack any intruder from all angles. Archers to cause the initial casualties and spearmen to cover the retreat. Food and water in the limestone caves by the river at the bottom of the south slope. The instructor you sent to train the bowmen knows his business and we practise arms at least once a day.' He grinned as they were interrupted by a yelp of pain from outside the window as Serpentius emphasized the need to keep the spear point low. 'Though some are less adept than others.'

Valerius took a sip of the familiar, earthy estate wine and tore off another piece of bread. Fourteen months and two Emperors had passed since his previous visit. He knew it was a gamble to teach slaves how to fight, but he trusted Lupergos's ability to choose his men wisely. Some instinct had told him it was a chance worth taking, and the burned-out farms and villas they'd seen on the way south had proved him right. With Fortuna's aid they would never be needed and the slaves could be rewarded either materially or with their freedom.

'We won't stand and fight, of course,' Lupergos continued. 'We'll aim to leave enough valuables on show to satisfy any raider. They may burn the house,' his eyes sought Olivia's and he unconsciously reached out to touch the swelling under her skirts, 'but it is the people who make Fidenae what it is.' He nodded grimly. 'We have even more reason now to protect what is ours.'

Valerius felt humbled by the look of loving affection his sister gave the Etruscan. Would any woman ever look at him that way? Domitia loved him, he had no doubt of it, but their love had been a series of transient affairs, never allowed to take root. That look in Olivia's eyes was proof that love, like anything of permanence, required time and nurturing to make it so. Olivia read his expression. 'Lupergos has plans for a new house.' She smiled proudly. 'Perhaps you would like to see them later.' She hesitated, and the shale dark eyes turned knowing. 'You were never the type of brother to make social visits, Valerius.'

There was a question in the statement, and he answered it. 'We are on our way to Rome, though I doubt we will be given any kind of welcome when we reach the city.'

Olivia nodded understanding, but she pressed no further, aware her brother was something more than a soldier, but sensible enough not to ask what. They discussed the political situation, since it affected them all. Valerius told of the Flavian victory at Cremona, but not its aftermath, emphasizing Primus's hopes that the war was already won and there would be no further fighting. He saw a shadow fall across Lupergos's face. 'You do not think this is the case?'

'All we want is for this insanity to be over.' The estate manager glanced at Olivia and she gave a little nod of agreement. Lupergos began hesitantly, as if he knew that what he was about to say wasn't what Valerius wanted to hear, but his voice grew in confidence as he outlined the situation. 'I am in Rome twice a week, selling our surplus produce on market day, and I tell you this: Vespasian has little support among the people. They may make fun of Vitellius's habits and his lifestyle, but Aulus Vitellius Germanicus Augustus has been a good Emperor for Romans who count their wealth in tens and not millions. Despite the fighting, bread is still cheap, and he is seen as wise and fair. To them, he is the legitimate occupant of the throne, appointed and approved by the Senate and people of Rome. And he still has teeth. Fabius Valens is said to be raising a new army in Gaul and Hispania. The Guard too, the men of the Germania legions who hailed him Emperor on the Rhenus, continue to support him. They say they will fight to the death and that they will never abandon him,' his eyes locked with Valerius's so the Roman understood the significance of his next words, 'but there is also an unspoken understanding that *he* will never be allowed to abandon them. They risked everything to put him where he is and they've yet to see their proper reward. If Vitellius is deposed, they believe the new Emperor will serve them as he did their predecessors, cast out and impoverished at best.'

Valerius listened with growing alarm. He'd never been deceived into thinking that this would be a simple task, but there'd always seemed a genuine possibility of persuading Vitellius to give up his throne peacefully. This talk of fighting to the death might be just that, mere words, but Lupergos's story had the ring of truth. Valerius reckoned he could discount Valens, at least for the moment – the earliest the Vitellian general could be on the march was in the spring – but would he be able to overcome Vitellius's fear of his own Guard?

More gossip. Marines of the Misenc fleet had mutinied and were forming a new legion to help oust Vitellius. The Emperor's brother Lucius had put down a rebellion in the south and burned the city of Tarracina, putting thousands to death. Batavian tribesmen on the Rhenus had concluded an alliance with their cousins beyond the river and Julius Civilis had vowed to march on Rome. True or false, no one at the table could know. Valerius understood stories like these often had a foundation in truth, but for the moment none of that could concern him.

'You say you go to Rome twice a week, Lupergos,' he said carefully. 'I doubt you are able to come and go as you please?'

'No,' the Etruscan agreed. 'Security at the city gates is heavy and you will not enter without an up-to-date pass. Every cart is emptied down to the boards and thoroughly searched. I doubt you could get a sheet of parchment into the city undetected. Once you are inside the Emperor's agents are everywhere, and the Guard has a presence on every corner.'

An idea began to form. 'When is the next market day?'

'Tomorrow.'

XXXIV

'Let's see your pass.' The gate guard at the Porta Collina had been on duty most of the night and his temper wasn't improved by either the hour or the weather. His comrades stood around stupid with lack of sleep, hating the chill December rain that worked its way through their cloaks no matter how much lanolin was in the wool, and the country farmers who forced them to stand out in it.

The tall peasant driving the bullock cart had already been stopped twice in the untidy scatter of suburbs outside the city walls. He sniffed and spat on the road at the guard's feet before reaching inside his tunic to withdraw a wooden token on a leather thong. The soldier studied the pass with a sour expression before carving another notch into it with his knife. 'Only another five days on this. Make sure you apply to the *quaestor's* office for a replacement or I'll take pleasure in kicking your sorry arse back to wherever it came from next time I see you.'

Still grumbling, the guard rummaged through the muddy vegetables and damp sacks of fruit. Meanwhile, his watch commander stared at the peasant and his companion, a rangy, unkempt figure with a pronounced stoop who had been walking alongside the cart leading an ancient-looking pig on a frayed length of rope. Without warning the commander marched forward and hauled back the driver's hood to reveal a hard, angular face with the pink line of an old scar running from eye to lip. There was just the slightest hesitation as the man met his gaze before dropping his eyes, but the surly defiance had already registered. 'Get off the cart,' he said brusquely. The peasant complied readily enough, but the rest of the watch straightened, sensing trouble. They were always happy to meet any show of resistance with a flurry of blows and kicks. 'You didn't get that scar working on any farm, friend. A sword did that, and I'd wager it's not the only one you could show me, eh? A soldier's scar. But you're not old enough to have completed your service. So you've either been discharged or you're a deserter . . .'

'All I want is to get these vegetables to market,' the driver grumbled. 'I . . .'

'Interrupt me again and I'll make you eat this.' The officer poked the club he carried into the peasant's chest. 'Where have you come from?'

'The Verrens estate, out by Fidenae. I do a bit of work on the farm on the faraway slope. Caradoc here, he's just a slave not quite right in the head that looks after the pigs. Please, master, if I don't get . . .'

'You won't get through this gate until I see your discharge papers,' the watch commander insisted.

'But that's not a thing a man carries about with him,' the driver pleaded. 'If I don't get this stuff to market early I won't get a decent price for it, and then what'll happen? Yes, I've served, I was in the First Italica, but they didn't want me any more.'

'And why was that?'

The man flicked his cloak aside and the officer stepped back, his hand automatically going for his sword.

'No place in a shield wall for a one-handed legionary.' The peasant shrugged and held out the mottled purple stump of his right wrist, like an unwholesome, flyblown piece of meat on a butcher's counter. 'No pension for old Lucco, either,' the cripple complained in his whining voice. 'I'd have starved to death if it weren't for my uncle getting me this job, not that it's much of a job. Imagine a Roman citizen being treated the same as a slave, I ask you.'

By now the guard commander was bored. He'd no interest in an old soldier's sob story. The maimed arm answered his question better than any discharge diploma and a long queue of carts was already building up on the road behind. As if to reinforce his decision the pig rubbed its wiry flank against him, emitted an enormous fart and splattered the cobbles with dark green shit.

'Venus' withered tits,' he cursed. 'Get that fucking beast out of here. The sooner it's turned into sausages the bloody better. On your way and find another gate to go home by, because if I ever see your ugly face again I'll break this stick across your back.'

The man Lucco bowed repeatedly and ran to the bullock's head, leading it forward through the gate, followed by Caradoc the pigman. To Rome.

'Not right in the head?' Serpentius said.

'If you were right in the head you wouldn't be with me.' Valerius rubbed at the stump of his wrist as they walked down the narrow cobbled track of the Alta Selita, three and four storey *insulae* apartments rising above them like cliffs.

The Spaniard saw the gesture. 'A shame about your hand.' Serpentius had carved the wooden fist Valerius normally wore on a thick leather stock that covered his wrist.

Valerius shrugged. 'I can't afford to wear it. Vitellius's people might have put out an alert, and we'd have been dead if the gate guard had found it among the sacks. In any case, we're here to negotiate, not fight.'

'You're forgetting Vitellius thinks I killed you in the arena at Cremona.'

Valerius winced at the sudden streak of fire across the top of his skull. He was still missing a finger's-width circle of scalp Serpentius had removed with a single bloody flash of his sword to make the end look realistic. It wasn't something he liked to be reminded of.

'That's true,' he acknowledged. 'But the man is no fool. He'll have spies in Primus's camp just as Primus has in his. If they've reported the presence of a one-handed man on the general's staff he may think a little harder about what he saw. He's nervous enough, that's for certain, judging by the amount of security.'

The Spaniard's dark eyes swept the area around them, taking in the little groups of Praetorians covering every junction. Rome was already a city under siege. 'He'd be stupid not to be.'

They reached the Vicus Longus and Valerius brought the bullock cart to a creaking halt.

'I still think this is a bad idea,' Serpentius muttered as he bent to tie the pig's tether to the body of the cart.

'Somebody has to sell the estate produce,' Valerius shrugged. 'And you'll get a better price than I will. You know what to do?'

'Oh yes,' the Spaniard said sourly. 'First I sell the pig . . .' He saw Valerius's look. 'All right. I check out the house up by the Temple of Diana on the Aventine for word of the lady Domitia. If I don't find out anything there, I seek you out at the villa of your old mate Gaius Plinius Secundus.'

Valerius nodded. 'It's up on the Esquiline, not far from the Fountain of Orpheus.' If anyone knew what was happening in Rome, it would be Pliny. He'd been surprised when Titus had mentioned his old friend's name as they'd discussed possible contacts in Rome. But Pliny had acted for Vespasian in some dispute with the Empress Agrippina in Claudius's time and they were still friends. Titus stressed there were no guarantees that Plinius would help them, but he believed the lawyer favoured Vespasian over Vitellius. Valerius's first instinct had been to search for Domitia himself, but he knew it would have condemned him as selfish and immature in her eyes. She retained her father's sense of duty and honour. What was the love of two people when balanced against the thousands or tens of thousands of lives that might be saved if he could only persuade the Emperor to stand down? 'Before I approach Vitellius I need to know how things stand on the Palatine and in the Senate. Things may have changed since Cerialis was here last.'

'Just be careful.' Serpentius looked around as the street began to fill up with people going about their business. 'I've found that the older we get the more difficult it is to stay alive.'

With just a hint of a salute the Spaniard was gone, the cart disappearing in a crowd heading down towards the pig market outside the Porta Salutaris. Valerius hesitated for a moment, shook his head ruefully and took the left fork towards Subura, down through the shallow valley between the Quirinal and Viminal hills. The persistent rain ran down his neck, making him shiver. He pulled up his hood and hugged his cloak tighter about him, dodging the nameless filth that flowed from the narrow alleyways into the gutters. It felt strange to be walking these familiar streets in another man's clothes. Each corner he rounded carried the threat of meeting someone he knew, or who knew him, and he instinctively pulled the hood close to hide his features. All it would take was a single shout. The chances of talking his way out of trouble were low and it would have been suicide to try to smuggle even a fruit knife past the guards.

But the hood had its disadvantages. A less wary man on such a mission might have ignored the rain and kept it back. Then, he might have noticed the similarly clad figure who slipped from a doorway and followed in his footsteps. Civil war breeds spies and informers the way a shaggy dog breeds fleas in summer. The spy couldn't even tell you who he worked for. He suspected it was the prefect of the Praetorian Guard, because his contacts had changed with each change of regime, even the subtle changes within changes that few people would notice. Then again, perhaps he was in the pay of the *vigiles,* the city police, which would make his ultimate paymaster Titus Flavius Sabinus, brother of the man whose forces were even now marching on Rome. But that was no concern of his. All that mattered was that he got paid and his family was fed. It would have surprised him to know that he was actually employed by a small group of clerks in the Palatium. They were pragmatic men who'd long ago recognized that knowledge was the currency of survival and whose network of agents kept them informed of any potential upheavals in their ordered lives. It had seen them through five changes of Emperor and would see them through many more.

Not that any of this mattered to the spy. He was a good spy. Not young or old. Not tall or short. Just ordinary. This was his city and you could see a hundred dull, bovine faces like his on any Roman street. It made him invisible.

Each market-day morning he made it his business to be at the corner of the Alta Semita and the Vicus Longus. The guards at the Porta Collina might change, but the spy was ever present. As always, he searched for something that didn't fit. Something a little different. A mannerism that changed from one day to the next. Someone in more of a hurry than usual. Today's sighting had been so obvious that at first he'd wondered if someone was trying to trick him. The spy had an excellent eye for faces. He knew everyone who came down this road at this time of this day. Sometimes faces would alternate, sometimes they would disappear for a few days. He'd never seen these faces before. A whip-thin, dangerous-looking character who walked with a stoop, but inexplicably straightened after he'd tied the pig to the cart. And the other, the one with the scarred face, who cultivated an air of peasant servility until he spoke to the first man, when his manner changed completely. Actors playing a part, was the spy's first thought, and the spy knew all about acting a part. After that it was just a question of which to follow. They made the decision easy for him. No one went on a clandestine mission leading a bullock cart and trailing a pig.

He kept pace with the figure in front, never letting him get far enough ahead to be out of sight, or have the opportunity to dodge into one of the narrow alleyways that honeycombed this district. He favoured the shadows beneath the shop awnings, sometimes on one side of the street and sometimes on the other. The way the other man varied his pace and stopped occasionally only made him smile because it confirmed his initial suspicions. Someone who also knew his business. Someone valuable. He meant the man no harm. He would follow him until he had his meeting, and, depending on the circumstances, perhaps to another rendezvous. After that what he needed was a fixed point of reference, or perhaps to get a signal to one of the patrols with whom he occasionally worked. They'd keep the man under guard until he'd made his report. Then it was up to them. Whoever they were.

He was so focused on his target that he had no warning of the arm that whipped out and dragged him into the alleyway. Not that it mattered, because he knew what was going to happen as soon as he felt the iron talons hooking into his flesh. Such a pity, he thought as he felt the sting of the knife across his throat and heard the roaring sound of his own death in his ears; he had been a good spy.

Serpentius wiped the curved knife on the man's cloak and walked quickly away. The instinct that something wasn't right was buried so deep that he'd almost missed it. He'd left the cart with a beggar with the promise of a denarius if it was there when he came back, and that he'd find him and cut out his heart if it wasn't. He'd known Valerius's route and the spy hadn't been difficult to spot. He wasn't a very good spy, after all. A good spy would have looked behind him.

XXXV

Pliny's house on the Esquiline Hill was an impressive three-storey affair that spoke of many years of inherited wealth and many more of benign neglect. The door was guarded, if guarded was the correct term, by a genial, slightly malodorous straw-haired creature as tall as Valerius, but broad as a two-horse cart in the shoulders. No doubt a retired veteran of Pliny's German auxiliary unit. With a grin that displayed teeth like a row of toppled standing stones the guard asked him his business before ambling inside to inform his master.

Valerius glanced around the small square to see if he could identify his watcher. He'd sensed the man's presence a few minutes after he'd left Serpentius and been perplexed when he'd disappeared. The square was enclosed by lime-washed walls, and over-loud vendors shouted their wares from every side. At one corner a pustuled beggar pleaded for a crust, but his eyes never stopped searching for a carelessly stowed purse. On another, attendant slaves waited for their masters in any blessed shelter they could find. Slowly, the minutes passed and he wondered if the servant, or more likely Pliny, had forgotten him. He sat down in the shelter of an orange tree and allowed his mind to wander.

He woke with a sharp cry of alarm. In the dream, his remaining hand had been hacked off by a fiery-breathed figure from the Otherworld who seemed to be a mixture of Vitellius and the Christus god. He flexed his fingers to make sure they were still in place and smiled. Fool. It was just a nightmare. Only then did he notice Gaius Plinius Secundus. Tall and thin, with a strong, dark-jawed face and bright inquisitive eyes, the former soldier stood over him with a quizzical smile and his writing block in his hand.

'You looked so peaceful that I didn't like to disturb you, and when you began to talk to yourself I thought it was a phenomenon worth studying. I hope you don't mind?'

Valerius raised himself to his feet, attempting to rub the dirt from his tunic. He was grateful the other man had decided not to notice his diminished circumstances or mention the other reason a former military tribune might turn up at the house dressed as a farm servant. 'I hope I didn't disappoint you. I was only dreaming.'

Pliny's eyes took on a distant look. 'Dreams can be most interesting. I like to try to interpret them, but I've never been particularly successful. I could try with yours if you'd allow me to?'

Valerius shook his head. 'No, Pliny. I don't think that would be very productive for either of us.'

'Another time, then.' Pliny took the rebuff cheerfully. 'Fascinating, though, how the dream manifests itself in the physical reaction of the subject. Your hand, for instance, was twitching in a manner that I've only ever seen in one that had been cut off during a battle . . .' He froze with a horrified stare at the stump of Valerius's right wrist. 'Oh, dear. I'm so sorry, my boy. I'd completely forgotten. You will never be able to forgive me, I'm sure. Please, if you can still bear my company, come inside.'

Valerius smiled and clapped him on the shoulder. 'If I was to make an enemy of everyone who forgot I left my hand in Britannia, Pliny, I wouldn't have any friends left.'

Valerius knew he must choose his moment well. Pliny devoured time the way a lion devoured its prey. Always on the move, always thinking, always taking notes on the little wax tablets he kept in his sleeve. A man who habitually lived a few moments in the future and occasionally forgot he needed to deal with the concerns of the present. Despite the age difference, the two men had always got on well as a result of their shared experiences in the legions. Valerius had served in Britannia, and Pliny, who was fourteen years the elder, had commanded auxiliary units for a decade in Germany. By rights, Pliny should have been enjoying a profitable procuratorship in some faraway province, but the gossips said he preferred not to attract the attention of the unpredictable Nero. Instead, he'd busied himself with unspectacular cases in the basilica. Plainly, he'd decided to maintain a similar low profile during the short reigns of Galba and Otho. By the time Vitellius had taken the throne Pliny's old friend Vespasian had already been hailed Emperor by his troops. Safer for the moment to stay at home with his library of several hundred books and his modest law practice.

'What did you think of the treatise I sent you on the cavalry's use of spears? I'm still not sure I'm right about the proper grip when closing with a mounted enemy.'

'I could see nothing out of place, Pliny,' Valerius assured him as they embraced. It had been more than two years and he was surprised the lawyer remembered. 'Although I know a few Thracian cavalrymen who would dispute the priority you give to mounted archers.'

Pliny led the way through a maze of corridors. At first glance, the interior of the house was a mirror of Pliny's mind: chaotic, cluttered, ungovernable and filled with pointless rubbish. But delve a little deeper and order might be discerned amongst the chaos. The scrolls piled three deep on a table in the reception area, for instance. Now that Valerius looked he could see each was labelled with its place of origin: Alexandria, Antioch, Athens and Atlantis. A bust of Aristotle weighed down one of the philosopher's own works. Pliny saw his glance and beamed. 'One of his lesser known pieces on zoology, and below it Zuma, for the African beasts. Ah,' his eyes found another treasure, 'I know you'll find this interesting. Herodotus, a first edition, and Thucydides, a little battered but still serviceable. Do you still have your copy?'

Valerius shook his head with a smile. 'No, I left it in Britannia.' The truth was that it had burned with the rest of Colonia as he'd watched from the compound of the besieged Temple of Claudius.

'One day I hope to read and catalogue them all; bring the whole world together: history, geography, botany, zoology and geology in one single book of many volumes.' The lawyer sighed wistfully. 'But sometimes it seems such an enormous undertaking.'

As they walked deeper into the house, Pliny showed off his treasures. 'Of course, this place once belonged to the poet Pedo,' he said proudly. He pointed to a faded wall painting of a fleet of ships on a dull blue strip that seemed to represent a river. 'A depiction of your hero, Germanicus, on his way to the northern ocean. Pedo recorded the voyage in one of his works, though it wasn't one of his best.'

Valerius picked up an oddly shaped piece of ivory, black with age, which lay haphazardly on top of a cabinet, but Pliny quickly retrieved it and placed it reverently back in position.

'The horn of a monoceros, a quadruped which exists only in farthest India.' He frowned. 'For some reason our only examples have come from the ocean, in fishermen's nets, or washed upon the shore, so perhaps they also have the capacity to breathe underwater?'

Skulls and skeletons, stuffed animals – some familiar, some outlandish – strangely shaped fish made of stone and the bones of some gigantic animal, greater even than the mighty elephant. And in pride of place an onyx box which Pliny opened reverently, but bade him not to touch for his life.

'The basilisk of Cyrene,' he whispered, revealing a shrivelled, snake-like creature about two feet in length and of obvious antiquity. 'The most poisonous of all living things. Its very presence breaks the stones and sets the grasses afire, and it is so venomous that if you plunged a spear into its body you would likely die.' In that case, Valerius wondered privately, how had it been killed? Pliny scented scepticism the way a rutting stag scents a ripe doe. 'A weasel,' he assured his guest. 'Only the effluvium of a weasel can kill the dread basilisk, though it dies itself in the struggle.'

He stared into the middle distance for few moments and his brow furrowed as if he was placing himself in the position of the doomed mammal. When he finished, he turned to stare at Valerius with a look of mystified innocence. 'I've quite forgotten why you are here.'

'I didn't say, Pliny. But I've been away from Rome for so long that I'm quite out of touch. I thought you might be able to tell me the lie of the land, as it were, socially . . . and politically.'

At the word 'politically' a stillness came over the lawyer reminiscent of the way a woodmouse hardly dares draw breath at the soft beat of an owl's wings overhead. His eyes didn't change, but his lips formed a little half-smile that Valerius sensed was entirely involuntary. Any more and you would have called it sly; instead it stayed just the right side of wary, but warned.

'Oh, I don't get invited out much,' he said casually, 'but socially, I believe, things are what might be called fraught. Before one can accept even the most innocent offer, one must first be aware of the make-up of the guest list, their relationship with one another and the host, and their, let us say, affiliations and interests. Too much of one thing and one might be accused of being in the wrong company, even, perhaps, of indulging in intrigue. Too much of the other and who knows where one might be in a few months. All possible hopes of advancement gone because one broke bread with the wrong person. Yet it can be equally perilous to refuse the wrong invitation. Spurned by one's colleagues, treated with suspicion by one's friends, and as for one's enemies . . .' He came to a stuttering halt with a glassy-eyed smile.

Valerius sensed that if he didn't take the chance now the moment would be lost. 'Titus Vespasian suggested I call on you, Pliny,' he said gently. 'And that was before he knew we were friends.' The other man froze but Valerius hurried on. 'I need to know what Vitellius is thinking. Who can he trust? Who is openly against him? Who will support him? And most important, who says they will support him, but will turn against him when the time is right? Do you think Vitellius can survive, Plinius?'

The lawyer blinked at the direct question and his face crumpled into a frown.

'Politically, yes, in the short term, but his long-term survival will not be decided by politicians but by soldiers.' His eyes turned accusing. 'As you know better than I, Gaius Valerius Verrens, since I can guess whence you've come.' Valerius didn't deny it, but he held Pliny's gaze

270

until the lawyer continued. 'Whom can he trust? His family and the Guard.' He unwittingly confirmed what Valerius had been told at Fidenae. 'More than any other Emperor I have known they are *his* Guard. I do not believe they can be bought, as so often in the past. They have invested too much in him to walk away. In some ways they are as responsible as he for what has happened, and they know that Vespasian's advisers also know this. To resume: Vitellius has the support of the people. You will note, Valerius, that I say people and not mob. The support of the mob can be won by circuses; that of the people takes more. They would have been happy to have Vitellius as Emperor, and happy if he won this war quickly and with as little bloodshed as possible.' Their eyes met and Pliny nodded acknowledgement of the unlikelihood of this outcome. 'He has been sensible in his treatment of those he rules, and, despite all the sneers about his laziness, his administration has been efficient. Things are dealt with quickly and fairly. They may laugh at his girth and his appetite, but they can tolerate that, because he is harmless. Yes,' Pliny said it as if understanding it for the first time, 'he is harmless, and after Nero, Galba and Otho, they would exchange any hope of military glory for the right to sleep easy in their beds.' He sighed. 'I support Vespasian, Valerius, and count him as my friend, but I wish more than anything in this life that he had persuaded his legions to take the oath to Vitellius.'

He reached into his sleeve, retrieved his sheaf of wax writing tablets and stylus and began writing. 'This is the make-up of the Senate as I understand it. One – a short list – for those who will support Vitellius to the last. A second for those already plotting against him: the majority.' He looked up from beneath hooded eyes. 'It is for your better understanding only. They will do nothing until Primus or Mucianus is knocking on the very gates of Rome. The only one who matters is Vespasian's brother, Sabinus, because he controls the urban cohorts and the *vigiles*. If he acts and looks like winning, the Senate may vote to remove Vitellius for their own preservation. Who knows how the Guard and the mob will react then.'

'Why does Vitellius not just arrest him?' Valerius was puzzled. 'He must still have half a dozen cohorts of Praetorians in the city.'

Pliny produced a thin smile. 'Because he fears to provoke him. As long as Sabinus stays quiescent, Vitellius can feel safe. He is like the sleeping dog who lies in your way on a forest path. Do you try to walk quietly by, or do you risk prodding him with a stick and having his teeth in your arm?' The sound of something large and sharp meeting meat and muscle echoed from another room in the house. Valerius's scarred cheek twitched at the familiar sound and he saw Pliny wince. 'The kitchen,' the lawyer explained with a resigned sigh. 'My loyal Tungrian guards have no notion of finesse. Half a boar and an open fire is the limit of their creativity.'

He handed Valerius the completed list and the one-handed tribune placed the sheaves in the pouch at his belt. 'Can you suggest any way for me to contact Vitellius without others knowing?'

Pliny smiled sadly and patted him on the shoulder. 'That, my dear friend, is something you will have to discover for yourself. But first,' his nostrils twitched as he caught the pungent farmyard scent of Valerius's ragged tunic, 'a bath and some new clothes. You cannot wait upon the Emperor looking and smelling like some itinerant pig farmer.'

XXXVI

Domitia Longina Corbulo studied the letter she'd written with parchment and ink stolen from the office of Titus Flavius Sabinus. When she was satisfied, she waited for the ink to dry, rolled the parchment into a tight scroll and used a thin strip of hemp to tie it. It had cost her several sleepless nights before she had made up her mind where her duty lay, but when it came to her the answer was obvious. Vespasian had been her father's friend and helped her escape after his death in Antioch, but she was a Roman lady, and, whatever his faults, Rome's Emperor was Aulus Vitellius Germanicus Augustus. She'd discovered a plot against the Roman state and it was her duty to expose it. On the other hand, she wasn't a fool, and neither was she disloyal to her host. The letter remained unsigned and contained no names and no specifics, only a vague warning to beware of a plot involving the *vigiles* and the Senate. Even without more details she believed the letter would inspire Vitellius to tighten his grip on the *vigiles* and force Sabinus and Saturninus to abandon their conspiracy.

'Tulla?' she called. 'You understand what you must do?'

Her maid appeared from the doorway, looking anxious, but fully dressed and in a dark cloak. She knew nothing of the letter's contents, but Domitia had, of necessity, been forced to reveal its final destination and her hand shook with fear as she accepted it. 'Of course, lady, but I still wonder if this is wise. If the master should . . .'

Domitia held up a hand. 'Hush, child.' She stood up and caressed Tulla's dark hair, though the 'child' was less than a year younger than her mistress. 'You will be in no danger. Go to the Forum and choose a suitable messenger from amongst those who hang about the basilica steps seeking casual employment. You will hand him a single *denarius* with the promise of two more if he returns to report the letter delivered.'

'To the Emperor's personal guard . . .'

'Find a public place and wait,' Domitia reminded the other girl. 'But you must position yourself so you will see him before he sees you. If he is accompanied by soldiers you must slip away as inconspicuously as you can.'

'But . . .'

'You know this is important to me, Tulla.' She fixed the slave girl with a mistress's stare. 'And of course, you too will be rewarded. Perhaps I will even give you your freedom.'

Tulla nodded, a swift darting motion like a finch pecking hungrily at seeds but always wary of the hunter's net. With a last frightened glance she disappeared through the doorway and Domitia sat on the bed and allowed all the tension to drain from her. She knew how perilous this might be. What if the messenger simply betrayed Tulla? Or robbed her? But Domitia couldn't go herself. It was not a question of courage. She knew Domitianus had his spies follow her every time she left the villa. It wasn't perfect, but it was the only way, and whether it succeeded or failed she had done her duty.

When a servant called her down to break her fast with the owner of the house she pleaded an indisposition. She knew she was no actress and even someone as self-centred as Sabinus would realize something was wrong. Instead, she kept to her room all morning, her fears mounting with every moment that passed without Tulla's return.

When she heard footsteps outside the curtained doorway she almost fainted with relief. But the curtain swept back to reveal Domitianus with a self-satisfied smile on his face that froze the blood in her veins.

In his right hand he held a tight-rolled parchment scroll which he tapped against the palm of his left.

'These are dangerous times.' The young man's voice registered hurt rather than anger. 'Who knows whom one can trust?'

It was clear he expected an answer, but Domitia clamped her lip between her teeth to prevent herself from crying out. She stood frozen in place as he approached her with all the blood-chilling, lethal grace of a cobra. Domitianus stopped just within reach and the almost unbearable, breathless tension stretched like a bowstring.

'You did not think I would have your slaves watched? How naive of you, and how like a woman. But this I did not expect.' The eyes lit up in the pale face as he shook the parchment scroll in his right hand. 'A lover perhaps? It would have been disappointing, but understandable. You prowl these halls like a trapped tigress; of course you would wish to escape. But now . . .' He reached out with his left hand and touched her cheek and Domitia knew she must not blink. For all his apparent serenity danger lurked close; a threat of terrible uncontrolled violence. The hand moved to her shoulder and lower, then lower still, but his eyes never left hers. 'Now,' his voice dropped to a whisper, 'there is truly no escape.'

She would have run then – the fear was so strong – had two *vigiles* not dragged an insensible figure into the room by the arms and left her lying on the marble floor. The beating had left Tulla's pretty elfin face swollen to the shape of a water melon and her eyes were bruised purple slits. A thin line of scarlet dribbled from the corner of her mouth to stain the creamy white marble. For the first time Domitia noticed that the knuckles of Domitianus's right hand were reddened.

'She will live,' Vespasian's son said carelessly. 'But no thanks to you. I'd have expected more from a Corbulo than this pathetic attempt at intrigue. They would have seized your messenger and beaten a description out of him. Your whore would have been taken and by nightfall she would have implicated you and everyone in this household. You see?' He paused to allow the reality of her situation to be fully understood. 'I have saved your life. And now I must decide whether to save it again. If Sabinus were to become aware of the contents of this scroll he'd have your throat cut, and your slaves' too. He is not a cruel man, but he would have no option.' All the time he'd been speaking his hand had been caressing her right breast, the fingers toying with a nipple made erect by fear. Suddenly his voice thickened. 'We'll discuss this,' he brandished the scroll, 'further. You will come to me tonight, and perhaps when we have spoken you will find that your captivity is not quite so onerous after all.'

With a final squeeze, he turned and walked from the room. As if in a dream, Domitia felt herself follow him to the doorway and draw the curtain. She couldn't breathe, but she knew that if she opened her mouth she would scream until she had no screams left.

Tulla's groan brought her back from the void. She was a Corbulo. A decision must be made. She remembered seeing her father, the eyes slightly open, the sword still held tight by his flesh. No, not her father at all. It was her father's body, but the essence of him, the spirit that made him who he was, had gone. It did not look so difficult.

She bent low over Tulla and smoothed the sweat-damp hair from her brow. 'My poor, poor child . . .'

XXXVII

'Publius Sulla, an old comrade from the Danuvius frontier, seeks an audience with the Emperor Aulus Vitellius Germanicus Augustus.'

The guard at the entrance to the great Golden House studied the petitioner. Steady grey eyes, sharp, angular features and, most striking of all, a mottled purple stump where the right hand should have shown beneath his sleeve. A noble face, the warrior's scars carried with pride; the man wore a patrician's heavy gold rings and a fine toga that would have cost the Praetorian a month's wages. 'Wait here, sir,' he ordered, and marched off to consult with his commander.

Valerius had used the name Publius Sulla before and he was confident it would get Vitellius's attention, especially in conjunction with the physical description of the man claiming it. The original Publius had been one of Vitellius's tribunes in the Seventh Claudia, an earnest young disciple of the mystic Christus, dead by his own hand in an earthen encampment in Dacia. It had seemed a reasonable enough subterfuge when he'd discussed it with Serpentius. Standing before this glittering jewel-encrusted edifice in the shadow of the enormous gold statue he realized it was as substantial as the diaphanous veil that didn't quite hide a courtesan's modesty. If he'd misread Vitellius's mood, the Emperor would throw him into his deepest dungeon to rot, or more likely have his throat cut at leisure. He counted on their old friendship to keep him alive in the first instance, and on Vitellius's well-tried instinct for survival to keep them both that way in the longer term. Vitellius had never sought the purple; his generals had forced it upon him when a refusal would have meant death. But he had been Emperor for eight full months, ruler of more than forty million people. Wielding that kind of power would change any man. The question was just how much and in what way?

The guard returned, accompanied by five others. A substantial presence for a single one-armed man. Yet their number raised a small glow of hope in Valerius's breast. It meant Vitellius recognized the name and knew the worth of the man who used it. In addition, the way the guards carried themselves gave no hint of a threat, only ill-concealed curiosity and a readiness to act in whatever manner the situation demanded.

'Come with us, please.'

They escorted Valerius through the entrance hall, along broad corridors floored with the finest mosaics, beneath ceilings of fretted ivory. Every turn brought new artworks from across the Empire. Pottery from Egypt, statuary from Greece, gold ornaments studded with gemstones imported from the eastern lands beyond Parthia. To right and left, painted plaster walls mimicked the antelope-grazed gardens that surrounded the house and the huge lake that was its centrepiece. No place for the mundane or the mediocre in Nero's masterpiece, and Valerius reflected on the over-inflated vanity that had inspired it. Nero had been determined to outdo his illustrious predecessors and stopped at nothing to achieve it. Much of the opposition against him had its roots in the enormous sums he'd invested in this place. In a way it contributed as much to his downfall as Corbulo's death or Galba's outraged sensibility. Had it been worth it, he wondered?

Eventually they turned through double doors and entered a vast, echoing receiving hall. At the far end, on a raised dais, Valerius recognized the golden throne that had once been occupied by Nero and later by Galba. It was empty. The soldiers led him forward to the foot of the steps leading to the throne and told him to remain there. They withdrew and he heard the doors close behind him. In the brooding silence that followed, Valerius's gaze drifted to his feet. A dark stain of what could only be dried blood cast his situation in a more ominous light. He was still wondering at its origin when an odd creaking sound reached him from the far side of the dais. First a great dome of a head appeared beside the throne, followed by wide shoulders draped in Imperial purple. Eventually, the entire substantial bulk of Aulus Vitellius Germanicus Augustus lumbered from the levered contraption that had saved him using the steps. The Emperor stood for a moment and stared at the man below with an expression of irritated confusion before slumping into his throne. Valerius took a step forward, but Vitellius stalled him with a raised hand and made him wait for a long moment before he spoke.

'So, Hero of Rome, this time you bring me not one ghost, but two. What portents am I to take from this after what followed our last such meeting?' If the words contained a disturbing mix of weariness, anger and uncertainty, those that followed held a definite hint of menace. 'I watched you die in the arena at Cremona. I saw the sword fall and the blood spill and I mourned my old friend Gaius Valerius Verrens. But hear this, Valerius, it would take but a click of my fingers to make it so again.'

'What happened was none of my doing.' Valerius didn't flinch from the Emperor's accusing stare. 'Otho offered a way forward without bloodshed . . .'

'Otho is dead.' Vitellius's bark carried all the authority of his office. 'And I am Rome's Emperor, and I say any blood shed was worthwhile.'

Valerius shook his head. 'They said you gloated over the bodies of the dead at Bedriacum, but I told them Aulus Vitellius would never have debased himself so.'

The big man hauled himself to his feet and stood shaking in front of the golden throne, a towering figure full of threat and power. 'The Aulus Vitellius you knew was not the Emperor of Rome. Those who died on that field were my enemies. Why should I mourn them?'

'Because they were Romans.' The words pierced the Emperor like a spear thrust and Vitellius groaned and sank back on the cushions. Valerius saw he'd been wrong. The outer man might be as corpulent as ever, but the inner Vitellius was somehow diminished. Aulus Vitellius could never have been described as a man of action, but at his core there had always been a great heart to match his great girth. That spirit persuaded him to use his fortune to buy grain to feed the starving of his province of Africa, when another would have let them suffer and prospered from it. It gave him the strength to survive the turbulent final years with Nero. And it inspired the courage to pick up Caesar's sword when the legions of Germania hailed him Emperor. Now, Valerius could see it was gone, sucked from him by the defeat at Cremona and the knowledge that the world was crumbling beneath his feet.

'Why have you come here?'

'I carry an offer from Titus Flavius Vespasian.' Valerius allowed his voice to harden. 'It will mean exile, but he guarantees you life and your family at your side. Your son will have his protection and the promise of advancement.'

Vitellius's domed head came up and Valerius saw a shudder run through the hunched figure. 'I did not accept your previous offer, from Otho; why should I even consider this now that I am Emperor by the will of the Senate and people of Rome?' Fury made his voice shake and the anger seemed to give him new strength. 'By the will of the Senate and people of Rome.' He emphasized each word with a bang of his right fist against the palm of his left hand. 'Titus Flavius Vespasian dares not stir from his fly-blown sand spit because he fears the might of Aulus Vitellius Germanicus Augustus. Instead, he sends his lackeys,' the plump features twisted into a sneer, 'including one Gaius Valerius Verrens. Why should I fear him? My army—'

'Was swept aside at Cremona.' Despite his best efforts, Valerius responded to the jibe. 'It no longer exists.'

'Armies can be replaced,' Vitellius countered furiously. 'I still have the support of the legions of Germania and Britannia, Gaul and Hispania. Even now they are marching to our aid.'

'Armies, perhaps, but not generals. Who among them can you trust, Vitellius? Caecina Alienus, the man who helped place you on this throne, has deserted you. He might have been no soldier, but he knew a month ago that you could not win. Five legates taken at Cremona, their legions humiliated and scattered.'

'The Guard and the people will fight. They at least will not turn their backs on me.' The look of desperation in the pale blue eyes was pitiful to behold. 'I could be a great Emperor, Valerius.' His beefy hands clenched into fists and his heavy frame shook like a man trying to bear the pain of an arrow in his belly. 'We spoke once of the Rome we both wanted. A strong Rome, a prosperous Rome, a Rome untainted by the stain of corruption. I can give you that Rome, Valerius, but only if you help me.'

It was not the cry of despair of an Emperor on the brink of disaster, but a plea from one friend to another. Valerius felt a prickle behind his eyes and something seemed to be caught in his throat, but he held the other man's gaze. The words had to be said.

'It is too late.'

A great roar of anguish and despair echoed from the marbled walls.

'Father?' Valerius turned to find a slim, dark-haired boy standing in the doorway with fear in his eyes. 'Father, is something wrong?'

A groan emanated from the man on the platform, but when Valerius looked again he was surprised to see Aulus Vitellius lumbering his way downwards one stair at a time. To his astonishment the Emperor's face split in a smile of welcome.

'I was just telling my old friend Valerius of the huge bear we killed in the woods outside Aricia. A passable imitation, don't you think?' He reached the floor panting with the effort. 'My son Lucius. Gaius Valerius Verrens, Hero of Rome.'

The boy's dark eyes widened, but he remembered his manners enough to produce a low respectful bow. 'You have won the Corona Aurea?'

'Valerius was the sole survivor of the Temple of Claudius in Britannia.' Vitellius's voice betrayed his indulgence. 'He fought off a thousand barbarian champions and won great honour for his Empire and his family. But that is for another day, Lucius. For now, you must leave us alone. We have important matters of state to discuss.'

Lucius bowed again. 'My apologies for interrupting you, sir. I was—'

Vitellius stepped forward and placed a protective arm around his son. 'Please, Lucius . . .'

The boy shot a startled glance at Valerius, obviously surprised at this public display of affection, before darting towards the doorway. 'One day I will win the Corona Aurea,' he shouted as he left the room.

When the door closed behind his son, the smile faded from Aulus Vitellius Germanicus Augustus's face and his shoulders sagged. He'd been a fool to appoint the boy his heir, he saw that now. So young and so innocent of worldly troubles, Lucius would have been devoured by the trials of office and the men who sought to take it from him. All it had done was increase the danger to him. The giant frame in the purple toga seemed to collapse in on itself like a punctured wineskin. Valerius stepped forward to steady his friend as he threatened to collapse.

'He does you credit, Vitellius,' he struggled to find the words, 'and you him.'

'Tell me how I can save them, Valerius,' the Emperor pleaded. 'That is all that matters now.'

Valerius repeated the offer he'd memorized in the headquarters tent of Marcus Antonius Primus, remembering a similar offer made all those months ago on the Rhenus frontier. Though the detail was different, both had the same aim: to end this ruinous conflict without further bloodshed. He prayed to Jupiter and Mars that the second was more successful than the first.

'You will be the guests of Vespasian on Sicilia,' Valerius assured him, 'your safety guaranteed by his public pronouncement that no harm will befall you. Watched, naturally, you would hardly expect otherwise, but free to go where you will within the confines of the island as long as you forgo politics. Lucius will take his place on the *cursus honorum* and the Emperor,' he saw Vitellius flinch at the word, 'will take an interest in his progress to high and honourable office. You will not lack funds. A sum of one hundred million sesterces has been set aside for your welfare.'

He searched Vitellius's face for some reaction. No matter the peril of his situation, he was asking this man to give up more power than any other had wielded. The outcome was not in doubt, but if he had the will and a general at his side, Aulus Vitellius could prolong the civil war for months or even years. He didn't have to fight a pitched battle. He could withdraw south and threaten Rome from the hills of Campania, while the German and Gaulish legions still loyal to him attacked from the north. But the man in the purple toga only nodded solemnly to each suggestion – until a single name slipped from Valerius's lips.

'First you must renounce your claim to the throne. When that is done, surrender yourself and your family to Titus Flavius Sabinus and . . .'

'Sabinus?' Vitellius's eyes widened in horror. 'How can I put my faith in a man who has been plotting to have me murdered for months? Sabinus would as soon have me killed as pass his next stool.' His voice shook with fury as he continued. 'He thinks I don't know about his intrigues with Saturninus and Trebellius. Aye, and the others, too. All the progress I've made, everything I have tried to do, has been undermined by one particular hand. The hand of Titus Flavius Sabinus. To place my trust in that man would be to put my head beneath an executioner's sword.'

'You have Vespasian's word,' Valerius urged, 'publicly pledged, that you can trust Sabinus. Only the city prefect controls sufficient forces to keep you safe after you renounce your claim. His urban cohorts and the *vigiles* will surround the house until Vespasian's legions arrive. There will be no reprisals against any Roman citizen who has supported you and the Praetorians will be granted immunity as long as they lay down their arms.'

'You don't understand.' Vitellius shook his head. 'Vespasian knows nothing of what is happening in Rome. Emperor, he calls himself? He is like the old beggar seeking pennies on the corner of the Forum in a pool of his own piss; blind, deaf and dumb. Sabinus has the forces to keep me safe? Sabinus does not even have the forces to keep himself safe. Six cohorts of Praetorian Guards are stationed in Rome and their commander can call on six more at need. Sabinus commands a few policemen and firefighters. The Guard could squash Sabinus like a grape in a walnut crusher. If they had their way he would already be dead. Only my forbearance has kept him alive, because he is Vespasian's brother. Sabinus has been the dagger pointing at my heart ever since I first donned the purple. If . . .' Valerius noticed a change in tone, almost as if another man had joined the conversation. 'If I am to trust Sabinus, I must know the exact dispositions he has in place to safeguard myself and my family. How many troops he has and who leads them. Where he will place them and his lines of retreat should they be overcome. How many senators will support him and their identities.' Valerius suppressed a growl of frustration as Vitellius listed his conditions. He was demanding that Sabinus reveal his entire strength and the foundations that underpinned it. If Sabinus conceded, he'd be placing himself and every one of his supporters entirely in the Emperor's hands. Vitellius saw his disquiet, but carried on relentlessly. 'Understand this, Valerius. If I am to place my family under his protection, I must know they are safer than they would be under my own. If I am to give him my trust, then he must give me his.'

'What if he will not provide this information?'

'Then you must persuade him.' Vitellius's voice regained its Emperor's authority. 'You will arrange a meeting between Sabinus and myself at the Temple of Apollo in three days' time, each of us to be accompanied by a single independent witness agreed by the other. My witness will be Silius Italicus, who was consul last year, and who I hope will be agreeable to Sabinus.'

Valerius's heart sank at the thought of another perilous, potentially fatal mission, but he knew Vitellius was right. If the two men had differences, better to work them out face to face. Who else had the insight into the minds of both Vitellius and, through Cerialis and Primus, Sabinus? If an atmosphere of trust was to be created, who else had the means? He still had doubts Sabinus would agree to the Emperor's terms. Yet even if all he could do was persuade the city prefect that a meeting was worthwhile, he would have achieved something. Eventually he nodded agreement. 'I will try. What hour would be best?'

Vitellius considered for a moment. 'The fourth, I think. Least likely to interfere with my digestion, which will make Sabinus's whining easier to stomach.' He saw the other man's look. 'Oh, I am not the Vitellius of old, Valerius. I have known power and I would rather keep it than not. I said you do not understand, and it is true. The only things that have changed since we met at Colonia Agrippinensis are the names of the people who hold my life in their hands. I am like the man being torn apart by two stallions. The legionaries of the Praetorian Guard are the same men who hailed Aulus Vitellius Emperor outside Moguntiacum. Whatever Vespasian promises, they will never believe he will leave them alive. Do you really think they will stand back and allow me to hand Rome to the man they fear? Titus Flavius Sabinus may be a cockroach I would rather crush beneath my foot than talk to, but the lives of my family are at stake. I would negotiate with Hades himself if it would see them safe.'

Valerius bowed and turned to go. It was only then he remembered the significance of the Temple of Apollo. Servius Sulpicius Galba had sacrificed a white bull at the temple on the Palatine on the day he'd been cut to pieces in the Forum.

XXXVIII

'If you have come here looking for employment in the urban cohorts you should know that whatever your merits I could never accept a cripple into their ranks.'

Titus Flavius Sabinus's sneering reference to Valerius's empty sleeve implied that a mutilated veteran's place was with his fellows begging in the alleyways off the Forum and only served to increase his dislike of the man. Sabinus didn't even have the manners to offer his guest a seat on one of the couches that shared the narrow room with painted busts of Sabinus's ancestors. Valerius found it difficult to believe this pompous, pot-bellied windbag could be Vespasian's brother and Titus's uncle.

'I merely told your doorman that I requested an interview with the Prefect of Rome.' He kept his tone solicitous, but just the right side of subservient. 'He was reluctant to allow me entry, but when I told him I'd served with you in Britannia and showed him my arm, he relented.'

The patrician eyed him suspiciously. 'I know every officer who served with me in the Fourteenth and you're not one of them.'

Valerius reached into the voluminous folds of his toga. For a moment Sabinus's face dissolved in alarm. He opened his mouth to call for aid only to close it like a wolf trap when he recognized what the intruder held in his left hand.

'Petilius Cerialis gave me this less than a week ago.' Valerius held out the object, a distinctive golden charm the former legate of the Ninth had worn at his neck. 'My lie was a small one, and in a good cause. I was with the Twentieth when I lost this.' Sabinus flinched as he bared the mottled purple stump. 'Sometimes it is allowable to do a small wrong if it leads to a greater good, don't you think?'

The prefect's eyes clung to the gilded bauble as if he were hypnotized. Valerius knew what he was thinking. It was all very well to plot and conspire, but the true leaders came to the fore when the time came to act. Judging by the paralysis that gripped him now, Titus Flavius Sabinus had spent many a long night sweating in his bed praying this moment would never come. His reaction confirmed the opinions of both Primus and Vitellius, and Valerius wondered that the one could place his faith in Sabinus and the other fear him. It was his brother, of course, the brooding power of Vespasian waiting patiently in the East while his legions marched on Rome. But it would take a man of decision to do what Valerius needed Sabinus to do. The fate of thousands depended on the patrician's fortitude. Was he capable of it? The washed-out eyes shifted and he found himself staring into the soul of Titus Flavius Sabinus. All he saw was doubt.

'I come directly from the Emperor.' He kept his tone deliberately dispassionate – a man discussing the price of a new horse – and as detached from the import of the words as he could make it. Still Sabinus's eyes widened at the use of the title and widened further at what followed. 'He is willing to give up the throne, but only on receipt of certain guarantees and assurances. Once he has them he will place himself and his family under your protection. He has asked me to arrange a meeting, on neutral ground, so you may judge his good faith and he yours.'

'Faith?' Sabinus exploded. 'That arrogant tub of lard has the insolence to question my faith after months of scheming to have me killed, poisoned as he poisoned his own son? Hemlock in my wine and my taster on his deathbed for three weeks after eating contaminated oysters.' Valerius had a feeling that if Vitellius had wanted Sabinus dead, the current conversation would be much more one-sided, but he kept the thought to himself. The Prefect of Rome eventually collected himself enough to ask what 'guarantees and assurances' Vitellius demanded.

Valerius outlined them one by one, watching the other man's face turn redder and awaiting the inevitable reaction.

'Jupiter's bollocks.' Sabinus struggled breathlessly to his feet and began to pace the floor. 'I might as well cut my head off for him. His Praetorians have done nothing but try to provoke my cohorts and *vigiles* into causing some kind of incident. I've kept them off the streets, all but my personal guard, and still they are taunted and spat on by Vitellius's preening peacocks, the leavings of the Rhenus legions. Now I am to tell him where to find them, who leads them and how they will deploy? Why don't I just have them march up to the Castra Praetorium and hand in their swords and save him the trouble? And not content with my head, he must have those of my friends in the Senate. I would rather oil the crack in his blubbery arse than give him what he wants. You ask too much.'

Valerius held his gaze. 'It is not I who asks, prefect, but your brother.'

Sabinus stopped as if he'd been hit by a sling pellet. 'I . . .' A choking sound emerged from his throat. 'I could have you whipped for such insolence.'

'Not insolence, sir, but the truth. End this war without further bloodshed and Vespasian will raise you up above all others. Only you have the forces within the city walls to protect Vitellius. *If* he surrenders, he will surrender to you and no other. He is finished and he knows it, but he must be able to end it with honour and he must be certain you can protect his family. Succeed in this and history will remember the name Sabinus alongside that of Vespasian. Fail . . .' He shrugged. 'Let us not think of failure. Whatever you do, you must not turn Vitellius away.'

Sabinus listened with his hand over his mouth as if he couldn't trust his tongue. Eventually, the hand fell away. 'Leave me now,' he said, his voice shaking. 'I must think on this.' He waved absently towards the window terrace and with a last frustrated glance Valerius stepped out into the gardens.

He walked through the dripping apple and pear trees towards the long balcony where he could look out towards the Palatine. Below him, tight-packed buildings clung to the slope divided by narrow, claustrophobic streets with only the foliage of an occasional tree to offset the sea of ochre-tiled roofs. But it was the Domus Aurea and its sprawling complex of gardens and lakes dominating the vista to his left that drew his eye. Behind that glowing golden façade Aulus Vitellius waited, balanced on a sword edge between life and death, teetering on the highest point of a precipice with his enemies crowding at his back and his family clinging in terror to his skirts. Few men had suffered more from the ravages caused by Vitellius's ambition than Gaius Valerius Verrens, yet standing here he felt nothing but pity for his old friend. From the moment he had been proclaimed Emperor Vitellius had had as little say in his destiny as the Celtic war chief Caratacus, brought to the city in chains by Claudius to commemorate the subjugation of Britannia . . .

'Valerius?'

He wondered, at first, if the whisper came from inside his head and he didn't dare turn in case he'd imagined it. An inner heat spread through him as if a hot spring had been tapped somewhere at his core. That voice. He swivelled and the breath caught in his throat at the sight of her. She stood less than four paces away, still slim and delicate as an desert antelope, beyond beautiful in a *stola* of rich aquamarine with a mantle of the same covering hair of lustrous chestnut that fell to her shoulders in ringlets. Yet his first thought was that Domitia Longina Corbulo's eyes had lost their vitality in a way that reminded him of the dark days after her father had died. A hundred questions filled his head, but only one mattered. Did she still love him? He moved towards her and would have taken her in his arms, but for the hissed warning.

'No, Valerius. We must not be seen together.' She took control. 'Two old acquaintances have met by accident, nothing more . . . for now.'

The 'for now' made his heart race, but he kept his distance though every fibre drew him to her. 'You are well, my lady?'

For answer she glanced across her shoulder towards the house.

'They said you were dead. I felt as if I were torn in two. If you had come earlier . . .'

'I was . . .' What was the point of explaining? 'You must come away with me.'

Domitia's eyes filled with a hope that faded as quickly as it had appeared. 'I . . . cannot. He would never rest until he found us . . .'

'Sabinus?'

'No, Do— Valerius!'

He was turning even before she completed the warning. A blurred figure raced between the trees and Valerius saw the flash of the blade swinging to rip at his belly. He blocked the thrust with his left arm, but his attacker was quick. A bolt of red hot agony shot through Valerius as the knife reversed and the point scored the bone of his wrist. But the pain only spurred him. Roaring with fury he used the momentum of the block to spin in a low crouch, ramming an elbow into the softness of his assailant's lower stomach. The blow drew an 'oomph' of expelled air and won him a heartbeat to whirl clear as the knife point swept round again, seeking his kidneys. It was only then that he recognized his attacker.

'You?' But Titus Flavius Domitianus had already resumed his attack. Hatred burned in the pale eyes and the knife hooked up towards Valerius's vitals. This time the Roman had no chance to block, but he'd been gladiator-trained by Serpentius and he reacted on pure instinct. He dodged left, sideslipping the blade and hammering his left fist at Domitianus's head as he swept past. The blow was aimed at the point of jaw and ear. If it had connected, the combination of fragile bones and some inner weakness would have stunned his attacker long enough to be disarmed. Instead, he struck a little high. The shock ran up his arm and Domitianus cried out as the impact made his skull ring. When he had time to think, Valerius could barely believe what was happening. He'd always dismissed Titus's brother as a coward who would only attack a man if his back was turned. Yet the man who came at him again was an entirely different animal, driven beyond fear by a primeval urge for revenge. Shrugging off the blow with a shake of the head, Domitianus darted in, feinting right and left

290

and seeking a killing opportunity. Somehow, Valerius always managed to drift outside the reach of the curved blade, but he knew quick feet couldn't keep him out of trouble indefinitely.

'This is madness, boy,' he warned. 'I'm here on your father's business. Together we can stop this war.'

But Domitianus was beyond hearing or reason. With a sinking heart Valerius knew he might have no choice but to kill Vespasian's son.

Domitia had been shocked into silence by the initial assault. Recovering her wits, she opened her mouth to scream for help only for Domitianus to fell her with a backhanded swing that smashed into the side of her skull.

Valerius saw her fall and felt a roaring in his head. All thought of the knife forgotten, he charged the other man. His rush battered Domitianus to the ground and Valerius threw himself on the young aristocrat, clawing at his throat with his left hand. Vespasian's son retaliated with a panicked slash at his eyes, and only a lightning movement allowed Valerius to switch his grip to the younger man's right wrist. With the wooden fist in place he could have battered his opponent into a featureless pulp, but Domitianus was left free to scrabble for Valerius's windpipe. As they rolled and bucked Valerius forced the knife point aside and smashed his forehead into Domitianus's face. The satisfying crunch of broken cartilage and the flood of blood brought a surge of exhilaration. Domitianus continued to curse and claw at his eyes, but Valerius knew he had him. His left hand, strengthened by countless hours of sword practice, worked at the younger man's wrist until he could feel the bones rubbing together. Eventually Domitianus could take the pain no longer and with a cry of frustration he let the knife drop free and tried to wriggle away. Valerius held his grip and pushed himself to his feet, hauling Vespasian's son with him.

All the madness was gone now and he felt nothing but cold hatred. Domitianus whimpered in terror as Valerius dragged him past a recovering Domitia to the balcony. 'This is Rome,' Valerius's voice was as cold as an Iceni winter. 'Take a good look at it. In a few weeks, perhaps in a few days, it will be your father's. But you,' in one movement he turned Domitianus and switched his grip to the throat, pushing him so the stone balcony was stabbing into his back, 'will not live to see his triumph.'

'No, please . . .'

Valerius looked down to where a sow suckled a dozen piglets in a pen forty feet below. He nodded and slowly pushed Domitianus back until his legs were in the air. 'How appropriate for a pig like you.' He smiled and Domitianus shrieked as he saw his certain death in another man's eyes.

'No! Please, no.' Had the cry been from Sabinus, Domitianus would not have seen another dawn, but it was Domitia who shouted. 'Gaius Valerius Verrens is not a murderer.'

Valerius closed his eyes and released a long breath. All the anger drained from him like wine from a cracked amphora. With a grunt of frustration he hauled Domitianus back from the brink and threw him to the ground. He looked from the fallen man to Domitia, at the thin line of blood leaking from the corner of her lip. 'Very well,' he said, in a voice still touched by death, 'but if you ever touch the lady Domitia again I will hunt you down and kill you, Vespasian's son and Titus's brother or no. Do you understand?' He nudged the prone figure with his foot. 'I said do you understand?' Domitianus mumbled something, and Valerius would have asked again, but Domitia gave an almost imperceptible shake of the head.

'I have decided.' Titus Flavius Sabinus appeared without warning from amongst his apple trees, where he'd watched the whole contest. He looked down at his nephew with a disgusted shake of the head and turned to Valerius. 'I will meet Vitellius.'

XXXIX

Marcus Antonius Primus looked out over the plain towards the hill-top fortress of Narnia that was the last major obstacle between his army and Rome. He could see the banner of the Praetorian Guard whipping in the breeze over the well-defended entrenchments, and what must be ten thousand spear points glittering in the morning sunlight. He sniffed the air, enjoying the invigorating damp grass scent that followed a rain shower, and the haunting cry of a buzzard made him shiver.

He shrugged off the moment and turned in the saddle to study the massed ranks of his legions. Five now, because he'd decided that with no sign of Mucianus it was safe to bring up the cohorts he'd left at Verona. More than enough to crush Narnia, but they'd suffer casualties, perhaps heavy casualties. He imagined his soldiers marching in open order into the teeth of the Guard's *ballistae* and *onagri* fire. No, it would not do.

'What was their latest position?' The question was directed at the young aide who had gone out earlier to negotiate with the Vitellian commander.

'That Vespasian is a usurper and Aulus Vitellius Germanicus Augustus is the rightful Emperor, as declared by the Senate and people of Rome.' The tribune prudently neglected to include the filthy insults that had been hurled at Vespasian and his legate. 'They are his Praetorian Guard and they will fight to the death for him.'

'You took the prisoner to tell him about the defeat at Cremona? Their commander understands that he is alone now?'

'Yes,' the aide said. 'The legate of the Fifth Alaudae. He was most forthright.'

'Their reaction?'

'I . . . I think they were quite shaken, sir. But they said that General Valens is already on the march from Gallia Narbonnensis and that Emperor Vitellius will prevail.'

Primus sighed. He'd hoped it wouldn't come to this.

'Arrange another meeting at the fourth hour. Tell them that I wish to meet personally with their commander.' He turned his mount and rode off to his headquarters pavilion.

An hour later Primus waited between the two armies as the Praetorian commander galloped out with his escort. There was no need of an introduction: Primus had served in the same Senate as Julius Sempronius. Sempronius completed the last few horse lengths alone and Primus nodded a welcome to the grim-faced Praetorian in the dark tunic and sculpted silver breastplate. 'I salute your courage and your resilience, prefect,' he said. 'But I hope you will consider this final opportunity to allow your men to surrender with honour, and to march out with their arms and banners without fear of reprisal.'

The Praetorian prefect took less than a heartbeat to consider the offer. 'The honour of the Guard can only be satisfied by my continued resistance, general. Aulus Vitellius . . .'

'I understand that you are expecting reinforcements from the north?' Primus interrupted the traditional defiant platitudes.

Sempronius frowned. 'It is no secret that Valens is on the way with the legions of Germania and Gaul.'

Primus nodded thoughtfully. He turned and waved the young aide forward. Sempronius looked at what he was carrying and his eyes widened. 'I . . .'

'General Gaius Fabius Valens, an honourable man, and a brave soldier, would correct your assumptions if only he were able.' Primus spoke courteously, but with a coldness that made Sempronius hesitate as the aide handed over the leather water bucket. The Praetorian glanced at the contents and Primus saw his face turn a sickly grey, all the belligerence driven from him in a single shocking instant. 'Unfortunately, as you see, General Valens has already made the ultimate sacrifice for Rome and his Emperor.'

'You will allow me to consult with my officers, general?'

Primus nodded his agreement and the Praetorian turned his horse and returned to where his escort waited out of hearing distance. He returned moments later after a short conversation with his aides. 'I will need an hour.'

'Of course, prefect.' Marcus Antonius Primus kept his face solemn so as not to add to the other man's humiliation, but inside his heart was soaring.

The road to Rome was open.

Olivia's eyes opened with a snap as she felt a hand shaking her shoulder. Instantly awake, she could have cried out with relief when she recognized Lupergos. He would normally have been sharing her bed, but tonight had been on watch in one of the mini-forts out by the road. Her relief was short-lived.

'They're coming.' Urgency made his voice shake. 'Armed men on the road and in the trees.' Olivia tried to still a surge of fear. They had been expecting an attack down the road, but this meant that their carefully prepared defences had been outflanked. Lupergos squeezed her hand in reassurance. There was no time to dwell on what ifs. 'Here, take this.' As she slipped into her sandals, he wrapped a cloak around her shoulders and handed her a leather sack containing food and water. 'We will try to stop them,' he held her to his body and the strength of it made her want to cry out, 'but at the very least we will buy you time. Granta and Cronus are waiting.'

She could have argued. She was his woman. This was his child inside her. He should stay with her. But the courage and certainty in his voice left the words unsaid. Instead, she kissed him on the cheek. 'May Christus be with you,' she said quietly. But he was gone.

The sight of her father's ancient freedmen attempting to look warlike might have seemed comical but for the determination on their faces. She nodded gravely and followed them from the villa. Led by two young slaves armed with bows they made their way through the gardens and up into the olive groves behind. The caves Lupergos had provisioned were at the bottom of the south slope by the river. Olivia had planned to take the well-worn path, but if the raiders had come through the trees they were just as likely to approach the house from that direction too. Better to stay under cover in the grove. After the recent rains the ground was treacherously slippery and the going slow. Before they'd travelled two hundred paces they heard confused shouts, barked commands and then the first screams. A moment later one of the barns burst into flame and the earth beneath the olives was transformed into a confusion of unearthly shadows. More screams of mortal agony followed and she flinched because they were much closer now. The two slaves exchanged a glance and without a word dropped their bows and ran off up the hill. Granta and Cronus seemed paralysed by the desertions and she slipped past them.

'Come,' she said crossly when they still didn't move. 'Enough of this foolishness.' Granta shot her a look of embarrassment and took the lead, the spear held threateningly in front of him.

Soon the bulky shoulder of the hill sheltered them from the direct light of the flames, but a dull glow allowed them to keep their bearings. Granta increased his pace only to freeze a moment later. As Olivia watched, the old man sank slowly back to merge with one of the olive trunks. Hardly daring to breathe, she and Cronus silently emulated the movement. Three rows of trees separated Olivia from Cronus and a shadowy figure ran between them, only to be catapulted forward with a terrible shriek. Olivia pushed her fist into her mouth to keep from crying out. A second figure appeared and hauled a spear from between his squirming victim's shoulder blades. The dark silhouette straightened and the head swivelled to study the darkness. Whatever he sensed must have satisfied him because when she looked again he was gone. Granta waved them forward, but Olivia's legs would barely carry her.

A sudden image of Valerius gave her renewed strength. *Lupergos knows what to do*, he had said. *Keep yourself safe, stay calm and he will join you. If you become separated just follow the contour of the hill until you hear the river. The caves are at the bottom of the slope to your left. Stay quiet and do not move, no matter what you hear.*

Granta halted so abruptly that Olivia almost walked into his back. It was a moment before she heard the sound of stealthy movement all around them. The whites of Granta's eyes shone like ivory as he turned to face the threat. Cronus would be doing the same behind her. Oddly, she felt very calm as she slipped the knife from its sheath. Whoever was making the sounds began to close in and she placed the point firmly against her breast. Her only regret was for the unborn child in her womb. She began to pray, the words soft as the wind whispering through the trees. 'Our father . . .'

A stocky figure holding a sword stepped from the shadows.

XL

Could it have been an hour already? Valerius fought to still his nerves as he waited in the bright sunlight outside the temple walls. How many thousands of lives depended on what was decided just a few feet away? He consoled himself that he'd done everything he could to bring about this moment when sanity should prevail. Now it was up to the two men whose voices were a distant murmur. When the negotiations were completed the Emperor and Titus Flavius Sabinus would leave the precinct separately, along with their witnesses – Sabinus had chosen Cluvius Rufus, the former governor of Hispania. If Sabinus acceded to his demands, Vitellius would abdicate within two days and place himself under the city prefect's protection. He winced at a stab of pain from his injured wrist. The wound had proved less serious than it felt at the time, but it still throbbed beneath the cloth bandage that one of Sabinus's servants had applied.

If all went to plan Valerius was to take word of the agreement to Marcus Antonius Primus. He'd also carry a letter from Vitellius which, as his last act as Emperor, commanded the Praetorians to lay down their arms and allow Primus to pass. Yet everything depended on whether two men who despised and distrusted each other could come to an accord.

Nearby, Serpentius kicked moodily at the stony ground and studied the gilded ivory relief on the rightmost of the big double doors. It showed a battle scene full of sword-wielding soldiers in armour and strange helmets, carving the arms and heads from cowering naked barbarians. 'What did you say this was again?'

'I told you. The Celts took the Greek shrine at Delphi and the Greeks didn't like it, so they marched up the mountain and slaughtered them.'

'No need to be so testy,' the Spaniard muttered, squinting and studying it more closely. 'They don't look like any of the Celts I killed in the old Taurus.'

'It happened four hundred years ago and the sculptor had probably never seen a Celt, or a Greek for that matter.' The doors creaked and began to swing open. At last . . .

Aulus Vitellius Germanicus Augustus needed the help of his companion to descend the creamy marble steps, but he moved with surprising speed between the statues flanking the temple precinct. Valerius cursed under his breath as his old friend approached the gate. Vitellius's face glowed pink beneath the chalky mask of his make-up and the deep-set eyes glittered. His gait and every sinew of his obese body signalled suppressed fury. Failure.

By the time he reached Valerius the Emperor was struggling for breath, though whether through his exertions or anger wasn't clear. His first words confirmed Valerius's estimate of his temper.

'How am I to trust a man so ruled by his fears? He had the insolence to accuse me of trying to have him killed, this . . . this . . . renegade whose assassins have stalked my every footstep since I first donned the purple. A man who lives only through my benevolence.'

'The terms?' Valerius walked by his side to where the specially reinforced chair and its six mute Nubian bearers waited.

Vitellius stopped abruptly and turned to him, nostrils flaring. 'Not even half, and that so meagre in detail and so reluctantly furnished as to be worthless. He gives me numbers, which are far below my own estimates, and dispositions which are as unlikely as they are unmilitary. If he is to be believed he can barely protect himself, never mind my family. No list of senatorial supporters, so I can gauge the true worth of his support, and thereby the likelihood of the people following them. No token of his esteem that might show proof of his goodwill.'

Valerius closed his eyes. It was worse than he had feared. Sabinus had probably told the truth about the numbers, but Vitellius's fears had exaggerated them for so long the reality could never match his expectations. Valerius understood the ways of spies; knew how they indulged their masters' fantasies by providing them with what they wanted to hear. He cursed Sabinus for his parsimony – a fine diamond brooch for Galeria and a colt for Lucius might have changed the tone entirely – and for his veracity, a poor trait in a negotiator with so little to offer. Yet surely there could still be hope?

Vitellius's guards formed up around the litter and Valerius had to push his way through as the bearers set off towards the Clivus Palatinus. 'The names mean nothing,' he said urgently as he trotted alongside, the rhythm of his feet over the cobbles making his words sound disjointed. 'You cannot expect Sabinus to present you with the heads of his friends on a silver platter. He is protecting them – you would do the same. In any case, if you are the man I think you are, you already know every senator who supports him, especially the ones who claim not to.' The golden curtain twitched and he gave thanks he had the other man's attention. 'Give me two days and I will track down every cohort and century Sabinus commands. I will give you their true capabilities, the strengths of their commanders and their present dispositions. If I can do that, and convince you of Sabinus's sincerity, will you agree to another meeting?' The curtain twitched again, but otherwise there was no response. As the chair reached the top of the slope Valerius made one final attempt at reason. 'Do not let your anger rule you as his fear does him, Aulus. There is no other way. I have seen these streets flowing with blood once before. Do not let history say that is Aulus Vitellius's legacy.'

A sharp word of command brought the bearers to a halt. The curtains drew back and he found himself face to face with the Emperor. 'Very well.' Vitellius glared. 'If you can satisfy me that Sabinus is truthful and sincere, I will meet him again. Report to me when your investigation is complete.'

Valerius stepped aside as the Nubians moved to the trot. He watched the litter bounce off down the hill with the escort of Rhenus legionaries pushing through the crowds like a ship's ram. Serpentius appeared at his side and Valerius greeted him with a resigned smile. 'I would rather face a charge of Parthian Invincibles than spend another day in Rome,' he told the Spaniard. 'But we don't have any choice. Come, we have work to do.'

'I think we can disregard the *vigiles* as a known quantity.' Valerius frowned. 'We'd have had word if Sabinus took three thousand night watchmen and firefighters off the streets. In any case, even properly armed they don't have the training or experience to take on a single cohort of Vitellius's Praetorian veterans without being slaughtered.'

It was almost noon, and Serpentius nodded thoughtfully as he lay on a bed of the lodging house Vitellius had provided, just off the Forum Boarium and fortunately upwind of the slaughter pens. 'That leaves us with the urban cohorts, and they're a different animal altogether. I've seen them at work breaking up the bread riots a few years back. They might only have been up against beggars, shopkeepers and drunks, but they knew how to handle themselves. Hard men who've done their time in the legions up on the Danuvius and in Syria.'

'And under Sabinus's direct command,' the Roman agreed. The *cohortes urbanae* had been formed by Augustus to augment the Praetorians who acted as the Emperor's bodyguard and Rome's last line of defence. Over the years an intense rivalry had grown between the two codes. The four cohorts each contained a thousand men commanded by a tribune, and were responsible for maintaining public order.

'But they're not in their barracks out at the Campus Martius,' the Spaniard pointed out. 'So where are they?'

'From what I could see, Sabinus has at least half a cohort at the villa in case the Praetorians come knocking on his door. He must have the rest hidden away somewhere Vitellius has no chance of getting to them. Without them, Sabinus has no influence in Rome and they both know that.'

'I was thinking I might have a sniff around the crossroads bars out by the Campus Martius,' the Spaniard reflected. 'Whores like to talk and there must be a good chance some of the regulars are sweet on the girls and will have let them know where they are.'

'That's worth a try.' Valerius signalled his agreement with a grin. 'While you're romancing the ladies and getting drunk, I'll check out the villa. That half cohort is getting its rations from somewhere and Sabinus must have a way of contacting the others.'

They agreed to meet back at the *mansio* at dusk.

Valerius stationed himself at the end of an alley on the street where the half cohort had its main guard post. It helped that the soldiers only had eyes for those approaching the roadblock and had little interest in anyone outside their perimeter. Still, it was dreary work. He fought boredom as the hours passed, watching the comings and goings with half an eye as his mind turned to his parting from Domitia.

His first instinct had been to get her away from the Sabinus villa and out of reach of Domitianus. It was Sabinus himself who urged caution and to Valerius's surprise Domitia agreed. Where in Rome would she be safer than in a house guarded by five hundred soldiers? Even if the worst happened and Vitellius fought till the last, Sabinus would maintain a defensive ring of iron around the Esquiline. Defensive, he stressed; he would give the Emperor no reason to attack.

The city prefect had seen Valerius's cold glance towards Domitianus, skulking away with his face bloodied and a fine pair of black eyes already developing. He will not touch her, Sabinus had pledged, or I will kill him myself, for the honour of my family. Domitia's eyes had sought Valerius. Where would they go in a city filled with dangers? What security could he offer? The answer was none. She would be a burden to him, she was saying. First save Rome, then save Domitia Longina Corbulo. That is your duty.

He wanted to tell her that he loved her and that he would do anything to be with her, but everything stayed trapped inside. He prayed that his eyes conveyed as much as hers, but the thought struck him that he might never know.

A flicker of movement down by the guard post returned him to the present. A man in civilian clothes presented something to the officer of the watch. When he'd been waved through the newcomer strutted up the street towards Valerius. Despite the lack of uniform something about the way he carried himself said soldier. Valerius waited till his quarry was past before slipping into the street twenty or thirty paces in his rear. Their route took them up towards the Porta Esquilina, the city's east gate, then right along the road that ran inside the city walls. This was an old commercial district, the Vicus Corvius, named for the merchant family who'd once owned it and a place of workshops and warehouses.

As Valerius watched, the man darted right into a side street. The Roman stepped up his pace and reached the entrance in time to see him disappear into an enormous brick-built *horreum*, one of the warehouses that stored the city's grain supply. And who was in charge of that grain supply? He smiled because the answer was the Prefect of Rome. This was Sabinus's secret hideaway for the urban cohorts. Where better to conceal three thousand men in a teeming city than the gigantic barns that could easily double as barracks? Better still, the *horreum* was perfectly positioned to allow the city guard to pour out and surround Sabinus's villa. Or storm down the Esquiline Hill and take the Golden House, the Forum or the Senate. He had what he'd come for.

Within moments of leaving the *horreum*, Valerius was cursing his stupidity. Of course they'd have watchers. He risked a glance over his shoulder to take a first look at his followers. In the van, Titus Flavius Domitianus was instantly recognizable by the battered nose and blackened eyes. He'd clearly neither forgotten nor forgiven the beating Valerius had given him. Unless Valerius guessed wrongly, Vespasian's son was hiding a club or a sword beneath his cloak. The bruisers accompanying him looked like the toughest and ugliest the urban cohorts could provide. His eyes flickered to the right and left seeking some sanctuary, but there was no help to be had among the shops and houses. Only the fact that the street in front was crowded with people walking in the same direction gave him hope. If he could only stay ahead . . .

The quickest way back to the Forum was through the pottery workers' district and past the Porticus Liviae. As he reached the public gardens dedicated by Augustus and named for his wife, he could hear a growing hum, like a swarm of bees somewhere in the distance. A shoulder that felt as if it was made of marble nudged him unexpectedly from the side and he turned with a muttered curse.

'Trouble seems to follow you around.' Serpentius grinned and a surge of relief washed over Valerius. Nine to two might seem poor odds, but he would take them any time with the former gladiator at his side, even unarmed. 'Here, keep this under your cloak.' The Spaniard slipped something from the sack he was carrying and Valerius laughed aloud as his fingers closed on the hilt of a *gladius*. Now let them come.

'I didn't get much information from the bars or the bar girls,' Serpentius said cheerfully, 'and no one seemed to be around at the barracks, so I thought I'd break into the armoury so that it wasn't a complete waste of time.'

'I'm glad you did.' Valerius kept half an eye on Domitianus, who appeared to have recognized the Spaniard and was keeping his distance. 'Judging by all this,' he nodded to the thickening crowd around them, 'the pot is coming to the boil.'

'Aye.' Serpentius gave him a significant look. 'It seems that the Emperor has some kind of announcement to make.'

'What? He can't . . .'

The Spaniard's savage face turned solemn. 'The word on the street is that Narnia has fallen and General Valens is dead. Primus and his legions will be here in three days.'

XLI

Aulus Vitellius Germanicus Augustus felt an unnatural emptiness as his household slaves helped him don the black toga of mourning. Like the only living thing at a feast of spectres, his was a world filled with shadows and blurred outlines; an eerily silent world, for no person dared speak in his presence. Hours earlier he'd been the most powerful man in an Empire of forty million souls – an Emperor under siege, but an Emperor still. Now? Now he was nothing. When the courier brought confirmation of Valens' death and the surrender at Narnia, he had felt like a moth pinned alive to a board. His mind ran in circles, his heart thundered in his breast and his wings had flapped, but never a twitch had he moved. Then, as true comprehension dawned, the old Aulus Vitellius died, the life draining from him as effectively as from a man who has cut his own wrists. What remained was a shell. A body without a soul, a life without purpose. No railing at the vagaries of fate for Aulus Vitellius, though Galeria achieved enough for both as poor Lucius cowered in the corner. Whatever happened, he must save his family.

He could fight on, he still had the means. The people would support him, the Guard still possessed the strength and the will to hold the city walls. His brother Lucius commanded a substantial force in the south. Yet all that meant nothing when balanced against the overwhelming strength facing him. Cremona, and now Narnia, meant the end was not in question. The one cost him the cream of his legions, the other opened the door to Rome. Eventually, he would be hunted down and defeated, and his family would be killed. Yet even in despair Vitellius's frantically seeking mind was able to find a tiny silken thread of hope. His negotiations with Sabinus had created the possibility of an end without bloodshed. He could give up the throne immediately, with dignity and honour, and hand over control of the city to Sabinus. His decision made, he sent word to the Prefect of Rome that he would make the announcement in the Forum at the seventh hour.

Only Galeria had been informed of his decision, but nothing escaped his court. The ashen faces of his faithful Asiaticus and the others told their own story. They wept as he handed out gifts: the bejewelled rings adorning his fingers and the deeds for the villas and estates they'd inhabited as a mark of his favour. Of the two, the rings were of more significant value. It would be up to Vespasian to agree the transfer of the properties and it would be a brave man who placed much faith in the iron general's predilection for forgiveness. Still, the gesture was a measure of his gratitude. These men at least, unlike his generals and the senators who had proclaimed him, had stayed loyal to the end.

For a moment he stood swaying, unsure what to do next. Galeria and Lucius would have run to him, but he shook his head and tried to remember. A revelation from the mists of confusion. Of course, it was the symbol of his reign. He stumbled to the dais and opened the rosewood box to reveal the sword of the Divine Gaius Julius Caesar. He had removed it from the Temple of Mars when Galba appointed him governor of Germania, carried it during his triumphal entry into Rome, and been sustained by it since. Now his fevered brain told him he must pass it on, a token of his humility – he would not call it humiliation – that Sabinus could hand on to his brother. He remembered the sword as he'd first seen it, one like no other, the hilt wonderfully worked in spun gold, with precious stones decorating the scabbard and a miniature legion's eagle on the pommel. He'd never noticed before how heavy it was, an almost intolerable burden, but he would carry it with him today.

'Come,' he said to his family and his courtiers, his voice gruff from the effort of keeping it from breaking. 'Remember this not as the day Aulus Vitellius lost Rome, but as the day he saved it.'

He led the way through the corridors and along the marble tiles around the great artificial lake. It was here Nero had re-enacted naval battles in the pomp of his reign, and he shuddered at the manner in which that reign had ended. Behind him came Galeria with Lucius, followed by Asiaticus, Silius Italicus – the former consul who had attended the negotiations at the Temple of Apollo – and the rest. By the time they reached the doors leading to the Sacred Way Vitellius was sweating heavily despite the chill wind. Awaiting him were his lictors, already assembled, and an honour guard consisting of a century of Praetorians. No trumpets or drums or golden chariot drawn by four ivory-maned horses, just a single litter, which Vitellius ignored.

'I will not be carried on this day,' he announced to the astonishment of all. He sensed Galeria's outrage, but nothing would divert him. 'Let Lucius take the litter as if it were my funerary procession. It is only right, for today is the last that will be lived by Aulus Vitellius Germanicus Augustus. It is the end of the Emperor.' The Praetorians remained ramrod straight, but Vitellius sensed a collective reaction run through them, like the barest ripple of breeze across a summer corn field. He knew the impact his announcement would have on them individually and as a body, but he could not consider that now. 'In a few moments I will be plain Aulus Vitellius, patrician of Rome, and at my Emperor's command.' Vitellius flinched as Galeria Fundana reacted to the words by wailing and tearing at her hair as if her husband truly was dead. A second litter appeared and the tiny doll-like figure was helped into it, still emitting her baleful, undulating howl. Vitellius heard the Praetorian centurion whisper an order to one of the escort and the rasp of nailed sandals as the man turned and set off at a trot for an unknown destination.

Heralds had gone out an hour earlier to spread word of the Emperor's announcement, but Vitellius was shocked by the size of the crowd awaiting him outside the gilded gates of the palace complex. They lined the Via Sacra ten deep, and so close his lictors had to push their way through with threats and curses. Hundreds – no, thousands – more filled the steps and colonnades of the temples and basilicas along the route. A shout went up when they recognized the Emperor, but it turned into a moan of anguish as they saw the dark colour of his toga.

Vitellius felt a surge of outright fear at the unexpected sound and tried to ignore the sea of faces turned in his direction. This was not how it was meant to be. For all his terror he had imagined a dignified procession and a short announcement. He would pass on Caesar's sword to Sabinus and walk away with the stunned silence of the crowd in his ears. But this? This was how a man must feel marching to his own execution.

His steps faltered as if he were walking into a driving wind, legs suddenly weak and his mind overwhelmed by what he could only describe as a vast wall of *feeling*. It seemed to pulse towards him in a wave, threatening to engulf him and all who accompanied him. Even his lictors quailed before the unearthly outpouring of emotion, until the Praetorian centurion barked at them to keep their formation. Vitellius himself responded to the order like a ranker and recovered his stride, the ceremonial sword of Julius Caesar held across outstretched hands.

Onward through the avenue of soaring columns, each topped by a statue saved from the Great Fire of – could it be only five years ago? Past the familiar temples and the basilicas, some of them still bearing the scars of the blaze, that had been such a part of his life. Another chill made him shudder. He already thought of himself in the past. The *regia* where he had so recently performed the duties of Pontifex Maximus. A familiar face flashed into view among the crowds on a temple step, the white scar on the cheek and deep grey eyes staring in weary astonishment. Gaius Valerius Verrens. Of course, he remembered, he had told Valerius he would wait. But surely he must understand that the news from Narnia changed everything? Vitellius set his broad shoulders and took strength from the face and the memories it brought. Their time in Africa together, he dictating the affairs of state and, by his side, always dependable, the man he thought of as his sword.

A new wave of remorse. If Gaius Valerius Verrens had accepted his offer of a legion everything might have been very different. This man would have moulded an army where Valens and Caecina had let it moulder. Primus would have been swept aside, or thrown back into Pannonia, Mucianus left with no choice but to retreat or starve, and Vespasian forced to negotiate. He suppressed a sob and searched for the face again, but it was already lost in the crowd.

'What's the idiot doing?' Serpentius didn't hide his puzzlement.

'He's trying to give away an empire.' Valerius had understood the moment he saw the sword in Aulus Vitellius's hands; the sword of Caesar, in its familiar gilded scabbard with the legionary eagle on the pommel. 'The trouble is, will they let him?'

He was referring to the crowd, but as they pushed their way through the mob it was clear another factor would soon come into play. From the direction of the Argiletum a compact column of fully armed Praetorians forced their way through the gap between the Senate house and the Basilica Paulli. Shields at the ready, they marched in columns of four through the Forum to form a solid wall surrounding three sides of the Imperial rostrum. It was an impressive display of strength, designed to intimidate or inspire, depending on your loyalties. A murmur of surprise faded to a hushed silence and the tension in that confined space became almost physical. Valerius saw Vitellius hesitate at the sight and realized this was not part of his plan. He had a choice now. It would require an instant decision, but the outcome of the entire day might depend upon it. He was directly to the right of the Rostrum Julium. All it would take was three steps to mount the stairs, where he could appeal directly to the people and, through them, to the Guard. Valerius willed him to act, but, after a moment's nervous hesitation Vitellius continued along the Sacred Way to the Imperial rostrum. When he spoke from here it would be to the members of the Senate, drawn up in the almost military phalanxes that declared their loyalties, or at least their current allegiance in the ever-shifting sands of Roman politics.

With the Spaniard snarling at his side Valerius barged through the crowd to a position on the basilica steps where he could see what awaited Vitellius. Senator Volusius Saturninus held pride of place, looking as puzzled as any of them, and Trebellius Maximus, locked in discussion with their mutual enemy, Titus Sextius Africanus. Verginius Rufus and Caecillius Simplex, one of the two serving consuls, hovered on the margins as if searching for someone. Where was Sabinus?

Vitellius reached the level of the rostrum and stumbled to a shambling halt. With a clatter of wood on stone the litter bearers eased their burdens to the ground. Now that he'd reached his goal the Emperor seemed unable to decide whether to mount the platform, and a murmur of impatience began at the back of the crowd. At that moment Aulus Vitellius reminded Valerius of a chained bear broken beyond defiance, its chest scarred and torn by the dogs. Hair matted with blood it had stood, shoulders slumped and head down, seeming to pray for an end to its suffering. Finally, the Emperor's great head lifted and he turned to the senators, his desolate eyes seeking what? Support? Acknowledgement? Pity? Whatever he expected, it was not forthcoming. Not a hand moved nor an expression changed. A hundred men he had counted as colleagues and even friends were as indifferent to his fate as the marble statues that topped the fluted pillars along the Sacred Way. Another man might have been over-whelmed, but Aulus Vitellius seemed to take strength from the scorn of his enemies. With a great heaving sigh he moved towards the stairs. The black and silver ranks of the Guard parted and he hauled himself unaided to the podium, the sword of Caesar clenched beneath his arm. Augustus had stood here in all his pomp; Tiberius, before his descent into debauchery and his retreat to Capri; Gaius Caligula's dangerous eyes had roved crowds just like these seeking out his next victims; Claudius, who could barely speak two words to a stranger, but whose stutter miraculously disappeared when he stood before a thousand; and Nero, of course, driven mad by excess and power. But no Emperor had ever stood here like this.

Aulus Vitellius looked out over the shining helmets of the Praetorians and blinked as if he was seeing the enormous crowd for the first time. Valerius had been wrong. Standing on the Imperial rostrum he ignored the senators and spoke to the people. With a last glance at his family, he began.

'I have been your Emperor for one day shy of eight months.' His voice shook as he spoke those first dozen words, but it didn't lack strength. Vitellius had never lacked strength, only restraint. A few shouts went up to sing the praises of his reign, but he raised a hand for quiet. 'I ask only that you hear me out till the end and judge me on the whole of what I have to say and not just a part. Just as you must judge the whole of my tenure. During that eight months I have been soldier and priest, Pontifex Maximus, a member of the arval brethren, and a commissioner for the performing of the sacred rites and for organizing the sacred feasts. Despite the constraints placed upon me by the profligacy of my predecessors I have endowed temples and funded the great games. As a magistrate, I always tried to be just, though I am aware,' his eyes darted left to where the senators remained frozen in position, 'that certain calumnies have been uttered against my name. I curbed the power of the soothsayers and I maintained the grain supply at a reasonable price in trying circumstances.'

He paused and the only sound was the whistle of the bitter wind through gaps in the ochre roof tiles of the temples. 'I did not seek to be your Emperor,' he continued at last. 'But when the legions of my province hailed me as such in the days after Marcus Salvius Otho murdered Servius Sulpicius Galba, how could I refuse them?' From the basilica steps Valerius noted that his old friend had overlooked the fact that Valens and Caecina had been on the march for a week before he heard that Galba had been killed. Still, it was a small omission on this day of days. 'I did not want to fight, but when Otho held a knife to Rome's throat what choice did I have? When my legions defeated his armies on the field of Bedriacum, I treated those who had been my enemies with mercy and honour. I executed only those directly involved in the slaughter of their Emperor. No man who profited from the reigns of Galba and Otho was impoverished by me. I took no estates nor disinherited any sons.'

Vitellius's head had slumped forward as he recited the litany of his successes and his mercies, but now it rose again. His gaze roamed across his audience so every man, and the few women among them, felt he was gazing directly into their souls. 'I have made mistakes,' he acknowledged with a long sigh. 'I placed my trust in a man who was not worthy of it and that man turned traitor against me. You all know that man. Aulus Caecina Alienus, who tried to sell my army to our enemies like a common market trader. I should have led those armies in the field, but I left it to another. General Gaius Fabius Valens is dead, and I honour him for his service and his loyalty. It was not through lack of courage or strength that I did not march with my legions, but lack of confidence in my ability as a soldier. I was wrong.' He drew the sword of Caesar from its golden scabbard. 'I believe my soldiers would have fought better knowing their Emperor fought by their side with the sword of a hero in his hand.'

Despite his entreaty for quiet a great shout went up from the crowd and the soldiers at the front surged towards him. Lead them and they would follow, whatever the odds. Caesar's sword would carry them to victory over the usurper. They wept at their Emperor's suffering and Vitellius put a hand to his eyes to dash away the tears of pride and regret and the realization that he had failed these people. His people. But that was not why he was here. For a second time he raised a hand for silence.

'There are different kinds of courage,' the enormous barrel chest heaved as he stifled a sob, but somehow he recovered himself, 'and believe me when I say that Aulus Vitellius would have had the courage to fight, and, if need be, to die with his soldiers. Yet sometimes it takes courage to do what is right, even when what is right makes a man look – and yes, feel – like a coward. A man might want to fight on for the sake of honour and pride, but when fighting on means more harm and suffering to his people is not that honour so tainted that it is no longer honour? Is not what is left pure selfish pride?' The fat hands shook as they sheathed the sword. 'I did not ask to be your Emperor. In truth, two men created Aulus Vitellius Germanicus Augustus, and one of those men is dead and the other in chains. I have failed you as a commander. The enemy will soon approach the gates of this city. If I force them to attack, fire and steel and blood will rain down on

312

the streets of Rome. Fire and steel and blood on the Forum where you stand. I cannot allow that. I will not allow that.' He held up the sword of Julius Caesar and his voice regained its strength. 'If Rome is to be saved from destruction and death I can no longer be your Emperor. This sword is the symbol of my office. I will hand it to a man capable of ensuring a peaceful transfer of power to Vespasian, should the Senate and people of Rome see fit to appoint him Emperor in my place. That man is Titus Flavius Sabinus, Prefect of Rome.'

By the pillar in the basilica Valerius experienced a surge of relief. This was Sabinus's moment. All he had to do was step forward and accept the sword and Rome could sleep easy tonight. But where was he?

On the rostrum, Vitellius turned to find the ranks of senators watching him with something close to horror. His numbed mind slowly comprehended that something wasn't right. What did those expressions mean? Every nerve had been concentrated on reaching this point, and he felt close to collapse now that he had come to the end. Where was Sabinus? He searched for the familiar, despised face. 'That man is Titus Flavius Sabinus, Prefect of Rome,' he repeated, desperation making his voice shrill. When it was clear there would be no answer he stumbled from the podium towards the Senate steps. 'Where is Titus Flavius Sabinus?'

A dozen more heartbeats passed without a reply. Vitellius was left standing with the sword in his hand and his carefully orchestrated plan stuck fast like a ship on a sandbank. He searched frantically for a face he recognized, someone who would save him from this. All he wanted was to hand over the sword and walk away. Instead, he felt like a small child lost without its mother and he experienced an irrational urge to weep.

He advanced through the lines of horror-struck senators with Caesar's sword offered out before him. Not a man moved to take it. Every one backed away, shunning him as if he were a plague carrier. At last, he found a trusted face, plump and bland, but a man he had promoted to high office. 'Gnaeus Caecillius Simplex, will you deliver your Emperor's sword where it is needed?'

Simplex raised his hands, but to ward off the evil being foisted on him, not to accept the sword. He stepped away, shaking his head in mute regret.

'Saturninus, old friend. You have been feasting with Sabinus of late . . .' But Saturninus had already turned away, and now they were all going. In moments the precinct was free of purple-striped togas.

His spirits rose momentarily as a familiar presence appeared at his side. 'Come, Aulus,' Galeria said quietly, 'we must return to the palace.'

'No.' He shook his head and Galeria was shocked at the almost childlike smile that wreathed her husband's face. 'The Temple of Concord. That is where we must deposit the sword. They can keep it for Sabinus. Not Concord? Mars Ultor then. Yes, that is where Caesar's sword belongs.' He changed direction, seemingly oblivious of the hundreds of people around him. As he pushed his way towards his friend, Valerius noticed the increasingly fractious mood of the Praetorian Guard. These were men whose futures were as entangled with that of Vitellius as ivy stems clinging to an oak tree. If Vitellius fell they would fall with him. By now Valerius had a feeling no promises from Sabinus would satisfy them. When he reached the Emperor's side their commander was already haranguing the mob in much the same terms from the rostrum steps.

'Aulus Vitellius Germanicus Augustus is the Emperor as appointed by the Senate and people of Rome,' the soldier shouted. 'Nothing can change that but the Senate and people of Rome. The Praetorian Guard is the instrument of the Senate and people of Rome, oathsworn to serve and protect the Emperor from all threats external and domestic. We will fight to our last breath and our last drop of blood to fulfil that oath.' His voice grew louder, so it could be heard even at the far end of the Forum. 'You will have heard the name Cremona. Cremona is an example of the mercy the people of Rome will receive from the rebels if they take this city. Do not be deceived by their lies. Cremona was surrendered without a fight, but its people were slaughtered just the same. They submitted, but their houses were burned and pillaged just the same.'

Valerius sensed a ripple of fear run through the crowd as though the Praetorian's words were a stone thrown into the centre of a pool. 'What can we do to stop them?' The plea came from somewhere in the centre of the great mass.

'You can fight,' the Praetorian snarled. 'The men of the Guard will not submit and they expect the people of Rome to fulfil their oath to the Emperor they appointed. Every able-bodied man must report to the armoury at the Castra Praetoria to be issued with weapons. An extra ration of grain will be distributed tomorrow from the fourth hour. It is the duty of every family to stockpile what food they can in case of siege.'

'On whose orders?' another man demanded.

'On the orders of the Emperor.' The Praetorian looked towards Vitellius, daring him to deny it, but the Emperor seemed to have drifted from this world part way to the next. Galeria opened her mouth to argue the point for her husband, but Valerius laid a hand on her arm.

'This is no time to provoke the only force capable of keeping you safe, my lady.'

The Augusta glared. 'Just because my husband has decided to trust you, do not think your writ runs in this family,' she snapped.

'What about the Senate?' the man in the crowd continued his argument.

'You saw the worth of the Senate. What do you think?' the Praetorian officer spat back to general amusement.

And he was right. Valerius felt a surge of helpless anger. If the Senate had supported Vitellius's abdication, even the Praetorians would have been hesitant about opposing the legitimate political power in Rome. But fear of being tainted by association had paralysed them. Instead, the only man who had tried to save Rome was the one man who no longer had the power to do so.

Vitellius had depended on Titus Flavius Sabinus to tip the balance against the Praetorians, and Titus Flavius Sabinus had betrayed him.

Where was the Prefect of Rome?

Valerius studied his surroundings with growing alarm. Vitellius was still trying to make his way towards the Temple of Mars Ultor, but the crowd barred his way, touching his mourning robes and imploring him to remain. Ominously, the Emperor's personal Guard stood back, taking their lead from the grim Praetorians in front of the rostrum. The men in black and silver looked capable of turning on the Imperial family at a word from their commander. Lucius plucked at his father's arm and tried to draw him back to the litter, but Vitellius only looked at him in confusion. 'Come, Aulus.' Valerius pushed his way to Vitellius's side and took his old friend by the shoulder. 'It is time to go home.'

As he helped the Emperor into one of the litters he sensed a malevolent presence somewhere close by. He looked up to find Domitianus staring at him with undisguised hatred from between the pillars of the basilica. Beneath his cloak, Valerius's left hand went to his sword, but by the time it was half drawn Vespasian's son was gone.

'Serpentius?' The Spaniard emerged from the crowd like a wraith at his call. 'I'll stay with the Emperor. You go to Sabinus's villa and try to find out what's happening.'

'And the lady Domitia?'

There it was again, that terrible conflict between love and duty. Valerius shook his head. 'Sabinus must be your first priority, but do what you can.'

XLII

'He was going to hand you the keys to Rome, but you were too frightened to take them.'

Titus Flavius Sabinus's left eye twitched at the undisguised contempt in his nephew's voice. 'It was a trap,' he defended himself. 'Did you not see the Praetorians? They would have butchered me the moment I set foot on the rostrum.'

'When courage was needed you showed none.' Domitianus continued his attack, stalking the room like a caged lion as Sabinus lay slumped in his favourite chair. Since the fight with Gaius Valerius Verrens the Prefect of Rome had seen a new and worrying side of Vespasian's son. Hatred and a burning desire for revenge had wiped away the boy and created a formidable and dangerous man. Not dangerous like his father, whose ruthlessness was tempered by natural decency, but dangerous and unpredictable like a snake. Allow him within striking range and you would regret it. If Sabinus was being honest this new Domitianus frightened him.

'A small escort, he assured me,' the prefect continued. 'A cohort of the Praetorian Guard was not part of our agreement. It is not too late. I will send a messenger to the palace to reopen the negotiations. An agreement is still possible.'

'Agreement?' Domitianus laughed aloud. 'Your messenger would not get within twenty paces of the Domus Aurea. The Guard has set up camp outside the walls and no one gets past without their sanction. The only agreement you would get is the confirmation that you are an old fool when they sent back your messenger's head.'

'Then we must protect ourselves.' Sabinus cringed at the plaintive, almost pleading quality to his voice. He knew what Domitianus was thinking. Could this be the same man who forced the River Tamesa with the Fourteenth legion? The man who helped destroy the mighty Caratacus? Well, Domitianus would discover that a man at sixty-five was not the same man he had been at forty. He no longer had the energy for ambition or the strength for hatred. He did not hate Vitellius. If anything he pitied him. Conspiracy was all very well, but the thought of action made him long for his bed and the ministrations of a pliant slave girl. And Domitianus was right. He was frightened. The grim, determined features of the Praetorians had made his heart quail, but not so much as the enthusiasm of the crowd for their Emperor. Perhaps he could have made the soldiers see reason, but the mob would have torn him apart. 'We will fortify the house, garrison it with the urban cohorts.'

'And wait to be burned out?' the younger man demanded. 'This house is indefensible and you know it, uncle. It is overlooked on both sides and the rear. Do you think a few more planks and grain sacks will stop a man like Gaius Valerius Verrens?'

'This is not about Verrens,' Sabinus snapped. Something in the younger man's eyes told him he was wrong. Domitianus's hand went to his smashed nose and he looked as if he were capable of doing murder. Sabinus tried to inject some authority into his voice. 'And the lady Domitia Longina Corbulo is a guest in my house. You would do well to remember that, Domitianus.'

Domitianus approached his uncle's chair with a cold smile. Sabinus noticed with a slight shiver that the young man had armed himself with a sword since his visit to the Forum. 'If you did not have the courage to accept Caesar's sword from the hand of Aulus Vitellius do not have the temerity to dictate to me, uncle.' He turned away with a giggle and Sabinus wondered, not for the first time, if his nephew was quite sane. Domitianus had told him about Domitia's letter to Vitellius giving details of his discussions with the Senate, but in a house full of conspirators what was one more? He knew for a fact that Domitianus had been trying to undermine his authority with the urban cohorts. He blamed himself more than his guest for her lapse. He should have been more careful, but he'd never been a man to concern himself with detail. The Corbulos had always been rather fixated on the subject of duty. The poor girl obviously believed she'd done what was right. Domitianus on the other hand had wanted her scourged and offered to wield the whip himself. Sabinus found their relationship, or at least his nephew's view of it, confusing.

'You—'

'No, Sabinus, *you. You* have half the Senate here wanting to know what you plan to do and hundreds more of my father's supporters outside. *You* have three thousand men of the urban cohorts going hungry and sick of being looked down on by the Praetorian Guard. *You* are the man who will have to explain why he failed when my brother-in-law Cerialis appears at the gates of Rome tomorrow and discovers them closed against him.'

'Tomorrow?' Sabinus's voice shook.

'Yes, tomorrow. Word came an hour ago while you were still having the vapours. His cavalry forms the vanguard of the army.'

'Tomorrow? It is not possible,' the older man repeated. 'They said another week.'

'You must act now,' Domitianus insisted. 'The time for waiting is gone.'

'No, I must—'

'Or do you have another reason than fear for your hesitation?' Domitianus's voice turned soft as a serpent's kiss and his eyes widened as if in sudden comprehension. 'Could it be that you do not fully support my father's claim to the purple? Could it be that the elder brother has aspirations of his own? Is that why you delay, uncle?'

'No, of course not, my loyalty is to—'

'Then act.' Domitianus towered over his uncle, his anger making him seem taller. 'Take your urban cohorts and the Senate and march to the Forum and make your own proclamation. *I, Titus Flavius Sabinus, Prefect of Rome, accept the offer of Aulus Vitellius, former Emperor, former Pontifex Maximus, to surrender the city to me to maintain order until such time as the Senate and people of Rome choose a successor.* You will reassure the Guard their positions and lives are safe, and a donative will be paid to ensure their future loyalty. The people will be free from hunger and unmolested because we will allow only the generals and their personal bodyguard into the city. Secure the Forum and you secure the city. Vitellius does not have enough Praetorian Guards both to man the walls and to cover any movement of the urban cohorts and the *vigiles*. Their only option will be to lay down their arms. The city will fall with not a life lost and Titus Flavius Sabinus will be hailed a hero. You cannot lose, but you must . . . act . . . now.'

Listening to those words, Sabinus felt a surge of his old energy. Domitianus was right. Through fear he had failed his brother when Vitellius had tried to hand over Caesar's sword. He must not fail him again.

'I will send a messenger to Vitellius to meet us at the Forum.'

'No,' Domitianus almost shouted. 'Did you not hear me? We cannot warn Vitellius without warning the Guard. Come.'

The senators had begun arriving at the villa in little groups soon after Vitellius left the Forum. Each of them sought reassurances about their own, and the city's, security from the man the Emperor had so publicly appointed as his political heir. About fifty of them jostled in Sabinus's receiving room, eyeing each other suspiciously and already anticipating the changes in allegiance required to prosper amid the new order.

Sabinus froze in the doorway at the sight of the massed ranks and he would have turned back but for Domitianus's firm hand on his shoulder. As his uncle stood quite speechless, the younger man realized he needed to act before panic spread. He searched the crowded room until he found the perspiring face he sought.

'Volusius Saturninus? My uncle goes to save Rome. He marches to the Forum to accept Vitellius's offer. Will you accompany him?' The veteran senator shuddered at being singled out, but he knew that to hesitate would cost him when Vespasian came to power. 'Yes, I will accompany him. I will place my life at risk to save Rome.'

'And you, Verginius Rufus? You have supported my uncle since the beginning. Will you fail him now?' Rufus saw his hopes of a lucrative province, the product of so much risk and so much indignity, fading. How could he refuse? How could any of them refuse? A few at the rear of the room tried to slink away, but Domitianus had placed a guard at the door and they found themselves corralled.

'My father thanks you and will reward you,' the young man told them. 'This is your day. A day of honour that Romans will speak of for generations.'

He disappeared from the room for a few moments before returning to his uncle's side. 'No going back now, Sabinus,' he whispered. He nodded at the senators, milling about looking shocked at their own bravery and wondering what came next. 'They need a leader, uncle. The die is cast and the outcome is not in doubt. But we must act quickly. I've ordered a century of the First cohort to secure the Forum and the centurions are assembling your entire strength. Now.'

Conflicting emotions flickered through Sabinus. Fear, dismay, anger at the way he had been manipulated, and finally resolve, because he knew Domitianus was right. He had no other option.

'Gentlemen?' He straightened to his full height. 'The Forum.'

He led them out, with Saturninus at his side, and the rest of the senators followed in twos and threes. Domitianus had already instructed his uncle's guards that they should be encouraged – herded like cattle if need be – to stay together. He held back slightly and spoke to two of the men.

Domitia had kept to her room since the altercation between Valerius and Domitianus, but the sense of anticipation among the guards and servants told her something was going on. The feeling had grown throughout the morning and now a murmur of sound brought her to the doorway just as the two guards appeared. They announced that she was to join Sabinus and that she should put on her cloak. Her first instinct was to tell them she would not be ordered around without an explanation, but their cold expressions told her she'd be wasting her time. She chose her warmest cloak – the blue one – and accompanied them to where Domitianus waited by the entrance.

'I hope you have an explanation for disturbing me, sir,' she said coldly.

To her surprise he greeted the question with none of his usual condescension. 'My uncle Sabinus is about to make history, and since you have always valued it I thought you might like to attend.'

He led her through the crowd of senators and the supporters and clients who had accompanied them to where Sabinus paced nervously, forced to wait for the urban cohort that was to escort him. They took their place among the politicians closest to the prefect. By now it was late afternoon and Domitia saw the skies were clear, as if autumn had ordered winter to take a step back for a day. She noted the uneasiness of the men around her and wondered how many of them were willing participants in the Prefect of Rome's plans. Eventually, the sound of marching feet heralded the arrival of the cohort. The tribune in charge assigned a century to escort the leading group of Sabinus and his reluctant political supporters. The rest would bring up the rear. Every man carried a sword, spear and shield and Domitia shivered as her nose caught a distinctive scent she had only experienced once before. The mixed odours of sweat, fear and something indefinable that was the smell of a man anticipating battle. The sight of the soldiers sent a murmur through the politicians and their supporters, but it faded as Sabinus led them out of the villa gates into the road. Their route took them down towards the Subura and in the streets around the Porticus Liviae traders, workmen and their customers gaped in astonishment at the silent, grim-faced soldiers advancing with such purposeful strides. Faces began appearing in the windows of the apartment blocks lining the streets and neighbours shouted questions to each other above Domitia's head. A cry went up when someone recognized the politicians in the midst of the soldiers.

'It's Sabinus. And look, there's old Metellus.'

'Are they being arrested?' The big-breasted woman hanging out of a second-storey window sounded pleased at the prospect.

'Fat chance,' an elderly man on the other side of the street chortled. 'Lean out a bit further, Liv, and I'll give you a squeeze.'

The woman disappeared with a suggestion that was at best anatomically unsound. On the street below a tanner appeared from an alley. 'What's happening?' he asked the owner of the next door bakery.

'It looks like they're taking over,' the baker frowned.

'Where's the Emperor?'

The baker didn't reply, but he began to hurriedly gather up his stock.

Sabinus marched onwards looking neither left nor right. Soon they were on the Argiletum and news of their coming must have preceded them because every door was closed. The only signs of life were the heads peering fearfully out of upstairs windows. As the procession passed in the shadow of the Temple of Mars Ultor, the head of the column seemed to stutter. Domitia frowned as she heard the unmistakable sounds of fighting: cries and screams and the clatter of iron on iron. Domitianus tightened his grip on her arm and dragged her towards his uncle.

'What's happening?' he demanded. Sabinus could only shake his head wordlessly. He pointed to the gap between the Senate house and the Basilica Paulli where the advance guard Domitianus had sent to secure the Forum could be seen bending over a dozen prone bodies. Blood flowed red over the dark paving between the rostra at either end of the Forum.

'This shouldn't have happened,' Domitianus hissed. Domitia looked at Sabinus and wondered that a human being could be so pale and still live. A soldier's daughter, her heart quailed at the implications of what she was seeing. She heard worried murmuring amongst the politicians in the procession behind, but her attention was drawn to the urban cohort centurion who ran up to report to Sabinus.

'A few of these Praetorian traitors tried to stop us, but the Forum has been secured as commanded. What are your orders, prefect?' A shout of warning rang out and the officer turned sharply in time to see one of the prone men leap to his feet and run off in the direction of the House of the Vestals. 'Get that man,' the centurion roared.

Too late. As they watched, the wounded Praetorian disappeared among the temples leaving only his shouts echoing between the marble columns. 'Murder! Betrayal! The traitors have risen.'

'Your orders?' the centurion repeated, but Sabinus seemed to have been struck dumb. Meanwhile, most of the senators and patricians had slipped quietly away at the sight of the spilled blood and the terrible consequences it heralded. Domitianus hurried after them, attempting to persuade them to stay, but none would even look at him. In desperation he dragged at Saturninus's arm, but the senator shrugged him away.

'We came here to witness a peaceful handover of power.' The politician's voice was edged with fear and heavy with disgust. He waved a despairing hand at the bleeding bodies lying on the black tiles. 'We wanted nothing to do with this.'

'Stay with us,' Domitianus urged. 'We can still win. My father's legions will be here in a day, two at most. Vitellius won't dare act against us.'

'Perhaps not,' Saturninus said. 'But this will bring the entire Praetorian Guard down on you. I see nothing here but blood and death.'

'He's right. That bastard will be off squealing to his Praetorian mates at the palace,' the tribune in charge of the escort cohort said. 'We can't hold the entire Forum against them until Primus's legions get here.'

'Then find somewhere we can hold,' Domitianus insisted. As he spoke his eyes were drawn to the looming bulk to his right.

XLIII

'This man says he is known to you.'

Valerius looked up to see Serpentius struggling like a chained animal between two big Praetorians. In the packed anteroom Vitellius's waiting aides backed away from the snarling figure in the doorway, appalled at the savagery written in every line of the Spaniard's face.

'These idiots have had me in the guardroom for an hour,' the former gladiator raged. 'They wouldn't listen.'

'Free him,' Valerius ordered, 'and return to your posts.'

He offered Serpentius a cup of wine, but the Spaniard shook his head. 'We've no time for that,' he rasped. 'You have to come now. Sabinus and the urban cohorts have seized the Capitoline. They've left a dozen dead Praetorians in the Forum and now the Guards' mates are on the way with blood in their eyes.' Something in his voice changed and Valerius felt a terrible foreboding. 'Domitianus is there. He's taken the lady Domitia with him.'

The room seemed to disappear for a moment until the iron grip of Serpentius's fingers on Valerius's arm returned him to reality. 'No time for that, my friend,' the Spaniard said. 'We must go. Now.'

'The Emperor . . .'

'He'll hear soon enough.' Serpentius was already on the move. 'But only the gods know what he can do about it. This city is like a scorpion stinging itself to death. It's as if people think the only way to avoid a repeat of what happened at Cremona is for Primus to be welcomed to a city in ashes with the streets already filled with bodies.'

They hurried through the gardens and past the lake, but by the time they reached the Sacred Way it was already filled with Praetorian units making their way towards the Forum. Valerius paused to look out across the sea of golden statuary, white marble and ochre tiles. On the far side the Temple of Jupiter Optimus Maximus stood like an impregnable citadel on the western of the Capitoline's two summits. The temple, the holiest in all Rome, was surrounded by a clutter of smaller shrines, arches and altars, each set in its own compound. To the right, across the dip of the asylum, more ancient and careworn, lay the Temple of Juno Moneta, on the platform known to all as the Arx.

'How many men did Sabinus have with him?' he asked Serpentius.

'A single cohort when he came down from the villa on the Esquiline. It depends whether he had time to bring in reinforcements before the Praetorians got here in any strength.'

Valerius turned the situation over in his mind. A thousand men. Not enough to defend the entire hill. Sabinus would have to set up strong-points to hold the stairs and the Clivus Capitolinus. That way he could fortify the temple precinct and hold out for days. The urban cohorts were a police force, but that force was made up of trained soldiers, and even the Praetorian Guard would struggle to winkle them out of such a formidable position. He only prayed that their commander realized that. Better to talk Sabinus out than have men slaughtered in one futile attack after another.

But when he forced his way through to the base of the hill he realized he'd prayed in vain. Cornelius Clemens, the stony-faced tribune in charge of the Praetorian force, had done all the talking he was going to do.

'You say you're here from the Emperor?' Clemens had encircled the base of the Capitoline mount with two of his cohorts; the others waited in formation on the Via Sacra out of spear range of the hill's jeering defenders. 'Well, you can go back and tell him we advised the traitor

Sabinus to surrender, only to have him respond with accusation, threat and insult. Do they think they can occupy the most sacred site in the Empire and expect us to let them sit there and taunt us? He even had the effrontery to claim the Emperor was responsible for the deaths of his own soldiers.' The man's face flushed with suppressed fury. 'Twelve of my men. Good men all, murdered by a gang of backstabbing traitors. Well, it doesn't matter where they hide or how long it takes, I am going to make them pay.'

'Perhaps it would be better to wait for the Emperor to arrive in person,' Valerius suggested. 'It might avoid more bloodshed.'

Clemens pushed his face into Valerius's, so close the one-handed Roman could smell the sour wine on his breath. 'Maybe you don't hear so well. Those were my men lying with their throats cut. The way I hear it, the Emperor won't be leaving the palace any time soon. My lads don't like what they hear about their tentmates surrendering without a fight at Narnia. If I don't order them up that hill then like as not they'll go anyway. Now take yourself out of here.' He threw a contemptuous glance at the mottled purple stump of Valerius's arm. 'This is no place for a cripple.'

'There's a woman with them . . .'

'More than one, so we hear.' Clemens softened a little. 'But if they're with that nest of traitors, they'll have to take their chances. I won't risk the lives of any of my men to keep them safe.'

Serpentius was waiting on the far side of the waiting Praetorians, beside the little circular shrine to Venus Cloacina. Valerius explained what he'd been told. 'So where does that leave us?' the Spaniard asked.

'I need to get Domitia out of there, but . . .'

'. . . the only way to get her out is to get inside first, and that isn't going to be easy.'

Valerius looked up at the towering bulk of the temple. 'The odds of getting through Clemens' cordon without his permission are slim. Even if we did someone would probably put a spear in us while we were explaining why we were there.' Neither man voiced the terrible reality of what would happen to the defenders if the Praetorians successfully stormed the hill. A soldier with blood in his eye wasn't going to be concerned about the age or gender of the people who got in the way of his sword.

'That doesn't leave us many options.' Serpentius paused as shouted orders were passed down the line of men to the foremost cohorts. He met Valerius's eye. 'And time is getting short.'

Valerius tried to still the fear that rose inside him. 'There has to be a way.' He ran back through the ranks to the command post. Clemens was briefing his officers, but he'd just noticed the several hundred people gathered among the temples surrounding the Forum. 'Jupiter's piles, where in the god's name did all these civilians come from?' he complained to one of his aides. 'Get rid of the buggers. What do you want now?' he demanded when he saw Valerius.

Valerius knew he only had one chance. He outlined the situation quickly and succinctly, one officer explaining a potential complication to another. 'The woman in question is General Gnaeus Domitius Corbulo's daughter and she is not with the rebels of her own free will.' He saw surprise and a degree of respect in the other man's eyes. 'I served with the general in Syria and before he died I promised I'd protect her, so you see my problem. It is a matter of honour and duty. If you're sending your men into the temple I'd count it a favour to go with them.'

Clemens' grim features twisted into a frown of calculation. His first instinct was to refuse the request outright, but he was a man who understood honour and duty. If there was a chance of saving the women – and one of them was Corbulo's daughter . . . He made his decision. 'If you're stupid enough to want to get yourself killed that's up to you. You can go in at the tail of the cohort. Just remember you're on your own. Once it starts no one's going to stop and help you. I take it you'll be accompanied by that murderous-looking bastard who's watching your back?' Valerius laughed. Serpentius would be pleased with the description. 'I doubt he'll have trouble finding the pair of you a blade and there's a pile of shields over by the steps of the basilica.' He was interrupted by a rattle of metal as the leading Praetorian cohort hefted their *scuta*. Valerius nodded his thanks and ran off shouting for Serpentius to fetch swords and a shield. When they were armed they took station at the rear of the last century. The black and silver-clad Guards in the final ranks turned to study the newcomers.

'We're safe now, lads,' someone muttered. 'Some aristo's come to lend us a hand, and he's brought his mangy old hound with him.'

'How about if this mangy old hound rips your fucking throat out when we're done with this hill?' Serpentius growled back.

'You'll be lucky if you can get up that hill, grandad.'

'Save your breath,' Valerius said before the Spaniard could continue the conversation.

Serpentius glared at him. 'We've done some daft things, but I reckon this is the craziest yet.'

'You know why we're doing it. If anybody's mad, it's you for coming with me.'

'Bloody women,' the Spaniard spat. 'A month ago we were fighting for Vespasian. Now we're attacking his brother, with no armour and one fucking shield between us. We might as well go the whole way and fight naked like those Celtic barbarians you were telling me about.' His face dissolved into a grin, then sobered again as the men ahead began to move forward down the Sacred Way towards the Capitoline.

It had begun.

XLIV

Valerius drew his sword when the ground began to rise beneath his feet and they turned from the Sacra Via on to the Clivus Capitolinus. Ahead, the first rocks and spears began to clatter against the upturned shields of the leading centuries as they trotted up the slope. Serpentius raised the curved *scutum* to cover both their heads. For the first time Valerius longed for the comforting protection of a *testudo* and the familiar weight of plate armour on his shoulders and chest. Serpentius had been right, this was madness. He wouldn't do Domitia any good by getting killed.

'Glad you came?' chuckled a voice from amongst the shields in front.

'This is like picking ripe peaches compared to Bedriacum,' Serpentius spat back, still holding the heavy *scutum* at shoulder height.

'You were at Bedriacum?' The voice gained a new respect. 'I was with the Twenty-first then. *Optio*, third century Second cohort. Who were you with?'

'The First Adiutrix and we kicked your arses for a while. Found your eagle yet?'

A centurion's bark ended the exchange as the column stuttered to a halt.

'That'll be the leading century up to their necks in the shit,'

Serpentius predicted. Valerius realized the Spaniard was right. Up ahead men were bleeding and dying as the centuries of the First cohort fought off a shower of spears and arrows and hammered at the gates where the road met the saddle between the two summits. Meanwhile, the rest of the column would have to endure.

Serpentius cursed as a rock clattered off his raised shield. To their right a series of columned porticoes flanked the road and from the roofs Flavian supporters and red-tunicked soldiers of the urban cohorts hurled spears, rocks and roof tiles on to the attackers who could only protect themselves as best they could. A growl of frustration escaped Valerius's throat. He knew what would happen if the leading centuries finally broke through the gates. One thing was certain: he was doing Domitia no good back here.

He shouted to Serpentius. 'We need to get closer to the front.'

'You mean where the spears are thickest?' the Spaniard said sourly. But he was already moving. They edged their way between the tight-packed column and the stonework of the porticoes. It took them directly beneath the defenders' missiles, but Valerius knew anyone trying to drop a boulder on them would have to expose themselves to a degree that would probably be fatal. The stalled attackers suffered the spears and stones with resignation apart from the odd howl when a point found its mark between the shields.

By the time they reached the lead century the gate to the Capitoline summit was already well splintered by their battering ram. It looked to Valerius as if a few more blows would see it split apart and he cursed as the *testudo* protecting the ram began to edge backwards. When it was clear of the worst of the missiles the unit's centurion darted out of the armoured tortoise and took shelter by the wall beside the two men in civilian clothing.

'Who the fuck are you?' the centurion demanded.

'Gaius Valerius Verrens, adviser to the Emperor, observing your attack.' The soldier's face twisted into a grimace as if he'd just bitten into an unripe lemon. Clearly the last thing he needed was any hint of Imperial interference. Still, he could hardly ignore the Emperor's representative.

'You can tell him that we would already have taken the place if those heathen bastards hadn't torn down every statue and column and used them to barricade the gate.' He licked his lips and spat. 'Defeated by gods and long dead fucking generals. Wood we can deal with, but we can't break stone, and there's no way round the gates, so we have to try something different.' He leaned against the wall and removed his helmet and head cloth to dash the sweat from his eyes. 'Give them their due,' he said with a grin, 'they're going to be hard to shift, but we'll winkle them out eventually. A few policeman and night watchmen are no match for my lads, even behind those walls.'

'What's the plan once you get inside?' Valerius asked, hoping for some detail that might help him get to Domitia Longina Corbulo before the Praetorian swords.

A shadow crept over the centurion's eyes. 'The only plan is to clean them out and kill everything that gets in our way.' He glanced at Valerius's missing hand and the old scars that marked both men as soldiers. 'You've been around. You know what happens when legionaries break a siege. We'll make it quick out of respect for their courage, but that's as good as it gets for those men up there.'

'They have a woman with them,' Valerius said. The centurion shook his head as if he didn't believe what he was hearing. 'I need to be with the first century into the complex.'

'Then you're likely to be dead. If I have anything to do with it, this will be the first century over the walls, but there'll be a price to pay. Honour and duty. The men they killed were from my front rank and there's a blood bill for that. Still, you look a handy pair and if you're prepared to take the chance for some floozy, who am I to stop you? Aprilis, centurion second century First cohort,' he belatedly introduced himself.

'How do you plan to do it?'

'That you'll have to wait and see,' he said as he set off after his men.

They followed, dodging the spears and boulders as the second century filtered back to re-form as the fourth in the column of attacking units. Valerius was curious how this fitted with Aprilis's boast that his men would be first into the temple complex. Perhaps the answer lay in the ladders that had appeared among the waiting soldiers. Not siege ladders by any means, builders' ladders, but long enough to scale a single storey. A roar from the far side of the Capitoline beyond the Tarpeian Rock announced the launch of a new attack and the centurion nodded grimly. 'The Third cohort are going up the Hundred Steps. Won't be long now.'

'Ready,' the shout came from the head of the column. 'At the double, advance.'

They retraced their steps up the paved roadway, forming *testudo* as they came under fire from the portico roofs. The first three centuries went ahead to resume the attack on the all but impregnable gate, but Aprilis halted his men in front of the most accessible of the pillared buildings. The roofs of these porticos backed on to the asylum, the area that dipped between the two Capitoline summits. Up here the building work never ceased and the defenders had easy access to piles of stone, the soldiers and civilians taking turns to hurl their missiles. But this time Aprilis had an answer to them. He roared an order and five ranks at the rear of the preceding century turned to launch a hail of spears that swept the defenders off the roof. Even as the *pila* were in the air the men with ladders ran to place them against the porticos and others rushed to mount them. Simultaneously, eight-man sections of legionaries formed *scuta* platforms and their comrades leapt on the swaying floor of shields to swarm the positions vacated by the defenders.

'After you, lord,' Serpentius invited. Valerius leapt on to the undulating surface and they supported each other across the painted *scuta* until they reached the wall of the portico. The roof was still beyond their reach, but the Spaniard formed a basket with his hands to boost Valerius up. Another hand clamped over his left wrist and he was able to haul himself on to the sloping roof. Half a dozen bodies littered the tiles, a few still groaning, but Aprilis's men ignored them to hunt the survivors who were fleeing towards the far side of the hill. Valerius scrambled over the peak of the roof and leapt on to the ground of the asylum a few feet below. A moment later Serpentius joined him.

'It's like killing rabbits,' a Guard laughed as he ran past chasing a terrified unarmed civilian.

But capturing the asylum, or even the Arx summit to the south-east, didn't mean they'd won the Capitol. The Temple of Jupiter Optimus Maximus was the true goal, and it still stood, massive and impregnable, away to Valerius's left, inside its own walled complex. Those walls were currently held by a weak force of urban cohorts, but Sabinus would reinforce them when he realized the threat to his flank.

'Aprilis!' Valerius called to the Praetorian commander as he tried to rally his men. 'The temple.'

The centurion raised his sword in acknowledgement and Valerius studied the task that faced them. Here in the dip between the two hills it only now became apparent how formidable an obstacle the walls were. The temple sat on a raised platform of sheer rock perhaps twice the height of a man, with the walls adding a further six or eight feet to the barrier. None of the ladders carried by the Praetorians would reach the parapet, not even if two were lashed together. Likewise it was too high to repeat the tactic of the shield platform. He suppressed a grunt of frustration. A mere few dozen paces away Domitia was being held captive. *Somehow* he had to get across that wall. He looked around, searching for an alternative. By now most of the defenders were dead, but a few were still attempting to escape from the rear of the Capitoline, where the rocks fell away steeply towards the streets below. Here apartment buildings nudged close to the hill, some of them almost backing on to it, and Valerius saw one fleeing soldier make a flying leap over the low wall and across a gap of eight or nine feet straight through a curtained window.

'There's one who deserves to get back home to his woman tonight,' Serpentius laughed appreciatively.

But the man's escape had given Valerius an idea. A pile of long planks lay beside the stones and building rubble that the Flavians had been using as missiles. 'Get Aprilis and his men to bring the longest planks and follow me,' he ordered. Instant understanding flashed across Serpentius's face and he ran off in search of the Praetorian centurion.

Valerius made his way to where the fleeing defender had disappeared through the apartment window. Brick built and unusually solid, the

334

insula block soared another two storeys above the height of the saddle. More important, the upper windows *overlooked* the walls of the temple complex.

Aprilis arrived at the head of his men and Valerius explained his plan, shouting to be heard above the clash of arms and screams of dying men that came from all around the hill. By now many of the porticoes were in flames and smoke filled his nostrils to remind him of the horrors of Cremona. He pointed to the window. 'If we can reach that building we might be able to get a small force into the temple complex.'

'Why not go down and in the front door?' The Praetorian looked dubiously at the drop between the *insula* and the hill.

'We don't have time,' Valerius pointed out. 'Those walls are going to be reinforced before long and then they'd slaughter us. It's now or never.'

Serpentius grabbed one of the planks and pushed it out towards the rectangular window a few feet below. It just reached the ledge with the near end a precarious thumb's breadth on to the surface of the asylum. Valerius looked down and caught a glimpse of a frightened female face. He prayed whoever was in the apartment wasn't preparing to push the plank away from their window.

'Do you want to live for ever?' Serpentius brushed past him and danced across like an acrobat, ignoring the bow in the wood that threatened to plunge man and plank on to the rocks below. 'I'll hold it steady. Get somebody to do the same at your end.' A guard came forward and Valerius stepped up on to the plank. 'Keep your eyes on me, and for the gods' sake don't look down.'

Every instinct told him to look down but, keeping his eyes on the Spaniard, he placed his right foot on to the flimsy bridge. The second step was easier, and with the third Serpentius was able to grab his arm and haul him into the cramped room. He was followed by Aprilis, who almost fell on top of him, and then the other soldiers tumbled through the window one after the other. A cry and a rattle of wood on stone announced that their temporary crossing had been momentarily severed, but Valerius could hear the sound of iron studs on wood as more and more soldiers crossed into the building. He noticed a woman and two children cowering in the corner of the room and gave them what he hoped was a reassuring smile before he followed Serpentius out into the main corridor. Guardsmen were already on the stairs, some of them still carrying the planks they'd recovered.

'Stay down,' Aprilis called as they darted into a room that faced the Temple of Jupiter and ducked below window level as a *pilum* thrown from the temple complex embedded itself in the plaster wall behind them. The centurion looked up at the spear and flinched as it was followed by a whirling oil lamp. Moments later, the curtain was alight and flames had begun to spread across the floor. 'This is going to be interesting.'

Valerius stepped forward with Serpentius, but Aprilis grabbed the Roman's arm. 'The second century of the First cohort isn't going to let a pair of civilians take all the glory.' He called out four or five names. 'Have your sections ready. When I give the order you get those planks across and men with them. For Rome.' A dozen voices echoed the sentiment, and Aprilis continued, 'Remember Metto and the lads who died in the Forum. If it happened to us do you think they'd let us down? Not likely.' He cursed as a second oil lamp fell into the room, the flames reaching out for cloth and straw. 'I hope you've brought those fucking *pila* like I told you. One volley on the order, then you cross.'

He sat back for a moment and closed his eyes. 'Shit. What are you waiting for?' he whispered to himself. 'Now!'

The spearmen rose and hurled their javelins into the defenders guarding the wall. Valerius heard the shrieks of spitted men and looked out as Aprilis's men rammed their planks forward to bridge a gap he now saw was considerably less than it had been on the lower storey. As the first boards reached the far side defenders rose from behind the parapet braving the spears to hurl the fragile bridges aside. Away to their right a group managed to get across only to be swamped by the enemy. By now the room was well ablaze, the flames licking at their skin.

'Fuck this,' Aprilis muttered. He stood up, pulled himself into the window frame and launched himself across the void, half sprawling on the opposite parapet and then rolling forward, already hacking at the legs of the Flavian defenders who instantly flung themselves at this new threat. The remaining Praetorians saw their commander's plight and followed his example. A few were hurled back into the abyss, but most safely made the leap to rise in growing numbers and carry the fight to the enemy.

Serpentius shook his head in wonder and shrugged at Valerius. 'You heard the man. What are we waiting for?' Without a backward look he bent his knees and sprang the gap like a leopard to land, sword ready, a warrior in his gore-stained element. Valerius watched helpless as three men converged on the Spaniard, thinking they were safe behind their shields. Serpentius danced forward, his *gladius* flicking out like a viper's tongue. In moments two of his attackers were down and the other had fled. The Spaniard left them to bleed and turned to urge Valerius to jump. As the Roman tensed to make the leap a new group of Praetorians burst into the room with a plank, bridged the gap and surged across. Grateful, Valerius followed them at a more sedate pace and Serpentius met him at the wall with a rueful grin. 'Just like a soft aristocrat to take the easy way.'

Valerius took a moment to study the scene around him. Aprilis had lost his helmet and blood ran from cuts to his head and arm, but he didn't seem to notice his wounds. The Praetorian rallied the survivors of his century into a defensive line to meet an attack from across the compound. The enemy officer seemed to be having trouble getting his men into position. Valerius's heart sank as he recognized Aemilius Pacensis, one of Otho's former aides and a man he knew and liked. Joining Aprilis, he thrust any such thoughts aside. On the far side of those men lay the Temple of Jupiter – and Domitia. The sound of renewed fighting came from the Clivus Capitolinus, where the Praetorians had resumed their attack with new purpose. It explained why Pacensis had so few men for his counter stroke. Sabinus couldn't afford to take men away from the gate and the walls above the Tarpeian Rock without fatally weakening the defences. But he was wrong. Because here, like a knife poised over his heart, lay the greatest danger. Valerius and Serpentius joined the line as Aprilis lost patience and launched his legionaries towards the confused Flavians. The numbers were equally matched and almost all were armoured and equipped with sword and shield, but that was where the similarity ended. Aprilis and his men had spent years on the Rhenus frontier honing their battle skills and sparring with the Cherusci, the Chatti and the Marcomanni. Fighting for survival was a way of life for them. The men facing them in the red tunics of the urban cohorts were trained in arms, but their recent experience had been breaking up bar brawls and bread riots and dealing with political upheaval. Pacensis shouted an order for a final rush, but the assault was tentative and piecemeal and the solid wall of Praetorian shields smashed the Flavians backwards. 'Kill the bastards,' Aprilis howled.

Valerius found himself swapping cuts with Pacensis, the patrician's handsome features twisted with fear and rage. 'Aemilius? Throw down your sword. It is finished,' Valerius urged. But the Flavian only attacked with renewed strength.

'Traitor,' he snarled. 'Turncoat. The name Verrens will be remembered for this infamy along with the Catilines.' Without warning his mouth gaped in a tortured shriek as a sword point found a gap in his armour and tore deep into his vitals. Valerius stepped back in bewilderment as his opponent sank to the ground, squirming spastically in his death agony. Serpentius faced him over the dead man, eyes glaring.

'Serpentius, why?' Valerius demanded. 'He was a friend.'

All around them men still hacked at each other with swords or wrestled together, tearing at their enemy with their bare hands, intent on smashing faces and skulls to pulp with helmet or rock. The slabs of the temple precinct flowed with blood and the air was heavy with the scent of death. Men wept, but didn't understand whether it was with relief or sorrow.

'He was the enemy,' the Spaniard snarled. 'How often have I told you that if a man comes at you with a sword you don't talk to him. You kill him.'

Aprilis's men finished off the wounded and would have set off after the survivors, but the centurion roared at them to follow him to the gate. As Valerius turned there was an eruption of flame and smoke. The *insula* they'd attacked from was an inferno and the fire had spread to a second building at the rear of the great temple. Even as they watched, the flames leapt the narrow gap and greedily sought out the ancient wood of the temple gables before flickering up the pediment and along the line of the roof. Smoke began to wisp from beneath the ochre tiles and Valerius was reminded of the Temple of Claudius in Colonia. When the Celts had fired the temple roof the end had never been in doubt. Even so, his mind struggled with what he was seeing. The Temple of Jupiter Optimus Maximus was more than just a place of worship. More than just a place where Emperors came to cement their rule. It was *Rome*. Men believed that as long as the temple existed, the Roman Empire and all it stood for would prevail. But the most sacred building in Rome was being devoured before his eyes.

XLV

'Mars' arse,' Serpentius cursed as he saw the extent of the inferno. 'What the fuck are we going to do now?'

Valerius was already on the move, ignoring the groups of Flavian soldiers who ran aimlessly among the buildings like rats trapped in a maze. At the base of the temple steps he recognized Sabinus, looking old and bewildered at the centre of a group of officers urgently seeking instructions. But it was clear no instructions would save them now. Dozens of Praetorians were already swarming through the shattered gate and across the columns and statues that Sabinus had gambled would hold them. To the left of the temple fierce fighting had erupted amongst the minor shrines at the top of the Hundred Steps. Men lay dead or dying, the maimed crawling to find what shelter they could. One soldier sat on the temple steps sobbing uncontrollably beside the corpse of a friend. Despite the smoke and flames pouring from the temple roof, more and more of the terrified Flavian supporters were rushing to the building in search of an unlikely sanctuary.

Sabinus's bodyguard must have been drawn in to the fight, because they were nowhere to be seen. Valerius saw his chance. 'Stay here,' he ordered Serpentius. He sheathed his sword and, taking advantage of the confusion, strode to where Sabinus was by now being confronted by a single brick-faced officer. Valerius brushed past the man and looked into the Prefect of Rome's face. 'You must surrender, sir,' he pleaded. 'There is no point in fighting on. Save what you can.'

'Get out of my way, fool.' A hand clamped on Valerius's shoulder and hauled him back. 'Cornelius Martialis does not surrender and neither does the Prefect of Rome. Your brother's legions are coming,' he hissed into the old man's face. 'Hold for a day and we will hand him Rome and reap the honours. There are only a few of these Praetorian bastards in the compound. We will hunt them down like rats. But . . . you . . . must . . . give . . . the . . . order.'

'It's finished,' Valerius insisted. He heard the officer snarl and the man's sword rose to chop him down. Even as Martialis struck, Valerius rammed the hidden dagger in his left hand up under the Flavian's chin, through tongue and pallet and into the brain. He wrenched the point free and Martialis swayed for a moment, croaking like a frog, before a fountain of blood spouted from his mouth and he collapsed to the ground.

Sabinus stared in mute horror at the dying man, but Valerius had no time for regret or indecision.

'Sir, you must—' Before he could complete his plea for surrender a terrified female scream froze the words in his mouth. He looked round and at the top of the temple steps the cloaked figure of Domitia Longina Corbulo was being dragged into the centremost of the three *cellae* – the inner sanctums dedicated to Juno, Jupiter and Minerva. The echo of her scream had barely died before he was on the move. Taking the steps three at a time he almost tripped as he leapt the body of the man who'd been weeping. When he reached the main platform he ran past the statue of the god dominating the *pronaos* only to find the copper-sheathed door slammed in his face.

Valerius stood in confusion for a moment, fighting for breath. His carelessness almost killed him. Something moved at the corner of his vision and he turned to find a black-clad Praetorian about to stick a *pilum* through him. 'No.' The cry was in vain until a sword flicked out from nowhere to knock the thrust aside and the spear point skidded off the metal door.

'We're with Aprilis and the second century First cohort.' Serpentius stepped between Valerius and his attacker. 'No point in killing your mates, is there, son?' His voice was the soul of reason, but the sword point hovering an inch from the soldier's breast told another story. The Praetorian's glare faded to be replaced by a look of confusion.

A shower of sparks fell past and Valerius looked up at the burning roof and knew time was running out. 'Get a dozen men and bring me one of the pillars from the enemy barricade.' The soldier stepped back, ready to question a civilian's authority, until he saw the certainty in Valerius's eyes. As he ran off the screams of dying men rose in intensity as his comrades broke into the outer *cellae* where the Flavians hadn't been quick enough to close the doors. Valerius tried to shut his ears to the sound, but the noise of men – and women – dying tore his heart. Roman killing Roman. Was there no end to the carnage he'd been trying to stop since Otho sent him north all those months ago?

Instinctively, he moved towards the doorway, but Serpentius put a hand on his arm. 'There's nothing you can do for these people, and you'll only get yourself killed.'

A woman's shriek scored the inside of his brain and he experienced a momentary thrill of fear before he realized it wasn't Domitia. He tried to remember her as she was the night on the Egyptian beach, with the remains of the tent glowing in the darkness. For a moment his head whirled with the honey scent of hair like spun silk and lips soft and sweet as ripe peaches. Of course, the reality was different. For all her efforts her hair had been thick with salt, smelled of smoke and the sea, and the skin of her lips was chapped and cracked. It had not mattered. The only thing that mattered was a tidal wave of passion that brought a man and a woman together with a force beyond nature and beyond the knowledge of the gods. He'd fought that memory for three years, certain that she needed to be free of him even if it was not what she wanted. But he would fight it no more.

At last the Praetorian reappeared at the run with seven or eight men carrying a marble column a foot thick and the length of a chariot pole. Valerius stepped aside and they hammered the column's head

342

into the centre of the door with a weight and power that rattled the oak back and caused a massive dent in the polished metal. The sound of splintering wood accompanied a second crash. The next effort smashed the double doors back and the Praetorians dropped the ram and poured through, ignoring Valerius's cries to hold back. Serpentius followed them, surging into the crowd and roaring for passage. Several dozen of Sabinus's urban cohort had escaped into the temple and the attackers paused for a heartbeat before launching themselves at the trapped enemy in a desperate hand-to-hand battle. Praetorian swords flashed, point and edge seeking out the nearest flesh and turning the air red. In the enclosed space the leaden stink of blood and the acrid stench of fresh vomit caught the throat like a hangman's noose, but it was quickly overwhelmed by a gust of smoke that filled the nostrils and lungs. Valerius looked up to where an ominous glow pierced the white cloud of smoke in the rafters.

'Domitia!' He roared out her name above the incessant clamour of iron on iron, demented shrieks and unheeded cries for mercy.

At the far end of the *cella*, Domitia crouched behind an altar with Domitianus's hand clinging to her arm like a slave manacle. She heard the shout and half rose to reply, only for Vespasian's son to shift his grip and clamp his hand over her mouth.

'Stay quiet, bitch,' he hissed. 'Don't you understand that I'm saving you?' The glittering eyes searched the gloom, waiting for his moment. 'Remember,' he addressed the four bodyguards hiding with them, 'when my father's legions take the city you will receive riches beyond your dreams. All I ask is that you buy me a few moments before you follow.'

The fighting drew ever closer, the clash of swords so loud she thought her ears might bleed. 'Domitia.' She heard the cry repeated above the clamour of battle and the screams of the dying. A familiar shape in the smoke made her heart beat faster.

'Now!' At Domitianus's order the guards hurled themselves over the altar and formed a protective line between the fighting and Vespasian's son. Domitia felt herself dragged back and she struggled desperately to break free. Something clattered to the marble paving beside her

343

and she cried out at the sight of one of the guards' still helmeted head staring up at her with a look of surprise in the dying eyes.

'Domitia.' The shout was closer now and somehow it gave her new strength. She tore at her captor until Domitianus removed his hand from her mouth to deliver a slap, but before he could strike she sank her teeth into his arm and he recoiled with a cry of pain.

'Die then, you fool.' He threw her towards the fighting and disappeared abruptly into the gloom.

For a moment she was too shocked to think. Her head whirled and smoke choked her throat. 'Valerius?' She tried to shout his name, but it emerged as a croaking whisper.

A shadow appeared in front of her. Valerius? No, the blurred figure wore the uniform of the Praetorian Guard. She turned to run, but her scalp seemed to catch fire as a hand whipped out to grab her hair, dragging her head backwards to expose her throat. A sword blade swept round before her eyes, so close she could see the pitting in the iron and the tiny nicks in the edge. Her life could be measured in seconds before it was dragged backwards, sawing across her windpipe.

For a moment she believed she was halfway to the Otherworld. Was it a trick of the mind or had the blade dropped out of sight? The man gave a grunt of surprise that rose into a brief cry of agony. At the same time the grip on her hair loosened and the weighty presence behind her vanished with the crash of a body falling to the marble tiles. She closed her eyes, her whole body shaking like the last leaf in an autumn storm. For a moment, she didn't dare turn, but a hand fell gently on her shoulder and guided her. She looked into his eyes and knew she was safe.

'Valerius.' The single word conveyed all the conflicting emotions that exploded in her brain. Relief and disbelief, joy and wonder – all that and love. Only love could make your heart thunder when men were bleeding their lives away within plain sight. Only love could make a stinking, smoke-filled charnel house feel like a wedding bower. Only love . . .

'If we don't get out of here we're all going to end up like roast suckling pig.' The harsh voice cut through her thoughts and banished all idea of love, and for the first time she noticed the whip-thin figure of Serpentius at Valerius's shoulder.

'Where is Domitianus?' Valerius ignored the Spaniard as his eyes searched the area around the altar.

'A door somewhere down there, I think.' Domitia pointed into the gloom at the rear of the *cella*.

'Good,' the former gladiator spat. 'Let him burn.' He turned to head back towards the entrance, but Valerius and Domitia stayed where they were. Their eyes met and she read the question in them. It was the last thing she wanted to say, but it had to be said.

'If he escapes he will never rest until he has hunted us down, Valerius.'

'Keep her safe.' It was more plea than order. Serpentius turned to protest, and Domitia stretched out a hand, but the Roman had already gone.

Reluctantly Domitia allowed herself to be led back to the doorway with Serpentius's sword threatening anyone who attempted to get in the way. By now the fighting was almost over and the remaining Praetorians carried their wounded to safety or crouched to cut the throats of any Flavians who still breathed. Most of the statuary and any portable treasure had already been removed, but two Guards hacked at a golden statue of the god on a throne, only to give up in disgust when they discovered it was only ivory covered in gold leaf.

When they reached the doors Domitia gave a convulsive sob and would have run back inside, but the Spaniard was ready for her. 'Don't worry, lady.' He carried her bodily down the temple steps. 'Gaius Valerius Verrens is not so easy to kill.'

But even Serpentius had to revise his opinion as the minutes passed and the Temple of Jupiter Optimus Maximus burned. A steady rain fell on the Capitoline, but it had no effect on the fire. By now the temple was a mass of flames, with thick red-shot smoke and sparks shooting hundreds of feet into the air. They watched the glowing doorway, praying every moment for the tall, one-handed figure to emerge, but eventually it became clear no one could live in that inferno. When the roof collapsed, sending an enormous bolt of fire into the afternoon sky, Domitia wept unashamedly and Serpentius was glad of the rain.

'A concealed passage led to the warden's quarters.' They jumped at the familiar voice from behind. Domitia threw herself into Valerius's arms, holding him as if she would never let him go. He lowered his head to kiss her hair, half smiling at the familiar memory the smoke scent brought back. 'Of course there would be a warden responsible for the upkeep of the place,' he continued, his voice almost dreamy with exhaustion. 'And he couldn't be seen walking in and out of the god's house with a bucket and cloths. It must have been the vault where they kept the Sibylline books. He'd made it comfortable enough.' He shrugged. 'Domitianus had cut his throat. The other entrance was by a stairway up through the rock from the Campus Martius side. I'm sorry,' he said to Domitia. 'We'll never find him now.'

XLVI

The Temple of Jupiter Capitolinus burned throughout the night, a terrifying beacon filled with apocalyptic portent for every Roman who witnessed the funeral pyre of Sabinus's hopes.

As Vitellius's Praetorians hunted down rebel survivors by the light of the flames Valerius led Domitia to a little temple dedicated to Fortuna Primigenia, left undamaged by the fighting. Serpentius guarded the door and they sat with their backs to the wall to wait out the threat. At first, they sat a little apart, but after a few moments Domitia shifted so her body touched his and her head lay lightly on his shoulder. Instinctively, he put his left arm around her and brought her close. She sighed, and he knew that despite all she'd suffered and witnessed she was smiling. The rhythm of her breathing and the steady beat of her heart merged with his, but it was the softness of her, and the curves and hollows that he remembered so well. The combination acted as a kind of elixir, sweeping away the blood and fire and terror of the long day. Something stirred inside him, and she must have felt it, because she raised her head to kiss him, first on the cheek and then on the lips, soft, then more urgent, so that his mind dissolved. For a few short moments there was no temple, no Capitol and no Rome. They were back on the Egyptian beach and she was in his arms beneath the cloak, moving softly with him in an act so natural he sometimes wondered if he'd dreamt it.

'What will become of us now, Valerius?'

He – they – must have fallen asleep, because the words woke him with a start and they were accompanied by a delicate yawn. He had been dreading the question, but his mind must have been gnawing at it, because he didn't have to think to know the answer. An answer that was no answer at all. Gaius Valerius Verrens, Hero of Rome, sole survivor of the Temple of Claudius, and commander of legions, had as much control over his future as a piece of swan's down caught by a gust of wind. Events had brought him here. Events to which he'd reacted, or events in which his actions had been dictated by others. From the day Titus had saved him from the executioner's sword his own will had meant nothing. No, from the day almost two years earlier when Vespasian had summoned him to take the message to Galba. Since that day he had given his oath to two Emperors and pledged it to a third. Strange that the man who held his fate and Domitia's in his chubby, bejewelled hand should be the only man he had wanted to give his oath to, and, perhaps, the only one who deserved it.

'We will go to the palace and seek the help of the Emperor,' he said eventually.

'That is not what I meant, Valerius.' She said it gently, knowing perfectly well he understood.

'When this is settled we will live on the estate at Fidenae where I was born,' he tried again. 'My sister is there now, but it is big enough and has sufficient water to accommodate two villas. We will plan the second together. I know the very place, down by the river among the trees, but sheltered and with a fine southern aspect. A small quarry for the marble, with slaves from Carrara to do the fine work. Big windows and room for the children to play.'

She allowed him his dream, waiting patiently before she spoke again. 'He will come for me, Valerius. For us. If he survives, he will be the Emperor's son, with power over life and death.'

'If he survives.'

'Yes.'

'Then he must not survive.'

Serpentius came to them an hour later and announced that the only troops remaining on the Capitol were either dead or guarding the temples that had survived the battle and the fires. They emerged into the soft, silvery light that is the prelude to dawn.

'Best not to take the Clivus,' the Spaniard proposed. 'The road is scattered with those foul little four-legged spikes we used against the Parthians, and the gods only know what else will be down there.'

Instead, they hurried across the asylum towards the Arx and the Temple of Juno Moneta, avoiding the areas where the worst of the fighting had taken place. They saw a light across a courtyard where someone had helpfully placed a lamp. As they came closer, Valerius realized that it was the first of a series and suddenly, with a feeling of terrible dread, he knew where he was.

'Perhaps we should find another way,' he suggested. But the reaction to Domitia's ordeal had finally set in and she was almost staggering from a combination of exhaustion and everything she'd experienced the previous day. It was clear that if they didn't take the quickest route they'd have to carry her. Serpentius shot him a puzzled look, but Valerius only shrugged and continued in the direction of the light, feeling like a moth drawn unwittingly to certain immolation. They reached the head of a steep stairway barely wide enough to accommodate the three of them. Valerius had his left arm around Domitia, who walked almost as if she was in a dream, her feet barely touching the ground. As they descended she staggered, almost bringing him down with her, and Serpentius had to grab her arm to steady her. A moment later they noticed something lying in their path.

'You were right,' Serpentius said through gritted teeth.

Valerius nodded and steered Domitia towards the wall. 'These are the Gemonian Stairs.'

They tiptoed through the scattered remains of a human being. A hand, still wearing a silver ring that Valerius thought he recognized, a foot with three toes missing, an upper arm, and a chunk of hacked-off thigh. Eventually a bulky obstruction, like the cushions of a cast-off couch, partially blocked their progress and they were forced to step gingerly past a headless, mutilated torso with the thick grey hairs of age on its chest.

'Anyone we know?' Serpentius tried to make a joke of the horror.

'It's difficult to be certain without the head,' Valerius said, 'but I think we've just said farewell to the shade of Titus Flavius Sabinus.'

The Spaniard turned to stare at him. 'Shit.'

Domitia sensed their disquiet and stirred between them. 'What's happening?' she mumbled.

'It's nothing,' Valerius assured her. Nothing but the certainty of more death, more iron and more fire. He had a vision of Cremona and the mutilated corpses stacked high in the Forum. He'd thought the burning of the Temple of Jupiter marked the end of Rome's suffering. It turned out to be only the beginning.

XLVII

'Sabinus is dead.' Valerius's words dropped like a stone into the unreal calm in the room overlooking the lake at the Golden House.

'We know,' Galeria Fundana said, stroking her sleeping son's curls. 'They sent us his head.'

Aulus Vitellius stirred on his couch. 'I tried to save him, but the Praetorians insisted.'

'We saved the others.' Galeria brightened, as if the lives of a few senators might be balanced against that of Titus Flavius Vespasian's brother.

Vitellius nodded, setting the great jowls wobbling. 'Saturninus has agreed to travel north to negotiate with Marcus Antonius Primus. Two cohorts of the People's Militia checked Cerialis and his cavalry in the suburbs yesterday and chased them back to Fidenae. We can still negotiate a peaceful settlement.'

Valerius frowned at the mention of Fidenae. It meant that the estate and Olivia were in the front line now. He wondered if the Emperor – yes, he was still the Emperor despite everything – believed what he was saying. He, Domitia and Serpentius had been turned away by successive sets of nervous Praetorians on the morning after the battle of the Capitoline. Eventually, they were forced to take shelter in an abandoned house in the Fourth District. It had taken all his

351

negotiating skills to persuade the Guards to send word to Vitellius of the one-handed man seeking an audience with the Emperor. By then, every city junction was controlled by members of the People's Militia, Vitellian supporters provided with weapons by the Praetorians from their armoury at the Castra Praetoria. He and Serpentius had been accosted four or five times on the way to the palace by men urging them to join and handing out swords, spears and shields to anyone who agreed.

'I have a request to ask of you, as a friend,' he said to the Emperor.

Galeria's head came up sharply, but Vitellius raised a hand for silence. 'If it is within my power to grant it.'

'The lady who accompanies me was held on the Capitoline against her will and is still in great danger. I would be grateful if you could keep her under your protection until I return.'

'You are not staying with us, Valerius?' It was almost a plea.

'I have one more task to complete.' Valerius decided he couldn't tell Vitellius of his plan to kill Domitianus. He hesitated and something seemed to catch in his throat. 'Once before, you asked me to give you my oath and I refused. I give it now, gladly, not to Aulus Vitellius Germanicus Augustus, but to Aulus Vitellius, my friend. When this is done I will return to share whatever perils you face or triumphs you achieve.'

Vitellius's lips twitched in a fleeting half-smile and in that moment Valerius understood that all the earlier talk of peaceful settlements had been a pretence to protect the Emperor's wife and son. He rose to take his leave, but Vitellius heaved himself up and followed him out to the corridor.

When they were alone, Valerius turned to his old friend. 'Disarm the militia and open the gates, Aulus. Take Galeria and Lucius south to join your brother.'

The massive chest heaved in a bitter sigh. 'Do you think so little of me, Valerius? Even if it were possible I would not leave my people.' He stretched out a plump hand and his fingers stroked a painted marble bust of his son. 'Aulus Vitellius's fate is not his to decide. You once told me that an officer should never give an order if he thinks it will not be obeyed. It was good advice. The Praetorian Guard are beyond my control. If I gave the order, they would ignore it. They are as much my jailers as my protectors. A week ago Aulus Vitellius Germanicus Augustus was the ruler of forty million souls. Today he is not even the ruler of his own house.' He laid a hand on Valerius's sleeve. 'May the gods go with you and aid you in whatever mission you undertake. All I ask is that when you return, make it your task to keep my wife and child safe.'

'It will not come to that, Aulus.'

Vitellius shook his head at the lie. 'I will always remember our time in Africa. A poor man rich in friends is wealthier by far than a rich one with none. Life was much simpler then.'

When he was gone, Valerius tried to shake off a terrible sense of foreboding. He walked swiftly along the corridor to the guest room where Domitia slept. She woke as he kissed her forehead, the wide, knowing eyes startlingly close to his. She clutched his right arm. 'Don't go, Valerius.'

He shook his head. 'You said yourself he will never leave us alone.'

'That was yesterday,' she said. 'I was tired and frightened. I didn't know what I was saying. Today, I order you not to go.'

'And if I obeyed, I would not be the man you think I am, or the one you deserve.'

She drew his head down to hers and kissed him deeply. 'Now will you obey me?'

He shook his head, and she turned her face to the wall. He stroked her hair. 'He may already be dead if the Praetorians have found him.'

She didn't respond until he reached the doorway. 'Valerius?' He hesitated. 'Come back safe. I can't lose you now.'

XLVIII

'Do you really think we'll find him in all this?' Serpentius searched the crowds who thronged the streets in a desperate hunt for the last available food. Vitellius had sent out heralds with a plea for calm during the negotiations with Primus, but it was clear not many people shared his optimism about a settlement. Most of the shops and stalls had already closed, their stocks sold out even at the exorbitant prices being charged by bakers and butchers, fruit and fish merchants who kept just enough back for their families. Rumour put Primus's forces anywhere between a mile and ten miles from the city and on the Via Salaria or the Via Flaminia, depending on whom you believed. They stepped back into a doorway as a century of Praetorians marched past with purposeful strides, silver breastplates gleaming and faces grim. Every man carried a black-painted shield with the familiar lightning bolts dissecting the boss, and a pair of heavy, weighted javelins.

'He won't have gone to his uncle's house.' Valerius didn't take his eyes off the soldiers until they'd rounded the corner. 'That's the first place the Praetorians would look for him. You said the last sighting of him was on the Street of the Ringmakers?'

'So they say,' the Spaniard shrugged, meaning believe it if you will. 'An informer told the Praetorians that Domitianus hid in a temple of Isis and in the morning the priests gave him robes and let him take part in their procession. My Praetorian mate, the one from Twenty-first Rapax, reckoned that was where he ducked out of the parade.'

Valerius chewed his lip. The Street of the Ringmakers was in Subura, and that was where they were heading. Vitellius had provided them with a pass that nominally gave them access to any part of a city scattered with informal militia checkpoints. Whether it would continue to do so depended on how much authority the Emperor still retained. Subura would give Domitianus the option of the Viminal or Esquiline gates, but Valerius doubted Vespasian's younger son would risk trying to leave Rome now. What was the point when his father's forces were coming to him? He would have friends in the city, but the Emperor's spies would have a list of them and no doubt their homes had already been searched. But Subura opened up another possibility.

'Not all of Sabinus's urban cohorts were on the Capitoline.'

'That's true.' Serpentius studied him with new interest. 'But most of the rest were rounded up and sent back to the Castra Urbana.'

'Remember that warehouse I told you about?' They had reached the junction of the Vicus Patricius and the Via Tiburtina and Valerius took the right fork up the hill towards the Porticus Liviae. 'The one where Sabinus kept them hidden?'

'Won't the Guard have searched it?'

'If they have it's just an empty building, but Domitianus will know about it.'

'So you think that little dog's turd could be skulking there?'

Valerius increased his pace. 'There's only one way to find out.'

When Valerius had last come this way the Vicus Corvius had been filled with bustling activity, but now it was deserted. The only sign of life was at the head of the side street that led down to the *horreum*, where two tough-looking men watched them suspiciously as they walked past. Valerius risked a glance and saw more men standing outside the warehouse doors.

'Soldiers trying to look like labourers,' Serpentius confirmed his assessment. 'It looks as if not all the urban cohorts have been rounded up. You were right, but I'm not sure how much good it does us. Even if

Domitianus is here we won't be able to get near him without a fight.'

'Maybe there's another entrance,' Valerius suggested.

They continued along the street and down another that ran parallel to the one with the watchers. The storehouse must have stretched the entire block, because much of the street was a blank wall, with a single opening at the height of the second storey. From the opening protruded a beam hung with a pulley and ropes.

They stopped and Serpentius considered the opening. 'If we could somehow reach that beam . . .'

But any thought of breaking into the warehouse was banished by the frantic blare of trumpets in the distance. 'Cornicens,' Serpentius said.

'And not too far away,' Valerius agreed.

They ran back to the Esquiline Gate where a sentry stepped into the street to bar their way. Valerius showed him the Emperor's pass and the man reluctantly allowed them access to the nearest gate tower. From the highest battlements they had a view across the sea of ochre-tiled roofs to the Campus Martius and beyond. His heart pounding, Valerius followed the line of the Via Flaminia past the distinctive conical roof of Augustus's mausoleum and out towards the Milvian Bridge. On the far side of the Tiber a dark amorphous mass seemed to shimmer and twitch and he knew he was looking at an army on the march. As the seconds passed it became clear it was actually a meeting of two forces. A battle. He watched a section of the mass detach itself and flow haphazardly back towards the bridge. Marcus Antonius Primus had been slow in coming, but now he was here and in numbers, and the Praetorian and militia defenders who'd hoped to stop him were fleeing back to the city.

'Look.' Serpentius pointed north along the line of the walls, where the tombs flanking the Via Salaria had been swallowed by the ever-spreading suburbs. The great red-brick fortress of the Castra Praetoria stood to their right and from its gates century after century of Praetorians marched out to meet a second Flavian column approaching down the old salt road. The Spaniard let out a bark of laughter.

'I don't see anything funny,' Valerius said.

'I was just wondering who in the name of Mars' hairy sac we were fighting for this time.'

Valerius blinked. It had never occurred to him not to defend his city, but the Spaniard was right. They couldn't fight Primus, because that meant fighting the Seventh Galbiana, the legion that had been *his*, if only for a moment.

'This time we fight for ourselves.' The words were uttered so softly that Serpentius almost didn't catch them, but the determination on Valerius's face carried its own message. And for Domitia Longina Corbulo.

Serpentius hesitated as they emerged from the tower on to the street. 'Domitianus?'

Valerius had already made his decision. 'We don't have time. A few cohorts of Praetorians and Vitellius's armed civilians aren't going to hold Primus and his legions for long.'

They hurried down the cobbled street in the shadow of the Old Anio aqueduct towards Subura and the Forum. When they reached the Porticus Liviae, Serpentius said he knew a quicker route. Despite Valerius's reservations they dashed through alleyways and between crowded *insulae* until they reached the Scalae Caniniae, a narrow, fetid stairway that wound between the poorer houses clinging to the lower slopes of the Mons Opius. As they reached the bottom of the first set of stairs they met a file of soldiers and armed civilians. Valerius stepped back to allow them to pass and momentarily became separated from Serpentius. The men had their heads bowed, and some of the older ones struggled for breath after their climb. They were urged on with curses and threats by the veteran in charge, a sallow-featured legionary in a ragged red tunic and armour that had seen better days. When they came abreast of Valerius he ordered a halt and the grateful men stood panting as he approached the Roman.

'I have orders to collect every able-bodied man for the defence of the city,' he said sourly. 'Join the rear of the file and we'll get you a sword when we reach our post.'

His tone allowed no argument, and he turned away expecting Valerius to follow. Instead Valerius pulled Vitellius's warrant from the pouch at his waist. The soldier accepted the wooden plaque with a suspicious grunt and inspected it as if it was a tin *denarius*. Eventually, he shook his head. 'The situation was different when this was issued. I need every man I can get to keep these bastard rebels out of the city.'

Valerius let his face relax into a deferential smile. 'But you said every *able-bodied* man.' He flicked back his cloak to reveal the stump of his right arm.

The moment the soldier's pale eyes widened at the sight of the mutilated limb he knew it was a mistake. Valerius saw the elements come together as if the man had discovered the answer to some long-lost mystery. With a bitter laugh of disbelief his hand swooped for his sword. Beneath the cloak Valerius groped for his own blade. Too late. Two men grabbed him by the arms.

'I know you.' The words burst from the legionary in a rasping snarl and the sword point came up to touch Valerius's throat. 'Old Lucca never forgets a face, not a face like yours in any case, or that wooden fist you wore then. You were outside the gates at Cremona before that bastard Primus burned it. Only you were in uniform. A tribune, wasn't it, but with a legate's sash. You're a fucking spy.'

'No,' Valerius insisted. Against such certainty, he knew there was little point denying his identity, but he had the Emperor's seal. 'Not a spy. An envoy to the Emperor. How do you think I got this pass? Yes, I was at Cremona, but there are negotiations taking place that you should not interfere with.'

'Negotiations,' Lucca snorted. 'The only negotiation those Flavians will get is a spear in the throat.' The men closest to Valerius growled their agreement. 'Right, lads, we're taking this spy to the *carcer* where they know how to deal with traitors like him.'

Valerius opened his mouth to protest, but a civilian with the pinched, feral features of a weasel prodded him with the point of his spear as a second man disarmed him. 'Why not just stick him now? We're needed on the walls.'

Valerius could see the calculations running through Lucca's mind. 'Take me to the Emperor,' he said desperately. 'Any one of his people will vouch for me.'

Lucca laughed. 'We're at war, in case you hadn't noticed. The Emperor has enough on his mind without wasting his time with a spy. No, you filthy bastard, it's the *carcer* and the strangling rope for you.'

Valerius looked round, hoping to see Serpentius. The Spaniard was nowhere in sight, but he would not be far away. 'Get to Aprilis,' the Roman called out. 'Aprilis will know what to do. And when you've found Aprilis go to Domitia.'

'Less of your lip.' Valerius grunted in agony as Lucca rammed the butt of a spear into his stomach and shoved him roughly down the stairs. 'First section with me, the rest of you get on up to those walls and make sure you don't let old Lucca down.'

Valerius had been in the *carcer* before, and the stinking, airless atmosphere, thick with the scents of urine, vomit, excrement and terror, was even less welcoming now. Rome's high-ranking prisoners were held here before execution. He doubted anyone would dare kill him without some sort of trial, but the inescapable fact was that he was trapped. The same pair of brutes who had tormented Lucina Graecina to her lonely, insane death stripped him of his sword belt and threw him in a barred cell at the rear of the prison. His only luxury was a pile of mouldy straw to sleep on, but he knew he'd been fortunate not to be flung into the bottle-shaped dungeon whose entrance was in one of the side wings. The jailers were unlikely to be shifted by threats or bribes, but he tried in any case, driven half mad by his inability to protect Domitia. 'Don't you know there's an army on your doorstep?' he raged.

'We have served five Emperors, and if another happens along we will serve him just as loyally,' the taller of the pair smirked. 'Never let it be said the keepers of the *carcer* are afraid of change. Now stay quiet. It wouldn't do to beat a gent like you, but we will if we have to. Your fate is sealed the moment you enter that door. The only question is whether you leave it alive or dead, and you have no say in that. Time means nothing here.'

Time means nothing here. Valerius paced the narrow confines of his cell cursing his impotence and the arrogance that had made him show the one attribute that identified him as clearly as a brothel sign. Five steps one way, three the other, then another five. Did an hour pass, or two? His imagination tortured him. What was happening outside these walls? For all Lucca's boasts, experience told him three cohorts of Praetorian Guards and a few thousand lightly armed civilians couldn't hold out for long against Primus. Vitellius must negotiate, or the city would burn. But Vitellius was hamstrung by fear and a prisoner of those same Praetorians who believed they had nothing to look forward to but an early death. A vision of Cremona haunted him, the bloody streets and stacked bodies, the flames and the terror, the raped women and speared babies. It could already be happening just a few hundred paces away. The treasures of the Golden House would be their first objective. Domitia would be at the palace when they came and the fear of it made him rage and rattle the bars of his cage, to the amusement of his jailers. Wasted energy. He must conserve his strength and prepare for whatever the day would bring. Soldiers can sleep anywhere, and though it was only a fitful doze tormented by memories and foreboding, Valerius eventually slept.

He was woken by hammering on the *carcer* door accompanied by the muffled sound of voices arguing. A few moments later the tall jailer walked in with a sour look on his face and the key to the cell in his hand. Behind him, grey with exhaustion, came Aprilis, his sword drawn and the blade still bloody.

'You were fortunate your Spaniard found me,' the Praetorian said, acknowledging Valerius's thanks. 'My comrades are killing all their prisoners as they retreat and they would have got round to you soon enough.'

'What's happening?' Valerius asked as the jailer freed him, muttering apologies about his treatment – 'a mistake has been made . . . unaware of your eminence, your eminence'. Valerius ignored him and Aprilis explained the happenings of the previous few hours.

'We tried to hold them at the Milvian Bridge, but they pushed us back up the Via Flaminia into the Campus Martius. It was carnage. The civilian militia threw their weapons away and ran. One minute they were fighting beside us, the next the scum were cheering the enemy and helping cut the throats of our wounded. A flanking column attacked up the Appian Way, forcing the Campus to be abandoned. Not long ago I had word that the Seventh Claudia had taken the Aurelian Gate. It meant we'd been outflanked and I was ordered to withdraw a second time. The only good news is that we still hold the Castra Praetoria and that's where we're going.'

As they emerged into the daylight one of Aprilis's soldiers stepped forward and handed Valerius a sword. He nodded his thanks as he draped the strap over his shoulder. 'I have business at the Golden House, but I will join you at the Castra Praetoria if I can.'

Aprilis shook his head, weariness making him impatient. 'You'll never make it. The palace is surrounded and might already be taken. The only reason the Seventh isn't here already is that our rearguard is holding them on the Velabrum. It won't be for long.' As if to confirm his words a roar swept like a wave between the Capitoline and the Palatine mounts, followed in moments by a stampede of retreating Praetorians along the Vicus Tuscus a few dozen paces away. Aprilis grabbed Valerius by the arm. 'You'll be no good to your lady friend with a sword in your guts,' he said. 'The chances are they'll treat her well enough if she's with the Emperor and his family. Stay here and you're dead.'

Still Valerius hesitated. These were his friends the Praetorian was telling him to run from. The two men were standing at the junction of the Sacred Way and the Clivus Capitolinus. At the far end of the Way he could see the walls of the Golden House where Domitia waited. But Aprilis was right. As well as the Praetorians streaming across their front, hundreds more were being forced back through the Forum. The centurion pulled him away in the direction of the Argiletum.

Before they had gone a few hundred paces they saw signs that the Flavians had been ahead of them. Clusters of dead and wounded legionaries and Praetorians lay scattered across the cobbles. Blood oozed into the central gutter.

'Third Gallica,' Aprilis muttered when he saw the insignia on the legionary shields. 'Where the fuck did they come from?'

They cleared the Subura and started up the slope of the Vicus Patricius. Behind them, Valerius could clearly hear the sound of fighting as the Praetorian rearguard tried to hold back the attacking Flavians. He considered cutting across the Esquiline to try to reach the Domus Aurea from the north, but every way was blocked. Instead, they were swept along like leaves in a swollen torrent as more troops filtered on to the street from right and left to swell the seething throng, a certain indication that Primus's legions were already in possession of most of the city.

'Vultures,' Aprilis spat as they ran past looters ransacking a jeweller's shop.

'What happens if the enemy already hold the Castra Praetoria?' Valerius gasped.

Aprilis turned to stare at him. 'Then we die where we stand.'

XLIX

The Castra had not been taken. They cleared the Porta Viminalis, lungs burning and legs shaking with the long run uphill, and there it stood: huge and impregnable, a massive red-brick square with walls three times the height of a man studded with towers at regular intervals. It had been the Praetorian barracks since the time of Augustus, but it was a fortress too, with the largest armoury in the city. Now the survivors of Vitellius's Praetorian Guard streamed from the Viminal gate or down the Via Salaria to make their last stand here. No surrender for these men. They were the veterans of the German legions who proclaimed Aulus Vitellius Emperor and they had no illusions about their fate if they were captured. Aprilis summed it up for all of them. 'If the bastards want to kill us it's going to cost them dear.'

Valerius knew that if he refused to draw his sword against the Flavians he'd be condemned as a spy or a coward, and the outcome would be the same in either case. He had already seen one man, a civilian accused of signalling to the attackers, being executed, his head rolling in the dust of the parade ground.

He tried to put Domitia out of his mind, but her face kept forcing its way into his head. His inability to protect her tore him like an almost physical pain. If he climbed one of the towers he would be able to see the roof of the Golden House, but he might as well have been in Parthia for all the good he could do.

Aprilis found him a silver breastplate, and offered a *scutum* with the silver lightning bolts of the Guard on the face. Valerius shrugged back his sleeve to show the mottled stump of his arm. 'All I need is a sword.'

Valerius had plenty of experience of sieges. Preparations for this one were more hurried and less ordered than they'd been at Placentia, where Valerius and Serpentius helped see off Caecina's legions. There was no shortage of *pila*, which lay stacked in bundles at intervals along the wall. What was in short supply were archers and artillery. The first could be relied on to make life difficult for anyone attacking the walls or climbing the big siege ladders, the second for breaking up the attacks with boulders the size of a man's head or the devastating five-foot 'shield-splitters'. But the most pressing lack was in manpower.

The Vitellians had begun the day with three cohorts and about ten thousand militia, a force barely capable of hindering the Flavian legions, never mind stopping them. When the Praetorians had been forced to retreat the armed civilians had melted away like snow in summer. Aprilis and his comrades had fought bravely to hold the Milvian Bridge and the Salarian Way, but they had been relentlessly forced back, taking casualties along the way. The Castra was defended by barely half the three thousand who had marched out to defend Rome.

Valerius reckoned the walls of the fort at around four hundred and fifty paces by four hundred, which meant less than one man to defend every pace of wall. That didn't take into account those needed to man the few *ballistae* and *onagri* in the towers. Nor did it leave any reserves, which, from his experience at Placentia, Valerius knew would be vital to respond to any breakthrough. There would be no care for the wounded, no rations brought to the walls. Every man would have to fend for himself. All Marcus Antonius Primus had to do was throw a legion at each wall, use his archers to keep the defenders' heads down, and the fort would be swamped. 'It is hopeless,' he warned Aprilis. 'We won't last a day.'

'Then what is your alternative?' the centurion challenged.

'You should surrender,' Valerius said flatly. He knew it was unthinkable for the Praetorian, but the words had to be said.

Aprilis's face reddened. 'Use that word again and I will kill you myself,' he said, and turned to walk away.

From their viewing point on one of the corner towers, Valerius watched the legions form up for the attack. He could see the symbols of at least five different units on the big shields that were visible from his position. Long lines of legionaries were waiting patiently in open order just out of range of the defenders' non-existent archers, the heavy *ballistae* arrayed behind them. The distant rattle of hammers identified carpenters knocking together the covered siege ramps that would bring the attackers within reach of the wall without exposing them to spears or arrows. In addition, Primus would have ladders every five or ten paces and the besiegers would swarm over regardless. He almost laughed. Siege? They'd be fortunate to last till darkness fell.

'We need to find somewhere to make a stand when they break through.' Valerius was surprised to find Aprilis back at his side.

'We might hold them for a while from the armoury.' Valerius left unsaid that the end would be the same in any case.

The Praetorian caught his tone. 'A man must fight to his last breath and his last heartbeat,' he said. 'What other way is there?'

Valerius didn't reply. The armoury was in the centre of the fort, part of a sprawling complex of buildings close to the *principia*. What did it matter anyway? Their chances of reaching it with the Flavian legionaries crawling over the walls were more or less non-existent. It was only a matter of time. And time was running out. By now it was dusk, but whoever commanded the siege was in a hurry. With an enormous rush the first catapult missile tore the air above them, the sound instantly followed by an echoing crash. It had begun.

Valerius adjusted his breastplate as the legionaries of the Third Gallica began their slow, inexorable march towards the west wall where he stood. Line after line of brightly coloured shields. The first of the smaller artillery pieces loosed their missiles and he heard a crash and screaming away to his left. It was going to be Placentia all over again, but at least at Placentia the defenders had reason for hope and optimism. Here there was only a grim resolve. Despair, fortified by a measure of truculent defiance.

He thought of the men who would climb the ladders. Men he had fought beside on the road to Cremona. *I won't kill unless I have to.* He must have spoken the words aloud because Aprilis laughed. 'Then you will certainly die here.'

L

'Come, child, this is no time for delay.'

Galeria Fundana's urgent tones dragged Domitia Longina Corbulo from the cocoon of her thoughts. The Augusta stood in the doorway, with an arm around Lucius. The boy's eyes were filled with a mixture of fear and excitement, as if this were some mildly perilous game rather than a matter of life and death. The massive bulk of Aulus Vitellius hovered protectively over them, his face pale as an alabaster statue. Vitellius hadn't shaved for a week and his cheeks were dark with stubble as if he was in mourning. In the distance Domitia could hear a muted buzz, occasionally punctuated by a shout and the frightening sound of the clash of arms.

'She is right, my dear. You will be safer in our villa on the Aventine than in the Golden House,' the Emperor said.

'But Valerius . . .' She shook her head. It was unthinkable that she leave without seeing him. He'd promised he would come for her and she must have the faith to wait.

'He would have been here if he could, my lady.' She turned in surprise to see Serpentius in the doorway, a look of weary resignation on his scarred features.

'Where is—'

'Safe. As safe as any of us are,' the Spaniard assured her as gently as his nature allowed. 'That must be enough for you.'

'He will have been delayed by the confusion on the streets,' Vitellius suggested. 'If the gods will it, he will find you before this is over.' She stared at him. Did he believe it was possible? She thought of the scarred features, and the eyes that had seen too much war. Gaius Valerius Verrens had survived the Temple of Claudius, the defeat at Bedriacum and the victory at Cremona. If any man could live through this it would be Valerius. The shouts grew more insistent and Vitellius paused as a guard appeared at his shoulder and whispered something his ear. Domitia saw a flinch of anguish, but he kept his features composed. 'Please,' he insisted. 'It is your duty to look after Lucius. We must not delay.'

Duty. The word had followed her since she was eight years old, prodding and insisting. 'A Corbulo does not have the luxury of choice,' her father had said. 'Only duty.'

'Very well,' she nodded. 'Come, Lucius,' she forced a smile as she took the boy's hand, 'we will count the sparrows on the way.'

Aulus Vitellius accompanied his family to the carriage that would carry them to safety and watched them ride away. Galeria stared rigidly ahead and little Lucius was already fascinated by the game Domitia Longina Corbulo had invented. Valerius's Spanish comrade trotted by their side and he was glad the former gladiator would be there to protect them. He should have sent them earlier, he knew, but the truth was he couldn't bear to be parted from them. Galeria Fundana was his strength, the rock that anchored him to his duty when the call of decadence became too loud to resist. Lucius was his reason for existing. He felt a fat tear trickle down his cheek. He had failed them. Utterly. He had promised to protect them, but now he had sent them out on to the perilous streets of a city under siege. Why? Because when the soldiers came the danger on the street would be infinitely less than here in this great glittering mausoleum. Alone at last – he'd sent all his guards and courtiers with Galeria – he wandered the echoing marble corridors, with their busts and their artworks, his legs shaking with fear and anticipation of what was to come. What did they matter now, all these shining baubles and this overwhelming sumptuousness that threatened to entomb him? When he'd been in debt he dreamed of a palace like this, but like the man who built it he'd been a fool. Vespasian was welcome to it – all of it. Better to have lived on bread and olives than come to an end such as this. He found himself in the entrance hall, with the enormous golden statue of Nero towering over him. He'd never replaced the head, but . . . His hand went to his neck. Would they? The Praetorians had sent him the head of Titus Flavius Sabinus and he had cringed from its accusing, glassy-eyed stare. The image triggered a new wave of panic. Vitellius staggered through to his private quarters, almost running now and with his heart thundering in his chest. The doors were locked, but he flung his weight at them, bursting them open. There, on the table, Caesar's sword. He reached for it with shaking fingers and heard the acclamation of the legions as they proclaimed him Emperor at Moguntiacum. CAESAR! CAESAR! CAESAR!

He'd never called himself Caesar, though other men had, but he'd carried Caesar's sword. Now he pulled it from its scabbard with that soft, familiar hiss. And almost dropped it. He had never seen it like this before, that gleaming, dangerous edge and the needle point. No longer an ornament, but a weapon of war. A killing weapon. How he wished Valerius were here. Valerius would know. Valerius would help him make the final decision. Tentatively, he raised his head and brought the point up to touch the folds of flesh at his throat. One thrust was all it would take. One thrust and it was over. But what if he botched it? Men took hours to die, sometimes days, with a wound like that. Could he bear it? No, there must be another way. He heard a childish mewing and felt a rush of revulsion when he realized it was from his own lips. *You are still the Emperor of Rome*, the rebuke was a silent scream, *for your family's sake and your ancestors', act like one.* He raised the point again, closing his eyes as the cold metal brushed the pulsing artery in his neck. *One thrust.* Shouts and the clatter of running hobnailed feet, skidding at the doorway. *Do it now.*

'You don't get away that easily.' Rough hands tore the hilt of Caesar's sword from his fingers, nicking his skin in the process. He willed himself to open his eyes and witness his bane, but the lids wouldn't obey his mind.

'Look at that,' someone else laughed. 'Caesar's pissed himself.'

'Don't bother about that, search him, and do it properly. There's enough of him – who knows what he's got hidden away under all that blubber?'

More laughter as they tore at his clothing, dragging his toga back and tearing at his tunic. Vitellius felt a wave of revulsion and humiliation as the toga dropped away and fingers probed at him. Finally, one of his captors grabbed his hands and wrenched them behind his back, the rope cutting deep into his wrists and making him cry out in pain. Another tied a second length of rope in a loose noose around his neck. Vitellius had an image of a bull being led to the sacrifice and his eyes snapped open in terror. Not even in his most terrible nightmares had he imagined it would be like this.

Ten or twelve soldiers were in the room. Most of them stared in bewildered amusement at the corpulent figure who had been their Emperor, while the others tore at cabinets and moved furniture in search of loot. Their leader, a blood-spattered centurion with a horror of a face, held Caesar's sword in one hand and the end of the noose rope in the other. The Emperor flinched as he jerked it sharply forward.

'Where's the treasure?' he demanded in a guttural southern accent.

Aulus Vitellius raised his chins and looked down his nose at his captors, and attempted to regain some kind of dignity. 'There is treasure all around you in this house. Take what you will; I have no further use for it.'

'Statues, paintings,' the man spat. 'An idol the size of an *insula* that isn't even made of proper gold. I mean portable treasure: money, ornaments, jewellery. The Golden House is supposed to be full of the stuff, chests of golden *aurei* and rubies as big as my fist.'

'A myth,' Vitellius lied. 'What little money and jewels were in the house went with the Praetorians when they withdrew to the Castra Praetoria. Perhaps you should look for it there?' The truth was that the wagon carrying Galeria had been fitted with a false bottom. Hopefully, his loyal guards would be burying the chests it held in the garden of the Aventine house. He had no time to enjoy this minor triumph before the centurion delivered a back-handed slap to his cheek that made his eyes water and the tears run again.

'Old Brocchus has been around long enough to know how to find treasure. You'll have heard of Cremona?'

'An infamy.' Vitellius shook his head. The slaughter of civilians at Cremona had grieved him more than any military defeat.

'Well, I know a jeweller at Cremona who didn't have any treasure right up until the minute I rammed a red hot *gladius* up his arse.' Brocchus grinned and drew the sword of Julius Caesar and placed the point in Vitellius's left nostril. 'We haven't got a fire to hand,' he smirked, 'so how about I start with a few bits and pieces. What's it to be, the nose or an ear?'

'You can't torture him, First,' interrupted one of the other men. 'He's . . . he was the Emperor. The high-ups are going to want to see him. Maybe even old man Vespasian himself.'

Vitellius felt a moment of knee-trembling hope. He lifted his nostril from the sword point and sniffed. 'Yes, I have information of the greatest importance for Vespasian. You will be well rewarded if you take me to your senior officers.'

'He's hiding something.' The speaker's face was poisonous with malignant intent. 'I think we should roast him until he squeals like the pig he is. We didn't come here to be fobbed off with a few statues and a fancy sword. No one would ever know.'

'You could feed a cohort for a month on a pig that size,' another man laughed.

'Use him as a table and a century could eat off him with room to spare.'

Vitellius tried not to hear the jibes and the laughter, but each barb stuck deeper than the last, and he almost didn't hear the reprieve from Brocchus.

'No, Julius is right. One of you bastards would blab if we killed him. He's more valuable alive than dead, and I reckon there might be a nice reward for this fancy sword, which, naturally, you'll all share in.' The looks told him they didn't believe it but Brocchus didn't give a fuck about that. 'Come on.' He dragged at the noose and Vitellius was forced to blunder after him, with half the other men following on and the rest continuing to ransack the palace. 'We'll take you to the general.'

But Brocchus had underestimated the crowd who'd gathered in the Forum reckoning it was relatively safe to emerge from their homes. Most were just thankful they'd survived, but some blamed Vitellius for what their city had suffered and these crowded round the pitiful procession to witness his humiliation. Brocchus growled at them to stay back, but he wasn't going to risk angering the mob over a stumbling fat man at the end of a rope. Vitellius was helpless against the spittle that splashed into his face and on to his tunic. Sharp fingers poked into the flesh of his enormous belly and tweaked the coarse hair of his beard. They shouted their hatred in his face and the tears streamed down his cheeks. He wondered that these screaming, contorted faces were the same people who had hailed him as Emperor a few short months ago, and more recently refused to allow him to abdicate the throne. No thought now of the luxuries he'd showered on them, the games and the tax benefits. They were passing through the line of pillars with his statues upon them and he saw that already the mob was preparing to tear them down. Without warning someone tripped him, and he fell to his knees, crying out as the cobbles tore the soft skin of his knees. Brocchus hauled at the rope, almost throttling him as he struggled vainly to rise. Another pair of legs appeared beside the centurion's and Vitellius looked up into the coldest eyes he had ever seen.

'I will take responsibility for this prisoner.' The man held his hand out for the rope. Brocchus opened his mouth to argue, but thought better of it. He noted the *phalerae* that signalled the other's long service in the Praetorian unit that Aulus Vitellius had disbanded, and the fifteen or twenty stone-faced veterans at his back. 'He's mine,' the officer repeated. Brocchus shrugged and handed over the rope, reflecting that the sword wasn't a bad trophy and there was plenty more loot out there. He didn't give the man he'd captured another thought.

Vitellius was hauled to his feet, and the soldiers formed up around him as their officer forced his way through the crowd. The mob stepped back from these hard-eyed men and the abuse faded, but for Vitellius the vision of a sacrificial bull was all the more vivid. His head sank on to his chest, but one of the soldiers drew his sword and slipped the blade under his chin, forcing it upwards. It seemed he must witness every instant of his humiliation. Past the rostrum, where he had tried to save Rome from this very fate, past the beginning of the Clivus Capitolinus, to . . . his first instinct was to struggle and pull himself away as he realized their destination.

The officer turned. 'It will be easier for you if you cooperate, but we will drag you if need be.'

'Please . . .'

The rope tightened, and he was pulled forward on to the stairs. The Gemonian Stairs. All fight evaporated from him and his heart fluttered like a trapped butterfly. Suddenly everything in his world seemed sharper. He could see the pores on the faces of his escort, the tiny rust pits on their swords and the fibres of their clothing. Every grain on the granite steps appeared visible to him. He looked up, hoping to see the sun, but clouds filled the sky and a light drizzle settled on his face. This was where Titus Flavius Sabinus had died, and he felt a twinge of regret for his old enemy. No man should die like this.

The little procession shambled to a halt and the tribune removed the rope around his neck, staring at him as if he wanted to remember the features for ever. When he was satisfied he spat in Vitellius's face, so he felt the warm phlegm on his forehead and in his hair. 'You destroyed my career, ruined my family and ordered my brother's execution,' the young man said, as if it explained everything that was about to happen.

'Yes,' Vitellius agreed, 'but I was your Emperor and it was my right. You have no right to do this.'

'My sword is my right.' As the tribune said the words, he plunged the blade into the other man's chest. Agony beyond imagining expanded to fill Vitellius's entire body. As he fell, his last conscious thought was for Galeria and Lucius, but then the next sword struck and the darkness closed in. In that moment, the reign of Aulus Vitellius Germanicus Augustus was ended. He had been Emperor for eight months and a single fateful day.

LI

The battle for the walls of the Castra Praetoria was over almost before it began. As Valerius predicted, Primus sent his siege towers forward to draw the defenders before launching squads of legionaries up the long ladders they carried into the gaps between. When the Praetorians rushed to meet the new threat, the Flavians burst from the towers and overwhelmed the weakened defences. In a siege, the first fissures must be instantly sealed or the cracks become gaping holes that undermine the entire defensive structure. Valerius could feel it happening around him.

A legionary in a red tunic rushed out of the darkness, his shield gone and his sword held too high. Valerius feinted to the right and hammered the hilt of his *gladius* into the man's face, battering him so hard he flipped over the parapet and fell to the rocky ground thirty feet below. So much for not killing. He had to kill to survive. And he had to survive for Domitia.

'They're over the wall in about five places,' came Aprilis's harsh, breathless shout from his left, as he exchanged cuts with another shadowy figure. 'If we're going back to the armoury we have to go now.'

Valerius's left-handed sword found a gap in his opponent's defence and the point pierced the enemy's thigh. Not a death wound by any

374

means, and he would have been happy to leave it at that as he retreated towards the stairs. But the injury only seemed to enrage the man and he clambered forward, roaring until Valerius silenced his shout with a backhand cut that almost took his head off.

They leapt down the stairs three at a time and ran towards the armoury through a welter of struggling anonymous figures. One man rushed at Valerius, but he dropped shoulder and with a Serpentius-taught gladiator trick flipped his attacker over his back into the dust, running on with barely a pause. Others had a similar idea and by the time he reached the armoury building the doors had already been barred. For a moment they were trapped at the entrance with Flavian troops converging on them from all sides, but someone inside must have spied the silver breastplate because the door suddenly opened and they were dragged inside.

'We thought you were already dead, centurion,' a tired voice said, and Aprilis clasped hands with another survivor from his century. 'We've done what we can, but perhaps you'd like to inspect our dispositions, sir.'

Aprilis nodded, but he needed a moment to recover his breath before he began. Like the rest of the Castra Praetoria, the armoury was solidly built of red brick with only a few barred windows; ideal for all-round defence. Valerius knew this was only a small part of it. They stood in a long corridor with doors on either side that opened on to narrow storerooms. A set of stairs led to the upper storey, and beyond them was another door that would lead to the open central courtyard where the armourers repaired Praetorian weapons and equipment on their forges. Men bustled about carrying benches and arms racks, turning every room into a mini-fortress, blocking the barred windows and using the torn-off doors to create barricades.

Aprilis looked over the preparations with quiet satisfaction, but few illusions. 'We'll keep them out for as long as we can,' he nodded. 'Once they get inside they'll have to take the place room by room and we'll make them pay.'

'Has this place been provisioned?' Valerius asked. Aprilis's expression told its own story even before he replied with a bark of laughter.

'Do you think we're going to survive long enough to starve?'

'Water?' Valerius remembered the terrible trial of thirst in the Temple of Claudius as the Iceni rebels had tried to burn their way in.

'We have ample,' the other Praetorian assured him. 'We filled every pot and amphora we could lay our hands on from the well in the courtyard before we closed it off.'

'Open the door or we'll burn you out.' The sudden demand was accompanied by a thunderous hammering and answered by a string of obscene suggestions. Aprilis calmly ignored the order. The door would take at least an hour to burn through and with a pair of the armourers' anvils behind it he would have plenty of time to react to the battering ram, when they eventually found one. For now, all they could do was wait.

Valerius left him talking quietly with the men who would defend the corridor and asked a passing soldier if any of the armourers were still in the building.

'Old Vulcan over there will help you out.' He pointed to a big man slumped at the end of the corridor using a whetstone to put an edge on a *gladius*.

'I need a shield.'

Vulcan, whose given name was Septimus, looked up at the man towering over him, his eyes taking in the battle scars that marked a veteran. But they were all veterans here. 'Plenty around,' he shrugged. 'Help yourself.'

'A special shield.' Valerius showed him the stump of his hand. 'One that I can strap on to this.'

Vulcan's eyes displayed new interest. 'Albanus,' he roared to one of the men barricading the nearest side room. 'Bring me one of those new *scuta* we were keeping for the ceremonials.' He winked at Valerius. 'Probably won't be needing them now.' He pulled a piece of cord from his tunic and Valerius saw it had been marked in short sections so it could be used as a measure. 'Let's see your arm.'

Valerius held it out and the armourer wrapped the string around the bicep and again just above the mottled stump. He nodded to himself. 'Easy. A couple of belts and a few rivets.'

A man handed the armourer a *scutum*, its face unpainted bare ash. 'I'll need an hour. Can you wait that long?'

'That would depend on our guests.' Valerius met his grin and Vulcan laughed and disappeared into one of the rooms, barking at Praetorians to get out of his way.

The one-handed Roman found a place to sit at the bottom of the stairs. As he listened to the muted cries and shouts beyond the door he closed his eyes and thought back to the final hours of the Temple of Claudius. In the confined space of the temple *cella* the atmosphere had been thick with the distinctive acrid scent of extreme fear and the stink of unwashed bodies. Most of those trapped by Boudicca's rebels were tradesmen and their families, estate owners who had missed the evacuation, and the temple's priests. Here it was different. The men defending the Castra's armoury had all expected to be dead by now. Every man had resigned himself to his fate the moment he took the decision to stay with his comrades. The fear was there – they knew that beyond these protective walls fellow Praetorians were being hunted through the barracks and slaughtered – and the sweat of their earlier exertions, but Valerius was heartened by the quiet calm apparent in the way they went about their business. What seemed like moments later a rough hand shook him and he realized he must have fallen asleep. He looked up into a soot-pitted face.

'Better be quick – I think our friends are getting impatient.' Vulcan showed him the rear of the shield with its two partially buckled straps just above the normal grip. 'Just slip your arm through there.' Valerius did as he was urged and thick fingers pulled the straps tight and fixed the buckles in place. Vulcan saw him wince and grinned. 'It's not going to be very comfortable, but it should do the job for a while.'

'I don't expect to be wearing it for long.' The smile on Valerius's face froze as his words were punctuated by the first hammer blow of a battering ram on the armoury door. He met Vulcan's eyes and the big man's blackened features split into a wry grin. 'A fucking silly place to die, eh?' The armourer darted a last frown at the door as the ram crashed home again before returning to his sword.

Left alone, the sound of the ram brought back the fate of the men

377

and women trapped in the Temple of Jupiter and Valerius was almost overwhelmed by a wave of regret. He would never see Domitia's face again, feel the softness of her skin or taste the sweetness of her mouth. He dragged the back of his left hand across his dry lips, nipping the flesh between his teeth to drive the feeling away. Serpentius had vowed to defend her to his last breath, and that must be enough for Valerius. Still, a part of him wished the Spaniard were here, for if any man could have found a way out of this death trap it would have been Serpentius.

'Must be a big bastard,' he heard Aprilis mutter as the ram struck again. 'They didn't even try to weaken the door with fire first. Steady, lads,' he said to the men crammed into the narrow passageway. The front rank knelt with their spears angled up towards the doorway at groin height and Valerius pitied the first men through the door because those lethal pyramid-shaped points would thrust beneath a shield and condemn them to a terrible, lingering death. Behind the kneeling men Aprilis had placed two further lines of spearmen with their *pila* ready to throw. Any of the initial javelins that killed an enemy would be a bonus; his best hope was that they'd force the owners to abandon their shields and expose them to the second volley.

The next strike splintered the door and suddenly Valerius had no more time to think as a horde of howling figures threw themselves into the gap, their yells becoming all the shriller as Aprilis's spears found their mark. In a heartbeat everything was a chaos of men ramming their shields at each other in the confined space and hacking at any exposed flesh, accompanied by the familiar disbelieving shrieks of the newly eviscerated. A man reeled past Valerius with his lower jaw hanging by a white shard of bone, the exposed tongue enormous below the dreadful staring eyes. Another slipped and was instantly pinned by a Flavian spear, leaving Valerius in the front rank. Swords hammered at his newly acquired shield and something hit his helmet with a clatter. The desperate fight reminded him of a seagoing slaughter to win a pirate galley, and he kept half an eye for the floor and the man who would stab a sword up into his vitals from below.

'Hold the line and take a step back,' Aprilis snarled throatily. Valerius followed the order, careful to maintain station with his neighbour and feeling the pressure momentarily relax in front of him. 'Again. Now!' As the defenders backed away past the first pair of doorways a flight of javelins swept from right and left to catch the attackers unawares, piercing neck and throat and bringing the assault to a stop for a precious moment.

'Back to the stairs!' Aprilis took advantage of the momentary pause. Valerius didn't wait for a second invitation, sprinting to clamber up between the fresh men waiting to resume the defence. Two or three of Aprilis's troopers were too slow, or perhaps they'd been injured, for their screams echoed in the cramped space as the blood-maddened attackers hacked them to bloody ruin. When they reached the narrow stairway the Flavians were met by a solid wall of shields two wide and four high, and from above a hail of spears arced down, hurled by Praetorians blessed with an inexhaustible supply. But this mixture of men from four or five legions who had converged on the armoury from all sides of the camp were undaunted by casualties. When one fell another took his place, clawing at the defenders' shields, hauling them apart to leave their holders exposed to the spears and swords of the Flavians. With a roar of triumph the first pair of defenders were torn from their places and thrown to the blades behind to be finished off. Then the process began again three steps higher and still the unrelenting hail of spears punched men back, only for them to be replaced again and again. A second pair of shields fell, and a moment later the third, and now a whole host of Flavians launched themselves up the blood-slick stairway, forcing the last shield-bearers on to the spearmen behind. At the back of the room, Valerius recovered his breath among the little band of defenders clustered around Aprilis.

He heard the Praetorian reciting a prayer, and to his surprise the words were those of the Christian cult. Aprilis saw his look and smiled wryly, as if to say it didn't matter now. Valerius closed his eyes for a second and muttered a prayer of his own, trying to fix Domitia's face in his mind. Not long. Aprilis waited until the attackers were pressing the spearmen. 'Now!' He hurled his exhausted men into the fray in a compact wedge, aiming his point of attack to drive the attackers back on to the stairs. Valerius knew even before they struck that they were too few, and the mass of Flavians absorbed the counter-attack as dry soil absorbs a shower of rain. Snarling faces and flashing swords surrounded him and he had to use all his strength and skill just to stay alive. At the edge of his vision he saw Vulcan fall, his body pierced by a hurled javelin. Something smashed into the back of his helmet and he fell to his knees. Screaming defiance he just managed to bring his sword round to counter a slashing blow that would have taken his head off before someone kicked him in the face with an iron-shod *caliga*. The blow knocked him backwards with blood in his mouth and at least one tooth gone. Worse, he'd lost his sword. With the last of his strength he managed to drag the shield to protect his body from the blades already seeking him out. He had a fleeting glimpse of Aprilis's agonized face as he was hauled across the wooden floor with swords hacking at his torso before the shield above him began to splinter and he screamed as something caught him a glancing blow on the knee. Somehow he thrust himself up, only to be pushed back, staggering against the wall with the remains of the shield ripped away. He raised his arms in a futile bid to keep the swords at bay.

'No!' A snarling centurion thrust himself between Valerius and the blades that sought him out. The one-handed Roman froze in disbelief, his breath a searing pain his chest, and his heart caught between beats. Gaius Brocchus turned with an almost serene smile of triumph. 'No quick death for this man,' he ordered his bemused legionaries. 'A spy and a traitor, isn't it, tribune? A stinking coward who played both sides against the middle.' He grinned, showing the sharpened teeth, and Valerius shuddered. 'Somebody's going to want you to burn, pretty boy, and old Gaius is going to be there to watch.'

LII

'You are found guilty of treason against the state.'

A murmur rippled through the crowd in the Forum. Every man had heard the overwhelming evidence against Gaius Valerius Verrens, enemy of Rome. How he had conspired with Aulus Vitellius to incite a civil war. How he had encouraged the sack and burning of the great city of Cremona. How he had, by trickery and deceit, delayed and confused the movements of the army of General Marcus Antonius Primus. How he had personally led the attack which resulted in the destruction of the sacred Temple of Jupiter Optimus Maximus, and how he had, with Aulus Vitellius, ordered the murder of Titus Flavius Sabinus, Prefect of Rome.

'I will speak for you,' Primus had said, when he visited Valerius in his cell in the *carcer*, 'but I cannot protect you. You are entitled to a trial in the Senate by reason of your rank, but Domitianus says he will not defile its stones with your presence. Until his father arrives from Alexandria, he is the ruler of Rome, and he is determined that you shall die. I have never seen such malevolence.' When it came to it, the evidence had been so conclusive that Primus had shaken his head and covered his face with his hands. Only Gaius Plinius Secundus had spoken up for Valerius.

Now, Domitianus's malevolent eyes stared with satisfaction at the

381

bound figure standing filthy and dishevelled in the space between the two rostra. Vespasian's son sat on a dais in front of the Senate House, surrounded by Primus and the generals who had saved Rome from the predatory clutches of Aulus Vitellius. Valerius met his enemy's eyes without flinching, unbowed despite his week-long incarceration and the certainty of death, determined to show no fear in front of the mob who crowded the steps of the temples and basilicas. He tried to ignore a right hand that throbbed as if it still existed, and the gash in his left knee that felt as if it was on fire. Domitia's face swam into his head and he wondered where she was, or if she had even survived. His jailers had delighted in telling him how the Flavians had hunted Vitellius's supporters through the streets and slaughtered them, urged on by those who had hailed him only days earlier. Surely Serpentius would have found a way to get word to him? Valerius had searched for the Spaniard among the crowds, but his ravaged features were nowhere to be seen.

Domitianus rose, his broad-striped toga hanging on his thin frame, and looking less like a ruler, however temporary, than a schoolboy making his first speech. He waited until the last whisper had faded and every eye was on him before he spoke. 'There can be only one sentence for such outrages.' He spoke in a high and grating voice that quivered with nervous energy, but it echoed in the silence and every man waited on his next words. 'That sentence is death.'

If Domitianus expected a roar of approval, he was disappointed. In his plea for leniency, Pliny had skilfully made play of Valerius's past military service, his gold crown of valour and status as a Hero of Rome. He had mentioned sacrifices, and every man could see the mottled stump of the condemned man's right wrist, and the honourable scars he carried from his service in Africa and Parthia. The lawyer had also cast what shadows he could on the evidence, and not every man in the Forum was fully convinced of the accused's guilt. Among the spectators were off-duty legionaries from the Seventh Galbiana and they formed little pockets of unease. Domitianus ignored them.

'A traitor's deeds deserve – demand – a traitor's death. Gaius Valerius Verrens will be taken from this place to the Circus Maximus and crucified . . .' A rumble went through the crowd at the dreaded word, the ugliest and most humiliating of deaths. A few men shouted 'No', but Domitianus continued with barely a hesitation. '. . . before the people of Rome he betrayed by his actions. He is hereby stripped of his rank, his lands and his possessions.'

Valerius waited until the sentence was complete before he spoke. He had walked hand in hand with death many times and did not fear it, but the means Domitianus had devised made him shudder. A quick end under the blade of an executioner's sword or even a criminal's at the end of a rope he had expected, but the cross?

'Condemn me you may, Titus Flavius Domitianus.' The shouted words echoed round the marble columns of the Forum in a voice powerful enough for all to hear. 'And kill me you may, but I will not bear being called a traitor in silence.'

Domitianus waved a hand to the nearest guard and the soldier raised his club, but a voice called out, 'No, let him speak.' The cry was taken up by others, till hundreds echoed the demand. Domitianus glared at them, but he waved the guard away.

'Very well, the traitor may speak,' he ground out, 'but know that words will not save him.'

'Everything I did, I did for Rome,' Valerius continued. 'When Marcus Salvius Otho sent me as emissary to Aulus Vitellius I went willingly, because I believed I could persuade him from war.' He shook his head. 'I was wrong. A shift was under way that no one man, not even Vitellius himself, could halt. So I took up arms against my old friend and I was proud to fight beside the First Adiutrix at Bedriacum. Was that the act of a traitor? You have been told that Vitellius deliberately freed me to spy on Marcus Antonius Primus, and that I attempted to delay him. I am no spy, but it was Titus Flavius Vespasian's wish that Primus should wait, and the general himself would tell you that if only he would speak.' Primus glanced nervously at Domitianus, but he stayed in his seat. 'It was Marcus Antonius Primus who sent me to Rome to persuade Aulus Vitellius to surrender and save needless bloodshed, and his plan would have succeeded if one man,' he let his eyes settle on Domitianus, 'just one man, had had the courage to step forward and accept the sword of Caesar from his hand. When Rome needed a hero, those who could have saved her instead fled to the Temple of Jupiter and left her to her fate.' The speech seemed to have drained the strength from him, and Domitianus gave a thin smile as his enemy's head dropped. But Valerius drew a long breath and his chin came up as he somehow found the will to continue. 'Perhaps I deserve to die for what happened in the sacred precincts of the temple, though neither I, nor any other, knows who cast the fateful brand. And for taking up arms against my former comrades. But I am no traitor. I swear it on the life and honour of Gaius Valerius Verrens.'

'Condemned from his own mouth.' Domitianus couldn't suppress a sneer. 'Let the sentence be carried out.'

Valerius made no attempt to resist as they came forward to bind him. He tried to put what was to come out of his mind, looking over the heads of the crowd to where a procession of men on horseback were approaching down the Argiletum. The leader wore a breastplate worked with gold and the glittering plumed helmet of a Roman general. His old enemy Gaius Licinius Mucianus had come to watch him die.

Mucianus forced his horse through the crowd to the dais and dismounted, throwing the reins to one of the guards. Primus darted a look of alarm as his rival approached Domitianus and saluted, earning a wary nod of recognition in return.

'I bring greetings from your father, the Emperor,' the general announced, 'and from your brother Titus. Your father sends word that he will return to Rome once his business in Judaea is completed and you have had sufficient time to arrange an appropriate welcome for him. He confirms your position in sole charge of the city as acting Prefect of Rome.' He turned to survey the scene around him as if noticing the thronged Forum for the first time. 'What is happening here?'

'Your timing is good.' Domitianus smiled. 'I am having this criminal put to death. You will no doubt enjoy the spectacle.'

Mucianus studied the prisoner and frowned as he recognized Valerius. 'My timing is indeed propitious.' He turned to an aide and the tribune ran forward with an open scroll. 'I carry a pardon for this man signed by the Emperor himself.' He handed the scroll to Domitianus. The newly appointed Prefect of Rome took it with shaking fingers, and when he came to the end of the document he raised his head with a look of puzzled amusement.

'But this is a pardon for a previous sentence of death, for cowardice in the face of the enemy.' He laughed. 'The Senate has convicted Gaius Valerius Verrens on the most vile charges of treason and I have just sentenced the traitor to death by crucifixion.' The sallow face creased into what he obviously believed was a benevolent smile. 'However, in recognition of my father's regard for the man's past service, I hereby commute the sentence to a merciful beheading. Send for the executioner.'

'Sir,' Mucianus stepped forward urgently, 'may I respectfully advise . . .'

'You may not,' Domitianus snapped. 'I will have his life.'

Mucianus continued to whisper to Vespasian's son, and Primus attempted to join the conversation, but Domitianus waved him away.

Strong hands pushed Valerius to his knees and he raised his head to see the bull-shouldered executioner walking towards him, a long cavalry *spatha* twirling expertly in his right hand. He recognized the brick-red peasant face of the man who had been within a heartbeat of removing his head four months earlier in a grassy Pannonian field. The soldier's face split in a wry grin and he shook his head. 'You should have run, son, and just kept running,' he whispered.

'Just make it quick,' Valerius said.

'You know the drill, lad. Head up and keep it still. Makes it easier on both of us.'

Valerius did as he was instructed, the wall of faces on the far side of the Forum a flesh-coloured blur. As a hush fell over the sacred space he took a final breath.

In the pause before the blow fell he was distracted by a slight movement at the corner of his eye. A wall of white entered his vision, moving from left to right, and his astonished eyes registered a procession of Vestal Virgins from the Temple of Vesta a few dozen paces up the Via Sacra. One face stood out at the centre of the little group and his heart stopped as he realized he was looking at Domitia Longina Corbulo. Domitia stared directly ahead, acknowledging neither the crowd nor the man kneeling in the centre of the square. Suddenly he knew.

'Strike,' he hissed at the legionary. He tensed for the stroke, but it never came.

'Strike,' he repeated, loud enough for every man to hear.

But the executioner was looking to Titus Flavius Domitianus for the signal, and Domitianus only had eyes for Domitia Longina Corbulo, who detached herself from the procession and serenely approached the platform, where a space miraculously appeared at his side. Their heads bowed together and Valerius watched in despair as a one-sided discussion took place. Eventually, Domitianus nodded gravely and stood, his face a picture of bewilderment.

'I have taken the advice of my generals. The sentence is commuted to exile.' He blinked and his eyes focused on Valerius. 'You will leave Rome within twelve hours and never set foot on the soil of Italia again . . . on pain of death.'

Valerius bowed his head and understood for the first time that there were worse fates than death.

LIII

'You should not have come here.'

The bitterness in Valerius's voice was like a knife through Domitia's heart, but to betray it would only have increased the pain for them both. Somehow, she managed to remain composed and apparently unmoved. 'Do not judge me, Valerius. I did what had to be done.'

'Your duty?' He spat the word as if it were a curse. She had arrived at the room where he had stayed before his capture as he was packing a leather bag for a journey that did not yet have a destination. Curtains covered the windows and the darkness was like a cloak between them, which was a blessing because it meant they did not have to look into each other's eyes.

'Not my duty,' she said without bitterness. 'What was right. Would you deny me the right to make a sacrifice to save the man I loved?'

Now it was his turn to feel the sting of the blade and she heard the agony of it in his voice. 'I would rather have died.'

'Yes,' she said carefully. 'I understand that, but ask yourself how Domitia Longina Corbulo could have lived if she had left you to your fate when she had the means to alter it.'

'I should kill him.'

'And have my sacrifice mean nothing?' She shook her head at his naivety. When she had made her decision it had felt like a death sentence, but once it was taken she realized she had the capacity to live with it. How many women of her class had the luxury of choice? 'Have I misjudged you so, Valerius? The man I love is brave and honourable and kind. He is not a fool who voluntarily throws himself to the wolf for no purpose. It is what Domitianus wants you to do, and you would die for nothing. I have given him my vow, and I will not break my word. You have often said I am my father's daughter. Would you expect me to dishonour his shade?'

Valerius fought for words, but he knew nothing he said would change what was. When the silence became unbearable, it was Domitia who spoke.

'Where will you go?'

'I don't . . .' He swallowed. 'To Titus, I think, if he will have me. If he does not want me, or if my presence threatens his position, then east; a sword for hire.'

'Better with Titus,' she nodded. 'I will send Serpentius after you when he has recovered.'

At first he thought he'd misheard her. 'Serpentius?'

'He was hit by a club from behind as he tried to save little Lucius.' Her eyes misted over as she remembered the moment, her heart in her mouth for Serpentius, the awful flood of blood from the pale flesh of the child's throat. His mother's screams. 'Serpentius is not invincible after all, Valerius. Neither are you. You may find him . . .' she searched for the proper word, 'changed. Since he woke it is as if he sees the world differently.'

Valerius sighed. Of course, the boy's fate had been certain from the moment Vitellius had named him his heir. But Serpentius? 'I thought he was dead.' His voice sounded very tired. 'Better then to send him back to his homeland. The gods know there is no more honour in riding with Gaius Valerius Verrens, enemy of Rome. If you could find a way to . . .'

'Of course,' she said. 'I will ensure he has the means, and more. It is the least I owe him.' Valerius finished packing the bag and straightened, meeting her eyes for the first time. She realized that Serpentius was not the only one who had changed. 'I will try to make sure that your property passes to Olivia,' she continued, 'and that the villa is rebuilt.' She saw his bemusement. 'It was burned. Deserters from one army or the other. She is safe, but a few of your people were killed.'

A bell tolled somewhere nearby.

'I will . . .'

'You should . . .'

Their words emerged simultaneously and faded in the same instant. She stepped forward into his arms and he held her, breathing in the fresh sweetness of her hair, trying to imprint every nuance of it on his memory. He felt dampness on his unshaven cheek and tasted salt on his lips. For a time it seemed neither could find the will to break the embrace, but eventually Domitia pushed herself away.

'You must go.' She turned away to the window.

He nodded. What else was there to say? He picked up the bag and walked to the doorway, hesitating as she spoke again. 'He has pledged to leave you in peace, but he will send them after you.'

Them. Assassins: backstabbers and poisoners.

'I will be ready for them.'

A soft current of air brushed the back of her neck.

'Valerius . . .' She turned back, not ready to let him go despite her entreaty. But where he'd stood was only darkness.

Historical note

The downfall of Otho at First Bedriacum in AD 69 would have marked the end of the civil war known as the Year of the Four Emperors, but for the ambition of Titus Flavius Vespasian, proconsul of Egypt and commander of the eastern legions. How long Aulus Vitellius would have lasted as Emperor is anyone's guess given his own character and that of his two foremost generals, Fabius Valens and Aulus Caecina Alienus, both of whom probably had their eyes on the purple. It's possible he would have survived thanks to the unswerving loyalty of the German legions who had placed him in power, but Vespasian's intervention ensured the question never arose.

Like his predecessor, Vitellius's short time in office seems to disprove his reputation. Suetonius represents him as a slothful glutton, but Tacitus, who was more contemporary, is a little more reasoned in his criticism. Revealingly, he says that Vitellius's most important edicts, the curbing of centurions' abuses of power and the expansion of the major Imperial offices beyond a small pool of privileged freedmen, were adopted by successive emperors. The Emperor also managed to keep the population happy and fed at a time when Vespasian had halted grain shipments from Egypt and Africa.

But one thing is clear; Vitellius was no general. When Vespasian's Moesian and Pannonian legions advanced on Italy he stayed in Rome or in one of his villas nearby, leaving the conduct of the fighting to Valens and Caecina. It was a big mistake. Caecina betrayed him at the first opportunity and would have gifted his legions to Vespasian but for the loyalty of his senior officers to their Emperor. Valens, sick and apparently having lost his appetite for the fight, wandered aimlessly until he was scooped up by Vespasian's loyalists.

Vespasian also avoided the front line, preferring to stay in Egypt, but for different reasons. It's suggested that he wanted the bloodshed kept to a minimum so that he could enter Rome in triumph as a protector as well as victor, and he might well have done so if Marcus Antonius Primus, commander of the Balkan legions, had obeyed orders and waited for reinforcements. But Primus was a man in a hurry. He'd been exiled for fraud under Nero and now he had the opportunity to resurrect his political career and wipe out the stain on his character. Instead of waiting for reinforcements from the Syrian legions he decided to attack Italy and moved on Cremona over the same ground that had been saturated in blood nine months earlier. Barely able to control his men and drawn into a battle he didn't want, he was forced to fight a night action which could have ended in disaster. Fortunately for Primus, without Valens and Caecina the Vitellian legions were more or less leaderless and he was able to fight his way through and take Cremona. However, the city paid the price for its support of the enemy in an orgy of blood, rapine and fire that probably cost Primus any chances of future advancement under the wrathful Vespasian.

Vitellius, now without an army, was still in Rome as the legions approached. It's clear he wanted to give up the purple and save the lives of himself and his family, but his Praetorian Guard of German veterans thwarted an attempt to broker a peace with Vespasian's brother Sabinus, who was still in the city. Sabinus attempted to take refuge on the Capitol with his nephew, the future Emperor Domitian, and a group of allies, but the Praetorians flushed them out and the Temple of Jupiter Capitolinus burned to the ground. Domitian survived, but when Vespasian's vengeful soldiers marched into Rome Vitellius was dragged from the Domus Aurea and butchered. Vespasian was Emperor and the Flavian dynasty had begun.

But what of Gaius Valerius Verrens? Disgraced and hunted, he must seek out the only friend he has left, the Emperor's elder son, Titus, and attempt to regain his honour against the Judaean rebels who are determined to be the Scourge of Rome.

Glossary

Ala milliaria – A reinforced auxiliary cavalry wing, normally between 700 and 1,000 strong. In Britain and the west the units would be a mix of cavalry and infantry, in the east a mix of spearmen and archers.

Ala quingenaria – Auxiliary cavalry wing normally composed of 500 auxiliary horsemen.

Aquilifer – The standard bearer who carried the eagle of the legion.

As – A small copper coin worth approximately one fifth of a **sestertius**.

Aureus (pl. Aurei) – Valuable gold coin worth twenty-five **denarii**.

Auxiliary – Non-citizen soldiers recruited from the provinces as light infantry or for specialist tasks, e.g. cavalry, slingers, archers.

Ballista (pl. Ballistae) – Artillery for throwing heavy missiles of varying size and type. The smaller machines were called scorpions or onagers.

Batavians – Members of a powerful Germanic tribe which lived in the area of the Rhine delta, now part of the Netherlands. Traditionally provided auxiliary units for the Roman Empire in return for relief from tribute and taxes.

Beneficiarius – A legion's record keeper or scribe.

Boar's Head (alt. Wedge) – A compact arrow-head formation used by Roman infantry and cavalry to break up enemy formations.

Caligae – Sturdily constructed, reinforced leather sandals worn by Roman soldiers, normally with iron-studded sole.

Century – Smallest tactical unit of the legion, numbering eighty men.

Classis Germanica – Fleet of galleys which patrolled and carried military traffic on the River Rhine frontier.

Cohort – Tactical fighting unit of the legion. Normally contained six centuries, apart from the elite First cohort, which had five double-strength centuries (800 men).

Cohortis urbanae – Literally 'urban cohorts', a kind of paramilitary police force in Rome, formed by Augustus and used to counteract the power of the Praetorians.

Consul – One of two annually elected chief magistrates of Rome, normally appointed by the people and ratified by the Senate.

Contubernium – Unit of eight soldiers who shared a tent or barracks.

Cornicen (pl. Cornicines) – Legionary signal trumpeter who used an instrument called a **cornu**.

Decimation – A brutal and seldom used Roman military punishment where one man in every ten of a unit found guilty of cowardice or mutiny was chosen for execution by his comrades.

Decurion – A junior officer in a century, or a troop commander in a cavalry unit.

Denarius (pl. Denarii) – A silver coin.

Domus – The house of a wealthy Roman, e.g. Nero's Domus Aurea (Golden House).

Duplicarius – Literally 'double pay man'. A senior legionary with a trade, or an NCO.

Equestrian – Member of the Roman knightly class.

Evocatus (pl. Evocati) – A Roman legionary who voluntarily re-enlisted after the completion of his service.

Fortuna – The goddess of luck and good fortune.

Frumentarii – Messengers who carried out secret duties for the Emperor, possibly including spying and assassination.

Gladius (pl. Gladii) – The short sword of the legionary. A lethal killing weapon at close quarters.

Governor – Citizen of senatorial rank given charge of a province. Would normally have a military background (see **Proconsul**).

Haruspex – Soothsayer, sometimes a priest.

Hispania Tarraconensis – Roman province covering a large part of what is now Spain.

Jupiter – Most powerful of the Roman gods, often referred to as **Optimus Maximus** (greatest and best).

Legate – The general in charge of a legion. A man of senatorial rank.

Legion – Unit of approximately 5,000 men, all of whom would be Roman citizens.

Lictor – Bodyguard of a Roman magistrate. There were strict limits on the numbers of lictors associated with different ranks.

Lituus – Curved trumpet used to transmit cavalry commands.

Lusitania – The Roman province which covered a territory that is now southern Portugal and part of western Spain.

Magister navis – A ship's captain.

Manumission – The act of freeing a slave.

Mars – The Roman god of war.

Medici – A Roman legionary medical orderly.

Mithras – An Eastern religion popular among Roman soldiers.

Nomentan – A superior variety of Roman wine, mentioned by Martial in his Epigrams.

Phalera (pl. Phalerae) – Awards won in battle worn on a legionary's chest harness.

Pilum (pl. Pila) – Heavy spear carried by a Roman legionary.

Praefectus urbi (Urban prefect) – The senior magistrate in charge of Rome, with command of the **cohortis urbanae** and the **vigiles**.

Praetorian Guard – Powerful military force stationed in Rome. Accompanied the Emperor on campaign, but could be of dubious loyalty and were responsible for the overthrow of several Roman rulers.

Prefect – Auxiliary cavalry commander.

Primus pilus – 'First File'. The senior centurion of a legion.

Principia – Legionary headquarters building.

Proconsul – Governor of a Roman province, such as Spain or Syria, and of consular rank.

Procurator – Civilian administrator subordinate to a governor.

Proscaenium – The area where plays were staged in a Roman theatre.

Quaestor – Civilian administrator in charge of finance.

Scorpio – Bolt-firing Roman light artillery piece.

Scutum (pl. Scuta) – The big, richly decorated curved shield carried by a legionary.

Senator – Patrician member of the Senate, the key political institution which administered the Roman Empire. Had to meet strict financial and property rules and be at least thirty years of age.

Sestertius (pl. Sestertii) – Roman brass coin worth a quarter of a **denarius**.

Signifer – Standard bearer who carried the emblem of a cohort or century.

Testudo – Literally 'tortoise'. A unit of soldiers with shields interlocked for protection.

Tribune – One of six senior officers acting as aides to a legate. Often, but not always, on short commissions of six months upwards.

Tribunus laticlavius – Literally 'broad stripe tribune'. The most senior of a legion's military tribunes.

Urban cohorts – Force founded by Augustus to combat the power of the Praetorian Guard. Used for policing large mobs and riot-control duties.

Vascones – Roman auxiliaries from a tribe inhabiting northern Spain. Gave their name to the Basque region.

Valetudinarium – A clinic or hospital.

Victimarius – Servant who delivers and attends to the victim of a sacrifice.

Victory – Roman goddess equivalent to the Greek Nike.

Vigiles – Force responsible for the day-to-day policing of Rome's streets, for fire prevention and for fighting.

Acknowledgements

As always, I'm grateful to my editor Simon Taylor and his team at Transworld for helping me make *Enemy of Rome* the novel it is, and to my agent Stan, of Jenny Brown Associates in Edinburgh, for all his advice and encouragement. My wife Alison and my children, Kara, Nikki and Gregor, have once more been the rocks on which this book has been built. My love of the Roman era never wanes, but it was rejuvenated during the writing of *Enemy of Rome* by a walk along part of the magnificent Hadrian's Wall with my friends and fellow JAFRAs Ben Kane, Tony Riches and Russ Whitfield, accompanied by historian Mike Bishop whose *Roman Military Equipment* is seldom far from my side. As with *Sword of Rome*, apart from the primary sources – Plutarch, Tacitus, Suetonius and Dio – Gwyn Morgan's *69 A.D., The Year of the Four Emperors* was my guide to a complicated and sometimes contentious series of events, and any gaps in my ever-advancing knowledge of life in the legions were filled by Stephen Dando-Collins's *Legions of Rome*.

ABOUT THE AUTHOR

A journalist by profession, **Douglas Jackson** transformed a lifelong fascination for Rome and the Romans into his first two highly-praised novels, *Caligula* and *Claudius*. His third novel, *Hero of Rome*, introduced readers to his new series hero, the one-armed ex-gladiator Gaius Valerius Verrens. *Defender of Rome*, *Avenger of Rome* and *Sword of Rome* followed and have established its author as one of the UK's foremost historical novelists. An active member of the Historical Writers' Association and the Historical Novels Society, Douglas Jackson lives near Stirling in Scotland. To find out more, visit www.douglas-jackson.net